Under a Watchful Eye

Adam L. G. Nevill was born in Birmingham, England, in 1969 and grew up in England and New Zealand. He is the author of the horror novels: *Banquet for the Damned*, *Apartment 16*, *The Ritual*, *Last Days*, *House of Small Shadows*, *No One Gets Out Alive*, *Lost Girl* and *Under a Watchful Eye*. His first short story collection, *Some Will Not Sleep: Selected Horrors*, was published on Halloween, 2016.

His novels, *The Ritual*, *Last Days* and *No One Gets Out Alive* were the winners of The August Derleth Award for Best Horror Novel. *The Ritual* and *Last Days* were also awarded Best In Category: Horror, by R.U.S.A. Many of his novels are currently in development for film and television, and in 2016 Imaginarium adapted *The Ritual* into a feature film.

Adam also offers two free books to readers of horror: *Cries from the Crypt*, downloadable from his website, and *Before You Sleep* available from major online retailers.

Adam lives in Devon, England.

More information about the author and his books is available at: www.adamlgnevill.com.

By Adam Nevill

NOVELS

Banquet for the Damned

Apartment 16

The Ritual

Last Days

House of Small Shadows

No One Gets Out Alive

Lost Girl

Under a Watchful Eye

SHORT STORY COLLECTIONS

Some Will Not Sleep

Cries from the Crypt

ADAM NEVILL

Under a Watchful Eye

PAN BOOKS

First published 2017 by Macmillan,

This edition published in paperback 2017 by Pan Books
an imprint of Pan Macmillan
20 New Wharf Road, London N1 9RR
Associated companies throughout the world
www.panmacmillan.com

ISBN 978-1-5098-2041-2

1 3 5 7 9 8 6 4 2

A CIP catalogue record for this book is available from the British Library.

Typeset by Ellipsis, Glasgow
Printed and bound by CPI Group (UK) Ltd, Croydon, CR0 4YY

Visit www.panmacmillan.com to read more about all our books
and to buy them. You will also find features, author interviews and
news of any author events, and you can sign up for e-newsletters
so that you're always first to hear about our new releases.

For Hugh 'Hershey the Wiseman' Simmons,
who helped me pull my finger out,
and who always manifested whenever I floundered.

'The longing had take
of love and sympa
shadowy world to whi

Mme. d'Espé

Contents

PART 1

YELLOW TEETH

1

Many Communications
Must Remain in Doubt

He just appeared at the edge of Seb's vision.

Tall, dressed in dark clothing and exuding a faint impression of menace, the motionless figure was standing upon the red shoreline like an affront to the pink, blue and yellow doors of the pretty beach huts lining the promenade. The sudden, intense scrutiny gave Seb a start. Momentarily, even a blurred face suggested itself inside his mind, peering about, though his imagination must have been responsible for that.

Seb laid his coffee and notebook down, turned on the bench and squinted into the distance. He was sitting near the cliff edge on the headland south of the beach, and even on such a clear day he'd never make out the man's eyes at that range. But had they been in the same room, and had he been glared at by an unseemly stranger, Seb's discomfort would have been the same.

Fifty feet below where Seb was perched between Broadsands and Elberry Cove, the empty sea stretched to a vague horizon. The coastline curved north to Paignton and distant Torquay, the claret shores and grey cliffs reaching for Hope's Nose. His thoughts had been wandering out there, seeking the elusive impetus for what he was trying to write, but his reverie was obliterated by this abrupt intrusion.

Under closer observation, what became more surprising was that the figure didn't appear to be standing on the beach. He seemed to be positioned a few feet out from where the sand ended. The man must have been standing ankle-deep in the shallows, or was perched on a submerged rock. This created the impression that the man was standing *upon* the water. A curious trick of perspective for sure.

From his raised position, Seb could see only the far half of the beach, but no more. A few dogs raced about, darting in and out of the gentle surf, and a few people dawdled and chatted near their frantic pets. Still too cold for bathers in April and there were no pleasure craft out that morning, but the sparse crowd on the beach appeared oblivious to this lone sentinel standing so near to them. Or was he so unsightly that they pretended the man was invisible?

If Seb wasn't mistaken, a growing stillness had also been imposed by the solitary dark shape. The cries of the seabirds were gradually softening to silence inside his ears. And through the spreading quiescence the sea's chop rose as his absorption increased. Soon the running water no longer sounded like the sea at all.

Seb felt himself drawn outwards to be engulfed in a moment detached from the world. The breeze dropped. He became disoriented and slightly nauseous. Louder was the gush of the water's current. His mind cleared and was uncluttered for . . . he didn't know for how long exactly, but probably only for moments. And then, from far away and behind his head, or from deep within his mind, he heard a voice call his name.

Sebastian.

A train's steam whistle shrieked as if imitating the cry of

the dinosaurs whose grinning and collapsed remains embedded the coastline where the limestone and brick-red breccia sands crushed each other. Seb flinched, but even his gasp seemed to have originated from a mouth behind his shoulder.

Two miles distant, the train carrying holidaymakers chuffed slowly into sight on the opposing headland, making its way to the great viaducts built by Brunel. Clouds of steam billowed and unravelled into vanishing rags of vapour. A long line of carriages, painted chocolate and cream, followed the engine's slow, military determination.

Seb had lived in the bay for three years, but the train still summoned images of Agatha Christie's world: flappers and gents with pencil-thin moustaches who dressed for dinner. And he clawed at this nostalgia as if it were buoyant wreckage in deep water with no sight of land. He near begged the presence of the train to return him to the world that he had known only seconds before.

And it did. His fixation with whoever stood on the shore was severed.

When he returned his attention to the beach, and scanned its red length, the watching figure was no longer there either. *Gone.*

A few days passed and Seb had nearly forced a rational explanation for the disquieting experience: he was tired, maybe his sugar level was low, he had been mesmerized by the sun-flecked water.

But when he saw the man again he knew who it was.

2
This Coat is Too Tight

Seb had set out his laptop, coffee and water in preparation for the morning's work on the book that he was struggling to believe in, let alone write. The work in progress barely resembled his previous novels, never rose beyond an imitation of effect and a perfunctory progression of plot, peopled by undefined characters that were mere wraiths of what had been intended.

It had taken him six months to acknowledge that his imagination was failing. The energy at his core was mostly spent, or had leaked away during the writing of his previous novel, a book written with the needle of his inner reader's compass spinning wildly, in a blizzard of doubt and vain hope, without settling upon any specific direction regarding the book's quality. He'd remained unsure about the manuscript when he'd delivered to his publisher, as had been his increasingly restless and disheartened readers when it was published.

In the past, the cliff-side gardens in Goodrington, with their panoramic views of the bay, had always been a favourite place to write. Settled on the same bench, he'd worked on two other novels that were special to him. The gardens above the beach huts and promenade, at the north end of

Goodrington, were at their best in spring. And that morning, far below his feet, the sea remained dark on either side of a great strip of sunlight. A door in heaven might have cracked to release what glittered on the water like a million pieces of polished silver, cast all the way to a misted horizon far out at sea. To his right, the surf lapped the shoreline with a pleasing rhythm. *If you can't write here, you can't cut it anywhere.*

Goodrington and distant Brixham might have served as architectural models of coastal towns when sighted at such a remove. Built up the slopes of the hillsides, the white houses with their red roofs were arrayed like Lego structures. Tiny brushes of treetops sprouted from within the settlements and even a toy railway cut behind the seafront. Torbay, and the only place where he'd found peace with himself. But had the place and his comfortable lifestyle made him too content? Was penetrating the surface of the world to recreate its meanings, in unusual and interesting ways, dependent upon times of adversity? He did wonder.

He worried that a flabby self-indulgence had replaced his purpose. Maybe wishful thinking about his books had usurped his critical candour. He'd seen it happen to other writers. Perhaps naivety had swapped places with wisdom and imitation had overrun his trademark strangeness. He also feared that an indifference to the reader had taken hold during the good years. Writing this book had been homework and a chore from the start. But worst of all, he had become *incurious*.

The palms and the pink and red flowers in the heather sighed, ruffled by a cooling breeze. He inhaled the sweet fragrance of the gardens, placed the computer on his thighs and fired it up.

Long forgotten now, but the first sentence of a new chapter had come to him that morning while he showered. Perhaps the sentence would have invoked the restless urgency that had once driven his writing, near panting alongside him, a mad dog with foamy lips. This opening line might have been the beginning of a scene that would drill through the grey weight of a dull mind to produce a fracture. From a crack would burst the flood.

But Seb never tapped a single key. Way down below, the same solitary figure that he'd seen four days before made a second unwelcome appearance. No features were visible within that spot of bone-white flesh, capped in black, but he was closer.

Once more, Seb suffered the impression he'd caught the figure's eye and that they were staring at each other across the cliffs and sea. Again, the man wasn't standing on the dry sand, but seemed to be in the water. *Or on it?*

Small shapes of children frolicked on the sands of a low tide, a group of people walked dogs, others just meandered behind this sentinel of the shoreline, but none regarded him.

Shielding his eyes, Seb rose and walked to the railing.

The watcher raised his chin as if this distant vigilance had become confrontation.

The effects of another mute communication with the same stranger, and in less than a week, was far worse the second time. Quicker and deeper was Seb's absorption into that scrutiny. As if struck by a cold updraught of air, he shivered and wanted to shrink to make himself smaller and harder to see. Braced by his own dread, Seb clenched his fists upon the metal fence until his palms hurt.

The swish of the surf, a murmur of faraway traffic, and

the oddly clear voice of a boy on the beach faded, until all that he could hear was water running in the distance.

That was not the sea inside his ears, either. This time he was sure about that.

Seb slipped behind the hedgerow, a cover reinforced by a pine growing at a lower level in the gardens. Relief from that distant assiduity was immediate, then cut short by the mention of his name.

Sebastian.

His thoughts slid sideways, queasily. He then feared that his head was dropping to the pavement, or that the ground was rushing towards his face. Where were his feet?

His name had been called from an inner distance and one that took form inside his imagination as a grey and misted space at the edge of his mind. He sensed the drab emptiness was entirely without borders and reached much further than he was glimpsing.

Tasting hormones of terror in a dry mouth, he emerged from behind the shrubbery. Moving his legs was too conscious a manoeuvre.

The stranglehold of the moment abruptly passed and the figure was nowhere to be seen. Not on the water, the sands, the promenade, or in the park behind the beach.

Seb gathered up his things and jammed them inside his rucksack, managing to lose his hat in the process, which slipped down the back of the bench. He was too tense to regroup his wits but restrained himself from breaking into a run. Instead, he followed the serpentine path into Roundham Gardens, the beauty spot on the headland.

And that was the first time that he didn't linger to admire the blue expanse of the bay. Distant Torquay was ever a mosaic of white buildings, built over the hills and cliffs, an instant dreamy transport into the Mediterranean. But to hell with the view. Hurrying through a row of pines, their long trunks curved and harrowed for years by the wind, Seb made haste towards Paignton harbour.

Even if the man had been intent on engaging with him, scaling the cliff-side paths behind Seb would have been an impossible feat in the time it had taken Seb to get this far, but he still repeatedly glanced over his shoulder to make sure that he wasn't being followed.

Hatless and harried, as he moved out of the cliff-side gardens, his mind cast about for an explanation for the irrational sensation. He feared an early onset of dementia, and the worst kind of end that he had imagined for himself. Secondary terrors skimmed over schizophrenia and other hallucination-prone disorders of the mind.

Or had he actually seen a man standing in the water? *The same man twice?*

He was shaken enough to consider that there was something unnatural about the figure. Perhaps the impossible had been achieved during that strange possession of his mind upon the cliffs; he was even close to believing in the presence of the supernormal. The very subject that had made his name as a writer for so many years. The paranormal had allowed him to become that rarest of writers too: one with a good living. But, regarding the numinous, though he had curiosity and fascination in abundance, he had no faith. Uncharacteristically eager to immerse himself into a crowd, he ran from Paignton harbour to a place he rarely went: the Esplanade.

Unencumbered by family and a confirmed bachelor –

having thrown the towel in on *all that* by thirty-six, fourteen years gone now – the seafront and its attractions had never been designed for him. But the holidaymakers at the tail end of the Easter holiday did not share his reticence. It wasn't yet May, nor ten in the morning, but due to the warm spring there was already a large gathering of retirees, young families and groups of prospecting teenagers on the front.

Seb mingled amongst the beach blankets, windbreaks and small tents on the beach and hurried across the shoreline in the direction of Preston Sands. Cutting up and onto the Esplanade by the pier, he was engulfed by the fragrant haze of fried sugar and hotdog onions, then beset by the incessant jangle of the arcade's dark interior. As if he'd forded back across the river Styx and rejoined the living, the assault on his senses was joyous.

He picked up a polystyrene beaker of sweetened coffee to calm his nerves and moved past the shrieks and hurdy-gurdy jingles of the small fairground, pitched beside the adventure playground on the green. Feeling protected and even invigorated by the noise, the very electricity and energy that was relentlessly maintained by a giant pair of throaty speakers, Seb moved to the outskirts of the scene to where the strollers and the stream of cyclists thinned. He found a bench facing the sea and slumped upon it.

Tall white hotels lined up behind his seat. The Lodges, Houses and Palaces still clinging to their Victorian identities. Their cosy familiarity served as a strong arm placed about his shoulders.

Sipping his coffee, Seb made a call to Becky. Recent events had suddenly brought forward one of those times when his need for company, intimacy and affection exceeded his desire for solitude. He'd forgotten what it was like to be intimidated. Yet, in the cliff-side gardens, he'd felt more than merely intruded upon, he'd come away feeling threatened.

As if superimposing itself upon the new scene about Seb, the watcher on the shore's black shape continued to stain his thoughts while he fumbled with his phone. A sense that he was still within the figure's orbit would not abate.

Becky's voicemail picked up. Conscious of saying more than usual in a message to her, he also cringed at the note of desperation in his voice. 'Hi, it's me. The weather is just fantastic . . . and it's been a while, so I wondered if you fancied a trip to the seaside . . . Anyway, I'd love to see you again, soon . . . There's a great new seafood place just opened in Brixham—'

Seb cut off the hesitant stream of inducements because another now called for his attention. The figure in black stood at the pier's railing between a noodle bar and a seafood concession. And he was closer.

Getting closer.

He couldn't have been more than a hundred metres away now, which added an even greater intensity to Seb's discomfort at being observed, and not only from the outside.

On his phone a recorded message played inside his ear, offering a menu of playback, re-record or deletion. And he wished that at least two options were available for far more than a recorded message. He suddenly wanted to undo the beginning of his adult life, because the man standing on the pier, and staring right at him, was becoming horribly familiar.

Can't be . . .

Seb stood up, upsetting his rucksack and coffee cup.

Two cyclists, riding abreast of each other, whirred past, their heads elongated by helmets into the shape of alien skulls.

Seb trotted across the beach road and slipped between two parked cars to reach the promenade. He clutched at the railings.

His fear was joined by a compulsive curiosity about the stalker's identity. But more importantly, how had he moved from Goodrington's shoreline and around the headland to reach the pier? There had been no one behind Seb as he fled the cliff-side gardens. He'd looked back often enough. Of course, it could just be coincidence, two similarly dressed men in different places fixing him with their stare. But Seb was beyond even trying to convince himself of this.

As he tried to make sense of the man's relocation to the pier, he could not suppress a competing suspicion that the figure had known where Seb was running to. *To wait for you.* And again, his reason was overrun by the notion that the man had arrived at the pier by other means, and by a method and design that Seb couldn't even guess at.

But if this was to be a reunion, his memory began to reopen some of its darkest rooms in anticipation. Rooms with doors long closed and double-locked.

On the beach below Seb a frisbee was thrown badly. A mother, with broad tattoos on her lower legs, roared at her young. An elderly lady spoke to her spouse and said, 'But I don't want you to feel any pressure . . .' Gulls cried above the rinsing action of the waves upon the sand. And all of these sounds retreated to a distance found only in day-dreams, or in echoes from the past.

Bewilderment and the swoop of vertigo made Seb press his

body against the railings to remain upright. An atmosphere of thinner air seemed to come into existence all around his body. He even feared that gravity was disappearing.

To the pier he looked beseechingly, his face pleading for a release and for that figure to make it all stop.

The man had vanished. He'd either sidestepped behind one of the little cabins at the side of the pier or had concealed himself within the crowd, *or even* . . .

Seb had no idea.

From an even shorter distance than before, he heard the sound of his name. *Sebastian.*

Again, the word might have appeared within the confines of his mind. It may also have issued from a range somewhere behind and slightly above his head. The only amelioration of his shock was provided by Seb's recognition of the voice. The speaker's face even appeared to him before quickly fading.

Could it be?

Seb turned about, and felt his vision drawn over the parked cars and to the man in black. He was now standing on the far side of the green within the shadow of the fir trees and behind a waist-high wall of breccia stone before the Hotel Connair.

He'd been on the pier mere seconds before. *Impossible.*

Seb could now make out the presence of lank hair and a baseball cap. A jaw covered by a black beard. The surrounding flesh issued an unhealthy pallor reminiscent of cream cheese, near-noisome at a glance.

The figure raised a long arm. The hand and wrist were as blanched as the face.

Seb moved hesitantly across the beach road. The world

looked as it usually did, though his vision twitched from shock. But the world was not the same. Where had sound gone? He might have been sleepwalking.

A car braked hard and Seb saw suppressed fury in an elderly face behind the windscreen that he'd nearly rolled across. He waved an apology to the driver and stumbled back to the bench where he'd left his bag.

The temporary suspension of the world ended. A universe of raw sound rushed like the sea into a cave and filled his ears.

A mournful chorus from the gulls upon their lamp-post perches.

The gritty bounce of a rubber ball on tarmac.

A car door slammed.

The grunt of a motorbike on the Esplanade Road . . .

The end of the episode left him shaken and as cold as a bather emerging into a crosswind.

The watcher behind the wall had vanished.

3
A Sack with a Narrow Opening

Breathless and barely recalling the journey home, Seb fell into the house.

Without the presence of mind to remove his coat and shoes, he ran upstairs and took to pacing the living room. He only paused to sweep up a brandy bottle from the drinks' cabinet. He chugged the brandy over a glass before resuming his anxious laps of the room.

By natural law it was impossible for a man to appear and disappear and then reappear.

A brain tumour?

There had been no headaches, no dizziness prior to these sightings. Nothing physically wrong with him for a long time and never seriously. Paranoia about his health ensured that he paid for regular check-ups and even annual, full-body screenings.

Dementia? At fifty? It was possible. He'd have to pursue some kind of test, and no doubt a search on 'Doctor Google' would fan his fear into hysteria.

Schizophrenia had been rife in his father's side of the family. Several relatives had seen terrible things and believed in them. One of them, a cousin he'd not seen since he was a child, had taken his own life. Two more had managed their

16

condition with drugs. They'd told him at his grandfather's funeral over twenty years before. That was the most likely scenario, the past returning in the form of a family taint.

He imagined selling the house and liquidating his invest-ments to pay for a long-term residency in a care home. He saw powerful psychotropic drugs sedating the ghastly visions of his near future. All alone in a white room, he imagined being unable to identify himself until his mind eventually winked out.

Seb scrabbled for the phone to make an appointment at the local surgery. Then put the phone down.

The memory of *it* on the pier, the sight of *it* in the shal-lows, reintroduced a hideous suspicion about the figure's identity.

Ewan?

Ewan Alexander? Why would he now be seeing Ewan Alexander, of all people, so near his home? A man he'd all but suppressed in his memory. Ewan was the kind of person you wanted either to forget, or to stare aghast at from a safe distance. It was the improbability of seeing him here, not just the nature of his appearance, that had shaken Seb.

Ewan had always been a tragic case, never physically threatening. He'd only turned nasty when Seb met a girl and escaped Ewan's influence. *God, remember Julie?* But Ewan had been as excluded and powerless as a man could be in life. A lost soul. Socially inept. A misfit. A chronic alcoholic. An eater of acid.

Brandy flowed. Seb's feet shuffled through the rooms of his sanctuary.

It wasn't him. Can't be.

Seb had not seen him in . . . *let me think* . . . twelve

years. Not since the last brief intrusion. That had been in London and Ewan had knocked on the front door and not just appeared out of nothing. He'd also called on the telephone the following year and left a garbled message intended for someone else. But that was all another lifetime away.

Seb opened the balcony doors and sucked the cool sea air into his chest. They had no mutual acquaintances. Ewan had no business being down here. But if he was here, then how had he done *that*?

Dear God. What if he was dead? That would have been his ghost.

Unable to appreciate the view, because of what might appear outside and look up, Seb retreated from the balcony.

Over at the kitchen counter he visualized the lone figure, watching amongst wind-beaten trees. He scratched through the ruin of his logic and attempted to convince himself that he was safe and sane, that Ewan Alexander had not been glimpsed in four different places in as many days.

The scaffolding of wishful thinking, that he was mistaken, or confused, or unwell, collapsed. His mind insisted on marrying an unhappy year, buried deep in his past, to that sickly face, crammed beneath a baseball cap.

He *had* seen Ewan that morning. And he had seen and heard *him* while feeling agitated, unwell, and even deranged.

So how did he cause that? Why had sound changed? How had the textures of the world dispersed, or been swapped with another place? Was 'place' even the right word? Environment? Sphere?

Ewan Alexander.

God, no. Not possible.

A lot had happened in the intervening decade since he'd

last seen his 'old friend'. For one thing, Seb had moved on. It had taken a long time, but he'd made a success of his literary aspirations. A goal that he and Ewan had once shared as students.

So had Ewan come to . . . *haunt him?*

Seb didn't want any reminders of that time coming back. Not now, not when he had everything just about right, give or take a book that he was struggling to finish.

The last time they'd met, in London, Seb had been convinced that Ewan was not long for this world. *When was that, 2003?* Surely no one could drink so much and avoid a premature grave. And the drugs? He'd watched Ewan neck neat MDMA from a brown bottle as if it was a shot of whiskey. Just one of his many assurances that Ewan's demise had been imminent a decade gone.

Ewan had been committed to self-destruction when they'd first met, in the late eighties. That was thirty years ago, in a Student Union bar, and even then Ewan had been too drunk to focus his eyes. He'd rambled and spat about music: Mercyful Fate, Venom, Bathory, stuff like that. Ewan's life had formed into the immediate shape of a slow, proxy suicide.

They'd only shared a house for one year. Much of which Seb had spent listening to Ewan through the walls, when the man was out of his mind.

So how could he still be alive?

But if he isn't, then . . . Even briefly entertaining the ludicrous idea made Seb breathless.

Another cascade of brandy splashed into his crystal tumbler. He slumped onto his favourite sofa in the living room.

A panorama of sea stretched round the rear of the house, visible through floor-to-ceiling windows. But the bay's wild beauty failed to offer its customary balm. Nor did the awards, pictures, ornaments and furniture provide their usual reassurance. In fact, Seb's advantages had developed a horrible feeling of impermanence. Wasn't that similar to how Ewan had always made him feel, even when he'd had so little to lose?

Seb didn't know what to do, so he remained seated, bewildered and sagging with the self-pity that follows misfortune and finds succour in inebriation. Eventually he moved downstairs and drew the blinds in his bedroom, then lay upon his bed. He needed to calm down and think things through.

Going to the doctors was still on the agenda and he'd try the following morning. *Can't go now, can't go pissed.*

But how do you explain something like this? He feared being sectioned.

In the gloom and silence, his memories of Ewan insolently pushed through his thoughts and trampled the happier times standing guard at the outer walls of his mind, the barriers against *back then*.

1988. Ewan was his first lesson of who to avoid in life.

Back then was horribly vivid as his mind hosted a carousel of dim, brownish rooms with thin curtains that were always closed, and spaces echoing with a drunk's rampages. Seb had written about that time in his first two books, and he'd succeeded in leaving Ewan out of those stories as a character. Even then, in the processing of memory through his writing, he'd been concerned that a fictional consideration of Ewan ran the risk of bringing him back from the past.

Those who live alone often speak to themselves, as Seb did in his bedroom. 'I was young. Inexperienced . . . and lonely.'

He'd been captivated by Ewan too, an older man. Shyness and courtesy had made him the victim of a misfit.

Their old house on Wylding Lane laid new foundations inside his thoughts. If every house had a face, then that one had suffered greatly, for a long time, and been forgotten behind barbed wire.

A concrete terrace, tide-marked by green mildew. A building slipping backwards down a muddy bank of a front yard with a broken gate. Sash windows clouded with condensation, or brittle with ice that resembled mucus, depending on the season. Every inch of kerb on both sides of the narrow road cramped by parked cars. Vehicles passing through all day long, and into the night, initiating noisy stand-offs.

Three bedrooms and communal areas untouched by improvements since the sixties. And within those narrow spaces, his old mate had never risen before four in the afternoon. Seb saw Ewan again, grey with a hangover, his eyes reddened, his breath gluey, a washed-out *Reign in Blood* shirt hanging from his bony shoulders, the cotton smelling of something you might walk downwind of in a zoo.

Ewan had been ten years Seb's senior, a mature student without maturity, his studies on the rocks. He'd been retaking a year of university. Only Ewan had failed the foolproof first year. *What is he even doing here? How did he get in?* That's what people had asked. Ewan's parents had paid for the course, and many other courses after it. Maybe to keep him away from them. But Ewan's parental contributions had been transmuted into strong cider and cannabis smoke,

21

which is why he'd been co-dependent on Seb for food and money, in a matter of weeks after he'd moved into the house on Wylding Lane.

That was Seb's second year and spent out of halls. Cut out of every other potential house-share going, he'd drifted too far away from the college, and that was when it really went wrong. Marooned inside a house with no central heating on the outskirts of town, with Ewan, his sole option. Two miles from campus in a neighbourhood for the abandoned, the jobless, the neglected seniors, vast but poor families: the uncared-for in the community. An area part-derelict, ashamed of itself, but curiously industrialized. A bottled-sauce factory had covered the area with the smell of molasses and diesel.

The mentally ill Indian girl who looked out of the window of a front room, across the road, all day, every day. She'd worn colourful saris that were like vivid colours in a black-and-white film made by an auteur.

Air so cold in Seb's bedroom it had bruised his skin blue that winter. Sleeping in his clothes and leather jacket under two duvets. The permanent odours of moist timber, the powdery rot of dew spots in the plaster beneath age-clouded wallpaper, and the kind he'd only seen before in crime dramas set in New York tenements. A hint of gas blended through raw sewage. The must of ancient dust under floorboards, mingled with what dirty shoes had left on carpets, where they existed. Cat piss despite there being no cat. A fridge that never worked. Food poisoning from belly pork. Chest infections. No toilet paper. Hunger. Cold. Stomach bugs. Grim.

They had both smelled. It had been too cold to take a bath in that house, though Seb had tried, once a week, in an inch of tepid water, and engaged in a feeble upward splashing of a cupped paw, like a monkey in a stream. He'd never managed to get a full sink out of the old immersion heater. But Ewan's odours had made his eyes water. An animal odour: cattle and ethanol, with a hint of shellfish left in the sun.

In one entire year Ewan had never laundered his few articles of clothing. Seb's own gaminess had eventually become a comfort, his bed a compost of sheets with the Turin Shroud on top, concealing a well-used mattress that he'd never dared examine. Fifteen quid a week.

Six lectures a week: Shakespeare's tragedies, the Romantic poets, the Victorian novelists. Seb had associated with the paupers, the derided, the murdered in every text. Ewan had cast himself as the dark, moody hero in every scenario, the prophet poet, the adventurer, the sage and mystic.

It was all coming back, a landslide in a landfill.

The open bin bag in the kitchen with no bin around it. The lino stained as if the rubbish sack was a giant tea bag. Oddments of crockery and cheap, dull saucepans piled across the counters. All debris from Ewan's odd mealtimes and hapless, hungover attempts at preparing food. Ashtrays heaped like mounds in crematoria. Living out of cans. A fiver a week on food. A diet of sausage sandwiches and soup.

Seb's inevitable retreat into his room, away from the tides of Ewan's squalor and noise that nothing could turn back. Smoking roll-ups and playing vinyl records. Handwritten essays. He'd thought himself a Dostoyevsky sketching notes from an underground, or a Hamsun enlightened by hunger, a Fante who asked the dust. But he was a nobody. Ewan had thought he was William Burroughs experimenting with acid, or a Bukowski drinking himself unconscious before the four-bar heater in the living room, twice each week, six cans of cider empty beside his long, curling form on the filthy rug, whenever Seb discovered him in the morning as he went out for classes, or food.

Ewan's own mountain of pain one long silence, caged behind those heavy-lidded eyes and never shared. Not even in rare moments of sobriety when he talked at length about Arthur Machen's *The Hill of Dreams*, or Algernon Blackwood's depiction of the numinous, Wakefield's ghosts or Blake's visions, and so many other diversionary things, from Shakespeare to Black Sabbath, from Shelley to Slayer.

That was the stuff that had drawn Seb in, his awe at a true outsider who might tutor his own sensitivity to the dark things that confirmed a belief in his own outcast status. Seb had read King, Herbert, Barker, Straub and Lovecraft before university, and he'd watched Romero, Cronenberg, Carpenter, Argento and Friedkin. But Ewan had shared M. R. James with him, M. P. Shiel, Aickman, Campbell, W. B. Yeats, Hughes, Baudelaire, Rimbaud, Bosch, Bruegel, Bacon, Spare, Resnais, Bergman, Kneale, and Lynch. Tipped him over with a wallop into another way of thinking it all through, another way of saying things, or not saying them at all and just letting them come out and *be there*.

He started you off . . .

But Ewan had never wanted to let Seb go, and by the end of that year, Seb had been unsure whether Ewan had cared about anything other than getting drunk or high, while using Seb like a carer, valet, apprentice, housekeeper, and admirer.

Seb had grafted at university and then grafted even harder afterwards. He owed Ewan nothing.

Had Ewan not always encouraged him to turn his back

on the material world, on family, friends? Poverty and the avoidance of responsibility and attachments being the only way to become a true artist, according to Ewan. And once Seb had flirted with that set of ideas, and set that course for himself, he'd felt unable to meet the world in any other way. Or had that been inevitable anyway? Was that the reason he'd been so attracted to Ewan in the first place? Had he seen his own destiny in Ewan? Or at least an inevitability in himself to become overwhelmed by his own compulsions? Seb didn't know, but their association should have ended in Wylding Lane in '88.

That year was merely the beginning. Ewan broke him in, and his mentor's legacy had continued through fifteen years of under-employment, often uniformed, often temporary, its only permanence low pay, augmented by occupations of sub-lets in the corners of cities inhabited by poor migrants and those who'd slipped off the edges. Those others had no choice, but he'd wanted to be an old-school writer and had been unable to resist Ewan's narrative. Perhaps Ewan's ghost had now returned to check on Seb's progress and to correct it, or regress it.

By publishing his early stories, the small presses had encouraged Seb enough to stay the course, though he'd remained anxious about what might befall him if he didn't make changes to his life. But what changes? A professional job? He'd been clueless about finding one of those. *Write one more book and then we'll see.* That had been his mantra. And at least Seb had grafted at the writing. He'd always been a grafter, determined.

When Seb's last parent went, his mother, he'd spent two years on antidepressants wearing a security guard's uniform, and then he'd got lucky. Horror became the new black in publishing and he was noticed.

But why had his own past noticed him now?

Seb remained in bed with the blinds down. Sometime in mid-afternoon he drifted to sleep.

4
Broken Night

A dream of winter, of charcoal skies and grey light. And he walks amongst people he does not know. People who move on their hands and knees. They appear helpless, perhaps lost, or even blind.

'Is the light over there?' he is asked.

'Have you seen my sister?' he is asked.

'I cannot get back,' he is told.

He is on the contoured hillocks of a golf course. A place he often crosses to reach the pub at Churston Court. And up and down those manicured mounds of grass he walks, but more quickly now to remove himself from those drawn to him who are given to crawling like infants. He won't look at them directly again. They're too thin and near transparent in some of their parts. The only face he looked into reminded him of creased, wet newspaper.

A wide, hazy sea lies directly ahead of him. Sounds of a distant crowd carries from the opposite direction. Seb turns and sees a large white building, three storeys high, the front flat and white like a vast mausoleum. A building he has never seen before. The patio before the entrance is full of people, and his mother's voice rises from the crowd. He wants to run for her. She has been gone for nine years, but he thinks he can see her, wearing a red coat.

Seb calls out, 'What?' and, in unison, the group points at the sky.

His mother's voice breaks free from the chatter of the crowd. 'Come back!' or maybe she says, 'Go back!'

He is a boy and has become a younger self in the way selves effortlessly switch within dreams. He remains on the golf course, but the grass is now sawdust, just like that of the butcher's shop that he used to visit with his nan, where it was scattered over the lino of a cold floor. Sawdust with blood mixed into it. The blood was dark and he was always told not to touch the floor with his small, questing hands. He'd liked the cold sausage and iron smells of the shop.

Seb's legs sink to the knee into the dust and wood chips, and he soon becomes breathless in an attempt to break free. Water flows fiercely somewhere nearby, as if from between the dunes. He cannot see it and fears the water will appear between the small slopes and cover his head and mouth.

Another enters the sawdust landscape, a thing with a covered head and a whitish body low to the ground. Seb can hear a wet snuffling and he is paralysed with his old terror of dogs.

Those others around him, who are crawling, scatter like crabs beneath upturned rocks. This new entrant moves eagerly to traverse the golf course as Seb flounders and twists and cries for his distant, unreachable mother.

That head, covered by a dirty sack, stiffens with an alertness that communicates an awareness of him, and an anticipation within its horrid form. When it turns to him,

Seb cannot find the strength to scream. He stops struggling in the blood-mired sawdust and cries harder.

Into this dream he comes to be sitting in his childhood home, on a green and brown carpet with a pattern that once made him think of chameleons. He sees a silver Christmas tree, a dimpled glass door, a plywood service hatch opening into a kitchen, and the images remind him of what will soon be lost forever. From out of the kitchen comes the sound of wooden sticks being snapped in half while a large, unseen form turns round and round and rubs against the cupboard doors.

When Seb wakes and sees the darkened bedroom and the vertical band of daylight at the edge of the curtains, his relief is immense.

Tracks of dried tears split upon his cheekbones. He is damp and hot, his muscles heavy and his mind groggy from the heavy sleep that overcame him in the middle of the day. But within the early bewilderment of waking, he is aware of a disturbance outside. A noise that issues a dreadful continuity with his dream.

Lying upon his bed, his thoughts stumble and he can't be certain if the sound is part of the worst nightmare he's endured in years, or whether it is a sign of a long animal moving around the external walls of the house, looking for access.

Into his mind creeps a sense of a sinewy body with a covered head, pressed into the bricks, and moving like a dog.

5
Incertitude

'There's so much I don't know about you,' Becky said, once
they had returned from the restaurant and settled in the
living room. Before they left the house earlier they had set
side-by-side on the sofa, but now looked at each other from
different sides of the room. It was the evening of another
day that hadn't passed without trauma.

Seb's frantic invitation to Becky had been accepted and she'd
arrived at the weekend, alighting from an afternoon service
at Paignton with a small leopard-print case in tow.

Her failure to disguise her shock at how he looked had
been immediate. A face unused to smiling, and a mouth un-
accustomed to talking, as a tired but frantic mind turned
upon itself, could not be concealed by a pressed shirt, smooth
cheeks and aftershave.

Seb had spirited her out of the station and into his car.
Her visit fell eight days after his sighting of Ewan on the
pier, and Seb no longer felt safe outdoors. Even though the
weather had distinguished itself with warm sunshine and
cloudless skies, he'd barely been outside in four days.

Seb had been reduced to darting to and from the nearest
shop to fetch essentials, all the time certain that a predator

watched him while planning its next strike. To prepare for Becky's visit, he'd resorted to home deliveries from a supermarket chain.

'God, I love your place . . . The view. Look at it! . . . How've you been? . . . I finished your book about the ship on the way down. It's different . . . Are you sure you're okay?' She'd said this as soon as they arrived at his house, while throwing her coat down and reacquainting herself with his home.

Seb's place was a modernized twenties townhouse, re-designed by the previous owners in a style that now resembled a picture in a Scandinavian design magazine: open-plan upstairs, light and airy, wood and right angles, bedrooms on the first floor and the living space on the second, all powered by solar energy. The ground floor had a garage for three cars and a reception area.

When Seb first saw the house, he'd liked the idea of going downstairs to sleep, but had never been able to account for the attraction beyond the novelty value.

'Any news on the new film?' Becky had asked, distract-edly. 'When's it out? Can we open the doors? I want to go on the balcony.'

'There's a cold wind coming off the water.'

'It's nineteen degrees.'

Seb had maintained the stiff smile that made his face ache. His nerves constantly jumped and the most innocuous sounds made him flinch. Though it was the departure of sound that he dreaded most of all, the unnatural silence that accompanied the harrowing presence.

Becky opened the balcony doors. Eyes closed, she inhaled deeply, savouring the coastal atmospherics in the way he'd forgotten how to. After a few minutes outside, she came indoors to sit beside Seb on the sofa. Glass of wine in hand, she'd sat tight against him and slipped a hand over his restless paws. 'You don't look that pleased to see me.'

'Don't say that. I've been counting the days.'

'Then what is it? You hiding a ring behind you?'

He blanched enough to make Becky shriek with laughter.

'I've . . .' He had been unable to finish the sentence. He'd made the decision to tell her about Ewan and had rehearsed an explanation. But what he needed to unload had suddenly seemed preposterous and left him feeling awkward, a bit ridiculous too, and even craven.

Becky had stretched out one leg and raised an eyebrow, coquettishly. 'I can't believe you haven't commented on these. I bought them for the weekend. You haven't even looked at them yet.' She was referring to the boots, spike-heeled and shining like eels to her knees. She'd worn them with a pencil skirt that had given her progress across the train platform a faint but enticing hobble. The susurration between her thighs would normally have electrified him. He should have been pleasantly uncomfortable with arousal, even greedy for her. After all, it had been a while, but now there was nothing *normal* about his existence and state of mind.

'They're great.' He'd unintentionally sounded unimpressed, and caught a shade of dismay in Becky's expression. It registered in a lowering of her satin eyelashes over the green eyes that had first attracted him to her.

'And you should see what else I've got on.' She'd stroked knees that appeared slippery with a sheen created by the afternoon sun that fell across the seat.

Seb had reached for her then and held her tightly. Not

with desire but with affection and relief. He held her like the friend that he so desperately needed – this pretty girl whom he'd always kept at an arm's length, and with whom he'd been unable to drop an act of indifference. He suspected she'd fallen for him during the six months in which they'd been lovers, without strings, and living in different places.

Becky found his ear. 'I want to go for a walk and a paddle in the sea. And I want to get pissed. But I'm not going out dressed like this. So let's get reacquainted properly in your room and then I'll get changed.' She'd reached between his legs and applied a gentle pressure. 'I thought you'd be a rock by now. Am I losing my touch?'

She wasn't and he'd wanted to say as much. She was as lively and cheeky, playful and sweet smelling, as kind and just as lovely as she had been, since the first time they'd met at a literary festival. Seb had wanted to tell her all of these things but he didn't, and not because of his reticence about taking an intimate friendship one step further. He'd remained quiet because he was cornered and muted by wretchedness. He was a man who felt twice his age and had no mental capacity for the erotic. Because of *him*, Ewan, or whatever it was that he was seeing.

During the previous week, Ewan had come for him again, and then again. And he was getting closer with each 'visit'.

Two days after the episode near the pier, and after the onset of a series of ghastly persecution nightmares, Seb had been compelled to leave the house. Needing to immerse himself within crowds during daylight hours, he'd driven to Plymouth. And while wandering the broad precincts of the town centre, he'd seen Ewan standing before St Andrew's Cross, at the bottom of the Royal Parade.

His clutch of shock had been instant, followed by a sense of being swallowed by a vacuum, or strange absence, his thoughts unravelling and transported somewhere else. Traffic, gulls, the crowd's chatter, a pushchair's wheels on cement, a ship's lonesome horn, and the clanking of a delivery van's door, all withdrew as if his hearing had lost its power source. But the face and murky mouth confronting him were distinct enough to reveal a most unpleasant smile, one triumphant and sneering.

There had been something more threatening about Ewan's appearance in Plymouth, too. He'd moved from out of the corner of Seb's eyes and deliberately positioned himself in Seb's line of sight, at the end of the street, and in the direction Seb walked, as if a meeting was inevitable.

Ewan had then passed away, without Seb being aware of the figure moving its feet. Two separate groups of people had crossed the monument from each side and Ewan had vanished.

Seb had seen more of Ewan that time. Streaks of white in the beard. What had looked like a dark raincoat was zippered to his neck and pulled in tight at his waist, covering the thin torso. Jeans too. Black jeans that were worn too tight for a man of his age, and were too short for the length of his legs. When they were students, Ewan's jeans were always too short, an inch of sock always visible above his dirty trainers.

Seb had returned to his car, but at once disliked being inside the gloomy parking level where he'd left his Mercedes and was alone. Hurrying to be anywhere but inside the shadows and silence of a multi-storey, he'd tripped up and scuffed a shoe, his jog up a concrete stairwell poorly co-ordinated. But Ewan was long gone by then.

Hoping that a short voyage on water would place him beyond the range of the visions, or whatever they were, he'd then intended to drive to Dartmouth, to take a boat to Totnes. This was two days later, but Ewan had appeared again, and at the side of a road a few hundred metres from his home.

Seb had been driving in the direction of St Mary's Bay and had turned into Ranscombe Road, only to then struggle to keep the car straight after seeing Ewan standing alone on the pavement. At full height too, without the shy man's stoop that had also been strangely absent during his previous appearances. At that point, Seb still refused to call them *manifestations*, but this would change.

What he'd seen of Ewan's face from the moving vehicle, and within the passing of a second, suggested an unappealing pallor embellished with a grimace. There was no smile. Just the bloodless features staring at him, with loathing.

A great discomfort, fuelled by fear and sharpened by shock, had impacted his senses and he'd veered towards the side of the road, at a parked vehicle. Forced to brake, a horn had then blared from behind. A tradesman's van had passed his car with a roar of acceleration.

Classic FM, on the radio, returned to the car's interior.

When Seb had looked up, Ewan had gone.

Seb had returned to the house, no more than half a mile away, and to a place that Ewan must have been telling Seb was now within his reach.

That same afternoon, Seb had intensified his frantic

online search for any information on Ewan Alexander. As with the other investigations, he'd found no trace of his old roommate. But, as he'd worked with the door to his office open, three bath-sheets drying on the balcony had moved at the edge of his vision. He'd swivelled his chair towards them, struck by a conviction that the towels had raised their corners, like hands, to beckon him.

Solely the work of his imagination, transforming the raw material of the inexplicable into the animation of ordinary objects. But he'd rushed to the balcony . . . only to hesitate when the sun umbrella under the pergola next door became a tall figure, bowing a concealed head.

Another illusion. But his blinds had come down in every window of the house that afternoon, and had not been drawn until Becky arrived on Saturday.

Too nervous to feel shame at his desultory attempt at sex, Seb had continued to top up their glasses. Having lived alone for twenty years, he'd vowed never to uncap a bottle before four p.m. Any self-imposed abstinence was long dead by that weekend. Becky had showered in silence and then dressed-down.

They had gone out for an early dinner in Brixham harbour, saying little to each other during the walk down the hill. Nodding now and again to acknowledge Becky's stilted observations about the loveliness of the quay, his focus had remained on the faces around them. Becky's disappointment in him was palpable but the least of Seb's worries, considering who might appear within the evening crowd at any time.

Guiltily, he'd also acknowledged that her corroboration was a motive for inviting her to stay. He'd wanted Ewan to appear so that Becky would see him. If she couldn't see him, then only God knew what was wrong with his mind. Of course, if she did see him and Ewan was really there, it wasn't great news either, but at least it would mean he wasn't going mad.

In the restaurant, Seb had pushed his lobster round the plate, while anxiously sipping several pints of Bays Gold. At some point between the first course and dessert, Becky's patience had reached fumes.

'I'm not going to ask you again, but something is wrong, Seb. You're different. Are you upset with me?'

'God, no.'

Her concern turned to irritation. 'You've got something to tell me. Are you breaking up with me? Couldn't you have done it on the bloody phone? I'd have thought an email would have been your chosen medium.'

'No, no, no. Please. Don't think that.'

'Then what is it?' She'd reached out and touched his hand, one that had barely released a glass since the mutually unsatisfactory tumble in bed that afternoon. And that's when his confession had begun to seep out.

'I'm worried about . . . something. My health. Mental health.'

'What is it? Has it come back? The depression?'

'I haven't seen a doctor. Not yet, because I'm not sure a doctor can help.' Seb shrugged. 'I think something has come back into my life. *Someone*.'

'A woman.'

'I wish it was that simple. Then I could do something.'

'Do something?'

'Forget the woman. There is no woman. I'm talking about a man.'

She'd looked relieved, but remained uncomfortable.

'And no, I am not coming out. You think that's why . . . back there, at the house? This has nothing to do with sex.' He'd paused to swallow a draught of beer. 'Becky, have you ever . . . hallucinated?'

'How much are you drinking, Seb? You haven't stopped since I got here. You know, living on your own, and writing those books, having to think about horrible things all day and night, while drinking, how can that be good for you?'

At that point, Seb covered his face with his hands, prickling with shame at how close he was to tears. The sympathetic ear, the warm familiarity of a companion combined with the drink, and he couldn't speak.

He'd gulped at his beer to rinse away the constriction in his throat. 'No, it's not that. It must look like that, but it's not. There was someone. Many years ago. A friend even, who . . . who I keep seeing now. Everywhere. But he can't be there. It's crazy.'

Even Becky had looked pale. 'You're telling me you're seeing someone who died?'

'I don't know. I've had no contact with him for years. The last time was brief. He showed up at my place in London about twelve years ago. I tried to help him, but then I had to get rid of him.'

'Why?'

'He was in a bad way. Drink. Drugs. That sort of thing. He'd wanted my help, but I didn't have any money. Not then. But I gave him somewhere to stay, for a bit. And tried to counsel him, that sort of thing. It was no use. He called me afterwards, the following year, and . . . I could have sworn that he was insane.'

'Christ.'

'Before that, a long time before London, we were room-mates at university. Way back in the eighties. It's a long story. But I never wanted to see him again after I graduated. No one who knew him did. He was . . . let's just say he was difficult.'

'Arsehole?'

'I thought so. But there was more to it, to him.'

'Was he dangerous?'

'When drunk and roused he might have been. But never towards me.' Ewan had physically restrained Seb once, after he took mushrooms. That was the only time Ewan had ever touched him, but he'd been strong.

'He put a value on me, our friendship. He didn't have anyone else.'

Becky had almost looked over her shoulder. 'He's down here?'

'I don't really know.'

'If you're seeing him then he must be.'

'That's what I thought.'

'I don't understand.'

Seb and Becky were as close as occasional lovers can be, which was not that close for this kind of admission, but he had no one else with whom he could confess. A fact that had made him sad. This was also how he felt when ill and alone.

'He's there and then . . . he's not there. He's appearing and kind of moving, or vanishing. He's been calling my name too. Not out loud. I can hear him inside my head.'

Becky had now been unable to disguise what looked like

deal-breaker discomfort. 'Get yourself checked out, like straight away. How long has this been happening?'

'Nearly two weeks.'

'Two weeks! And you haven't been to a hospital?'

'No, because I'm not convinced . . .'

And if memory is stimulated by a scent from one's past, and Seb had read his Proust, then what engulfed their table inspired a vivid sense of Ewan in 1988 – the long face, the forehead and cheekbones oily and red from intoxication, the morbid and haunted look that came into his eyes as if another personality inhabited him when drunk. And if the devil also appears when you speak his name, then Ewan Alexander might have been sitting at the next table.

Seb could actually smell him. No mistaking it. Layers of sweat saturating a leather jacket rarely removed in any weather. Sebaceous and harsh, but piny with fresh alcohol over stale booze, wafting from his clothes and from the furniture he'd sat upon, lingering in the rooms he'd passed through.

'You smell that?' Seb's voice was no louder than a whisper.

'You're freaking me out. Where, Seb, where is he?'

'There,' he'd said in a voice so tight it hissed. He'd pointed at the windows facing the docks.

And behind that miserable statement of a man, the masts of the boats had wavered like the banners of a dishevelled army. No longer a vague apparition at a distance, Ewan had practically been in the same room. Becky's voice had faded as the volume of the world was turned down.

When Seb had looked right at Ewan, who was near pressed against the window, the chink and clatter of tableware and the murmur of the other diners had retreated.

Music failed inside his ears. It was as if Ewan had come that close to take the glare off the glass, to peer into the interior of the restaurant. He'd known Seb was inside, but not at which table.

When Ewan's murky eyes had found him, and in such attractive company, the bearded face had stiffened and those black eyes narrowed with a hateful intensity. Loathing mixed with a sharp, sudden pain, that Seb remembered seeing in his old friend's eyes many years ago, when that face had been much younger, and when Ewan had discovered that Julie and Seb were an item. Ewan had seen the beginning of the end then. Seb's relationship had crippled him with jealousy. Thirty years later Ewan had not forgotten the slight.

The end of the spell had made Seb dizzy enough to grip the table with both hands. The noise and tumult of the world refilled the room and Seb's ears.

'Where?' Becky had said. 'Where? Where are you looking? The windows? Which one?'

The state of that form and the length of it – how could she have missed it? A hoary face and the bedraggled hair, as if Ewan had climbed out of the harbour, grimacing with teeth better suited to a face from prehistory.

She had seen nothing. Seb knew she was only trying to make him feel better when she claimed that she *may* not have looked at the right window. But she must have done. There were only two panes of glass behind her chair and she'd looked right at them. Ewan had been standing in plain view.

He'd then vanished behind a passing waitress.

Stunned, and unable to unthaw his mind, Seb had remained still with shock.

Schizophrenia, or the terrible decline of dementia, and probably dementia with Lewy bodies. He'd done his research while searching for Ewan online. You could get that at fifty. Was that worse than the alternative explanation?

Even as a child Seb had been prone to frowning. His natural expression was often described by others as humourless, dour and intense. It made some people wary. But his scowl concealed his insecurity. In photographs of himself he could see his own morbid pessimism and an aversion to conflict, his sensitivity to criticism. None of which he'd shaken off from childhood. Seb harboured grudges. Mere slights, or casual teasing, he was unable to forgive. Ewan had been similar. But as Seb had stared in horror at Ewan's appearance against the window in the restaurant, the dark shape of the intruder had produced a dim reflection of his own scowl upon the glass, and he'd realized that the most perplexing contradiction in his hallucination theory was how Ewan's visage had also aged, and realistically. Perhaps too vividly for the imagination alone to depict. Surely he would see a hallucination of Ewan as he remembered him.

He also reminded himself that madness was the most creative human condition. Any alternative explanations of a supernatural cause defied natural law to such an extent that it was, simply, an unbearable proposition to entertain. But if Ewan was dead, and that truly had been his apparition, then *it* was following Seb like a revenant. And there was nothing that he could do to escape it.

Seb now felt safer back at the house. Maybe because he still hoped that Ewan couldn't get inside. *Otherwise he would have done so.* But the idea of him doing so nearly encouraged Seb to expel what little of his dinner he'd managed to swallow.

This really wasn't what Becky had in mind for the weekend either. Her discomfort had grown with Seb's agitation in the restaurant. He'd drunk more since their return to the house and now paced the living room at a tilt and weave that he couldn't correct, no matter how hard he concentrated.

'What did he actually do to you?' Becky asked, not unreasonably.

What did he do! They'd be here all night. How did he encapsulate such a force of disruption? There was no stopping him on the subject of Ewan. *Out with it all.*

Becky appeared shocked by Seb's intensity as he began to unwind and rewind his memories of Ewan. Images from time reflowing like a tide of sewage raised by floodwater, swilling through his mind and into the sanctuary of his clean, modern home . . .

Ewan's big red fist leaving dents in the doors. Death metal. Black metal. The sounds of hell making the speakers of that midi system in his room crackle and spit like fat in a fire, hell fire. Reefer smoke, pungent like grapefruit and sausages, filling the unlit hallways under dead bulbs they'd never had the money to replace. Coins in the meter, Seb's coins. Vomit in the bath. Cheap bread. Horror films on VHS, all night. Cans and cans and cans of cider, the empties filling bags in the garden. Fingertips turning orange from nicotine. Teeth turning yellow from neglect and tobacco and strong tea.

Yellow teeth. Black bearded mouth. A billy goat. Purple gums and yellow teeth. Dog mouth. Dog ivory.

'The mess, the stench, it filled every room in that house.

It grew across every surface and around my feet. It came inside my room.'

'Students.'

'No excuse. And it was far worse than that. The squalor merely started it, the opening skirmishes. There was the question of money. Promises and promises to repay the loans that I gave him. Money I could ill afford to hand over from a student grant. He never paid me back, but his parents were loaded. Oh, he kept that quiet until I met them, just once, at the end of the year. This guy who ate my pitiful supplies had been to a private school. A boarding school. His father was an officer in the air force. Top brass too. His stories, his promises, they were as worthless as his literary ambitions.'

Becky shrugged. 'He used you. I think everyone meets someone like that. Most often in a relationship.'

'He knew so much, you know, about ideas, bits of philosophy. It all seemed so *cool*, for a while. And I took it all in, was taken in, and . . . seemed to become *of him*. I cringe with shame when I think of who I was back then.'

'Seb, that was a long time ago—'

'I read more of his books than the set texts on my course. I even grew my hair long because Ewan wore his long. I started to drink and smoke weed. But he could not, at any level, acknowledge what a terrible person he was to be around. And I learned why, because confronting that was never in his best interests.'

This information hardly prepared the ground for the other stuff he wanted to tell her. There was always something else that was never right about Ewan. 'There was something he kept hidden. It often crept out of him. That was much worse. The things that made everyone else avoid him.'

'Like what?'

'Standing and staring, in total silence, at the mud and broken concrete in that wretched back yard. Coming and going at night. The sobbing in his room, for hours. Ranting outside my room when I started seeing Julie . . .'

God, Julie. Remember Julie?

Ewan had also boasted about dreams so lucid he'd considered them to be journeys through another place that existed, where *others* had been on hand to guide him. Druggy, pisshead nonsense, but from Ewan it always felt a little too believable, a possibility. And Ewan had claimed to have seen figures, faces above his own when he woke in the early hours, forms standing upright beside his bed, voices in the attic.

There were those dreaded silences when he'd thought Ewan had died in his room. *When he hoped he'd died so it could end* . . . Silences capable of a further lowering of the house's temperature. Sometimes the absences had lasted for days.

'Poor guy. Might it simply have been about *her*?'

'Julie?' He could almost smell her red hair again. 'No. By the time she appeared, and that was in the third term, we hated each other. I was counting down the days until I finished my exams, so I could get my deposit back and leave him behind. He'd been chucked out of college by then.'

'What was he like the second time? You said he came to see you in London.'

'Much worse. And it wasn't a visit as such. He found out where I lived and followed me home. He must have done.'

Seb could still remember his shock when he'd first seen

Ewan in West London. That had been a few days before his first visit to the house where Seb had lived in Hammersmith. He'd seen the tall but hunched figure in an old blue raincoat, muttering anxiously to himself while never looking another in the eye. Pacing, agitated, jobless, alone, whispering and getting closer to the one thing that he considered companionable.

Seb had avoided him. He'd ducked into a second-hand clothes shop, and the second time had hurried into the Hammersmith and City Line station.

So how had Ewan found him back then? How had Ewan known where to look for Seb in the first place, in West London? Seb had never been certain, and given recent events was even less sure now.

Ewan had claimed he'd called Seb's mother and that she had volunteered his Hammersmith address. Seb had mentioned this to his mother that Christmas and she'd no knowledge of the phone call. Ewan had lied.

Once Ewan had finally left his room in London, after one barely endurable month, Seb had checked with four friends from university with whom he still maintained email contact but no longer saw. None of them had heard from Ewan since he'd been kicked out of college, fourteen years before.

He'd only been able to assume that Ewan had figured out he was living in Hammersmith from a Friends Reunited profile, and had headed there and come across Seb in the street, or when coming out of the tube station, before following him home.

Ewan had always liked to play the enigma card, to know things that Seb did not. It was partly how he'd maintained the balance of power when they were students.

His old friend had resorted to begging Seb to let him stay and to sleep on the floor of his room. And his need for shelter and support had become a wheedling insistence, cries for help from an old friend across successive visits. He'd claimed he was sleeping rough and had nowhere else to go. Dishevelled, drunk before noon, his big face held in a cage of long fingers, the nails black with dirt, he'd sobbed while Seb had fidgeted on the office chair set before the small table where he'd written one of his small press collections and the majority of his first two novels.

That had been a hot summer too, but Ewan had worn a battered jacket, zipped to his throat. And a black cap, similar to the one he wore now, jammed tightly onto his unwashed hair.

At the time, Seb's take-home pay from the bookshop had been a shade over eight hundred pounds each month, and he'd saved a thousand pounds from several years of temporary work. He'd rented a small room and had a few friends. Not much, but a massive improvement on Ewan's situation. Even so, Ewan's shocking and inebriated state had made Seb acutely afraid for his own future. He remembered that much. Ewan had served as a warning of what might become of Seb if his literary ambitions were thwarted.

He'd allowed Ewan to sleep on the floor of his room for a night that became a week, that dragged into a month. His orderly room was transformed into a slurry pit of free newspapers, empty sandwich cartons, cider cans, dirty crockery and black hairs.

When Seb knew the temporary arrangement showed signs of co-dependency, he'd asked Ewan to leave and also requested that he no longer visit the house. By then, his two female housemates had expressed strong aversions to the house guest. His relationship with Katie and Cleo had never been the same after Ewan had finally sloped off. The girls distrusted Seb merely for knowing a person like Ewan.

'But what had he been doing, before he came to see you?'

'After he was chucked out of uni? From what I could work out, he'd quickly forfeited his refuge at an impressive family home. He also claimed he'd had some involvement in squat and commune scenes. That kind of thing. By reading between the lines of his spin, I figured he'd stayed pissed for fourteen years.'

Though, Ewan's anecdotes in London had also made Seb feel glum. He'd only struggled uneventfully in bad jobs while grinding away at his writing. Ewan had lived like a writer, though not written anything.

It had taken Seb ten years after university to complete his first two collections and to see them spark, briefly, in the underground caves of the small and swiftly vanishing horror presses of the nineties. At his first convention in 2003, he'd been surprised to discover that he had at least one hundred readers. He'd near broken himself just to get that far.

Ewan had just *known* that Seb's books were no good.

Seb had then finished another two books in London, novels, before his big break at forty. He'd finished another seven since and watched them appear in other languages. Two had become films. One of the films was actually good. The other one had been more successful at the box office.

Ewan's work still had not appeared in a single collection that Seb was aware of.

'He still called himself a writer, and mocked me! What did he ever produce? A few short stories!'

One or two unusual ideas and startling images that Seb could just about remember, but nothing more, because Ewan had never been more than a dilettante. Seb had been committed from the beginning. Seb finished books, Ewan scratched out fragments. Seb read, Ewan had stopped reading other writers and, thereafter, believed he knew what books were all about with a glance at a cover.

Becky continued to frown. 'So Ewan was a kind of mentor. He helped you become *this*.' She wafted a hand at the awards in the living-room cabinet and at the framed poster of the first film, the good one.

Seb cleared his throat. 'There was some value, yes. He introduced me to things. But he didn't write my books.'

She shrugged. 'But what does anyone know at that age, Seb? You had a kind of late older boy crush on this guy, who wasn't who you thought he was. That's not uncommon, but I can see you've given it a bit of thought.' A hint of mockery lingered in her voice. She was finding his testimony hard to take seriously, but he'd had eight days to think of little else. 'It's like you're talking about a girlfriend too. A bad relationship.'

'Strange as it sounds, you make a good point. Both times, I think Ewan was unable to live without me. There was nothing sexual in his co-dependency, no latent desire, nothing like that. But there was a need in him, like an addiction, for acceptance. He'd been alone for a long time before he met me, and then again in London. Nothing had worked out for him. Ewan still needed someone to understand and approve of him, while he exhibited some kind of personality disorder that was counter-productive to him ever achieving his needs. His investigations into himself were never honest.

He never understood himself. What he saw was not what anyone else saw. He was never free of who he wanted to be. But he couldn't see who he was.'

'Maybe he did know, but the truth was too sad to acknowledge. Or maybe he was a total narcissist. A psychopath. No conscience. And you were his perfect victim. That might explain why he's tracked you down. You might not be hallucinating, Seb. Because that's what I don't get, why you keep seeing him . . . or think you're seeing him now.'

'That makes two of us. No one can appear and disappear like that. It's no trick. And it doesn't explain how . . . *everything* seems to change before he appears.'

6
Down the Last Valley

A sense of having been amongst a group of whispering people, who were moving through a cement culvert, receded from his mind.

Seb could see the darkened room surrounding the bed.

Becky was already sitting up, her fingers spread across her cheeks. A gesture she made if something upset her in a film.

She said, 'Can you hear it? Outside?'

Her frightened eyes increased the disorientation of Seb's own rousing. And he could hear something too, a noise that he shouldn't have been able to hear from inside the bedroom. For the second time recently, he believed that a large animal was moving along an external wall of the house.

Becky had gone to bed before him. He'd stayed in the living room and moved from beer to bourbon. She'd been asleep by the time he joined her, which was only when his mind had finally exhausted itself, adrenalin having run through him like rusty water mixed with ethanol, to leave him shaky. He'd always assumed that his apprehension before he retired led to the frequency of the troubling dreams. But if Becky had heard it too . . .

They both saw the blinds moving over a window that

Becky must have opened. He hadn't noticed it was open when he came to bed, and now they were too frightened to get out of the bed to close it. The disturbance outside neared the open window.

Other objects in the dark room became clearer, as if the room was close to a source of illumination. Though the soft light's origin was not visible, the outlines and shapes of the bedroom furniture offered some familiarity.

But when Seb finally sat up, he saw that a tall man was standing at the foot of the bed, on his side.

Becky now slept soundlessly beside him, unmoving, her face turned away.

How?

He realized he'd just dreamed Becky being awake. But his shock at having passed from a dream into the actual room, without noticing the seam, was worsened by the lingering silhouette of the figure.

Seb couldn't see a face, but was certain the form belonged to the man they'd been discussing for most of the evening. Ewan Alexander was inside the house.

Seb didn't speak or move. Bewildered and cold with shock, he waited expectantly until he noticed that the ill-defined head of Ewan did not appear to be looking down at him, but was angled away. The head was turned to the window, the one that had been open just before. It was now closed and covered by the unmoving blind.

From inside his own mind, or perhaps these sounds originated from within the room, Seb heard several muted voices that ran over each other.

He was reminded of when Ewan used to talk to himself,

when he was drunk and he produced streams of nonsense in odd voices, spoken quickly and horribly. When they were students, Seb had often overheard him doing that in his room. Back then it had been much louder as if there were other people inside his room. It was something Seb had always put down to drugs, that ability of Ewan's to speak in tongues. He'd also imagined that he was overhearing a cartoon filled with devils.

When the stench hit him, Seb stuffed bedclothes against his mouth.

He'd never smelled anything as foul since the time he'd entered an empty tube carriage, years before in London, and then quickly realized why the carriage was deserted. A pile of clothes had lain discarded on a seat. The foetid odour arising from them had made the unventilated space unbearable. The refuse's odour had attained a specific pitch, when the smell of an unwashed human body became akin to the stench of regurgitation. He'd been more aghast at the circumstances that had forced another citizen to reach that state, and to undress on public transport.

Seb felt fully awake now . . . but realized he was lying in the bed beside Becky again. She was asleep and lying in a new position, facing him.

Two dreams. One into another. Am I even awake now?

Seb sat up.

The figure was gone from the end of the bed and so was the smell. Or so he thought, though he may have detected a residue of oily sweat in the air. Maybe the second dream had been so vivid that his nose was deceiving him.

He left the room and lit up the hall, then the other three empty bedrooms. He checked the two ensuite bathrooms and a little dressing room nervously, checking for legs and feet under the suit bags on their hangers.

Turning the lights on and clearing his throat as if to provoke an intruder, he went upstairs and searched the living room and dining room, the kitchen, his office, the small utility room. All were neat and empty, the windows closed and locked.

Seb moved to the ground floor. There was a short hallway down there, a spare toilet and the door that opened into the garage, the latter occupying most of that level. He found nothing unusual. All was secure, pristine and as empty of life as it had been when he'd gone to bed. Only he and Becky were inside the house.

It wasn't yet four a.m., and he'd not turned in until one in the morning, but he had no desire to return to his bed.

Hours later, dawn had already come and gone when the phone's trilling jerked Seb awake on the sofa. It was his agent, Giles White.

'You might have seen them, Seb. Another hundred went up yesterday. I'll be doing all I can to get them removed with the help of your publisher, first thing Monday morning. So don't worry about a thing.'

Seb's head wasn't the only thing that remained thick with sleep. His voice was as much a gargle as it was a word. 'Sorry?'

'The reviews. I'm afraid that sock-puppeteer has been at it again.'

Stupid paper-thin story, poorly developed characters, clichés.
Piss poor. Keep it in the toilet and wipe your arse on it!!!
Avoid at all costs!!! Don't waste your time, even if it's a

free download or you find it in a bargain bin in a charity shop.

A chore to get through. Have no idea what all these people think is frightening about this tosh. The 'author', and I use this word lightly, knows nothing about the wonder and terror of the supernatural.

Total tripe. Author's friends are giving him five stars. He's a total fake.

Lazy . . . completely unsatisfying . . . worst book ever . . . no stars . . . free books are better than this . . . worst book I've ever read . . . how did this rubbish ever get published . . . couldn't have been more wrong, bored me to tears . . . worst book I've ever read . . . 'convaulted' (but must have meant convoluted) . . . gave up halfway, gave it to a charity shop . . . one of the worst books I've ever read . . . rubbish . . . waste of time . . .

The reviews had piled up on Goodreads and Amazon, all penned by his old enemy who went by names that were now so tediously familiar: goddess50, hindererfolk, phakerevealer, crookidityidity62, sixthsenser, keirosmaster, parasoma_guru, arosoma+mage, vastjetblacknessboy, praiserofnothingness, extremelyrelaxedsleeper, perceptualmaestro, weightlessness-&freedom, nonexistanttravellar, terminationofliars, hazzard-ouscognition, vitalvehicle, summerlandman.

Seb had *mostly* stopped caring about bad reviews years before, and mainly because he'd stopped reading them. He found they taught him little about his books other than that they confounded many expectations, or were simply not to the taste, or even sophistication, of some readers. And *their* taste was often mistaken for an arbitrating authority on quality. Many commentators appeared to want attention at any cost. The need to be heard and acknowledged the motive. Others were just unstable.

A glance at the new crop of stinkers revealed the traits of the hater that his books had mostly encountered over the last two years. He'd assumed the sock-puppeteer was an undiscovered writer. User names often changed, but the puppeteer still occasionally littered his reviews with literary terms, as if possessing some expertise, or believing that he did, while attempting to adopt an ordinary voice to disguise a more knowledgeable status.

The earlier reviews had been composed more carefully. There had been some affectation of erudition and attempts at wit. But the author now repeated himself with hyperbole, and with the telltale emphasis of 'ever' and the four exclamation marks. The juvenile toilet analogies were repeated as imagination failed and the fatigue from repetition set in. These notices were shorter and shriller.

The puppeteer had roared for two years, but Seb had work to do and readers who waited.

His agent and publisher had complained to the retailers and review sites favoured by the puppeteer, but these days, who had the staff to deal with the great numbers of people who passed through and left their graffiti everywhere? Even bad reviews suffered from discovery hell.

'What you doing?' Becky stood in the doorway. She looked ashen and tired and was wearing his gown. Her feet were bare, her hair tousled.

'My agent called me. My number one fan is back.'

'Oh,' she said distractedly. 'How many this time?'

'Triple figures.'

'New book?'

'Yep, taking the ratings down to one star overall.'

'Can I make coffee?' she asked and Seb suffered the impression that Becky was no longer listening.

'I'll make it. I'll get us some breakfast too. I have some rolls. Bacon and eggs.'

She smiled and asked him if he'd slept.

'Barely.'

'Snap.'

'Why? Sexual frustration and hysteria after my floundering yesterday afternoon?'

'Stop fishing. That was no big deal. I think I just had the worst dream of my entire life.'

Seb had to swallow. 'Dream?' He didn't add *me as well*, but his surprise at Becky's admission was tinged with the reckless excitement that precedes a corroboration of the unlikely.

Becky mock-shuddered her shoulders. 'Really weird. I don't want to remember the bits that are still fresh. I'm off seafood for a bit, that's for sure.'

Seb followed her into the living room and took to the kitchen reluctantly. He was desperate to know what had upset her in the night. But he didn't want to rush her and felt that this wasn't the time, so they proceeded to eat the toasted rolls, coffee, juice, bacon and eggs when they were ready. He knew she liked the fare as an occasional treat, and only when she was away from home.

The food, a shower, then an hour of being awake in a house bright with sunlight slowly brightened Becky's mood, but not Seb's. His own nightmares and the bad reviews were fresh intrusions, and his paranoia was sufficient to attribute the reviews to the same force that had recently pitted itself against him. Though a connection between the two would be hard to prove. The reviews had continued for years, the sightings of Ewan were recent.

As he showered and dressed, Seb became angry. He still had no clear idea whether he was seriously disturbed, or if, by some miracle, Ewan Alexander had mastered the ability to appear and vanish from his sight like an illusionist. But this was his world, the real world, a place of comfort and technology made comprehensible by science. He liked it and refused to let it go. Admitting to himself that he was hiding at home, and cowering behind a female guest too, didn't come easily, but he'd found a strength during Becky's visit that had been lacking when alone. He wanted to fight back now, wanted to strike out at whatever it was that had crept in. Going about his business as usual would be a start.

'I suggest we take a walk through the woods to the cove,' he said. 'Then grab a late lunch at the Court. Fancy it?'

'Absolutely. Love to.'

That settled it. They'd go out as a determined front.

But things can change.

'Us both having bad dreams?' he said later as he pulled on his coat in the hall. 'It seems odd that we both had night-mares last night. No dickie tummies and we both ate different meals.'

Becky grimaced as she came down the stairs, rummaging through her bag. 'Mmm? It was so strange because I was sure I'd woken up.'

'Really?'

'Oh, yeah. I was in your bedroom. I could see everything clearly, as if the landing light was on and shining inside the room. And there was someone outside the house, crawling or something. It sounded like someone was rubbing themselves against the wall, or dragging themselves down the side of the house. You were asleep and lying with your back to me. You didn't wake up. And the window was open. I was too scared to get up and close it, you know, before this *thing* got in.

'I could hear these voices too. Tiny voices. They were tiny elderly voices. Old people. A crowd of them. They were in the room somewhere, like in a corner that I couldn't see, or in the air above the bed. It was horrid. Where does this stuff come from? I never remember dreams. It must be you! Your fault, freaking me out about that face at the restaurant window!'

With some difficulty, Seb opened the front door.

He parked at the pub and led Becky to the stile at the edge of the farmland bordering Marriage Wood. This was an area of 'outstanding natural beauty' according to UNESCO. The wood would be carpeted with bluebells and Seb thought this area might enchant Becky, and perhaps help make amends for what he'd put her through that weekend.

If the treetops in the wood were a wind-blown chaos in a gale, the ground remained oddly still and Seb liked the airy, vaulted spaces extending for hundreds of feet between the myriad trees on the slopes. When Seb wandered through the wood he usually only came across occasional dogs and their owners, in the foot of the valley before the trees leapt up the slopes and loomed over the trails below.

Amidst the sweet beech and larch that morning, and all the way to the sea, they came across no one. He led Becky along the main trail, passing the ruined limekilns that once produced the materials that built Torquay and fertilized the surrounding land. He pointed out to her the excavation craters that pitted the earth, all overgrown with ivy, as were the pale slabs that suggested ruins of a greater antiquity.

The intended destination was a sheltered cove where the water became an enticing aquamarine colour as it deepened, while the shallows were so clear that a photograph failed to reveal the water's surface. Seals often frolicked in the cove, or followed those patient fishers, the grebes, around the shoreline and towards Brixham harbour.

As they lost sight of where they had entered the trees, and before they were in sight of the stone gateposts at the rear of the cove, Becky stopped walking and sucked in her breath as if she'd trodden on broken glass. Seb turned to see what was wrong. 'What?'

She didn't answer him, but appeared troubled by something she'd seen. Her head was angled to peer up the slope on the right side of the trail.

Seb moved to where she stood and noticed that her face had adopted an expression identical to the one accompanying her narration of her dream. She whispered, 'I thought . . .' Then added, 'Doesn't matter.'

Seb followed her stare and peered through the trunks, part furred by khaki moss and black ivy. The bonier branches had once given him the idea that such trees might resemble the magnified legs of insects. 'What is it?'

'I could swear . . . up there . . . there was an arm that waved.'

She wasn't making much sense and struggled to find the words in the right sequence for whatever had caught her eye. 'Sometimes trees look like people, don't they?' She tittered after she'd spoken, embarrassed. 'I've been reading too many of your books.'

Seb didn't suggest a return to the car. That would involve going back the way they had come. Instead, as they were almost clear of the trees, they could follow the coastal path into the harbour.

They continued towards the cove until Becky stopped again. 'There!' Her voice was quiet, but tense and insistent. 'God, it made me jump.'

'It?' Seb stared at the ridge above them. 'Where?'

'I'm not pointing,' she whispered, as if nervous about drawing even more attention to herself.

'Someone is up there? Where?'

'Watching. Looking right at us.' Becky seemed to retract her head into her shoulders as if suddenly cold. 'Do you see? Or am I imagining it? Jesus, what is that? Something over their face?'

'Who? I can't see . . .' And then Seb did see *something* that he had initially mistaken for a profoundly twisted tree.

Surely people can't grow so tall. Though if that was a person, then it was someone that must have been standing behind a groping branch, with a body that matched the trunk's woody contortions, while peering down at them.

Or were they? It wasn't easy to see who was up there, nor easy to guess why anyone would be on the ridge. And if that was a man, then his legs must have been obscured by the thick nettles between the trees. What was visible, however, made Seb think of Ewan.

Becky touched his arm. 'I don't know . . . Seb?'

His concentration rewarded him with a suggestion of a figure in dark clothing, even a formal suit that was tight on a pair of impossibly long arms. And if he could see a hand then the hand was pale enough to be mistaken for limestone, or fungi attached to dead wood. The *hand* was positioned as if a long arm had been extended to grasp the fallen timber before it.

The only other detail that struck Seb was a covered head. *Was that a head?* If it was, there was something about the position of the head, and how it was cocked but held still, that made him feel unwell with fear. And whatever was looking at them from within the hood compelled Seb to look away. A meeting of his eyes with those distant and indistinct black holes was too great an ordeal.

Becky sucked in her breath. 'Oh God. It's moving.'

Seb flinched, then looked up again and saw a flurry that later reminded him of a dancer able to swing the upper body to one side while their feet remained planted on a stage.

'Who do you think . . . ?' Becky began to ask, and then stopped as the indistinct shape seemed to slide, or maybe withdraw backwards, and so quickly that Seb almost missed the movement. Sideways it went, briefly, as if on runners, and the manoeuvre issued no noise. But Seb's next impression was of the form not so much moving away, but shrinking into the undergrowth.

'A deer?' Becky muttered. 'Sometimes they . . .' But she never finished the suggestion. Neither of them had seen a deer. And what they had glimpsed was no longer there at all.

There had been a vigorous breeze in the tree canopy when they'd entered the wood, but there had been no sound around them on the path during the sighting. Birdsong was audible again, and the reintroduction of sound made Seb realize that they'd both been transfixed in a soundless glade of the wood, for several seconds.

'The birds,' Becky said, in confirmation that something strange had occurred for her as well. She looked to the tree-tops, that now swayed and loudly swished their leaves once the unnatural pause in the air currents ended.

A pressure of fear pushed through Seb's eyeballs.

Becky didn't seem to be faring much better, even though *it* was over. 'I really didn't like that,' she said. 'They didn't look right.'

Seb didn't have anything to add. Had that been Ewan, though, with his appearance altered?

Had he not seen a similar form scampering through the sawdust of a bad dream? Whatever had been watching them, and perhaps even waiting for their approach, must be connected to Ewan's sudden reappearance in his life.

Becky's collaboration as a witness failed to produce any relief. Whatever was now happening to him was worse than losing his mind, because if that *thing* . . .

'Now you know,' he said.

They hurried to the cove, not exactly running, but walking uncomfortably close to a jog until they were standing on a pebble bank.

Listening to the surf roll stones up and down the beach, they caught their breath and stared at the water as if the bay presented a barrier across their escape route.

'Sorry, but is there another way back?' Becky asked, almost formally.

'On the coastal path. There's a track up there.'

He now hated himself for asking her to visit. He may have put her in the path of harm, without understanding the threat beyond receiving a sequence of murky and elusive impressions that came by night and day.

'That was just someone . . . someone out . . . We had a bad night, Bex. I said too much yesterday. And we drank a fair bit. It's made us jumpy. Innocent things are starting to look sinister. The other day on my balcony . . . the towels . . .' He didn't believe a word of what he said, though the thing in the trees may have been nothing but a glimpse of someone wearing a baggy linen hood, with eyeholes cut into the front. *But why would they do that?*

He didn't examine the idea verbally, and he also believed it unfair to share an impression that the hood had been similar to the bags that were tugged over the heads of the condemned on the gallows, in times long gone.

'Yes. Maybe,' Becky said, as if she were speaking to no one in particular.

The return journey via a new route around the wood was uneventful, though on the section of the path parallel to where they'd seen a figure on the ridge, Becky moved closer to the stone wall opposite the encroaching trees. Seb only noticed because he'd done the same thing.

'Seb, will you take me to the station?' she said when she saw his car.

'But lunch—'

'I want to go home. Now.'

7

The Same Event in a
Converse Direction

Ewan was on the drive.

Seb alighted from his car and fell backwards, casting an arm across the roof to keep his feet.

He closed his eyes, counted to three and reopened them.

Ewan remained, grinning. He stepped forwards and the gravel crunched beneath the soles of his shoes. *He* was *there*.

It was *him*, and the strange aural effects accompanying the previous sightings were absent. Things were going to be different this time.

Seb's first impression confirmed the continuance of an old theme, inebriation embellished by neglect. Even then, the changes in the man's appearance since London were shocking. Ewan had been to places and done things that Seb could only imagine.

The man's greatest burden in life may have been a grotesque head. A large skull, flat at the back, atop a flabby neck showing no definition to the shoulders. The squashed upper section of his face, with a low brow and near-porcine nose, quickly and regrettably became familiar. Sometime during the intervening years his eye sockets had suffered a lumpy reformation with scar tissue, from knocks or tumbles. That bit was new and made the entire spectacle freshly monstrous.

The tired complexion now showed the effects of poison or liver damage. Between the cap's peak and the moustache, across the cheekbones and forehead, the sallow skin was blotched with broken blood vessels. Greasy white patches streaked the unkempt beard as if individual moments of crisis had bleached clumps of his facial hair.

Seb's biggest aversion yet was reserved for the mouth. The last time he'd seen Ewan there had been something disconcerting about the terrible condition of his tobacco-stained teeth, but at the threshold of his home in Brixham, he experienced the same disgust he'd once endured when confronted by the genitals and anus of a baboon in a zoo.

Ewan's mouth was feral and grotesquely genital. Perhaps it was the unkempt fringe of black beard that made those lips appear so bruised and engorged to emphasize the square, gappy teeth. And they were stained brown-yellow, like two rows of dried corn inside the smirk that hadn't changed since he'd appeared on the drive.

This was the worst face that Seb had seen in his life. Finer feelings seemed to have been blunted, and the sensitivity to the nuances of another's discomfort erased. There was nothing contemporary about Ewan any more. He was a savage.

Trying to keep the tremor from his words, Seb heard himself croak, 'What do you want?'

'You'll find out,' Ewan replied in a voice that had always been too high and thin for his appearance, near effeminate in tone and public-schooled. His voice had also altered, was now roughened by catarrh and deepened by age.

Despite his fright, Seb still suffered a mad desire to laugh at this visage before him. To howl desperately at the oily hair, near dreadlocked and hanging like old rope from beneath the baseball cap that was jammed onto the crown of the big head.

Not wanting to become trapped against a wall, and needing a space in which to think and to evade an assault, he abandoned the car and angled himself away from the house.

Intent on pursuing the effect of surprise, Ewan anticipated the manoeuvre and steered Seb towards the front door, one hesitant step at a time.

Had this scene been in one of Seb's novels, there might have been a scuffle and a strong show of resistance from the lead character. But this was no novel, this was his life and he was no fighter. The situation made him understand how we imagine we are people that we are not.

'Sebby, my old mate.' Ewan tittered and held out a large hand, the skin red and marbled like corned beef, the nails black with dirt. His eyes were still dark enough to make the pupils indistinguishable from the iris. And with him so close, the intensity of his stare was made worse by its hint of sadistic amusement and need.

'You dropped your hat when you ran away.' At the end of the long fingers drooped the hat Seb had lost in the cliffside gardens in Goodrington. 'I went back and picked it up. I could have hung it on a fence spike, but I didn't think you'd be going back there for a while.'

After this, it was hard for Seb to process how Ewan came to be inside the house so quickly. Concussed by his own fear and bewilderment, he retained nothing but a hazy recollection of scuffing his feet to the porch, where he suffered a reluctance to remove the house keys from the pocket of his jacket. During that time, Ewan had kept closing. Hemming him in and making the strength hiss out of Seb like the air from a tyre. Later, he'd likened himself to an elderly person, herded into their own home by a thief driven reckless by intoxicants.

The hallway had seemed to blur brightly around Ewan's black eyes and their penetrating expression of triumphant mirth.

'No. No way.' Seb did manage to say that much in the hall, but his resistance was brushed aside with the waft of one dirty hand. Ewan pushed past him and Seb coughed in the smell wafting from the trespasser's coat.

Shutting Ewan out would only have deterred the inevitable. He would get in another way. *Had he not already?*

He needed to know why Ewan was here. The invader's purpose remained undisclosed, but Ewan wanted something for sure. Seb hoped it was only money.

Following the horrible experience on the drive, the silence of his home, the white walls, the absence of dirt, the right angles and the open spaces took on an aspect of fragility. He might have even been taking a last look at a building marked for demolition, or one perched on an eroded cliff. All that had nurtured and protected him, and confirmed him as a success, now appeared as if it were destined to be lost.

Ewan took an insolently casual moment to look about himself in the stairwell, and at the stacking evidence of affluence that confronted his weather-beaten face. The luxury made his scruffy presence even more dramatic, wild and incongruous.

The intruder's focus shifted to the framed book covers and prints of the film posters. His posture stiffened. There was a poster of *Apparitions* on the hall wall and Ewan seemed ready to remove the frame from its hooks before smashing the picture against the floor. Instead, he snorted dismissively and climbed the stairs, assuming the lead in the way he had done twenty years before when they were students. Did he believe that dynamic still existed, with him the dominant half of the friendship?

Alcohol fumes combined with his other odours and trailed behind him, suggesting a tangibility akin to an unclean mist.

Ewan went straight on up to the second floor, light on his feet, but swaying. He glanced into the kitchen and study, but only paused, as if stunned, when he saw the view of the bay through the living-room windows.

'What do you want, Ewan?' Seb repeated, while stricken with a suspicion that he was following a dangerous animal deeper inside his own home. 'You've been following me.'

When Ewan spotted the glinting metal and sparkling crystal of the awards that Seb's writing had acquired over the last decade, his eyes narrowed with the most severe displeasure thus far displayed. In the bookcase beneath the awards, the shelves were lined with the colourful spines of Seb's first editions, and the foreign-language editions gathered from over thirty countries.

'Yes. Very nice.' He nodded as if proving some point to himself. 'Very, very nice, indeed.'

The house offended Ewan. Perhaps he expected Seb to have put his life on hold, or to have made a catastrophe of the last three decades as Ewan had clearly done. But why show up now, and why not ten years ago when his trajectory as an author went vertical?

Ewan thumped his body down upon the sofa like an

oafish teenager. A crack sounded, either inside the sofa or from the tiles beneath the rug.

Seb started, as if the spell holding him rigid for so long was broken. 'Careful! Jesus Christ!'

'Oops,' Ewan said, and tittered.

Anger surged like a hot bile to the back of Seb's throat. *Too late now. He got inside. He's inside now.*

His rage quickly transformed into dread at the sight of those gangly limbs sprawled in a horrible suggestion of entitlement upon *his* couch. Ewan's jeans may have once been blue but were now blackened with filth. On his feet, a pair of beaten shoes were split across the bridge of the toes. The soles had been ground to a rubber membrane by the endless, purposeless walks of the transient.

Shiny with stains and ripped in two places, the original colour of his anorak was also impossible to determine. Ewan made no move to remove his coat, and for that Seb was grateful. It suggested the visit might be short.

'Why are you here?'

'Hasty, don't be so hasty. All in good time. And aren't you going to offer me a drink?' Ewan's words were slurred and that may have accounted for his disinclination to say much since he'd appeared. 'Come on! Have a drink with an old friend. It's been ages. And look at you, the bestselling writer! It looks like one of those Sunday magazines in here!'

Ewan glanced around the room again, gently shaking his head as if in exasperated despair at what confirmed his worst suspicions. Seb clearly hadn't followed the script. But he knew that Ewan was being disingenuous. A maddening, searing jealousy was burning him up. He'd seen evidence of that before, not least over Julie.

'One drink, an explanation, and then you'll have to go.'

Ewan changed his expression into a poor attempt at appearing offended. 'Am I keeping the literary genius from more important matters? I mean, I haven't seen you in years and you're already trying to get rid of me.'

'I didn't ask you to come here. Or to . . . *you know*.'

Ewan grinned. The rictus conveyed that he could do something extraordinary that Seb didn't understand, and Ewan wasn't going to be very forthcoming about it either, or anything that he didn't want to talk about. He was playing by different rules: persistence and manipulation, implied threats, intimidation. Perhaps a precedent was being set for their coming interaction. The grin, the demands for drink, the posture of the careless body spread across the sofa, were the only statements of intent being offered at this stage.

To avoid Ewan's black eyes, but also to regroup his wits and to think on his next move, Seb went into the kitchen to fetch drinks, choosing two bottles of low-strength beer. He didn't know what else to do. He was too jittery and risked more indecision, so he busied himself with the cupboard doors and glasses, suppressing the tremble that had possessed his hands. He was out of practice with any conflict, save what came at him online.

He thought of the police and fingered his phone inside the front pocket of his jeans. But what would he say?

He then thought about taking a knife from the drawer. That idea made him recoil the moment he entertained it, because holding a weapon was as preposterous as the current situation.

He'd probably remain civil and restrained, unemotional,

and the insight made him loathe himself. Ewan counted on Seb being Seb.

He returned to the living room, unarmed and holding two glasses of beer.

Ewan was looking over the first editions and fingering them roughly with his grubby hands. He'd returned a book to the wrong place, left another carelessly protruding from the shelf, a third was laid flat. The disorder transfixed Seb. It was another reminder of the past, and perhaps a premonition of his future if he failed to get rid of Ewan quickly.

'Drinkie-poos,' Ewan said, and took the proffered glass. 'I have to say, you don't seem very pleased to see me.'

Seb felt an urge to lash out, to strike the oily face hard. A tremor passed along his arm; though, like the bullied who are manacled by the restraints of reasonable behaviour, this was an impulse that would never become action.

'You're surprised by that?'

His terror at the dreams and Ewan's appearances remained trapped inside his mind like an energy that would not earth. He realized he'd do anything to avoid a continuation of *that*. Provoking the unstable was never a smart move either. Their responses to resistance could be as desperate as their circumstances.

'Our lives have followed different paths. Clearly.' Seb tried to add the last word in a neutral tone, but it dragged itself sarcastically from his mouth.

'First you run away and now you're all tense. Relax, Sebastian. Aren't you interested in what I've been up to?'

'I've enough on my own plate.'

'I think you are, just a little bit.' Ewan winked. 'You couldn't even begin to understand what I've done. What I've achieved. And, judging by what I've seen of your books, you've gone a bit off course as far as all that is concerned.'

'All of what?'

Ewan tittered and shook his head as if Seb had embarrassed himself.

'I don't follow, Ewan. As far as what is concerned? In what have I been lacking?'

Ewan's eyes protruded as if from a burst of excitement. 'True mysticism! And enlightenment.' Between the two men, a flotilla of spittle droplets fell through the sunlit air.

'My ambitions were never so grandiose. I just wanted to write well.'

'Yes, well . . .' Ewan raised his eyebrows. 'Never mind, but at least you've done all right out of potboilers, though there's no accounting for taste.' He watched keenly for Seb's reaction. Satisfied he'd inflicted another small wound, he changed the subject, directing proceedings. 'How long has it been now?' Ewan asked, distractedly, with a befuddled frown, pretending that he didn't know.

'Ten years, at least,' Seb said, knowing it had been exactly twelve since the smelly shape had last stunk out his living space.

'Long time.' Ewan was about to repeat his heavy slump onto the sofa, but caught Seb's eye and lowered himself more carefully, parodying the action of a person sitting upon delicate furniture. 'Too long! So I thought it was about time that I paid you a visit. All very nice, I must say. You've been lucky.'

Ewan swigged from his glass as though desperately thirsty. Perhaps he wanted to give an impression that doggishly gulping the beer was more important than anything

Seb could possibly say in reply. Ewan followed this by ex-aggerating a satisfied gasp. Foam flecked the black hair around his wet mouth.

Seb moved to the balcony doors. 'Lucky? Yes, very lucky, Ewan. You could say that I've exceeded my own expect-ations, and by some margin. But I've also worked hard. All that advice writers offer about commitment and dedication has some validity.'

Seb opened one door and found the briny draught imme-diately welcome. It was late, the sun was going down and the afternoon had turned chilly, but he was feeling sick on account of the smell, and the sight, of Ewan.

'Brrrr,' Ewan said loudly, and eclipsed the end of Seb's sentence, impatient with his host's attempts to defend himself. In the past, he'd often make noises and engage in distracting movements, when drunk, if an argument wasn't going his way. He'd never been able to listen to anyone for long and liked to obliterate other personalities with his manic energy. Seb thought it doubtful the tactics had changed; attack and give no room for counter-attack.

Ewan had always thought he was quick too, while having no insight into what a ridiculous boor he was. More and more was coming back to Seb now, and chiefly those things that he'd been happy to forget.

Seb warily settled into his favourite chair, the one closest to the balcony. 'So what are you doing here, Ewan? I'm get-ting tired of asking the same question. What is this about?'

The question summoned a grimace from Ewan. 'You haven't got a clue, have you? Not really. About anything. You never did. You always were a bit like that. Couldn't grasp the bigger picture. You were a bit, dare I say, clueless?' He pursed his lips and took an affected sip of his beer.

Seb wanted to throw the television remote into Ewan's face, as hard as possible across the short distance. He thought instead of the distant black figure standing in the sea and quelled a shudder. He had to know how Ewan had managed to appear like that. *So let him speak.* From whatever the unwanted visitor shared, conclusions could be drawn later.

'I tried to read a couple of your books,' Ewan said, creasing his nose as if recalling something worse than the smell of his own clothes. 'Oh dear. Oh dearie me. But I can see that you put a lot of work into them.'

'Ewan. What do you want?'

'Did people really like that story about the hospital? I have to say, I found it all a bit silly. Afraid I didn't finish any of the others I found in the library either. I tried. But you've clearly done all right out of it.' He looked around himself again with an expression that suggested he wanted to begin vandalizing the room. 'People will buy anything, though. All about marketing these days, branding, isn't it?' He shook his head, exasperated but knowing.

Seb cleared the irritation from his throat. Suppressing it was giving him heartburn. 'It clearly attracted you down here. What are you after, an endorsement?' *I have seen the future of horror and he hasn't taken a shower in ten fucking years.* Seb smiled to himself. Two could play this game. 'It's been a while since I've seen you on the shelves of WHSmith. Better to actually finish a book first, Ewan.'

'You think I envy all this?' Ewan shot back. 'It's hardly that. I'd actually be a bit embarrassed if I was churning this out.' He indicated the bookshelves. 'Pulp, isn't it? Is that what you wanted to write? Is that all writing is worth to you: money? You missed the boat somewhere along the line, Seb. But I didn't come here to talk about your books.' There was a sarcastic tilt on the last word, as if intonation alone could belittle the actual works. 'I didn't come here to pay homage. I'm quite sure you get enough of that from the pillocks out there. Though they haven't got a clue, not about writing, have they? And they haven't got a clue about the other stuff either.'

'What other stuff? I'm intrigued as to what the point is that we've all missed.'

Ewan silenced him with a big hand that wagged a finger in remonstration. 'Don't you think that something so special might be a bit private, sacred even? So all in good time.' He held up his other hand. 'My glass is empty.'

'Bar's closed.'

'Open it. What's the point of having all of this if you can't relax and have a drink with an old friend.'

'You're hardly that. Do friends stalk one another?'

'Stalk!' Ewan found this incredibly funny and slapped a thigh. 'You haven't seen anything.' And he fixed Seb against his chair with his eyes alone. Eyes bloated with inebriation but shining with diabolical intent. 'But I think you're waking up now and getting the picture. And about time, I'd say. About time you got a bit real. If you were worried enough to run away on the beach, you'll be quite surprised, shall we say, by what else I can do. I might show you sometime. But I wouldn't be in any hurry to see it, if I were you. It's not some magician's illusion. I'd say that only a tiny handful of people in this world have ever pulled off what I can pull off.'

Seb did his best not to react to the threat and kept his voice calm. 'What picture can I not see? I still don't follow.'

'Oh, don't be coy. Some of us have spent our time a bit more wisely, instead of writing silly stories about . . . about . . .' The drink appeared to be affecting his memory. 'Ghosties and things. But you don't understand what's really out there, or here, and really close by, do you? Not really. You're in the dark like everyone else. You don't even know what it is that you're trying to write about. That's all fantasy. So I thought I'd show you something real, something special, something that requires a lot more skill than just sitting around in here, pulling some ridiculous story out of your head. Ha! And you are privileged to have seen what you have seen, but you don't even know it. You can't handle it. Just like I suspected. Dearie, dearie me, you really have missed the boat. But at least I'm here to help you now.'

Seb wasn't sure whether his fear or his loathing would choke him first, but the situation felt akin to being taunted by someone who was pointing a gun at him. 'Help me with what? I'm fine as I am.'

Ewan looked at his glass. 'We can get into all of that later. Today, I just wanted to say hello and have a drink with an old mate. Get reacquainted before the fun begins.'

'Fun?'

'Oh, yes. You've got a lot to learn.'

'About what?'

Ewan grinned. 'About what's really going on. Where it all leads.' He gazed around the room again. 'I thought your stuff would have a bit of edge, like I tried to show you, when I started you off, back at uni. But you've lost the plot.'

'You started me off, did you?'

'Don't deny it.' Ewan looked at the bookshelves. 'You wouldn't have written one of those books if I hadn't helped you.'

'I don't think that's—'

'You hadn't read anything until you met me. You didn't know anything. Think about it. You could say that all of this –' again his hands took in his surroundings – 'is mostly down to me. My influence. And you've never acknowledged it.'

To make such a declaration would have entailed Ewan checking the acknowledgements in each of his books, as well as reading the interviews he'd given about his origins as a writer. This made Seb consider the fresh spate of trolling reviews. He wondered if Ewan had been behind those from the start. Perhaps, for years, Ewan had been maliciously harassing his books online. 'Do you really believe that, Ewan?'

'Believe it? It's a fact. You'd never read Machen or Wakefield, or Aickman, Blackwood, none of the *believers*, until you met me. I even lent you my books. And, judging by what you've written, you didn't read them all that carefully.'

Now Seb's entire body was rigid, white and uncomfortable with suppressed rage. He stood up. 'I'm not getting into this. I'm not debating my books with you, or anything else for that matter. But I can understand why you're upset. It doesn't appear that things have worked out for you, Ewan, though that has nothing to do with me. But I'm not really surprised that you're pissed off and pissed up. Nothing's changed there, has it? Same old resentful Ewan. But you made your bed and I have made mine, and it's time you took off.'

'I've only just arrived. I'm not ready to go yet.' He winked and grinned his yellowy grin. 'You must be a little dissatisfied with how it's gone, surely?'

'No, as a matter of fact, I—'

Ewan interrupted, raising his slurred voice. 'Was it worth it? Not very rock and roll is it? Gadgets and baubles, trinkets! I remember you telling me how you were going to drive across America. Live in a forest in Norway. Or was it a Greek island? Have you done any of that?'

'No. But I—'

'Ha! Didn't think so. You've just become some fussy, pretentious, stay-at-home pulp fiction type. You haven't done anything! You haven't lived, man! Or seen anything. You're a bit of a fraud, if I'm honest.' Ewan's mouth had become sloppy. His eyes were becoming increasingly unfocused and he was struggling to express what Seb suspected was a rehearsed spiel. Ewan may have waited a long time to say all of this.

Seb's anger would no longer keep silent. 'I'll tell you what I did, Ewan: I read. I actually read books, and a great many of them. I learned from them, and from better writers. And I sat still, at a desk, and I wrote. I figured out the basics of the craft. And while I wrote for years without much recognition, I paid my bills doing boring, soul-destroying jobs. I stood on my own two feet and I supported myself. I had no choice. My parents weren't rich.

'I had some breaks. A lot of people helped me for sure, agents, editors, even critics, but I wrote my way out of some bad times. Only I could do that, alone. I have no control over the bigger picture, but at least I was consistent and I worked.'

Ewan tried to interrupt. 'Listen to him!'

'And I acknowledged my failings, Ewan. Confronted them, addressed them. And I searched myself, wrung myself out to see if I had anything to say, to see if I could make a contribution. Year after year. Half of my life making writing a purpose, including over a decade of indifference from publishers. Eventually I was noticed, because I stuck at it.'

'Noticed by who? Some twats in London, with their soirees and festivals and launches. I've seen them. Been to those things. No one has a clue. No one. They're not even fun. No one even knows how to have a bit of fun.'

'Fun? Is that the goal? The party's over, Ewan. It ended in 1990 for everyone but you. Your own approach doesn't look like much fun to me. I mean, Christ alive, have you looked in the mirror recently?'

Ewan glanced down his body. 'What?' he asked in what appeared to be genuine surprise.

'What have you produced? Where's the body of work? You're what, nearly sixty? Was this the endgame that you had in mind?'

'Oh, I've been working. And writing! Oh, yes, but not some ridiculous crap they sell in some crappy supermarket. Some shit that mums read to pass a few hours. Oh, no, you don't need to worry about that!'

'I'm not worried. I don't care.'

'Oh, I think you will be quite surprised by what I have been up to. By what I have produced. And we're talking about the real deal here. Something that will matter when it comes out. Oh, yes.'

Seb no longer thought about the vanishing act, or the lone sentinel watching from afar, or the figure up in the trees of Marriage Wood. Ewan had attacked the most important thing in his life: his writing. 'Matter to who? You? And when what comes out? And when? How do you even know your writing is any good? What kind of scrutiny has it been put under? Does it not need any informed appraisal? Maybe not, because you just know that it's brilliant. Still the same old Ewan. Delusional. Pissed and lazy. Just another entitled prick with family money. And that must have been pissed away by the look of you. Or were you cut off? Did your folks finally realize they'd sired a money pit? An ungrateful one at that. Your greatness doesn't extend more than one millimetre further than your own grubby skull, and it never did. You keep telling me that I'm clueless. *Me!* That I've missed the boat. But I am inclined to believe that when the boat left port, you were still asleep in the park, unconscious on a bench.'

Ewan grinned and lowered his voice in a way that suggested the coming of danger. 'Listen to yourself, playing at being some literary toff. Pretentious. Mannered. Some cosseted Hay-on-Wye ponce. Who do you think you are, M. R.-fucking-James?'

He roared with laughter at his own jibe. 'It's that voice. That horrible voice in all of your books. It's fake. It's not you! You're working class, for God's sake. A prole trying to write like a toff!'

'You don't have a clue about—'

Ewan rose, swaying, from his seat, gesticulating with those dirty claws, swinging his big red hands excitedly through the air. The last of the beer in his glass cut a foaming arc across the room and splashed over a table, the back of the sofa, a wall. 'You're the joke! You. Clueless!'

Seb clenched his fists. 'You son of a bitch. My furniture!'

81

'Oops.' Ewan found the spillage funny, but looked oddly sheepish too, as if finally realizing that he had gone too far and risked losing control of his advantage.

Anger had all but closed Seb's throat. He was shaking but he took a step forwards, and this time Ewan retreated. 'I worked . . . so hard. For years.'

'Misguidedly. It must be said.'

'You went to a private school! You were born into privilege. Did you think I'd forgotten? You've never stood on your own two feet. You've never worked, have you? You've never even had a job. What's your excuse? You don't have one. What have you got to show for yourself? Nothing. You're undisciplined and feckless, an overgrown adolescent. And you come here, to my home, to terrorize and criticize me? You call *me* a fraud? You try to threaten me with that . . . with whatever it is that you are doing? Are you so poisoned by envy?'

Part-way through Seb's assault, Ewan had looked shocked, and even slightly remorseful. But the swinish grin eventually returned and the expression in his eyes darkened. 'There, *that*. That's more like it. You're not trying to sound like bloody Walter de la Mare any more. That's a bit more real. You're making progress already.'

'Piss off!'

'Even better. But you still don't get it. You can't even see that I came here to help you. To do *you* a favour. To share something that'll . . . well, that'll make you a better writer for starters.'

Seb returned to his chair, trembling. Instability was contagious. He'd not been truly enraged for years, but was now unable to see straight. 'I'm calling the police.'

'Ha! And tell them what? Did I break in? No, you let me in. I'm just an old friend who's come a long way to see you.'

'Who's been following me, watching me, harassing me. They'll take one look at you and know the score.'

'Call them!' Ewan was excited again, as if Seb had succeeded in initiating one of his rehearsed ploys ahead of the planned time. 'Get them to come here and escort me off the premises. Go on, do it! What are you waiting for?'

Ewan's eyes shuttered up and down to refocus, probably from the effects of whatever he'd been drinking, or even taking, before he'd arrived. 'You won't call them because there'd be no point. Because I can come back, at any time, and you know it. I presume you'd like to get a good night's sleep now and again? And to be able to go shopping, and on dates with that tart, without me just popping up, here, there and everywhere?'

He raised his long arms into the air and waggled his fingers spiderishly. 'At any time, day or night, I can just call on you. If I want to. Tell you what, why don't I go right now and then come back in a few hours when you're fast asleep? How does that sound? We can get together then. You won't need to get up and let me in, either. I'll let myself in and we can resume our little chat, while you're asleep or awake. I really don't mind. What do you say to that?'

Seb felt his anger rapidly cool.

'Now where's my bloody beer? I'm parched.' Ewan wafted a hand in the direction of the kitchen as if to hurry a servant along. 'Well, go on then, get them in!'

Snoring grumbled from the adjoining room.

By nine, Ewan had finished his fifth drink and the last of

83

the beer in the fridge. After a final salvo of slurred, repetitive reproaches, he'd fallen asleep on the sofa where he'd remained sprawled. Within the soiled clothes his relaxed limbs had looked terribly thin in contrast to the small belly and flabby neck.

He'd briefly snapped awake twice, his expression near unrecognizable, doleful and confused, as if he had been struggling to identify where he was. Ewan was not only drunk, but spent.

Reluctant to close the blinds, in case the gesture intimated that Ewan had been accepted as an overnight guest, Seb had opened a window and left the room. He'd then remained in the kitchen for an hour, his elbows set on the granite counter, chin cupped in his hands, hungry but nauseous. He realized he knew as little now of Ewan's reasons for seeking him out as he'd known before the man had entered the house.

The time for shaking Ewan awake and asking him to leave had passed. Even if he had managed to coerce him off the premises, he imagined Ewan making a nuisance of himself on the drive, shouting drunkenly and frightening his elderly neighbours. If he did go away, he'd only turn up again, and who could tell what shape he'd be in?

He would have to kick him out in the morning when Ewan was sober, but only after forcing him to make clear his intentions.

Seb left the kitchen and retired to his room just after eleven, his chest tight and his mind racing.

He undressed, reflecting upon how he had slept in the same bed with an attractive woman the previous evening, inside his smart, modern house. A place where he'd been

surrounded and confirmed by the evidence of his achieve-
ments. The sudden change in his circumstances seemed
absurd, even unmoored from reality. But that was how Ewan
had operated in their house at university, and in his room in
London, by infecting an environment physically, and in
other ways too.

Not this one. Not this time.

It was preposterous. At the age of nineteen, when he
didn't know any better, he had made the mistake of befriend-
ing a dangerous misfit. How could he still be paying for the
error at the age of fifty? Maybe he would continue to pay
for it until one of them died.

Until he fell asleep, Seb listened to the snoring that rever-
berated through the ceiling.

8

I Can See in an Absence of Light

When sleep came, its condition was fitful and harassed by an awful dream set inside his house, though the interior was enlarged enough to hold him and Ewan, and those *others*, forever.

Seb was much changed, into a naked thing, luminous as a pale worm in dark clay, a skeletal, hairless creature without genitals. A crude operation had been performed between his legs and the wound had been stitched shut with the brown twine that he kept under the kitchen sink.

Exhausted by the long marches down the never-ending hallways of the building, he had struggled to see through a mist. Dim light the colour of mercury illumined little.

Crouched behind Ewan, the ranting giant, whose crown of hair had stuck to his skull and neck, Seb had felt perversely safer.

Like a bearded prophet with a paunch, naked save for a loincloth, Ewan had forged ahead on his thin legs, and swept one arm about in the air as he read from a cluster of dirty papers. Incanting words that Seb never caught, Ewan forced a swift pace. He wanted no delays in their reaching the far-off stutter of pale light that soundlessly flickered ahead.

Behind Seb others crawled. *They* were old, filled with fear and eager for him to lead them to a place that he was unaware of. He preferred not to look at them, but heard their bare hands and knees bumping upon the floorboards that soon turned to wet bricks. He also caught snatches of their nonsensical entreaties as he moved.

'Is the light over there?' someone asked.

'Have you seen my sister?' another said, as if in answer.

'I cannot get back,' a voice uttered in a tone that verged on panic.

Up ahead something waited within the distant whitish static. Perhaps something on the ceiling was worshipped, or just longed for. It never became apparent to Seb, but the crowd considered the light to be a way out of the damp culvert that ran with cold, black water.

Eventually Ewan discarded the papers and took to swinging one of his old shoes like a priest's censer. The shoe was filled with soil which Ewan used to fingerpaint a figure onto the moist bricks. Childish images of the same thing, but all the worse for the crude composition that depicted a long, hunched form that moved about on all fours, with its head concealed inside a bag.

'We find ourselves and we find the way back,' he said to Seb, and someone behind Seb shrieked, 'Yes!' in what sounded like a paroxysm of devotion.

Seb was soon holding aloft his best salad bowl, a vessel choked with filth so that he might resupply the tatty shoe in Ewan's hand. And down that masonry chute they all stumbled while Ewan spread the graffiti.

At the threshold of the room of the flashing light, Ewan had leaned down and looped a belt around Seb's throat.

Then dragged him into a flickering space where the sound went backwards.

With his legs beset by a paralysing sensation of pins and needles, Seb was hauled around a floor that reeked like an ape's enclosure in a sun-baked zoo. Whimpering with determination to reach the light, he found himself slipping back the way they had already journeyed, until he staggered anew across the wet bricks of the culvert.

Occasionally, someone would scream from above, someone hanging upside down and reaching for him with their long arms. But within the herd of thin, muttering people, Seb kept moving towards the light.

The end of the nightmare was horrible without containing much specific imagery. Seb woke, suffering an impression that his body had just been suspended within a dark space, where gravity had ceased to exist. His feet had risen above his head towards *something* close to his soles. Whatever was above him had suggested itself as a large, open mouth, moving in circles as he struggled to keep his body on the mattress.

When Seb awoke, his face was taut with dried tears. He sat up, panting for breath, afraid, and almost too alert to have been asleep. Fragments of the dream struck him with an unnatural vividness.

He sensed that his mother and father had been inside the stuttering light. Had they called out to him? He wasn't sure when he woke up, but a sense of them had made him yearn for the intermittent light with a ferocity that should have broken him from the nightmare.

He remained dazed and shaken for several minutes. Recollections from the previous evening seeped into his mind.

He hated himself for how quickly he'd become immobilized by cowardice.

Seb looked at the clock. It had gone two in the afternoon. *How?*

He'd been exhausted for weeks. He then tried to explain the nightmare with the intensification of his feelings of victimization. They could be responsible for the awful claustrophobia of the dream, which made him resent Ewan even more than he already did, if that were possible. Ewan had reached deeper into his existence. His physical pollution of the house, and his maddening, autistic will was but the first level of torment. It was as if Ewan was now unwilling to be without him at any time, even as he slept.

Seb swung his legs out of bed.

Pausing in the corridor outside his room, he could hear footsteps upstairs. Feet shuffling and bumping, interspersed with a low chatter from the television.

A cupboard was opened and closed, the dulled sound audible through the ceiling. A light clicked on. The ring-pull of a can was cracked and emitted a hiss of gas. The noise of the television rose higher and a picture in the hallway vibrated. A solid object fell to the floor of the living room, bounced and rolled.

Seb went up, drifting through a familiar scent cloud; the sweat of cattle, the kidney and shellfish of a male groin too long unclean, and something else like burned bone, binding all of the other flavours together.

Coughing to clear his airways was futile. The entire building was filled with the stench. It was seeping out of the living room that Ewan occupied. No doubt the miasma had filled the kitchen and his office too.

Imagining that he might smell Ewan everywhere, and on all of his things, for weeks brought Seb close to a convulsion. That's how it had gone down in London. Ewan's odours had been absorbed by the upholstery, thickened in the confines of wardrobes and drawers, and drifted from every book cover and ornament, his spoor ever present for weeks after he'd gone.

Ewan could not remain here. Seb would have to run to town and withdraw money, should he need to pay for a room for Ewan until he knew what the man wanted. One payment and that would be it, just like in London. He loathed himself for contemplating this appeasement, but was unable to think of another way of ridding the house of this stinking menace.

He'd need to do some research and consult a solicitor about obtaining a restraining order, but didn't imagine that getting one would be easy. The police and courts would have to be involved. Maybe police intervention would frighten Ewan enough to stop appearing. Though Ewan might also move his tactics up a notch. He'd promised as much. Explaining his predicament to the police, without appearing mad himself, was something Seb also struggled to imagine.

On the first-floor landing, Seb broke out in a sudden and uncomfortable sweat. From the kitchen, on the floor above, he heard the whoosh of the boiler. The central heating was on. Electric lights burned in every room on the next floor, save the living room, where only the television screen's white light flickered around the door, which had been left ajar.

Into the lounge Seb burst.

And was immediately disoriented. The television blared

and flashed in the darkness. Canned laughter crackled the speakers. The floor thumped and transmitted the sound into Seb's chest.

The screen was showing a music channel: Scuzz.

A warm day out too, but the balcony doors were closed and the blinds drawn.

Stale cider and fast-food smells competed with the other odours. Seb coughed to clear his airways but it sounded more like retching.

In the gloom on the far side of the room, Ewan's gangly shape was slumped into Seb's favourite chair. One shoe had been removed and Ewan had placed a discoloured foot upon his lap. Only when something exploded white on the television, did Seb see the full horror of that foot.

Yellow teeth gritted and nose creased, Ewan concentrated as two of his dirty claws scratched the psoriasis on his instep.

'Jesus,' Seb said, at the same time as his foot connected with an empty cider can and sent it skidding into another two empties beneath the side table. They were all labelled as a brand of extra-strong cider.

His thoughts bumped into each other and careened away into nothingness. He only retained the presence of mind to locate the remote control on the coffee table. He snatched it up and turned the volume of the television down.

Ewan pulled the remnant of a black sock over his foot and ankle. 'It itches,' he said, smiling.

'I'm not surprised.'

When they'd cohabited, Ewan had always staked out the living room as his own territory, and sat too close to the screen like a child that had never been told otherwise. He now seemed intent on repeating the habit, in line with turning the room into an unnerving facsimile of his old bedroom in Wylding Lane. A disorderly nest.

Seb was choked more by exasperation than the smell. Did that make him forget what he wanted to say? Perhaps the intense way Ewan looked at him was disarming. Ewan had no time for the glance. His eyes were still and he looked at Seb like a cat that Seb remembered from his childhood. A cat that would sit and stare with black eyes that had always made him feel uneasy and guilty, as if its suspicions of Seb's unacceptable thoughts had become more than a hunch.

Ewan, like the cat, was really expecting some kind of challenge or attack. Those were the eyes of someone incapable of trust, who pushed his luck and awaited reprisals.

Suffering an aversion to meeting Ewan's black eyes – one that writhed in his gut – Seb looked away.

About the living room were the books that Ewan had taken off the shelves, flicked through and discarded, open and face-down. A first edition of an Oliver Onions collection lay beside the chair that Ewan had slumped into. An empty cider can was placed upon the dust jacket.

Seb rushed across the room and retrieved the book. The jacket was marked by a drying ring of liquid that smelled vinegary. 'Jesus Christ!'

Ewan sniggered.

'Do you know how valuable this is?'

Ewan shrugged. 'It's just a book.'

'My book!'

'Oops,' he replied in a placid tone before he giggled. 'Would you listen to him?'

'Listen to me!' It was then that Seb noticed a stained

rucksack and two bulging bin liners arranged messily beside Ewan's chair. *Luggage.*

So Ewan had been out that morning, while Seb slept, to fetch *his things.* Another two cans of extra-strong cider were balanced on the arm of Seb's favourite chair. A king-size Mars bar and three bags of crisps lay upon the coffee table. The provisions must have been inside Ewan's grubby ruck-sack, or procured while Seb had been lost to the world and dreaming of another place.

The front door locked itself once it was pulled to. Seb laid the book down. 'You . . . you've been out. And then you let yourself back in. How? How the hell did you get back in here?'

'With a key.' If anything, Ewan seemed surprised that he was being questioned about how he came to be sitting in Seb's chair with the bags beside his feet.

'Key?' Seb queried, beginning to feel soft-limbed and weightless again from the sheer preposterousness of the situation.

'It was on a hook in the kitchen.'

Ewan had taken the spare front door keys from the hook on the back of the kitchen door. *What else had he taken?* Seb noticed that the door to his office was ajar.

'That's it! Police.' Seb ran for the landline phone.

Ewan was amused. 'I went to collect a few of my things. I have something very interesting to show you. I told you about it yesterday.'

Seb's fingers paused on the phone. He invested every ounce of dismissive incredulity he possessed into his voice. 'I'm not interested in anything that you have to tell me. You took my keys and let yourself into my house! A private building. Are you bloody insane?'

'I didn't think you'd mind.'

There was a plate on the floor, smeared with tomato sauce. Takeaway papers were screwed up beside the plate. At the sight of those, the room seemed to judder in Seb's vision. *He's eating in here!*

Seb took a deep breath, then placed a hand against his racing heart. He sat on the sofa. 'We need to talk.'

'What about?'

'What do you think?'

'I've been waiting ages for you to wake up.'

Seb closed his eyes, steadied himself, lowered his voice. 'You can't stay here. Put the keys on the table. Right now.'

Ewan stared at him, his expression wilting to pitying amusement, the eyes swimming with inebriation.

'Look at this place,' Seb said, his voice hampered by his panting breath. 'Look at what you've done to it, in a matter of hours.'

Nonchalantly, Ewan surveyed the room. 'Sorry, what am I looking at?'

Seb slapped his hands against the sofa cushions. 'Can you not see?'

'What do you mean? I can see plenty. It's you I worry about.'

With an upturned face, Seb appealed for support from some higher power. He could not let himself be drawn into another exchange with Ewan, one that promised to be baffling, devoid of reason and conducted in this atmosphere of his unwashed body and clothes.

'I want you out. Now.' Something squealed in Seb's voice, which made him sound foolish and impotent.

'Sorry, why?'

'You were never invited! And the mess! The bloody mess. It stinks in here! You are ruining my books. My things. Everything.' Holding his head in his hands, Seb added, 'Jesus, Jesus, Jesus. This is my home. You are not welcome here. What are you doing here? What are you doing to me?'

Ewan's expression maintained a weary, intoxicated puzzlement. He sniggered again.

'This is no joke.' Seb's voice broke again. 'I know you have problems. But you are your own worst enemy. And they're not my problems. You need to leave.'

Reaching over the side of his chair, Ewan picked up a can of cider. Leisurely, he took a throaty swig. Observing this simple, unapologetic and carefree act made Seb realize that he despised Ewan so intensely that he wanted him destroyed. *Wanted* to destroy him.

'Did you not hear what I said? You have to go.'

'Sorry, go where?'

Seb raised his hands into the air. 'How do I know? That's not my concern. Anywhere that's not here. Wherever you crawled out of.'

'No,' Ewan said, with a shake of his head. 'Can't go back *there*.'

'Home. Your mother, if she is still alive.'

'She is, but no. She's done her bit.'

History was determined to repeat itself on a foetid loop of greasy hair. With a tremendous concentration of will, Seb kept his voice steady. 'I don't want you here. Find a room somewhere.'

As if carefully considering the advice, Ewan took another casual swig of his cider. 'Not really my scene any more.' He started to laugh. 'And I don't have enough money. Those rooms are also terrible places. I've lived in a few. I prefer it here.'

Seb could barely hold enough air inside his chest to speak. 'Does any of what you're saying strike you as absurd?'

'I don't follow.'

'You just show up here. At my home. It's been twelve years since you pitched up in London, and you were hardly welcome there either. We weren't even close when you dropped out of college. In fact, we hated each other. But you . . . you come here, and get inside and just . . .'

'What, sorry?'

'Refuse to leave when I ask you to. Is this some kind of revenge?'

Ewan shrugged.

'This is my home. I decide what happens here. Do you understand that?'

'I think you're missing the point –'

'No! You are missing the point. This is a private residence, not a drinkers' hostel. You have no rights here. You even took my keys. My keys! I could have you arrested with one phone call.'

Ewan looked at the can in his hand. A glum, morose expression took over his face.

'Can you not see that I am a very private person?' Seb persisted.

'So am I. But this is big enough for two people. Ample.'

'What you think is irrelevant. You're just not listening to what I'm saying, are you?'

'I am.'

'Then get the fuck out!' Seb pointed at the door. 'I don't want you here. I don't want you anywhere near me, ever.'

'No.'

'What?'

'You're confused. You've just missed the point.'

Seb thought on who he should call first, the police or Social Services.

'Somewhere along the line, you got it all wrong,' Ewan said.

Seb's face was in his hands again. This time he clawed at his scalp. He couldn't bear to look at Ewan. He spoke into the floor instead. 'I'll find you somewhere to go. I'll pay. We'll meet on neutral ground. You can show me whatever you want to show me and then you can piss off. How's that?'

There was a long silence. 'It's a nice offer. But I'm not so sure it's the right thing to do. You see, I don't want to live on my own any more. It's too hard to keep everything going. It's better I stay here. And we've so much to discuss. I need to set you right, and you owe me.'

Seb stood up and wrenched open the blinds, nearly breaking them. He threw the balcony doors wide. Ewan blinked in the sharp, lemony light.

Seb clutched at the chip paper and seized the top of the nearest bin liner beside the chair that Ewan was slumped in.

Ewan leapt up. 'Leave it!'

Seb dropped the bin liner and stepped away, his scalp prickling.

Ewan's eyes were wild, the cheeks flushed, the thick lips trembling. 'Don't touch that!' He made an effort to calm himself, his eyes fixed upon the bin bags. 'Just leave that.

You have no idea what I went through to get that. No idea how valuable it is.'

This was the closest Ewan had come to the drunken rages of their undergraduate days. And now that he was on his feet and excitable, he began to weave. He pointed a dirty finger at Seb's face but didn't speak, or couldn't think of what to say.

Seb thought of shut-ins living amongst stacks of old newspapers and heaps of garbage, every item of vital importance to some incomprehensible inner life. Ewan had drunk himself insane and his goal in coming to Devon was to surround himself with refuse and filth in Seb's home. To take revenge on Seb for his success, while sealing himself off from a world that he could not function within, with Seb for company so that he didn't get lonely. Seb wanted to scream.

Instead, he said in a strengthless voice, 'I want you and all of this out of here. Gone.' What he said sounded like a platitude, half-heard at best and ignored by a naughty child. His resistance seemed to disperse around Ewan's head.

He tried another tack. 'I'll give you something to wear, otherwise you'll never get a room. I'll pay for a week in a guest house and then you're out of my life. It's that or the police today. I can get a restraining order like that.' Seb clicked his fingers. 'You are so far out of line, so stop playing dumb.'

Ewan never reacted, and continued to totter on the spot.

Heavy with a particular type of exhaustion that can only be inflicted by drunken imbeciles, Seb edged his way out of the living room, intending to go downstairs. He'd leave the house and call the police on his mobile phone. The handset was inside the pocket of his jacket in the hall.

'Some things are the way they are for a reason,' Ewan said. 'And I can come back at any time. You know that.' He nodded his oily head to emphasize the subtext.

'And if I refuse your demands then you're going to give me bad dreams and will keep appearing to me like some sinister creep, forever?'

Ewan laughed. 'Now you're being dramatic. Getting ahead of yourself. We're not there yet and we've a lot to get through. If you really want me to leave, I will, but only after you've considered my proposal.'

'No deals.'

'If I find myself in a police cell, Sebastian, I promise you that I will return here every day and I will make your every night a living nightmare. And when you leave and find somewhere to hide and think that you are all safe and cosy, guess what? I'll be standing at the end of the bed. And the more I do it, the worse it'll get for you. That's how it goes.'

Ewan's voice softened, or lost its strength towards the end of the threat. He'd begun confidently enough but didn't appear comfortable with what he'd just promised. 'You have to understand that what I do is dangerous. It carries a grave risk. Not just for me. We're in this together now, whether you like it or not.'

A strange, cold sensation prickled Seb's skin. He shivered. 'Why? Why are you doing this to me?'

'I need help and you owe me. You know you do.' Whatever Ewan decided was the truth would always be in his self-interest with no room for deviation. Nothing had changed on that count either.

'What have you been messing around with?'

Ewan smiled as if acknowledging a long-overdue respect.

'No one else would believe me. Though you might, because I've given you a glimpse of something truly miraculous. You have no idea just how incredible this is. And it's going to change everything. Oh yes, for me and for you too, if you just stop freaking out over a few spills here and there. Maybe things will be different for everyone else too, out there, when we're done.' He stretched a long arm towards the balcony windows and spread his dirty fingers to encompass the world.

Again, nothing specific had been mentioned, nothing but hyperbole with a dose of self-importance. Ewan was playing the messiah in possession of rare and forbidden knowledge. *Just like old times.*

But Seb had no real idea who this person was any more. Ewan had never been so unstable. He looked even more primitive and dangerously delinquent than he'd done the day before. It was already pushing three p.m. and Seb was losing another round. But where could Ewan go at this time, in this state? He had no money. If Seb gave him some money, could he trust him to stay away? And he still didn't know how Ewan did *that*.

'You've still told me nothing. Do better. And I want you to give me your word that you will piss off once I've heard your spiel?'

'Spiel! Oh dear. I think you may find it to be a bit more significant than that, my old mate.'

'I am not your mate.'

Ewan flopped himself into the chair. The wooden feet dug into the varnished floorboards.

Seb closed his eyes.

Ewan stared at the bay in the distance and tried to keep

his slurred words together. 'You know, I once went to William Blake's old house. And to Peckham Common. The place where he said the angels were in the trees. They're still there. I could see them. That's when it progressed to a new level for me. My gift was always there, even when I was a kid. But I have learned to see other things. In other places.'

Seb shivered. 'Is that right?' His voice sounded tiny in the silent room.

'There's plenty of things you can see without light.' Ewan stretched his legs out, slurped from the can and gasped with satisfaction. 'Even with your eyes closed.'

'I bet.'

Despite his delusions about being a poet at university, Ewan had often transformed into a bully when drunk. 'You'd better not be thinking of laughing at me.' The subtext was obvious.

Seb stiffened.

Ewan grinned with the sadist's cruel delight at another's unease, offering a full reveal of his yellow teeth. He wanted to be feared and respected.

'I've done a lot of thinking about you,' he said, drawing Seb's horrified eyes to that dark, wet mouth. 'About what you have said about writing. And you were wrong. I was right.'

'Make it quick.'

'Tut, tut. That's not the spirit.'

'Just get it over with!'

'What happened to you, Sebastian? You don't even know how to enjoy all of this!' Ewan threw his long arms into the air. 'And as you will see, all this –' he windmilled an arm – 'hardly matters in the order of things.'

'Order of things?'

'Oh, yes. As you will see.'

'What will I see?'

Smiling as if humouring a fool, Ewan knelt on the floor beside his chair and began rummaging through the bin bags. There followed a brief struggle with the contents until he pulled out a dirty collection of paper, held together with a rubber band. 'I want you to read this. Just for starters.'

The ends of the paper were brown and dog-eared. Seb thought of the previous night's dream and became queasy. The whole situation and its coincidences were unreal. It was as if he was being incrementally separated from the world. Even his thoughts were becoming ill-defined.

'It's all nicely written out.' Ewan walked to the coffee table and swept away the bags of crisps. One of them was open and the contents scattered noisily across the floorboards. 'Oh, dear.'

Ewan straightened the dirty papers on the table. When he removed his hands, the top page curled back upon itself. 'So here it is, if sir would be so kind.' He pointed at the sofa, motioning for Seb to sit. 'We may as well get started. You've a bit of catching up to do.'

'With what?'

'One thing at a time.'

'Is that something you've written?'

'Indeed.' Ewan beamed as if he were presenting a long-awaited manuscript that Seb should feel awe before. Ewan drummed the black fingernails of both hands on the top page and cleared his throat. 'I give his lordship, *Breathe in the Astral*.'

Eyes bulging with excitement, Ewan stood back and

waited for Seb's enthusiasm at a chance to read the dirty sheets of paper.

Seb could smell the manuscript from three feet away. He shivered with disgust and didn't want to touch the paper, let alone read it. It must have been sealed inside a bin bag for long periods of time, amongst soiled articles of clothing, while the author wandered endlessly, drunkenly gibbering about angels in trees. Ewan needed a psychiatrist.

Seb glanced at the top page. 'It's not even typed.'

'You asked me what I had been doing for ten years, well here's your answer.'

There couldn't have been more than a hundred pages on the coffee table. Ewan had never seemed more ridiculous. 'You spent ten years writing that?'

'Not just writing it. A lot of preparation was involved. Poetry doesn't just happen you know. You may think it, it . . . it . . .' The great poet couldn't express the sentiment. Instead, he staggered around the bin liner and delved deeper. There were a number of cardboard box files inside. 'This is the secondary material we will use. You need to read it. You'll see what's what.'

Teeth clenched and on display, he strode across to Seb's shelves and pointed at the first editions. 'Never mind this,' he said, rolling his eyes. 'I think it's time we moved on from all that.' He took the baseball cap off and scratched the scalp beneath. 'Time you involved yourself in something a bit more ambitious. Something that matters.'

It was the first time Seb had seen the hat removed. Ewan's hair had retained the shape of the cap and that was how Ewan's head had looked in the dream. A fresh gust of scent molecules drifted from the unhealthy, tangled hair.

'Everything will make sense and you will see why I'm right. So you best get started.' The cap went back on the head. Ewan now seemed happy with how things were going. So this is what he wanted, someone to pay attention to him and his crazy ideas.

Seb only wanted to physically destroy him, to entangle his fists in the terrible hair while smashing his head against a steel radiator. He rose to his feet and turned to the door. 'Forget it.'

Ewan stumbled to block the door. 'It's very important that you read it. You've never read anything like it. Never.'

'Step aside.'

'No, no, no, no, no, no,' Ewan said in a sing-song voice that Seb found odious. 'What are you afraid of? I sense a little insecurity creeping in here. Oh, dear.'

Seb's vision flickered. 'You solipsistic moron. I have a life! What do you know about anything? Look at yourself. When was the last time you even washed your clothes?'

Ewan pursed his discoloured lips. 'Mmmm. Let me see. About two years. About that. You see, where I have been there wasn't even hot water. None of this phoney comfort for frauds.'

At the mention of the duration Seb felt his face drain of blood.

'Couple of years since I've had a bath, so what? The flesh is irrelevant. *This* has nothing to do with the body! It isn't even about the mind. This is the soul-body that I am writing about. The soul-body, you fool! Have you any idea how long the preparations last to even get a glimpse? To take that path, to unlock yourself and go on that journey? Read my book and you'll see. You'll all see things a little more clearly. You've missed the boat! Same as everybody else. All you hacks. You've all missed the boat.' Ewan tapped his head knowingly. 'But I haven't.' He refused to move away from the door.

Ewan had no respect for him, his privacy, his possessions. He was just here to pitch his awful manuscript and to take advantage of him in every possible sense.

Too enraged to speak coherently, Seb opened a window. He pushed his head out and gulped at the air. He was suffering from more than a fear for his own safety. He was also afraid of what he might read in the lunatic's dirty papers. The contents might infect him with whatever had deranged Ewan. Not a bad story for a horror novel, he thought, but this was no story. It was real and happening to him.

Seb went and sat on the edge of the sofa, his body angled forwards, his hands gripping his naked knees. 'You came here because you want me to read that?' Seb pointed at the dirty papers and at the bin bags.

Ewan grinned.

'This is something you have been writing, and you think that I will, what? Help you get it published?'

'Oh it will be. By whoever reads it first. It just needs a little polish. Then it needs to be placed into the right hands. That's where you come in.'

Seb kept his tone level. 'So, let me see if I have this right: you expect me to read this, edit it, and then take it to my publisher? Maybe you also expect me to champion you as a writer?'

'Yes, that would be good,' Ewan said in a tone of eager

acknowledgement. 'That sort of thing,' he added. 'Maybe we can show your editor first. You know, like an exclusive.'

'So you thought you'd threaten and coerce me, the man who has now given you shelter twice, and the only person to ever offer you friendship at university? This is how you repay me? You've become aware of my success, but you hate it, and you hate my books. Maybe you've even been reviewing them too, when not working on your masterpiece?'

Ewan looked uncomfortable but pleased with himself that he'd been found out. His own subterfuge amused him. He couldn't stop grinning.

'You've shown me nothing but contempt and yet you expect my help. In fact, you believe that you are entitled to my assistance, because you loaned me a few books in 1988.'

'Oh, it was more than a few books. It was ideas. Music. A new perception. Direction. I opened your eyes to a whole new world. I started you off. It's not my fault that you took shortcuts and sold out. If you'd listened to me you might have achieved something unique. You have no idea how far I've gone, beyond all this.' Again the dismissive swipe of a big dirty hand, loosely directed towards the entire world. 'You could even have had a bit of fun along the way. But you've still done all right out of me. Time to pay the piper, my old friend! And until you read it, you have no idea how important my book actually is.'

'Important? It's not a book. It's a pile of dirty paper. Handwritten and kept inside a bin bag. You think I am going to spend my precious time reading it and rewriting it?'

'More of a structural edit and a bit of typing. It'll be worth your while.'

'What?'

'Yes, you'll get to be the first person to read it. I tried some of the publishers in London, but they didn't read it.'

'Hang on, you took *this* to a publisher?'

'I went to see a few.'

'You actually went to *see them*?'

'At their offices, yes.'

'You walked into publishers' offices with your . . .' Seb eyed the bin liners and decided not to describe the submission. 'And you asked them to read *that*?'

Ewan nodded. 'They didn't understand. If they'd read it they would have recognized something special, something a bit different from all the crap they churn out. You see, there's nothing like it out there.'

'Out there? You're aware of everything *out there*, I assume?'

Ewan sneered. 'All that silly middle-class crap. Stupid fantasy. It's not real. I've been in plenty of bookshops. It all misses the point.'

Seb felt a profound pity take him over, one that depressed him but also brought him close to hysterical laughter. Ewan had broken new ground on the frustration, futility and desperation of becoming a writer.

And nothing was ever going to be as vital as his manuscript. Ewan's discoloured eyes had lit with an unstable intensity. He leaned forwards and tapped the soiled paper. 'This really happened. Everything in there is the truth. What it's all about, life, existence, consciousness, and what comes next. All the evidence of everything that matters is in those bags. And we need to get started. There's no time to waste. I've been through . . . you just can't imagine . . . just to get here. I don't want to waste any more time. I want to get this out there quickly. This is a great opportunity.'

'For whom?'

Ewan didn't seem to hear him. 'The writing's fine. In fact, it's very good, I think you will find. But the material needs reorganizing. What you do with your books, you know, the structure? That sort of thing. It needs that.'

'Structuring, revising, and even typing up? Big job.'

Ewan remained insensitive to Seb's sarcasm. 'But when it's done it'll be something else. And you've done this before. On those.' He wafted a hand dismissively in the direction of the bookshelves. 'It won't be a problem for you. And my book is nearly there. I'm a bit tired. I need a break from it. But all this needs is a little TLC. Though I'll be reading what you've done to see if it's right. We can go through it, section by section, after you've finished and I'll check it over.

'I call them verses, not chapters. You'll find it's a bit of everything, poetry, philosophy, you name it. Unique. You could even say it's theological, a religion. It'll be one, I'm sure of it. And when it's all nicely typed and ready, we'll take it to your agent. He can negotiate with your publisher, like he does with your stuff. But that's ten years' work on that table and in those files. I don't want to get ripped off.'

Seb had nothing more to say. He'd run dry of everything, language, hope, even feeling that particular kind of despair constructed from boredom and pity. He yawned, stood up and left the room.

Ewan appeared puzzled by Seb's departure. 'Where are you going?'

Downstairs, Seb closed the door to his room and killed the lights. Still wearing his dressing gown, he slumped onto the bed. Physical and mental exhaustion slowed his thoughts towards paralysis. He slipped earphones inside his ears and selected Beethoven on his MP3 player.

When Seb felt able to leave his room again, in the early evening, the first thing he smelled in the corridor outside his bedroom was Ewan.

During the hours he'd been alone in his room, he'd decided he would read the stinking pages of Ewan's manuscript. He'd do that this evening. If Ewan then refused to leave his home, and to take up residency in a guest house at Seb's expense, he'd call the police. He would risk whatever it was that Ewan decided to cast at him, whether he was awake or asleep. If this didn't end now, he sensed that a turning point in his life was imminent. One just ahead of him that would swing him about and compel him to revisit the hardest and unhappiest years of his life. It was that simple.

Still tired and delicate, as if hungover from that day's binge of emotion, Seb went upstairs and checked the living room.

Ewan wasn't inside but the television was still on, as were the ceiling lights and a lamp on a side table. The bulging bin liners and rucksack were still in place beside Seb's favourite chair. Cider cans littered the floor, the rug was stained in three places and the floorboards were tacky from spillages.

Seb turned the television off. The house fell silent.

He searched for his guest and found him behind a closed door on the first floor, passed out, mouth hanging open, lying on his back. He'd eventually gone into one of the guest bedrooms and climbed onto a bed, fully dressed. There was a long, arcing smudge of dirt at the foot of the white duvet cover. Seb anticipated burning the bedclothes in the garden later.

Maudlin and feeling sorry for himself, Seb returned to the living room, removed the empty cans and dropped them into the recycler. Ewan had also eaten three bags of crisps, two Magnum ice-creams that he'd found in Seb's freezer, and put bread in the toaster but forgotten about it.

Methodically, Seb cleared away the mess.

At seven he rinsed the mop he'd used on the living-room floor a final time and straightened his spine, rubbing his lower lumbar. And immediately became dizzy as if the blood had drained from his head.

Blinking rapidly, he tried to clear his eyes of the red motes of light that fell through his darkening vision. The ambient sounds of the room, and the sea beyond the nearby cliffs, retreated as if sucked down a drain. Sensing a scrutiny from behind, he turned.

Ewan stood at the far end of the dining room, seeming taller than ever, his form entirely dark save for the bloodless face. Seb dropped the mop.

Ewan smiled and stretched out a long arm to point into the living room, to somewhere near Seb. Through the unnatural silence came Ewan's voice, but in a tone that was older and gentler, even emotionless. For a moment Seb was unsure whether the voice sounded from within the house or inside his head.

Work to be done.

Seb stepped backwards and submitted to an overpowering compulsion to look down. The first thing his startled eyes settled upon was the stained covering sheet of Ewan's manuscript, spread out on the coffee table. *Breathe in the Astral.*

Seb peered back at the doorway. Ewan had vanished.

Through the open balcony doors returned the distant buzz of a lawnmower, the soft hum of a car engine, the song of the thrushes in the garden below.

Inside the kitchen, a room now pungent with lemon disinfectant and bleach, there was no sign of Ewan.

Unsteadily at first, but gathering purpose as he moved, Seb walked downstairs to the bedroom that Ewan had occupied.

And found him lying upon the bed. His eyes were closed but twitching. His chest rose and fell.

You have no idea. No idea. Ewan's voice announced itself from behind Seb, or again from *within*.

Seb turned as if he were turning inside a dream, and in the hall outside he saw the black form of a man, Ewan, who stepped away, out of sight and deeper into the passage.

Seb forced himself to follow. He heard no footfall, not even his own, and passed into an empty hallway. There was no way that Ewan could have hidden himself in so short a time by making it into another room. Besides that, the man was still stretched out on a bed in the spare room.

A noise erupted from the room where Ewan slept. A deep moan that rose and broke into a whine. The sound of an animal in pain.

By the time Seb was peering through the doorway, Ewan was making the noise of a man choking to death. His freakishly double-jointed hands had also bent inwards and shook about. Tremors returned along his forearms to his shoulders.

His spine suffered a spasm, arching his body into the air. Gangly legs kicked spastically into the duvet, before bending at the knee and thrusting out from his pelvis at odd angles. His eyes opened and rolled white as the muscles in his face convulsed. Froth gathered in the messy beard.

Staring in shock and revulsion, Seb feared Ewan's neck was close to snapping when it pulled the big head backwards. The entire weight of his upper body appeared to be supported by the crown of his skull. One of Ewan's lower legs bent back behind his thigh and his body jumped as if electrocuted, onto its side. The muscles of his arms shuddered violently and the contorted form propelled itself, or bounced, off the bed and onto the floor. Out of sight, a coconut crack issued from the connection of a skull with a wooden floor.

The seizure – because Seb was certain that he was witnessing one – continued on the floor, where Ewan's body thumped about, his thin legs kicking while his torso bent backwards from the waist. The bearded face gulped at the air between mouthing words.

The electricity in Ewan's nervous system gradually earthed. The spasms of his muscles subsided, and soon his body merely twitched.

Seb was clutching the doorframe with fingertips that had turned painfully white. He also acknowledged a desire for Ewan to die, right there. The moans rising from the floor, that evolved into sobs, only caused him disappointment. Suppressing the vengeful feeling, he entered the room.

Ewan lay still and wept. The only movement remained in his long hands as they gingerly pawed about his head, in the place where it had connected with the floor and maybe the headboard too.

Ewan was unaware of where he was. His eyes were wide open, the stare unfocused, tears adding a sheen to his cheek-bones. On the carpet beside him lay a small plastic baggie. It contained speckles of a blue-white powder.

Maybe chemical assistance was required for him to perform this unnatural transference. Seb had clearly seen Ewan in the entrance of the kitchen, and again, though less distinctly, in the hallway between the bedrooms. He had seen these *apparitions* while Ewan lay upon *this* very bed.

Seb recalled Ewan's silhouette standing in his room when Becky had visited. But from where had he *travelled* then?

He wondered if he should call an ambulance. He supposed he should, but resisted the idea because a sullen, recalcitrant part of him wanted Ewan to remain incapacitated as oxygen deprivation caused permanent damage to his brain.

For a while, he did nothing while a confirmation of the impossible sank through him. He just stared at the reduced, traumatized, weeping figure, until prolonged exposure to it initiated a shiver of disgust across his skin.

A fuller awareness returned to Ewan's eyes. When he tried to speak, he croaked. Raising one limp hand he managed to say, 'Water.'

'Is that what happens when you do this? When you perform your great miracles?' Seb asked, and recognized the goading tone in his voice.

Ewan said, 'Help me,' piteously. And it was only then that Seb saw a fellow human being in distress, one hurt and frightened and helpless. It was only then that he went to fetch water.

9
Sinking in Darkness, Rising in the White Room

Jittery himself, Seb helped Ewan back onto the bed. His own shock was steadily becoming a trauma. He couldn't see the end of it.

He went to the bathroom and washed his hands, wishing he could cleanse away the entire mess that Ewan had imposed upon his life. Even his shirt reeked of the man. He stripped it off and dropped it into the linen basket in his bedroom.

All this time, his head crowded with options: calling an ambulance, driving Ewan to a hospital, finding Ewan's mother – *she must be nearly ninety* – scouring the local listings for hostels, and perhaps even initiating a committal by a psychiatrist.

When he returned to the guest bedroom, Ewan was asleep. Mouth open, head back, his body limp upon the covers, he snored quietly, whistling through his nose.

I wish you'd died.

Seb shut the curtains, closed the door and went into the living room. Pouring himself a large brandy, he peered into the corners of the room and out to the balcony. His eyes finally rested on the darkened kitchen doorway at the far end of the dining room. *Where next?* And would he come again in that horrible, hooded form? The thought prompted Seb to say, 'Never. Not again. That was the last time. It has to be.'

He briefly imagined bringing one of his heavy crystal awards down upon that greasy head that was staining an Egyptian cotton pillowcase in his spare room. A revenge fantasy because he'd never do it. *Or could he, if pushed any further?*

Would death be any kind of barrier to Ewan's influence? Was there any way of permanently getting rid of him, besides subjugating himself to Ewan's demands and hoping for the best? Seb had to assume that a long period of time was destined to elapse before his usefulness to a man with a unique ability to terrorize his victims was exhausted.

He checked on Ewan throughout the evening, repeatedly cracking the door to peer inside. He listened to the whistles, throat clearing and mumbles that arose from the man's sleep. Alcohol, perspiration and the sebaceous miasmas of neglect eventually encouraged him to keep the door closed. He wished he'd opened a window in the room, but didn't want to go back inside until Ewan was awake. God knows what might happen if he did.

Sick with apprehension, Seb cobbled together a light tea in the kitchen. When he discovered three hairs that were not his in the butter he lost his appetite.

Just before midnight, Ewan roused. Seb heard the bedroom door click open on the floor below.

He raced down to catch sight of Ewan going into the bathroom, hobbling, head lowered, shoulders slumped. After a cascading urination, Ewan shuffled back out.

Seb called out from the bottom of the staircase. 'Ewan!'

He was ignored. Glum, haggard and hatless, Ewan continued on his way down the passage and re-entered *his* room. He shut the door. The muffled noise of bedsprings depressing were detectable as the uninvited guest returned his weight to the mattress.

It was the continuing contempt, the callous disregard for his feelings and rights, the man's affected ignorance of deep social transgressions, that broke another chunk from Seb's levee. He flooded again with a hot white anger.

He thumped down the passage and threw the door open. 'After what you pulled this afternoon, you are not staying here!' But even as he spoke he could see that Ewan was in no fit state to move. He was exhausted, ill and bedridden. Close to a complete physical collapse.

He's making you responsible. Co-dependent, again.

That was part of Ewan's strategy. Insults followed by cries for help, grandiose literary delusions swiftly augmented by a childlike vulnerability, drunken rages interspersed with an obliviousness to any injury inflicted upon the reluctant host. Ewan had never changed. The actual sight and scent of him was maddening.

His instability was also infectious. Seb knew this. It shook him up and then shook him apart. Ewan was loosening rivets in the scaffolding that kept him balanced. His own slide to despair was already in place. His entire existence was a construct of routines and activity born of self-discipline, of tight controls over his environment, counter-checks imposed upon apathy and listlessness, his potential for lazy thinking, persecution fantasies, paranoia, anxiety attacks and recourse to the drinks cabinet.

He hadn't written a word in three weeks or addressed his correspondence. Had not shopped properly, slept much or eaten adequately. He'd lost the ability to relax since his first sighting of Ewan on Broadsands. The script of his life was being rewritten while he impotently monitored the edits.

'Don't even think about getting comfortable.'

Face drawn, the cast of his mouth doleful, the eyes pained, Ewan didn't bother to defend his position. He was inside now. *Try and move me* was communicated by the collapsed posture upon the bed.

Seb entered the room and fought with the blinds, then angrily threw two windows open. Pitch black outside. *Another night with him here.*

Ewan's sorrowful eyes watched Seb patiently, affecting innocence as if Seb were being unfair at an inappropriate time.

'What happened? This afternoon, what was that? A fit? Are you epileptic?'

Ewan swallowed. His voice croaky, he whispered, 'It takes a lot out of me.'

Ewan's creepy appearances were not effortless miracles. They exacted a high price. Perhaps the processes were even life-threatening. Seb hoped so. 'And you're taking drugs in my house to facilitate your stalking.'

Ewan didn't blink, but his silent admission of how difficult this awful *trick* was to enact encouraged Seb. For the first time since his arrival in the area, not everything was going Ewan's way, and Seb saw his first advantage.

Until he regained his strength, or a modicum of it, Ewan would probably play the invalid card, in the same way that he'd played the poverty hand in London. Digressions until he'd regrouped and consolidated his baffling, controlling presence.

'I want answers. You want to lie around in bed, then you'd better start talking, or you are bloody history, tonight. I don't know who to call first, a doctor, a psychiatrist, the police, but you are out of here and this all stops, unless you start making sense.'

The threats made no impact. Ewan continued to study Seb's face as if trying to understand why Seb would feel this way. He'd expected terror while craving awe and admiration.

The period of silence extended. Seb came close to shouting to break it. 'Well?'

'Do you have anything to drink?'

'No!' Seb slapped his hands against his thighs. 'How can you even consider alcohol? I thought you'd died.'

'Have you read my book yet?'

'No, I haven't even looked at it. Let's just say I've had other things on my mind.'

Ewan attempted to shake his head, dismissively, upon the pillow that was looking unhealthily dark since his head had been upon it. He winced and kept still. 'We can exist in another place.'

Silence resumed its frustrating command of the room.

'And?'

'If you've never sunk in the dark room and risen in white light, you won't understand. Nor believe that it's possible.'

'Let's just say my scepticism is on pause right now. So what is this? Some kind of . . . I don't know, ritual magic, or hypnosis—'

Ewan didn't like speculation, or any attempt at a definition that wasn't his own. 'This has got nothing to do with magic.' He said *magic* as if the very word disgusted him. 'What's magic? Magic doesn't exist. And I don't have any time for any of your intellectualism either. Not for this. You don't know this. It has nothing to do with religious dogma either. It's different.'

'So no magic, nothing spiritual –'

'I didn't say it wasn't spiritual. It has nothing to do with organized religion, but it is spiritual. That's exactly what it is. But the religious can't handle it, not any more. They're incapable of accepting the truth.'

'This is a psychic thing?'

'Hardly. That barely begins to explain it. That's like one itty-bitty piece of an incredible fresco on a ceiling above us all, but one that no one can see, in the most beautiful cathedral. A tiny piece that has fallen to the floor of this . . .' He looked about himself at the tastefully styled room, but in revulsion. 'Do you remember any of the poetry you read, at uni? You did the same courses as me. *He hath awakened from the dream of life!* You know that?'

'Shelley.'

'*No sudden heaven nor sudden hell for man.*'

Seb shook his head.

'Oh, dear, *the writer* . . .' Ewan rolled his eyes and intended to continue in that vein, but noticed Seb stiffen. 'Dearie, dearie me,' Ewan muttered instead, and then said, 'Tennyson. And the poets had more idea than anyone else, especially Blake. This has to be felt, deeply. There has to be faith.

'A man called Heindel tried to define it. Tried to describe the enlargement, the growing, that can take place in our awareness. He argued that because we exist physically in time and space, we can only recognize ourselves in that same time and space. But imagine shedding the physical body, the vehicle, and the time and space that imprison us physically, to become *a double* in another place, one nearby, that has no time or space. Imagine *projecting* into a place that intersects this one.'

Ewan sighed when he saw the look of incredulity grow on Seb's face. He closed his eyes. 'It's hopeless. I'm tired.'

'I'm still intrigued.'

Ewan moved higher up the bed, using an elbow. 'It's all in my book.'

'Pretend that you're pitching your book. Every book needs a pitch.'

Ewan scowled, then seemed to lack the energy to sustain the expression. 'The body . . .' He looked at his own as if such an appraisal was a subject unworthy of consideration. 'The body is a prison cell. Once you know . . . once you understand that, you can have nothing but contempt for the body. Inside them we don't even know what it is to be alive. You're only really alive when you leave your body. That's the irony, but you cannot believe the potential we have.'

Ewan frowned as if confronted by an infant. 'Let me make it simpler for you. Imagine if all of your sadness and pain, everything that troubles you, all of it, anxiety, grief, disappointment, anger, were to go. Imagine how you would feel if all of the misery of being alive just fell from you. You can't. Because you've never projected. You can't imagine the ecstasy. To become so strong, like you cannot believe. Powerful. You're suffused with . . .'

'There's nothing here –' he looked askance at the room again – 'that matters. This existence is a shadow of what our souls can experience at a higher level. A place where I can go. Where time and space are no longer my captors. You cannot imagine the freedom, the elation. And you never will until you die. But imagine if you could experience that before you died. I have. You asked me what I've been doing for all of those years since I saw you last, well, there's your bloody answer.'

What Ewan had said, the very diction he'd used, made Seb feel uncomfortable and also mortified for Ewan. This talk of souls, ecstasy and of being 'suffused' was appalling, the discourse of the charlatan. Seb hated the very sight of him more than ever, this reeking, unwashed drunk, with the tangled ropes of hair spread across his bed linen, the weather- and drink-blasted face. He was reminded of emaciated holy men in India, mad hermits, swivel-eyed cult leaders, greedy preachers, the low animal cunning of the vulpine clairvoyant, and he placed Ewan amongst their absurd ranks.

Ewan rolled onto his side to clasp the glass of water on the bedside table.

Seb tried to conceal his sarcasm but knew he'd failed as soon as he began to speak. 'It doesn't appear that this enlightenment of which you speak so highly, and this ability to transcend space and time, have done you much good. To be honest, Ewan, I'd be inclined to feel a little short-changed by your epiphanies if this is how you end up, at your age. I mean, wouldn't it have been better to have stayed in this *other place*, wherever it is that you go?'

'Doesn't work like that. We're not supposed to be there.'

'Evidently. But when I . . . when I have seen you out and about, you hardly look your best either. If I am going to be honest, you look like you're stuck in hell. You also always return to your body, the prison, and that's not much better, is it?'

The jibe caused Ewan pain. If it was possible he went even paler. He now looked harried too, if not haunted, as if being forced to remember something not only unpleasant but frightening. 'Hell' may have been the trigger.

When Ewan resettled himself, his eyes had developed an expression that seemed to reach beyond the room, like an intense focus on something in the past. 'It wasn't always like this. It's not all darkness. There's light, a light that you cannot imagine. Like nothing you've ever seen. That's why we travel. Once you've seen it . . . Nothing is the same again. Nothing.'

Seb was convinced those had been the first truthful words he'd heard Ewan say since arrival. 'Light?'

Ewan's face appeared younger, the eyes alive with something other than scorn, spite or deviousness. It looked like genuine wonder. 'It's not the same as the light here. It's so bright and yet so soft. It defines everything more vividly. You can see the beauty of everything. What you see becomes new, changed. There are no shadows. The light casts no shadows. No glare.

'Paradise. Summerland. The Third Sphere. It's been called all kinds of things by people who have been ignored. But these people have been *there*. And it is the only place where we can be free and happy. Completely free and intensely happy, always. Even if it is dark where you find yourself, you take that light with you. Your presence is the light in the unlit places. Your soul is the light . . . trying to return.' Ewan continued to stare at nothing in the room as tears filmed his eyes.

Seb sat on the floor, resting his back against the chest of

drawers. Trying to appear as if he were not humouring Ewan, though he still found it difficult to suppress his scorn, he said, 'How do you do it? How do you get *there*?'

Ewan didn't seem to hear him. His lips moved, though he wasn't speaking to anyone but himself. Eventually, he smiled. 'You don't, unless by accident, or during an accident. A near-death experience will do it. Or while upon an operating table. Or unless you are born with a loose . . . it's known as the vehicle of vitality. And if you are in possession of one that is improperly moored, it allows you to *drift*. It was only the determination of some people, who'd travelled accidentally, to relive the experience that made it possible for this to ever be controlled. As much as it can be, but never fully.'

'There are techniques?'

'They have to be practised for years, in the right environment, and under the supervision and control of mentors before it's feasible. It's not easy, what I do, oh no. For most it's impossible and always will be, no matter how hard they try. But not for all. And I have been preparing and learning a great secret for years.'

Seb barely managed to repress the derogatory snort that had gathered behind his face like a sneeze.

'But the first time was an accident. You see, I nearly died. Massive fit. Maybe from bad gear. I'd separated my consciousness before, using LSD, and other things. Loads of times. I'd known about this experience years earlier, before I first met you. As difficult as the books were to get hold of, I'd even read everything that Hazzard ever wrote. Both of his books before I was twenty-one.'

'Hazzard? M. L. Hazzard, the writer?'

Nodding his head, Ewan narrowed his eyes knowingly.

Seb knew of M. L. Hazzard. Aficionados of the weird would probably be aware of him too. Years before, Seb had read a couple of Hazzard short stories in long out-of-print horror anthologies, but he'd never forgotten one of them. 'Many Communications Must Remain in Doubt', it had been called. A simple but affecting story of a man who continually haunted a beautiful young woman by travelling in spirit-form to her home each night, to watch her undress, before lingering by the bed to inhabit her space and scent. Eventually the woman wakes and the narrator reveals himself, but wearing a goatish mask, the horns extending into the air. The man had wanted the woman to believe that he was Pan, and that she had been chosen for special instructions, but she dies of fright. She had a heart murmur that the stalker never knew about. The story ends with a description of a paranoid man in a house that he hasn't left in two months, on the other side of town, as he hides a goat mask in the loft, between a box of Christmas decorations and some board games from his childhood. He makes a cup of tea, but his hands are shaking and he can't speak.

The anthology in which Seb had first read the story had actually been one of Ewan's books: *Night's Longest Hours*. Derleth may even have been the editor. It had been published by Consul, Seb thought, someone like that, and Ewan's copy had been bound in sticky tape.

'I tried all kinds of things to achieve what the Master did.'

'Master? Who, Hazzard?' But before Seb said any more, he began to feel cold. *The goat mask?* Could a hood or sack be put to the same use in the interest of striking terror into a man? That black form in the trees of Marriage Wood that he and Becky had seen, and crawling across the golf course in the dream, what had that been? Ewan must have used a costume to make his point more dramatically.

Seb thought about the rucksack in the living room and wondered what he might find inside it. He shifted about on the floor and rattled the chest of drawers. 'Please, continue. You were saying, the first time, it was an accident.'

'Yes. I nearly died, or even died. They weren't sure afterwards. But I felt myself die. And it was the most peaceful thing that I have ever experienced. I was aware of it. All of it. *Dying*. Actually dying. Totally aware of it, as if death was magnified inside my mind. My toes went first, then my feet, then my legs. They just became absent. My abdomen, my chest and then my neck just shut off. But the focus of my consciousness in that room was intense, everything was so clearly defined around me. I was shutting down, but I was more aware of the world than I had ever been.'

Ewan paused to swallow and moisten his lips. 'But then I was looking at myself. Standing upright and looking down at myself. Like in Hazzard's stories, I was looking at myself from nothing. I was in two places. I could see myself on the floorboards in a room in that terrible house. My eyes were open but totally vacant . . . I wasn't there any more. And I remember thinking how thin I looked. And how long my body was, as if I'd never realized what I actually looked like. It wasn't the same as looking in the mirror. I looked . . . strange.

'That didn't matter, that body on the floor. I felt nothing for it. But I still knew that it was *me*. I knew that I had split. I didn't care that I had separated. I felt euphoric. I was *euphoria*.'

Ewan lay back and briefly closed his eyes in bliss from recall alone. 'The experience was so gentle and beautiful. I was in love and loved more than I had ever been . . . It was more powerful, more transporting than the effect of any drug that I'd ever taken. Here was true joy. I was free. It was all over, the struggle. I was completely free of myself. And yet, I understood everything too. Or I was about to understand and . . . about to *know* everything, instinctively and all at once. It was like I was on the edge . . . of *that*.

'I watched one of the two people that I was with, and he touched me. I could see the back of his head. I watched him shake me really hard. And I suddenly fell forwards. It was like stumbling in a dream, like stepping off a kerb that you haven't seen, or a step that suddenly appears under your foot. There was this sickening jolt and I woke up on the floor, back inside that body that I had just been looking at. My body. And the experience was over. Completely.

'I cried because I had come back. For the first time in my life, I really wanted to die. I wished that I had died. That was the first time it happened and it changed my life. It changed everything.'

Seb realized that, if his experiences in the last two weeks had never happened, Ewan had said nothing that couldn't be explained as the result of drug use, mental illness or a combination of the two. 'The first time?'

'I was taken to hospital and kept inside for a few days. They ran tests. I was in pretty bad shape and I was diagnosed with epilepsy. I'd had a couple of fits before, but nothing like that one. I thought it was because of what I'd been taking, impure stuff, for years, living rough, you know? But it happened again, in the hospital, on the ward. Maybe I had another fit, but a milder one. I don't know.

'I found myself standing beside the bed, looking down at myself. That time it didn't last long. As soon as I became aware of what I was doing, I fell back, into myself, and I was awake again in a hospital bed, inside this long, dark room. The ward. But it hadn't been dark when I was standing beside the bed. The room had been filled with light. Beautiful, soft light. I had seen everything inside the room. I only realized later that *I* had been the light.

'I knew something special was happening to me. It didn't make me afraid. Not at all. I couldn't think about anything else afterwards. It was like that had been a sign. A message. I'd been guided and this was my new purpose, to understand and control a gift. This was something unique that I could do. This was the *thing* that I had always been looking for. It's like *it* found *me*. There was nothing that I would ever do in my life again that could compare to that experience. I had travelled, truly. My soul had detached from my body.'

'When did this happen?'

'2010. Though there were plenty of signs before then that I was right for it. Compatible. I thought poetry was the route for my awakening, music, drugs, a lifestyle, a way of living, of *being*. Subconsciously I had always been searching for *it*, without being sure of what "it" was. But nothing compares to this, no other human experience.'

'You learned to . . . what, harness it?'

Ewan shrugged. 'Not really. Not for a long time. Not until . . .' He didn't finish the sentence and reached for the glass to drain the last drops of water. Seb suspected it was a deliberate evasion.

'I tried. God, did I try. You have no idea how hard. But you gotta let it take you. You don't decide. You just put yourself by the door and hope that it opens, like Hazzard said. Took me a long time to realize that. And sometimes it would happen when I was sitting down, drifting off, day-dreaming. But mostly when I was lying down, before I fell asleep. It can't be forced. The fit shook something loose, though, a latent, innate gift.'

'What about the fits? Don't you need medication? To see a doctor? I mean, it's pretty bloody serious. Don't you care about your health?'

Ewan glanced at Seb as if the question was stupid. But within the look was the answer: of course Ewan didn't care. Why would he care, when he thought he'd found something greater than life itself? Something that he believed would transform his own dull and painful existence.

'It started to happen without the fits. They weren't always involved, thank God. I had inhibitors, medicine for my condition. But sometimes, quite randomly, when I was resting, and really tired, I just seemed to step outside of my body. Sometimes as I was going under, falling asleep, I'd feel myself rise up and out. I would open my eyes and be wide awake, fully conscious, but looking down at myself, from the ceiling. I would be *floating*. I could also wake in the early hours of the morning after a dream and I would sit up, but my body would still be lying down.

'Around that time, it even happened in a cinema. I was standing beside my seat, about three feet away, in the aisle, and looking at myself sitting down. I had no recollection of even leaving my body. I was just *there*.

'I had to go home for a while, after the first fit, after my diagnosis, and I remember my mother came into my room one morning. She had a cup of tea and my medication to make sure that I took it. I remember watching her enter the room and approach the bed. My body was inside that bed. But *I* was standing in the corner of the room, watching her.

'As soon as I became aware that it was happening, I would always return to my body, with this jolt. A sickening kind of click or crack and I'd be back inside my body, and feeling weak and tired and disappointed again.

'I knew I had to be relaxed. Extremely relaxed. Especially my muscles. So I took relaxants when I could get them. My mother had medication for anxiety attacks, and those tablets helped. In combination with medication I used yoga and meditation. I studied those for the years when I was at my mother's. I had to get everything right, the body, the mind, the environment, the situation, otherwise it was hopeless. The room had to be warm too. And I would begin my breathing exercises. I would put my whole body to sleep, one part at a time.'

Seb writhed at the idea of the selfish prick taking his old mum's medication, but Ewan remained enraptured by his own recall. 'I would begin the process with the little toe of my right foot. Have you any idea how long it can take to make one toe go to sleep? I mastered it. Eventually I could turn my body into a dead weight and that mass would then dissolve. The facial muscles were the hardest parts to get right. But I would become so deeply relaxed, my body so limp, that I wasn't awake or asleep. I was *between*. That's crucial, to get between states of consciousness. I learned that, once I had reached my eyes, the final part of myself, I needed to imagine a void, a hole, a great emptiness between my eyes.

'Eventually, in my mother's house, in the room I kept there, this blank, white room, where nothing could distract me, I found myself near the ceiling, looking down upon myself again. And forty-three times thereafter across two years. I kept a journal. I made it happen forty-three times. Imagine it!'

Ewan slumped back and released an exasperated sigh. 'Our minds are the key, or what is held inside our minds is the key. But our minds are also the jailors. Anxiety, or surprise, or shock, or any conscious activity can disrupt the experience. I could not linger, as so many others had done before me, in that state. There was instinctive panic. A primal anxiety, the dread of not being able to return. The survival instinct, it's in the body. And nothing that I could do about it. Unless I stopped taking my medication. Then, I would leave my body so dramatically during a fit, and the experience would last for longer, and more intensely, while my body was in shock. Only while my body was close to death could the soul-body better escape.'

'You're not taking the meds now, are you?'

'I don't have any,' Ewan said in a voice as piteous as Seb had heard yet.

So that he could terrorize Seb, Ewan had put his health in the gravest danger. 'Jesus Christ.'

'There was no way it was all a daydream, or a hallucination, a delusion. Where I ended up is hyper-real. My acuity was incredible. I could even see dust motes. Every colour was beautiful. I put a print in my room, a Van Gogh, and I saw what he had seen, but barely managed to transcribe into a great painting.

'Everything around me was living, emitting, transporting.

Twice, when I was drawn upwards and suspended, I even managed to touch the ceiling. Where the paint was rough, the sensation in my fingertips was so exaggerated that I could have been touching broken glass. Where the paint-work was smooth, I could have been touching sandpaper. And I was willing myself to move. Don't you see? I was moving on the ceiling of that room. You can't imagine it.

'So where else could I go? What else was possible? And the light! My God, the light. If you saw a glimpse of it right now, in here, you would weep. You would dream of it every day for the rest of your life. You would crave it. That is how moonlight should be, enchanted. It was my spirit that was generating that light. *Me*. The inmost light.

'Soon, I was beginning to notice myself too, as a form. My ability was evolving. It was adding limbs that weren't really there. I even put a mirror in my room and angled it so that I would see myself if I separated. And I managed to see myself once, in the air while my body lay beneath me on the bed. I could see part of myself, just adrift, floating. I'd wanted to see myself, so I had focused on seeing myself, and I did. There were two of me in that room.

'I could think too. And remember things more clearly than at any other time in my life. But it's not like reasoning. Everything just came to me at once, in a flash. I could see, hear, feel everything more acutely. It's not a dream. I was *more* conscious. I was more intelligent. I'd never been so wide awake and never experienced such a wonderful feeling. The weightlessness as you ascend . . . The vitality you feel. The delight in seeing the world so bright and alive in a way it never was before. There's no pain, only joy.

'And in that form, I could also see three hundred and

sixty degrees without turning my head. I only had to *want* to see behind myself and I could. It was subtle. A nuance of the experience. So I knew that I could also look beyond a wall, or a ceiling, or anything solid if I so desired. Sometimes, I would be looking down at myself in the bed, with everything below me appearing small, while behind me was infinity, a vast blackness.

'What if I could also move further away from where my physical self lay, and I could travel beyond the room? That was my thinking. I sensed that movement to other places could be instantaneous. And in time it was.'

Ewan grinned his yellow grin. 'As you can attest.'

'Someone else taught you how to go further.'

Ewan's grin became a smile though it was less pleasant than the previous expression. 'I'm tired. If you want to know more, you'll have to read my book.'

Even after what he'd just listened to, Seb found it difficult to want to know that much. 'So what happens now?'

'That's entirely up to you.'

'You can't stay here.'

'Only until you've worked on my book. This is a great opportunity for you.'

'I'll be the judge of that. And I don't believe you, or trust anything that you say. That's my main problem. There is also a massive collection of fragments in my living room, scattered inside two bin bags. I don't have the time to work on that. So I'm happy with a synopsis of the remainder of your story. The part that takes you from your mother's spare bedroom to *here*.'

'That's far too complicated. You wouldn't understand, or believe it for that matter. I'm afraid that would be a bit too much for you. Better to read it. The manuscript is a bit more considered.'

'It's the *bit more* that concerns me. And you clearly have no intention of going anywhere, and neither do I, so spill.'

Ewan immediately became uncomfortable and adopted a more serious tone. 'I don't feel comfortable talking about it. Not right now. I don't feel well. For fuck's sake, I've had a massive bloody fit and you're interrogating me.'

'That's not why you won't talk.' Seb wanted to be more than a little astonished by the story he'd just heard, but he found that he couldn't get past the situation, nor past what use Ewan's great 'gift' had ultimately been put to. He also knew that he had heard an incomplete version of events. An embellished version probably existed inside the bin bags too. Ewan was not an honest man and he was playing for time.

'Let me guess, Ewan: the next chapter ended badly for you. Just like everything else in your life. Yet no lessons were learned. So here's an interpretation of my own: you are attempting some desperate last resort at my expense, because you've nowhere else to go. This is the end of your line. Right here.'

Ewan had closed his eyes before Seb finished.

Seb woke. Sat up quickly. Fought his way free of the duvet and clambered off the mattress as if that could remove him from *where he had just been* while asleep.

He had not registered seeing any walls in the large, partially lit space that he'd just dreamed of. Behind the figures surrounding him, the borders had dissolved to black. Those *others* had been suspended in the air.

Seb couldn't recall a single face now, only suggestions of the naked and grey condition of the bodies bumping together, *up there*.

From each navel, including his own, a snaking silvery cord had disappeared into the darkness of the floor. The stems had appeared as flexible and rubbery as flesh, while shining like liquid mercury.

Awake, he now thought of those cords as strange metallic weeds. He also thought of fungal growths in caves, mushrooming from out of rock.

All of the *people* in the dream had been agitated. They had talked in hurried whispers while moving their arms in small circular movements as if they were underwater. Beneath them, where a floor should have been, water had flowed. Black water without a trace of foam or a reflection. An underground stream in some kind of cavern and the people had been anchored to its bottom by the silvered cords extending from their abdomens. The water had rushed across the bottom of the room and travelled into a darkness without definition or relief.

He'd scraped his fingers at the ceiling and slapped it with his hands. The surface had issued a hollow sound but been too hard to break. He'd known that he would never escape the tunnel.

The only illumination in the space had come from a dim, metallic light issuing from the figures themselves and from their silver cords, as they all drifted. And either the surface above them was lowering or the water was rising. An elderly man beside Seb had wept, as if knowing they would soon submerge in the fast current and be swept away into nothingness.

Nearby, out of his view, a woman had said, 'Sink. Heavy, heavy. Sink deep.' She'd seemed excited by the prospect of doing so.

Others had begun to repeat that phrase as if it were a command or prayer. As his anxiety had also turned to a dreadful joy, Seb had felt a compulsion to contribute to the chorus.

The water rose and his cord shrivelled like a disused umbilicus. Where it grew out of his abdomen the flesh had turned black. The stem then issued a far weaker light.

He'd woken.

What had Ewan said earlier about it being time he was *involved* in something more ambitious? Involved in something dangerous; had that been the inference?

Seb looked about the bed. His room was dark but the silhouettes of the furniture were visible. Light didn't so much shine beneath the door from the passage outside, as seep inside. A soft, grey light tinged a glacial blue.

When he opened his bedroom door he realized that the lights in the corridor were switched off. Despite that, he was seeing too much of the passage without the aid of electric light. This dull glow in his home suggested an overspill, one steady and unflickering, but from where did it shine?

Streetlights above the front drive were too distant to penetrate the building. Without interior light the house remained dark at night. The source confounded him.

The television upstairs? Was Ewan in the living room again?

As he tried to fathom out the luminosity in the corridor, his awareness of a peculiar discomfort grew. This was nothing physical, like being hot or cold. What he tried to dismiss as an after-effect of the nightmare persisted as apprehension. He suspected he was about to meet someone unpleasant. The very atmosphere of the building had altered and now swelled with the anticipation of a presence, or the arrival of *something*.

Taking shorter breaths, if he took them at all, Seb was reminded of how he'd felt when Ewan appeared to him outdoors. A static prickle passed through the fine hairs on the nape of his neck and needled his scalp.

Ewan. Ewan must have been projecting again.

Whether by shaking or punching the man awake, Seb would stop whatever was being initiated. But before he took a single step towards Ewan's room, Seb turned in the direction of the staircase because of what he could now hear.

The sound was coming from above him. Though the noise was muted through the walls and ceiling, someone was in distress and weeping upstairs in the living area.

Ewan?

As quietly as he could manage, Seb walked barefoot to the stairs and went up. He'd only taken a few steps when the weeping ceased and was replaced by a voice, or voices, that stayed low and whispered together sibilantly.

The light on the staircase had now changed, and he would have been surprised if a television could transmit an illumination capable of making the walls and stairs appear so drab, if not neglected.

Seb continued up.

Within the strange light his own home now appeared much older. He peered about the landing and was made to think of shuttered and locked-away places, where dust and dross gathered behind boarded windows, and flat surfaces turned grey and powdery. Unrestored and lacking in human habitation for decades.

Before Seb made the landing, the distant murmur of voices was accompanied by the noise of dry paper shifting about the wooden floorboards. It could have been the riffling of a book's pages by a breeze.

From where he stood, he could see that the doors of the study and utility rooms were closed. The television was mounted on a wall and was out of sight, but the set emitted no light. It wasn't switched on, so the light wasn't coming from there.

Just out of his sight, on the far side of the living room, the paper was soon being strewn about as if loose leaves were being subjected to a hurried investigation.

What he could see of the living area, which reached to the windows and balcony beyond, might have become a basement. One in which his furniture had been stored for years. The light was faint and grainy, with a hint of tarnished silver, as if it were passing through gaps in the walls. Picture frames were black holes. Bookcases were inky rectangles. The corners of the room and balcony doors were lost entirely to darkness.

The unnatural light aged whatever it fell upon. He suspected he'd re-entered his most recent dream and become engulfed by the ghastly illumination of the watery tunnel.

Where was the source?

The voices?

'Ewan?' he called out, but too quietly. 'Ewan! God's sake, what are you doing?'

His voice startled a fresh activity within the living room,

and he was relieved that he could not see what had cast its shadow onto the far wall.

Those lengths of what might have been the impossible shadows of wavering tree branches soon took shape as peculiarly long arms held out before a wasted body, topped by a large head.

The murky suggestion of shadow then rose up higher and felt about, as if blind and unsteady when upright.

A heavy object struck the living-room floor and Seb's heart may have stopped for several seconds. He assumed that a sighting of *whatever* was inside the room would be foolish. 'Who's there?' he cried out, the force of his voice compelled by panic.

A soft thump.

Scratching.

The shadow on the living room wall grew within his sight.

Taking three steps at a time, Seb fled down the stairs. As he descended, his last glimpse of the shadow repeated maddeningly inside his mind. That sense of a figure dropping to the floor, then rising to all fours. It groped about as if more capable, and in possession of a much longer reach, when positioned low to the ground like a stalking animal. As the shape had moved fluently about the room there had been a swishing sound, reminiscent of a heavy cloth sweeping floorboards.

The muttering that followed him down the stairs was human-like, though much reduced, before it degraded into something canine.

Seb reached the foot of the stairs and turned for the ground floor. He would have kept going had the last flight of steps not looked so impenetrably dark. He was also certain that the darkness down there swelled and bustled with a curious energy of its own.

As he hesitated, the back of his neck tingled afresh, in anticipation of both an attack from below and a blow from behind. One glance over his shoulder was sufficient for him to notice movement on the staircase wall. What could have been human limbs commanding an unnatural extension, struck out and snatched at the air, and in a manner uncomfortably similar to that of a magnified insect. And if those were the shadows of hands, then the nails extending from the digits were long enough to qualify as claws.

The scream that followed was reminiscent of the distant shrieks of the apes in Paignton Zoo, which could be heard miles away on a still day, as faraway territorial disputes were conducted on the contoured cement of their enclosures.

Seb pounded down the passage and threw himself inside his bedroom. Using what felt like a superhuman strength, he raised one end of his antique chest of drawers and hauled it across the floorboards, scraping the skirting-board paintwork. He dropped the heavy article part-way across the door.

At the windows he tore open the curtains.

His shaking fingers began a futile clawing at the window locks. He turned the steel security key backwards and forwards, momentarily forgetting that the key required a simultaneous press and turn to release the window. By the time he remembered this, he'd become paralysed with terror at the sound of what moved through the passage beyond his bedroom.

A shriek outside was followed by a heartfelt sobbing and a string of muffled words intoned in some kind of entreaty for mercy or succour. The piteous whimpering of a grown man had recommenced, and directly outside his door. A sound that passed inside his room to inhabit his nerves.

When the crying ceased, a nasal whine shook Seb enough for him to make another attempt to unfasten the window lock, while knowing that the drop from the first floor was too great. *Two broken ankles.* He was trapped.

The whine passed away in the direction of the stairs.

Not breathing, Seb listened and received an impression that the intruder was conducting a search, albeit blindly.

It entered the empty bedroom on the other side of the wall. A grumble whined into a bestial snarl. With horrible clarity, Seb imagined an old mouth that opened too widely. One filled with yellowing teeth.

Shouts of distress issued from Ewan's room, further down the passage. Such was the strength of Ewan's bellow his cries passed through several walls.

Seb crouched under the window and hugged his body into a ball.

Ewan flung wide the door of his own room and shouted, 'No! No! Get away! Get away! No! No! I'm trying to help. I'm only trying to help!' This was swiftly followed by the sound of Ewan's feet slapping towards Seb's bedroom.

Seb watched the door handle being snapped up and down from outside. Ewan was trying to get in, and desperately enough to employ his feet, knees and hands to bang at the door, shaking it in the frame.

'Let me in,' Ewan whimpered, his words near breathless. 'No!'

Ewan made a narrow gap through which one of his arms, whisking in an anorak sleeve, came through to swipe about inside as if he was trying to push Seb away from the other side of the door. When Ewan's hand found the obstacle, the chest of drawers, he slammed his shoulder against the door, lower down and closer to the door handle. The barricade rocked back and forth.

Around Seb, the air swelled with an unbearable anticipation.

Ewan spoke again, though not to Seb. He seemed to be talking to someone else, *out there*, in the corridor. It was hard to understand all of what he was saying, but the child-like tone of his voice surprised Seb. 'No. You can't . . . Don't.' Ewan was pleading. 'I'm doing what *he* wanted. Get away!'

Ewan resumed hurling the full weight of his body against the wood until the barrier jolted forwards. Soon after, he was inside the bedroom. He slammed the door and turned round, his ungainly body wedged behind the chest of drawers. 'Here,' he said, panting, but as if to a room full of people.

Seb had never seen Ewan so witless, so blanched and jittery, his eyes so wide and the yellow teeth bared horribly as his fear chattered out. 'They know. They followed. They know. They know.' Ewan's muttering then became inaudible.

He had no idea who Ewan was speaking about, but Seb got to his feet and began clumsily tugging on a pair of jeans with shaky hands. Socks and a hooded top followed. His shoes were downstairs. 'What . . .' Seb said, but was too shocked to finish the sentence. He finally managed, 'Has it gone?'

Ewan seemed to notice Seb for the first time. Strands of greying hair were stuck to his bearded cheeks. He raised a hand to bid Seb be silent. 'We have to get out,' he whispered, and rolled his eyes to look up at the ceiling. 'It will come inside.'

Seb suffered a sensation of his body dropping through thin air. When he regained his bearings, he felt weak and sickened with a fear that would not relent. Memories of the animal shrieks returned to his memory and resounded inside his skull. He went for the bedside lamp and clicked it on.

'No,' Ewan said, in a desperate whisper.

Seb ignored him and made for the main lights.

'Idiot! If it gets in you'll see it . . . properly.' He shook his head. 'You don't want to do that.'

The receipt of this detail had Seb reaching for the chest of drawers to steady himself. His legs wanted to go out from under him. Ewan's body odour served to revive him.

Trying to make as little noise as possible, he returned to the bedside table and turned off the lamp. When halfway across the room on his way back to the door, Ewan said, 'In here. There . . .'

Ewan clawed his way around the door and disappeared, shutting the door behind himself, sealing Seb inside with the room's most recent arrival.

Reluctantly and fearfully, Seb turned to see what had startled Ewan. And even though no electric light brightened the room, the air was now lighter than it should have been, or had been only moments before. Like the living area had been, the room was drained of any colour but that of a dull mercury, and the visible furniture was aged with the instantaneous affliction of antiquity.

The air billowed with an otherwise invisible presence. Though it didn't remain concealed for long. In a far corner beside the bed an indistinct shape appeared close to the floor.

Motion became manifest too, as each taut second passed to reveal the *form*, moving about on the floor in a series of jerks.

Before the paralysis snapped from Seb's limbs, the shape rose and its sickly luminance cast a shadow. Impossibly, a silhouette appeared on the wall and the ceiling above the bed, and upon the other side of the room too.

The form expanded and contracted quickly at the edge of Seb's vision, though whether this was from the weird atmospherics or from pure shock he did not know.

Seb yanked the door open.

A desperate sob became audible within the room that he departed. It was louder than before and filled with more distress than he'd known any living thing capable.

He closed the door behind himself, but as he'd turned he'd glimpsed movement in the mirror of the wardrobe, and received an impression of something sticklike but agile and too tall to be human. If that had been a head topping the form, the head had been covered. Seb suffered a notion that eyeholes had been cut out of whatever concealed the face. The suggestion of its arms extended and grasped at where he had just been standing.

As the noise of the apparition's grief transformed into something doglike, Seb fled, barely keeping his footing on the stairs to the ground floor.

When he reached the hallway, Ewan was still fumbling with the front door keys in an attempt to get out.

10
Hinderers in the Passage

Bent double, and gripping knees that shook from the exertion of bolting from the house and running to a stagger, Seb stared at Ewan with all of the murderous loathing that his mind could summon.

Ewan lay on the grass beside him, facing the sky, insensible with exhaustion. His eyes were closed.

They'd stopped running a mile clear of the house. If Ewan was running then he should be too; that had been his thinking and had brought them here. The ragged jog had ended after Ewan collapsed upon the dewy grass, at the top of a path that led deeper inside the Berry Head Nature Reserve.

Beneath the lightening sky, the hedgerows and garrison fortifications formed the mounds that surrounded them. Elevated hundreds of feet above the sea, the atmosphere was thinner and colder.

Exposed to the vast sky and the expanse of the sea, the great spaces enlarged Seb's fear until he doubted he'd ever felt as insignificant. He knelt in the grass. Moisture passed through his jeans and fired shivers across his back and neck. He'd grabbed shoes as he passed through the front door, but in his haste to escape he'd failed to tug a jacket free from the rack in the hallway.

Anxious at the movement of the nearest shrubs in the breeze, he stood up again, rubbing at the outside of his arms, and looked about himself.

Between his desperate inhalations of the cold air, Seb finally felt able to speak. 'What was that? What was it? You brought that into my home . . . last night . . . that *thing*. Are we safe?' The final question, and the way he'd said it, made him feel pitiful.

Ewan rolled onto his side. He sounded asthmatic, and was either sick or cleared his chest of phlegm. A shake of his tangled head served as a delayed response to Seb's question. 'Never,' he gasped.

Sweat frosted in the runnel of Seb's spine. 'What? Is *it* here?'

'No . . . Not yet, anyway.'

'Not yet?'

'I can't feel it.'

Seb realized he couldn't either, that nauseating apprehension and the onset of an unnatural scrutiny. He moved closer to Ewan and stood over him. 'You bastard. You brought that . . . that thing into my bloody life!'

'I didn't think they . . .' Ewan never finished. Instead, he said, 'What did you see?'

'See? Something that shouldn't bloody exist!'

'What did you see? Tell me.'

'A . . . a shape. Long . . . like a shadow. An animal, a man, I don't know this time. What did you do? What? To bring it here?'

'I never.' Ewan wheezed and then swallowed noisily. 'Not intentionally. What do you mean, *this time*? You've seen it before?'

145

'Before you showed up, never. You prick!'

'But you've seen it? When?'

Seb recalled his dream, the one in which he'd been chased across the golf course, right before he'd heard something brushing itself down the side of the house. Becky had dreamed of it too and heard the same thing. Their walk in Marriage Wood had been interrupted by something just as unpleasant.

'It was in the woods near here. Over there.' Seb pointed towards the cliffs inland. 'Something was in there, waiting for us. My girlfriend saw it too. The day after you appeared at the bloody window of that restaurant. It wasn't right. Didn't look right. Not normal. And I've dreamed of it. Because of you. You bastard.'

Ewan placed his long, dirt-smeared fingers over his face and shook his head without speaking.

'I thought it was one of your tricks. Why can I see it? Tell me! Am I in danger?'

Ewan ignored him until Seb began shouting, 'Am I in danger? You put me in danger! Am I in danger?'

Ewan took his hands off his face and spoke without looking at Seb. 'You're probably fucked. We both are.'

Seb wanted Ewan dead. Wanted to end the whole idea of Ewan by dragging the scarecrow body to the cliff edge and hurling it down to the rocks. He imagined the oily head breaking apart like a coconut shell. 'Get rid of it! Just piss off and get rid of it!'

Ewan struggled to sit up. His mouth and beard glistened. 'I've never seen it here. *He* must be involved. Oh, Christ.'

'Here? Who? *Who* is involved?'

'I was only told about those *others*. They were used as

threats, in the past. But I've sensed them, when I projected . . . That one could be directed? I didn't believe it . . .'

'Who? Who are they? What do you mean *directed*?'

'You don't want to know.'

'I bloody do!'

'You wouldn't believe me if I told you. And there isn't time. It's *all* got to go back. There's been a misunderstanding.' Ewan struggled to his feet while Seb tried to figure out what Ewan was saying. 'It's all got to go back today. You have a car.'

'What?' Seb grabbed Ewan by the collar of his anorak. 'You're going nowhere until you stop this. So fix it! Stop it!'

'How do you get rid of what's not there?'

'They are . . .' He didn't know how to phrase the question. What kind of horror writer was he? 'That thing . . . it's leaving a body, yeah? Like you do?'

Ewan shook his head dismissively, even contemptuously, at Seb's feeble comprehension. He tried to prise Seb's bloodless hands from his collar, but ended up holding Seb's wrists.

The subsequent grapple felt increasingly hopeless and pathetic the longer they stood there, Seb without a coat in a dawn wind that whipped off the bay.

'You tell me,' Seb roared at Ewan. 'You tell me what that was!'

'I have to go. It's not safe. Get off me.'

'Safe? What? Not safe for *who*? For you?'

Ewan pulled back and Seb went with him, barely staying on his feet. 'Where are they?' Spittle flew from his mouth and peppered Ewan's face as he demanded the information he was also reluctant to receive. 'The people who are projecting a malicious version of themselves, that's what they are doing, isn't it? Where are they, the bodies? Who are they? What has any of it got to do with me?'

'Versions? That's not a version,' Ewan said with a returning spike of the usual sarcasm. 'That is what *they are*.'

The only thing preventing Seb from punching his old *friend* was the weakening effect of his own fear. He gathered himself. *Stay angry.* 'Bullshit! Where are they? Where do they live? That thing with the sack on its head . . .'

Ewan was almost crying when he asked, 'What? What did you just say?'

'What?'

'About a bloody sack?'

'The head, it was covered. In my dream and then . . .'

Ewan stared at the grass, his eyes protruding. 'Len,' he said to himself. 'Thin Len. You saw him.'

'What? What are you saying? Who is Len?'

'Oh Christ. Thin Len.' Ewan clawed his face. 'They're not living. But they exist.'

'You better start making sense or I'll put you down for good, you prick!'

'A child-killer. He was a murderer. He was hanged. I thought he was a myth, a story.' *But he's not*, or so Ewan's hapless, drawn face seemed to communicate.

Seb could hear himself wheezing, but he managed to pant out, 'What?' in a tearful voice.

'Let go!' Ewan roared. They struggled again, briefly wrestling and twisting around each other upon weak legs, until Ewan lost his balance and pulled Seb to the ground.

Seb regained his hold on Ewan's greasy jacket.

'Piss off!' Ewan batted at his hands and kicked at him while remaining on the ground as if he were too tired to get back up again. 'You think you can understand? They are the parallel. Hinderers.'

Seb let go of Ewan and raised himself to his feet. He looked about the common in bewilderment. 'What? What does that mean?'

As if confronting some terrible truth, Ewan dropped his face inside his hands. Perhaps he suffered a revelation that had been much postponed. 'Hinderers in the passage. That's what they're called. I was told *things*. I glimpsed something, but only when . . . when I went further.'

'What are you saying?'

Ewan appeared too frightened to continue. He began to shake, his face creased as if he were about to cry.

'Hinderers in the passage? What bloody *passage*?'

A palsy took over Ewan's hands.

'They're *dead*?' Seb asked, his own voice a ghost of itself.

Ewan nodded. 'They reside *over there*. Oh, Christ.'

'Where? Where?'

'Discarnate. Trapped . . .' Ewan's attention drifted from Seb and he mumbled to himself in what sounded like a weird stream of consciousness, gibberish but alarming gibberish. 'The subnormal of the mist. People of the mist. They can't ascend. There's no physical body. Don't you get it?' He looked at Seb and raised his voice close to a shout, 'And for *him*, Thin Len, this was never about choice!'

'What are you saying? How can I see it? How?'

'Hades. They drag vestiges of the body veil through the halfway place. They repeat . . . they rage blind for decades, centuries . . .'

Ewan struggled to get to his feet, then began glancing

149

about himself in a baffled, childlike fashion that made Seb feel much worse.

Ewan paced in a small circle, his long hands clutched to his scruffy cheeks. 'To stumble and crawl in the blackout, in the mist . . . to be denied ascent.'

He muttered other things that Seb didn't catch, but he did make out, 'To be in terror, always. The confusion . . .'

Seb grabbed Ewan's shoulder. 'What happened to the bloody light! The unlimited freedom? The power, the strength, the vitality and the marvels of the marvellous, Ewan? Where is it now? I didn't see a bloody trace of it back there!'

Ewan grinned at Seb, but only with his mouth because his watery eyes were still stricken with the horror of some terrible epiphany that had settled inside his ugly skull. 'The paradise belt. They'll never know it. They don't conform to earth or paradise conditions, you idiot.'

'Idiot? You fuck!'

'They're in the greylands, fool. They're shades.'

Holding his face, Ewan resumed walking, but in tighter circles. 'Jesus, Jesus . . . The gliding of the double.' He closed his eyes and swallowed.

'The gliding of the frickin' what?'

'Oh God, that I should have seen it . . .' Ewan began to actually cry. His chest heaved out sobs. This wasn't an act to gain sympathy and he again reminded Seb of a small boy. 'I should have not seen that. I never wanted to. Never, no. But it's me! Me, it's crossed over for me. They sent it. The light is dimming for me. But I won't . . . I won't . . .' Ewan had lost his train of thought, along with his wits.

'This thing, the hinderer, you said it can be *directed*?'

Ewan nodded once, quickly. 'Looks like it.'

'It came after you, not me?'

'I have to get away from here.'

'Please do, but first—'

'Money. I need money.'

'Now, there's a surprise.'

'You have enough. What do you need it for?'

'What?'

Ewan's eyes narrowed and he displayed his discoloured teeth. 'All those savings!' He spat at Seb's feet. 'Bloody ISA. High interest bonds. From writing that shit! You won't miss a couple of grand. Five, six, seven, that'll do it.'

'What?' Shock left Seb dizzy. Ewan had been through his personal financial records. When he'd been asleep, Ewan must have rummaged through the bank statements in his office. Seb's body shook with anger, disbelief, confusion, the cold. 'You . . . you went through my files.'

Ewan wrinkled his nose. 'So what?'

Seb went for him, swinging his limp arms. He landed a punch on Ewan's chest, and another blow on the side of that greasy head.

Ewan partially ducked out of the third swing, but Seb reached for his jacket, the throat, that tangled hair. He wanted to tear Ewan apart with his bare hands.

'Get off.' Ewan broke from Seb's clutches, then snatched at one of his forearms. And with a strength that surprised Seb, Ewan swung him around in a circle until his feet left the turf. When Ewan let go of his arm, Seb's feet didn't regain the earth for several seconds.

Pain seized his diaphragm as the air was forced from his

lungs on impact with the ground. He landed hard, rolled through the wet verdure, momentarily unsure of where his arms and legs were. When his lungs finally filled, his will to fight was gone. He wanted to be sick.

Ewan's shoes skittered in their haste to leave him behind. Off through the grass he went, a raggedy vagrant, returning to the stony path they had staggered up to reach the common. But Ewan was not trying to get away from Seb. He was going *somewhere* to save himself. Seb's fate meant nothing to this old *friend*. It never had done.

He brought this into your life and now he's running away.

An hour later, Seb stood outside his house. The front door was open but he made no attempt to enter. Merely looking inside at the familiar coat rack and framed pictures made him feel like an invalid handicapped by his own terror. He might have been a ghost himself, revisiting a place from which he'd been expelled and could no longer claim as his own.

All the time wondering if *something* was waiting inside, he repeatedly scoured the windows to make certain that nothing was looking out. Perhaps it crouched in its own sickly luminance, in a dim corner of a room, a form indistinct but exuding the gravest threat to his mind, life, and *what came after*.

'Oh, Jesus,' he said and bent double to let the dizziness pass. A sudden recollection of that shadow on the wall, its motion, its reaching for him, had made him giddy. Mere suggestions of the thin arms and much-changed hands were literally sickening. And the grief in it, the guttural noises of a beast insensible with rage, *the sight of it rising* . . . He could not bear to remember how he'd felt when Ewan had shut him inside the bedroom with *it*.

He now felt a great need to sit down, to be comforted. The incremental death of his own scepticism had left him a very nervous man, somewhat bewildered and increasingly prone to mutter to himself and to twitch. A rapid ageing seemed to be upon him. He knew he stood at the boundary of new terrain in which he had no guide and no foreknowledge.

Without doubt, the dreams had come *with* Ewan, like a cerebral infection transmitted by psychic means. And what could he understand of the black passage and its watery bottom, in which strange umbilical growths had anchored a congregation of strangers?

The distant face in the woods and its every intimation of malevolence, its derangement, had been no act of the imagination either. It was the same thing that had crawled along the outside wall of his home and hunted him across the golf links in a dream. These had been premonitions and forebodings of what had started to *become*. Right here, *around* him. And had not the very materials of the world, ordinary items like a sun umbrella and his own bloody towels, become charged with a supernormal character before his very eyes?

There was an existence beyond this one, then, though what evidence of an afterlife he'd encountered brought him no comfort or hope. Attempts to comprehend this halfway place, this *passage*, where 'hinderers' existed, enlarged his mind into what may have been an antechamber of madness.

You're probably fucked.

Ewan had truly disrupted the world that Seb had taken

for granted. Not only with squalor, but by creating a new environment where the unnatural existed. 'Ewan, you bastard.'

Preposterous. He was afraid his mind was coming apart from the sheer strain of what was trying to enter it. Reason would not respond, or even meet this new reality halfway. Only his imagination sufficed.

Perhaps *this* state could only occur at certain times, though, and only near Ewan? He wanted to believe that, because the alternative didn't bear thinking about. He just wanted this all to stop.

The prospect of removing Ewan from his life, by any possible means, now seemed justified. But feeling that murderous impulse was not the same as carrying out the task. Though who would miss Ewan? He'd damned himself a long time ago. It was obvious that Ewan had long forfeited more than his health and personal happiness. Ewan had come here with the purpose of threatening, extorting and blackmail through means too unique for belief, or for referral to the law.

That thing had been an agent for someone else. Ewan had mentioned a 'misunderstanding'. There were others involved in this too. Collusion didn't strike him as improbable. But collusion with *what*?

Seb's sole task must now be the prevention of a further tarnishing by association. But where was Ewan? Had he come back here?

He had nowhere else to go.

Seb drew the latch on the shed door, a wooden hutch at the foot of his rear garden. From within the jumble of tools that smelled of oil and rust, he removed the steel-bladed 'moon', a lawn-edging tool. At the very least he'd make

Ewan understand that he could never come back to this house in any form.

As Seb approached the open front door, the softening of his limbs resumed, and his arms were rendered numb by the idea that the 'moon' would be of no use against what had followed Ewan here.

Hinderers.

Thin Len. Child-killer. Hanged.

'Ewan.' His first attempt to call out in an authoritative tone failed.

'Ewan!' Still not loud enough and no one upstairs would hear him. Maybe that was the point.

'Ewan!' Much louder and, as soon as he'd spoken, Seb tensed to flee.

No response arose from within the house.

Seb stepped inside.

Silence amidst the fragrance of the morning's damp air that had seeped inside. No sound of movement upstairs either, but he couldn't prevent himself from imagining *another* up there, holding their breath, if respiration was even relevant in these circumstances.

Expecting the sudden brightness to provoke motion, Seb flicked the upstairs lights on.

Nothing stirred.

His own heartbeat was affecting his balance, but he moved up the first flight and peered about the passage.

His bedroom door was closed. Same with the doors of two of the spare rooms. Ewan's room was open. Before they'd scarpered like terrified children to the nature reserve, two hours earlier, Seb believed, this was how they had left the house.

Holding the moon's semicircular blade before him as if it were a bayonet, he crept further inside. Opened the first guest room and scrabbled a hand about to flick the lights on.

Nothing inside, at least nothing visible. The second spare room was the same. His bedroom appeared banal in its ordinariness. The chest of drawers was still skewed at an angle behind the door and the blinds were open, but the room appeared empty of whatever had assumed an awful version of the living in the early hours of that morning.

Seb slipped inside and opened the windows to rid the room of an odour of male sweat.

Ewan's room was as it had been the last time he had checked on his uninvited guest's recuperation. The duvet was crumpled from where Ewan had been lying upon the bed, fully clothed. The glass of water remained on the side table.

The bathroom was clear.

This was the house he had known only a few days before. At least for now.

He tried to convince himself that *this*, whatever he'd endured, could not continue if Ewan wasn't around. From now on, at all times, he would need to rely upon the curious alarm signals of his instincts.

Gripping the moon tighter, and switching on every light that he passed, Seb moved to the living area.

When he saw that Ewan's bin bags and rucksack had been removed, a surge of hope left him dizzy.

The kitchen and study were also safe.

Besides a taint of stale cider, and Ewan's clothes, all other physical traces of the man had vanished.

Seb searched the house again, from top to bottom, though with more confidence during the second pass. Once he felt safe enough to shut the front door, he went back upstairs.

He slumped on the settee, holding a highball glass heavy with bourbon.

He's gone. Ewan had really gone. He still had the spare keys, but Seb would get the locks changed. He'd also call the police and report Ewan as a nuisance. He'd even describe this whole experience as a stalking, and would mention the threats, blackmail attempts, and anything else that he could legitimately ascribe to Ewan's actions.

He needn't mention the *other things*.

The course of action seemed so simple, but Seb was still stunned by how the man had overrun his life. The invasion seemed to have lasted for months, not weeks.

Was it truly over now? Another brief surge of wishful thinking only foundered when he again considered the previous night's visitor. He imagined that such a force would not be as easy to dispel as the vagrant who had summoned it.

No, I mustn't, I cannot think that way. His connection to *it* was Ewan, and that doorway was going to be decisively and permanently blocked now. That would end the matter. *Surely*.

Seb didn't want to be on his own. He called Becky. No one else would have any understanding of his plight, and even she might struggle with recent developments. But at least Becky had experienced something *uncanny* – a word he'd overused in his own fiction, but had never been able to apply to his own life, until now.

She answered quickly, 'Seb. Hi,' though the wariness and lack of warmth in those two words was obvious.

'Becky, thank God. You just won't—'

'I'm on my way to work. I can't talk long. Later's better,' she added, but only in appeasement as if apologizing for her sharp tone. He'd expected her to ask after him. She didn't.

'Okay. I wouldn't have called you if it wasn't important. But things have happened, or changed since I saw you. You remember when we were in the woods, near the cove? And that dream? Well, this has all just gone to a whole new level. I—'

'Seb. I don't know what to say about *that*. I'm trying not to think about it at all. It's hard to say, but the whole weekend freaked me out. You did too. I'm sorry, but you did. Everything was all wrong from the moment you met me at the train station. I'm still trying to shake that whole weekend off. I need more time. And I'm really sorry, but I don't know how I feel about *things* now.'

'Becky, *he* came! He came here, to the house. The man I told you about. The one I have been seeing. He showed up.' He paused to rub his head, as if to loosen the right way of expressing himself. 'Jesus. But there is . . . *another* that came with him. This is not easy to even talk about, let alone believe, but he brought *it* with him. Brought it here. It got inside the house last night. Becky, I'm in danger.'

'Seb, I'm sorry. But I really do, genuinely, have to go. Now.' It sounded as if she were running up some stairs, somewhere in distant London. He could hear her heels and her breathlessness. 'And I'll admit, I don't have a clue what to say to you. I don't even know what you want me to say. Sorry. We never . . . Well, we were never that . . . Close isn't the right word, is it? But you know what I mean. It makes it hard for me to . . . understand this place where you are right now.'

Seb tried to swallow a lump of misery, the size of a plum, that had formed in his throat.

Becky switched tack and tried to make him feel better. 'But we did try and talk about this, didn't we? You remember? And I'm not sure what I can tell you now, that I haven't already said.' Was that a sliver of embarrassed condescension for his piteous need for support? Or was he only imagining a serious reduction in her respect for him?

Seb levelled his tone. 'I just wanted to talk to someone. To tell you what it's been like. That was all. A friend. Someone who might understand.' And as soon as he'd spoken he recognized and disliked the passive aggression in his voice.

'Seb, don't be like that. Please. We don't know what happened, but whatever we thought happened, or saw . . . it frightened me. It really did. I know that much. It still does. I don't even want to think about it. I don't know what you are . . . going through right now—'

'Going through? You think I am making it up?'

'I didn't say that.'

'I've done nothing. It all just started to happen when he appeared. I told you.'

'He? This guy you told me about, the university friend who never did the dishes? Well, yes. You started seeing him, and things . . .' She could barely bring herself to say it because she thought he was mentally ill.

Seb barely heard what she said next and only comprehended it after she'd finished speaking. 'You weren't yourself, Seb. Not at all, when I was with you. I'm sorry, but I've been thinking that sometimes when people are unwell, they create an atmosphere around themselves that's a difficult place, a bad place even, for other people to be in. It kind of infects everyone else, you know?'

'But it's not me, it—'

'And that's how I explain this to myself. It's like that weekend was all a part of where you are right now. Where your head is.'

'Becky! For God's sake, this is serious. He came here, to my house. Physically. He wanted me to do things for him. He made demands. Blackmail. He demanded money from me today. He's been making threats . . . Those reviews, well guess who wrote those? He—'

'Seb, sorry. I have to get off the phone. This is all terrible and don't think that I am being unsympathetic, but I think you need to see someone. A doctor. I really do. And if someone is trying to *get* at you, and whatever, then you need to call the police. Not me. I don't know what you want me to do? Sorry, I really have to go. Bye.' Becky ended the call.

Part 2

THIS PRISON OF THE FLESH

11

I Am Not Here Any More

Seb listed several prompts for himself on the hotel notepad. They were reminders of what he wanted to say and might deter him from saying other things, or the wrong thing, when he spoke to a police officer. The list helped him organize his thoughts, if one even lingered long enough to be seized. His mind was alternating between states; it was either a hornet nest that had been tapped hard with a stick, or a sluggish trickle of basic sentience.

A voice with a local accent answered the call he'd made to the police station in Brixham, and Seb cleared his throat. 'I'd like to make a complaint.'

Complain he did. And so encouraged was he by the unexpected strength of his voice, and the apparent interest at the other end of the line, that he was asked the same question three times before the query registered. 'You say the man's name is Ewan Alexander?'

'Yes, yes. That's right.' At this point Seb understood that the name was already known to the local constabulary.

'Stay on the line, please. I'm putting you through to the DCI.'

After returning home from the Berry Head Nature Reserve, Seb had drunk steadily throughout the previous day and rendered himself unfit to contact the police at that time. Unable to countenance another night in his own home, he'd also taken a cab across the bay and checked into a hotel in Torquay. He'd then spent a night in a large and comfortable room. A night that passed without the kind of disruption he now dreaded to the point of nausea. After a long and heavy sleep he'd woken refreshed at noon.

He still retained a sense that his sleep had been marred by hectic activity at various times during the early morning. Though he had no recollection of any specific details of what had bustled within his sleeping mind. For that he was relieved, and he hoped for a repeat experience at the same hotel tonight.

If Ewan had returned to the house while Seb hid in Torquay, the spare key that Ewan had stolen would no longer fit the front door lock. Emergency locksmiths had been busy the previous afternoon. While they worked, Seb had pretended to neaten the edges of his lawn with the moon implement. So Ewan wasn't setting foot inside the house again, at least not physically.

Seb had also called and requested a comprehensive clean of the property for the coming afternoon. He'd dispose of the bed linen that Ewan had used while the cleaners were on site. Anything his uninvited guest had messed with in the kitchen would be recycled.

He was regaining control, at last.

Inside his hotel room, sat by the window and staring at the bay, he'd also begrudgingly contemplated the prospect of working again, something he'd not considered for a fortnight. Ewan's disruption had been catastrophic, to his life and writing. But, as a man prone to anxiety over deadlines and contracted commitments, even in circumstances such as these, Seb ruefully mulled over the fact that only four months remained until his new book was expected at his publishers.

If he didn't resume work on the novel soon, and he couldn't see how that was possible, an extension would be needed. Perhaps a schedule change would be required and he knew how his publisher loathed those.

Nor could he guess how he'd find a way back into the problematic first draft, or how he'd recover the voice of the female narrator. Another impression formed: that the ideas, story and characters of his work in progress had been rendered thin and unconvincing by recent events.

At least he knew what his next story would be about. Maybe for that alone he owed Ewan.

Perhaps he should abandon the work in progress and just write the story of the past few weeks? After all, it was all that he could think about now. *But in four months?* It usually took him over a year to write a book. An extension would buy him some time, and he needed to find out how much time. He also had to know what his editor thought about him delivering a different book to the one contracted two years before.

A voice appeared inside the ear he'd pressed into the phone's handset, and addressed him by name, 'Mr Logan.' The police officer was taking the call outdoors and introduced himself as Detective Chief Inspector Brian Leon, CID. In the background Seb heard the swish of traffic and two other people conducting an intense conversation nearby. A dog barked and was reprimanded by its owner. 'You say this chap has been making a nuisance of himself?'

'Yes.' Seb was ready to repeat what he'd told the officer at the station, but didn't have an opportunity.

'Where are you now, sir?'

Because of nerves, his mind blanked and he couldn't recall the name of the hotel. As each second passed, he also felt as if he was implicating himself in a police matter. He found the room service menu and gave the detective the name of the hotel.

'I see, but you live locally?'

'Yes, in Brixham. But it's precisely because of Ewan Alexander that I'm staying here.'

'Is that right?' The detective took his time digesting the information, which increased Seb's perturbation. 'You told my colleague that you saw Mr Alexander yesterday?'

'Yes.'

'When was the last time you saw him yesterday?'

'Between four and five a.m., I think. That was the last time I saw him, but not since.'

'Bit early?'

'Yes . . . he was, er, staying with me.'

'Staying with you?'

'Well, in a manner of speaking. But the circumstances were not entirely satisfactory. To me, that is. Which is why I am making a complaint.'

'Can I ask you to stay where you are, sir? I'd like to ask you a few questions in person.'

'Of course,' Seb said, and suddenly wished that he could take a drink.

'I'll come and meet you.'

*

166

After he'd identified Ewan's body at three in the afternoon, Seb knew he was incapable of saying much that would make sense to the police.

He was also at risk of making an absurd statement. So he remained silent during the drive from the hospital to the police station. And during the journey, he attempted to thaw his mind from shock, in order to process the enormity of Ewan now being dead, as well as the implications for him.

The detective then left him alone in an interview room to nurse a mug of instant coffee that went cold between his limp hands. He hadn't been arrested and wasn't in custody, but in the small region of his mind able to function, after seeing Ewan's corpse in a hospital morgue, he couldn't be sure that he wasn't a suspect.

Even now, the police might be watching him via the camera fixed beneath the ceiling, in one corner of the room. Wouldn't they be adept through mere observation alone, at determining guilt or innocence?

What he had been told, but still struggled to accept, was that Ewan had died sometime during the night before. He had died at a guest house in Paignton, near the seafront, and inside a locked room.

The front door to the guest house had been closed and mortise-locked at ten p.m. The proprietors, an elderly married couple, had seen no one enter the building after ten p.m. The detective had shared that much with Seb after arriving at his hotel, at noon. While Seb had lingered and shivered up on Berry Head, too scared to go home, Ewan must have collected his bags from the house and made his way to Paignton.

There had been a disagreement too, between Ewan and

the proprietors of the guest house, about payment owed on a room, which Ewan promised to settle later. After that, Ewan had apparently locked himself inside the same room he'd occupied for the fortnight preceding his brief stay with Seb.

Inside the single room, which he never left, Ewan had begun drinking. The owners of the B&B had heard the clink of cans inside one of his bags as he'd come in that morning. He'd died in the night. Six empty cider cans were found in the morning. So Ewan had been getting his load on. As had Seb, but across the bay in Torquay, and in far more comfortable surroundings and without the assistance of cheap cider. He'd supped half a bottle of Courvoisier to get through his own night.

There had then been a brief disturbance around three in the morning from inside Ewan's room: 'Cries for help. That sort of thing.' The detective hadn't shared much more. But for Seb, that small detail had been sufficient for him to form his own ideas about what had transpired behind drawn curtains. He never shared his theory with the detective. Though, God knew, he was tempted.

From the moment Seb met DCI Brian Leon, the police officer's tone and mood had issued a weary acceptance concerning Ewan's demise. He'd also seemed indifferent to the possibility of foul play. The sounds that Ewan, presumably, had made during the night in his room at the guest house were short and never repeated: 'A quick scream. That kind of thing. Two or three, then silence. Quite upsetting for the old couple who own the place.'

Unable to summon any response from Ewan, the owners of the guest house had let themselves into Ewan's room at nine and found him dead. 'Beside the bed and under the window, with his arms still reaching out, like he'd been trying to get the window open. He'd pulled the curtains down on one side.'

At that point in the detective's recitation of the details, Seb wasted no time informing Detective Leon about Ewan's epilepsy, and of the fit that he had witnessed inside his own home. He'd also swiftly attested to drunkenness being the probable state during Ewan's last night alive. After all, Ewan's sounds of distress could be attributable to someone suffering a bad turn while drunk, and the guest house owners were also certain that Ewan had spent the night alone.

After the proprietor of the guest house had called an ambulance, the immediate clues to Ewan's death were apparent to the first paramedics on the scene. As far as they, and then a doctor at the Torbay hospital were concerned, Ewan had died of heart failure. The doctor added a footnote that the cardiac arrest may have been triggered by shock, though this assumption pended further examination.

The irony of the situation didn't escape Seb. He wouldn't have found himself in an interview room at the local police station had he not made the nuisance complaint about Ewan. There was nothing to connect the two of them. Seb had accidentally volunteered information and tied himself to the death of a visitor to the area.

Ewan had also given the guest house a false name, 'M. L. Hazzard', and had paid in cash for twelve days of the fourteen days that he'd previously stayed in the room. The bill for two nights, plus the one in which he had died, were still outstanding. Ewan had also cited Arthur Machen as being his next-of-kin in the register, along with a false telephone number. The owners hadn't thought they'd see him again, so were surprised by his return on the afternoon preceding his death. He promised to pay the outstanding bill and an extra night later that evening, but he never came out of his room alive.

Even after death, it seemed, Ewan was able to preoccupy and disrupt Seb's life as much as he had done when alive.

Just before the detective reappeared in the interview room, the worst of Seb's initial shock had begun to subside. He'd also identified his predominant reaction to the news as relief with some guilt. Until a fresh anxiety was inspired by the thought that a visitor to Ewan's room was capable of stopping a man's heart, and by merely appearing beside the bed.

If it gets in, you'll see it . . . properly. You don't want to do that. That's what Ewan had said, after forcing himself inside Seb's bedroom, two nights earlier.

Seb had come close to being sick in his lap when he'd first endured this notion of an assassin that could materialize beside a bed.

Ewan had given it a name: *Thin Len.* The hanged child-killer. He'd described it as a 'shade', a 'hinderer', and up on Berry Head he'd gibbered to Seb about the 'gliding of the double'. What else had Ewan said, during that time when his wits scattered at the mere idea of what had been sent after him? *But it's me! Me, it's come for me. They sent it.*

Within the theatre of his own mind, Seb had then rescreened the activities of several previous evenings he'd endured at his home, and with a vividness that left him feeling fragile.

After the detective had entered the room, he noisily pulled

out a chair from the other side of the table. 'So you are saying he wanted money from you? That was his reason for his travelling to the area?'

'Yes, as far as I am aware. And he wanted me to write a book for him.'

When Seb divulged this information, Detective Leon seemed to encounter new ground, concerning the motives for blackmail and extortion. It took him a while to think of a response. Eventually, he asked for more details and Seb continued with the story he'd rehearsed in his hotel room, while desperately hoping that the police officer would fail to recognize the significant process of editing that Seb was employing in his statement.

'But, I'm not entirely clear, Mr Logan, on how he came to be staying with you in the first place? In effect, he was your guest.'

At the first hint of a cross-examination, Seb wondered, and not for the first time that day, if he should request legal representation. At all costs he had to avoid describing the full facts of the phenomenon surrounding Ewan's arrival in Torbay.

His voice less steady than it had been moments before, Seb attempted to explain himself. 'I'd seen him around, as I told you. He'd been following me, watching me. Getting closer. And when he turned up on the drive, I was actually opening the front door. I'd just dropped a friend off at the train station in Paignton. And, well I . . .' Seb struggled to admit that he'd been terrified. 'He was, technically, a friend. An old friend from college. And he'd pretty much done this before, when I was living in London.'

'You said earlier this was twelve years ago. The last time you saw him?'

'That's right. So I thought I'd find out what he wanted, and I hoped to encourage him to leave me alone. But he stayed. He became drunk. He was already half-cut when he arrived, but he carried on drinking. It got late.'

'This was the first night, Sunday?'

'Yes. He wouldn't leave when I asked him to. He then suffered this terrible fit. I mean, it was awful. I thought he'd died. I'd never seen anything like it. And I didn't have the heart to eject him after that, so he stayed for a second night.

'I was at a loss as to what to do. Should I call you, an ambulance, or some department in Social Services? He was suffering from fits, using drugs, virtually homeless, an alcoholic. I offered to pay for a room for him but he refused. And that's when we had our biggest disagreement, that second night. A massive row. There were several leading up to it, in fact, because of the outrageous demands that he was making. I just couldn't get rid of him while he laboured under this assumption that he could just occupy my home and force me to write a book for him, as he sat around getting pissed. It just made me see red.'

'You never called us.'

'I thought . . . that I could deal with the situation myself. It was also embarrassing. I didn't really want to draw attention to it. But the general aim of his visit was to extract assurances that I would help him. Then came the demands for money. He'd been through my personal financial records to find out what I was worth.'

'I see. Did these disagreements ever become violent?'

Seb flushed hot then cold, and then hot again when he

knew that the detective had seen his reaction. He thought of the scuffle up on Berry Head, and of the potential subcutaneous bruising on Ewan that might have been caused by the tussle. 'A bit, yes. Early yesterday morning. I finally got him out of the house in the early hours, and chased him off into the nature reserve. There was some pushing at one point, and . . . Afraid I am no fighter, but it did become ugly at one point. This was after he demanded money from me. I'm afraid the red mist just fell again at that point.

'He knocked me down. Despite his lifestyle, he was still bloody strong. And then he ran off. That was the last time I saw him, early yesterday morning. He went back to my place to fetch his bags. I didn't want to stay at home after what had happened, so I took the room in Torquay and had the locks changed at home. From what you've told me, he obviously headed to this B&B in Paignton, and . . .'

The detective nodded, in what might have been agreement, because he'd probably already checked on Seb's whereabouts with the staff at the Commodore Hotel. Seb hoped that the detective had done so too, because the hotel's security cameras would reveal that he'd never left the hotel premises last night, and couldn't possibly have killed Ewan in a guest house in the next town in the bay.

'You don't know where he was staying before he arrived in the area?'

'I have no idea. He was very selective about what he told me. He liked to be enigmatic, you know, about himself, and where he'd been. But I had the impression he'd been involved in something unpleasant, some kind of group. He was reluctant to talk about it. I don't know any more because he never gave me any details. Nothing, in fact. I think he'd just run out of options, so he came looking for me. He knew about the success of my books. That was my general impression of his motives.'

The officer nodded again, his eyes thoughtful, but otherwise inscrutable. 'That's very similar to what his mother said this morning.'

'She must be getting on.'

'Eighty-eight. But she hadn't seen the deceased for three years. She said her son was studying. She couldn't tell me much more. The only time she ever heard from him, he would ask her for money. It's odd, but it was my impression that she was a bit wary, or even frightened of her own son. But she'll have someone take care of the funeral arrangements, and she doesn't want his effects sent back to Manchester.'

Seb thought of the two bin bags full of paper. He imagined them being hoisted into the back of a rubbish truck and he felt a wild and vindictive desire to laugh out loud. When the feeling passed, he considered it incredibly sad that Ewan's jumble of paper, his great work, which was *destined* to change the very perception of the world, should suffer such a fate. The sum total of Ewan's life, and his literary delusions, were going to a landfill or recycling plant. As was any recorded evidence of the reckless but remarkable things that he had actually achieved. It was a postscript that Seb would have struggled to invent in one of his own stories.

The detective checked through the shorthand notes on his pad. 'I'm also going to assume he'd worn out his welcome with anyone else he knew. Anyway, there'll be an autopsy to confirm cause of death, and we have his old medical records now. But unless anything else shows up, I doubt we'll be in touch again. Thank you for identifying the body.'

The officer stood up. 'Are you all right? We can recommend counselling for victims of this sort of thing.'

'No, thank you. It's all left me a bit dazed . . . I'm not entirely sure how I feel.'

'That's quite normal. Even a bit of guilty relief that it's over, eh?' The police officer smiled faintly, but knowingly. 'I'll have someone drop you back to the hotel.'

'Thank you.'

'Might be a bit of material too, eh, for the next book?'

This was the detective's first acknowledgement of what Seb was known for locally. He didn't know how to react, or even if he should. Levity seemed inappropriate.

DCI Leon remained unapologetic. 'My wife's read some of your books. She always liked that one about the moors.'

'Oh, well, do thank her from me. That's nice to know.'

'Though she had a few problems with the last one about the ship. Can't remember what it was called, or what she didn't like about it.'

12
Second Death

So this is where Ewan died: 15 Beach Road.

The street was lined with two-storey townhouses, each building painted a different colour, from coral pink to duck-egg blue, with picnic benches on tiled forecourts and tall palms clattering their fronds behind low front walls overrun by an easterly wind.

Permanent signage the length of the street advertised Sky TV, room rates, AA star ratings and Rosette restaurant awards. Perhaps the road looked a little tired between seasons, but under a blue sky at any time of year, it effortlessly conjured impressions of family holidays, cosy rooms, carveries and suntanned granddads holding pints of Bays Topsail in the lounge bars.

Seb had always been fond of Paignton, particularly the seafront and the streets that led to the Esplanade. To him the little hotels were a living installation of English comforts, veritable Larkin poems twinned with facets of a living social history; places where the working class, and mostly the retired and those with young families, still came and stayed for their annual holidays and long weekends.

The area hadn't been gentrified like Dartmouth or Totnes, so the town remained more affordable and retained a post-war echo. Moving with the times where necessary, but retaining the seafront for ordinary people. Those had always been his impressions whenever he walked inland from the long promenade. But Seb knew he'd never look at Paignton in the same way now.

To the east, gulls shrieked over the pier and the shoreline. Beyond the cinema, the pirate-themed mini-golf course and the Shoreline restaurant, where he liked to eat crispy squid, the sea stretched into a vast, euphorically blue distance. The near-empty fairground on the green flashed and blared.

A man passed on a mobility scooter, his Jack Russell trotting alongside the whirring carriage. Seb moved aside, then returned his attention to the Beach Haven Hotel. This shouldn't have happened *here*. Ewan had no right bringing *that* here.

A retractable green awning covered the front windows on the ground floor and the rooms above were concealed by nets. The hotel's rates were stencilled in white type on a staircase window. It looked all right. Neat and clean, the trees in good condition, the paintwork freshly mint green on the masonry and a bright white on the sills and around the doorframe. Seb bent over to open the tiny gate and entered. The front door was locked but the hotel was still advertising vacancies. He rang the bell and waited.

Three uneventful days and three tense nights had passed since Ewan had died. Seb had spent much of that time on walks in the nature reserve, around Torquay's marina, and out to the lighthouse at the end of the slipway in Brixham. But whatever he'd been doing, he'd found himself incapable of thinking about much besides Ewan.

He'd also spoken with his agent and answered the most

pressing emails from his publisher and the three film production companies adapting his books, but hurriedly. His ties to a life preceding the reunion with Ewan had failed to reform in his mind as important. As unpleasant as his re-acquaintance with his old housemate had been, he'd been taken to the edge of the truly remarkable. The experience left him wondering if he'd be able to write about anything else. His perception of the world, and himself in it, had been fundamentally altered. Seeing the world through new eyes made him ponder if the sensation was similar to being devout.

An elderly man came to the guest house door. He was portly enough to fill the doorway and protrude out of it. Muscled arms emerged like hairy logs from a short-sleeved shirt, and as the morning brightness struck his face, his tinted glasses blurred the definition of his deep-set eyes.

Seb introduced himself, before stumbling through an explanation of his association with the guest house's recently deceased guest. A connection that instantly made the man tense and too bemused to react. But Seb's earnest offer to cover the missing payment on Ewan's room did elicit a delayed response. The man's accent was thick West Midlands. 'You say he was a friend of yours?'

'Once, but not for many years. I hadn't seen him for a long time, until recently. All the same, I was still shocked, and I still am, when the police told me that he'd died.' Seb looked up at the building. 'Here. But he'd been staying with me for the two days before he passed away. He wasn't very well.'

The man continued to weigh Seb up from the threshold.

Seb reiterated his desire to cover the unpaid bill. 'It's the least I can do, for some kind of closure. It's very odd, but I feel some kind of obligation to him. I'd also like to ask you a couple of questions . . . about *how* he died. I mean, that night . . . It was so sudden and the police didn't tell me much.'

The man finally relaxed and introduced himself as Ray, though Seb could appreciate how any mention of Ewan would cause reactions ranging from caution to outright horror. 'You better come inside and talk to the wife. She's better at this sort of thing.'

Seb was introduced to Dot, who came out from an office to stand behind a counter set in an alcove under the staircase. A front desk small enough to suggest a lectern. Even then, a vast array of brochures, stationery and equipment had been arranged upon it. Somewhere from the office behind, a telephone rang.

'I'll get it,' Ray said, and then nodded his plump, hairless head to indicate Seb. 'This fella was a friend of the one in number three.'

When he saw the look of dread on the woman's face, Seb quickly redefined the 'friendship' for her, and found himself repeating the short speech that he'd edited and improved through repeat usage to explain his association with Ewan.

He also endeared himself to Dot by producing his wallet and then his credit card and insisting that he cover Ewan's unpaid bill at the Beach Haven.

Seb was not entirely comfortable with the idea that he was paying for information, but what he desperately sought was a grim reassurance that Ewan had died because of a fit. That his much-weakened constitution and poor health, after decades of hard living, alcohol and substance abuse, had *mostly* been responsible for stopping his heart. Seb needed to believe that whatever *it* was that had been hunting Ewan could not kill a man by appearance alone. The idea of death by such an agency, and then a victim's fate post-mortem, was the destination to which Seb's thoughts had recently flowed, circled and then settled.

Dot returned from the office with a set of keys attached to a large plastic fob. Coming out from behind the tiny counter she said, 'Come on up. I'll show you the room.'

Ray shuffled from the office and stood at the foot of the stairs, reluctant to join the tour.

The little hotel was clean and plainly decorated. Clearly a business in which much pride and hard work had been invested, and this amplified the indecency of Ewan's transgression. But Ewan had long stopped caring about anyone not committed to his obscure and selfish cause. What little sympathy Seb had conjured for him since his death evaporated.

When they stood outside number three, indicated by a brass number fixed into a newly white door, Dot said, 'We came up in the morning because he still hadn't paid. And you should have heard him in the night. He woke up the lady on the other side and the couple upstairs. We heard it too, me and me husband, but then it went all quiet in here.' Dot nodded at the door as she unlocked the room. She didn't share Seb's sudden nervous reluctance to see it opened.

'He liked a drink, that was clear, but he kept hisself to hisself and didn't bother no one. Don't think he went out much. Never ate breakfast here. Don't think he was up in time. Only saw him eat once and that was chips.'

Seb followed Dot into the room. It was small but well

kept. There was a bed with a fitted cabinet on one side, a wardrobe, a tiny desk and a flat-screen television attached to the wall.

'We've given it a thorough clean and it needed a good airing.' Dot paused and wrinkled her nose. 'Between you and me, I don't think he ever used the shower.'

Seb cleared his throat. 'He certainly had his fair share of problems.'

'It's hard to tell with people these days. You know, with all their tattoos and piercings and things, but we've never been quick to judge, like. Live and let live, we've always said. You can't jump to conclusions, but we were in two minds about letting him have the room in the first place. When we started to, you know, really catch wind of him, it was too late and he'd paid for twelve nights. He said he wanted to keep the room for a few more nights so we held it for him, but he never paid up when he came back. We felt a bit sorry for him too, you know. He seemed lonely. Depressed, like. And with the drinking we was just kind of counting down the days till he moved off. But that's where we found him, by the radiator, under the window.'

Dot shuffled to the window as if to recreate the scene for Seb. 'He was down the side of the bed, somehow, with his arms up like he was trying to climb out. Still in his clothes. I don't think he had any other clothes with him, just bags of paper when the police went through his things. They wore gloves too and wouldn't take his stuff with them. You could see they didn't even like touching it, cus of the smell, like. Said someone would come and fetch it, but they still haven't. Bags of paper he had with him. Fancy dragging that round with you? Horrible sound he made, though. Screams, you know, and really sudden, like.'

Seb nodded, trying to appear as thoughtful as he could manage. 'No one heard anything else that night?'

'Well that's the strangest thing, because the lady down the hall, now she said she thought she'd heard someone else in his room on the night before Mr Hazzard died, when he wasn't here, like. Sorry, Mr Alexander. But we never knew that at the time. He'd give us a false name. But the lady down the hall mentioned these noises she'd heard in Mr Alexander's room to Ray – a complaint, to be honest, about the chap in three. She's not here no more, otherwise I'd ask her to tell you what she told me. But she told us that she saw someone the night before he died, on his hands and knees, and moaning like he was unwell. Out in the hall. Or this fella on the floor might have been crying. We never saw no one come in though. The lady across the hall thought he was blind drunk, like Mr Alexander often was.

'But, as I said, this was the night before Mr Alexander come back and passed away. It was ever so strange because this lady was really frightened. Really put the wind up her, as my old dad used to say, cos whoever she saw had his head inside something, like a sack or pillow case. That's what she said. Never heard anything like that in my life, have you? She shut her door quick, like, and told Ray in the morning.'

Seb felt that he should say, *how odd*, or *how strange*, but the constriction of his throat strangled a response.

Now that she had a listener, Dot's story became irrepressible. 'But I says to her, like I'm telling you now, that Mr Alexander was not even here that night. Could not have been. No way, I says to her. Me husband wakes up when anyone comes through that door of a night. And we were nearly empty as it is. There was only the lady in two and a couple up on the next floor. Elderly like, and they're always back in their room by nine. So it couldn't have been a friend of Mr Alexander's. How would he have got in here, for one thing?

'We'd checked with the maid who does the rooms in the mornings and she said his bed hadn't been slept in either of them nights that he wasn't here, so he weren't here. No way. But it gets stranger, really odd, like. Because the elderly couple up in five had said that on the day before Mr Alexander came back, that they had seen someone in here too, this room. With summat over their face, and looking out the window as they came in from the garden, and it give them quite a shock. They come in and says to Ray that the fella in number three needs his head seeing to, you know? That his jokes weren't funny. If there'd been kids here, they said they might have been really frightened.'

Seb had to concentrate on making himself speak loud enough to be heard. 'They saw something . . . someone?'

'Hard to say and I only heard this through me husband. And when I asked them the next day, the Gibsons, like, they didn't want to talk about it. You know, it made them quite angry. But Mr Alexander wasn't even here that day. Hadn't been in his bed and, like I said, we would have seen him come through the front door.

'It must have been the curtains and the light, you know, on the glass. That's what I reckon, but *they* swore blind that they saw this fella in this room, at the window and looking down. Clearly like. They said he was wearing an old suit too. That's right. It's the details that make it so strange. I mean, an old black suit, with this big head, they said. Mrs Gibson said it was like a horse's hood, you know. A horse with a white sack over this long head, but with eye holes cut in it. I mean, I don't know what they were on themselves. Because they said he shrank too. Got smaller, you know. Then he wasn't there at all.

'But don't you think it's odd that the lady in number two says she saw something very similar in the hall, outside this room?'

Dot pulled a face as if she'd bitten into something unpleasant while she let Seb imagine what she'd described for him. 'I don't like anything like that, you know. It does my head in. And no one has ever said nothing like that, not here, and we've had this place thirty years. But it made me think, you know, about this chap in number three. It was another reason to not want him staying here. I'm not being cruel, because we're as open-minded as the next person, but it still seems odd that the other guests should start seeing things. I'd like to say that they was making it all up, but I'm not sure that I can.'

After his tour of the place of death, Ray helped Seb carry the two big bin bags and Ewan's rucksack to Seb's car, parked at the kerb out front. Ray and Dot were visibly relieved to get 'shot of them'. With the police reluctant to take them off their hands and Ewan's mother not wanting it, Ray and Dot hadn't known what to do with the three bags and had left them in their office.

'We was gonna give it a few weeks and then put 'em out for the bin men,' Ray had said, before Seb drove away. 'They're a bit whiffy, even with the windows open.'

13
Indeed, I Have Seen my Sister

[Society of Psychophysical Research – SPR. Vol. 4.
Case No. 37. 1963. 'Mr B']
*This place that we appear in, I know, is analogous to
the world I left, and to its time and the natural laws
that govern it. We can see the world we leave exactly as
it was before we left it, though the light is very different.
But we also stand at the gateway to immortality, to
eternal life. Of this, I have no doubt now.*

*I have actually taken my first step on the journey
that begins after bodily death, and have renounced my
will and been in the presence of something far greater,
perhaps even God. But to also preserve my individuality,
to be myself but changed and better as I venture deeper,
is a miracle in itself, and the greatest journey that a man
can embark upon. H was right and I have remained
sceptical of my wife's obsession for far too long.*

*H commands my utmost respect, he has my faith.
Like Christ, a comparison my wife so often made, he
has remained steadfast in his beliefs, despite derision
and persecution. He has been committed to his purpose,
as we must be.*

*

Seb had returned home and placed Ewan's bags on the floor of his office. And then circled them for hours. Several pots of coffee had succeeded in palpitating his heart and making his skin clammy.

After the shock of Ewan's death, he knew he was teetering on the brink of a new obsession. Despite the carousel of the past few weeks, sweeping him from terror to rage and back to terror, an awakening was underway within his imagination; a stirring of whatever had first compelled him to dedicate his life to writing fiction, over thirty years before. That unstable core of impressions and ideas was excavating itself from the rubble of the dulling process that had engulfed him across the previous two years.

The unpleasant smell arising from the bags, however, proved inexhaustible and spread to fill the office. Seb opened every window on the top floor and cast wide the balcony doors in the living room to disperse the stale odour of Ewan and his dusty paper.

For an inspection of the rucksack, he'd backed the car onto the drive and worn gardening gloves to examine the contents in the garage.

He'd immediately shovelled the articles of clothing into a refuse sack, as well as a pair of shoes, the soles worn paper-thin from Ewan's wanderings. An old Nokia phone he put to one side. The battery was dead and there was no charger. An antique Sony Walkman with a broken lid was unearthed, along with twenty compact discs of music, including Bathory, Emperor, Blood Frenzy, The 13th Floor Elevators and Coil. Seb tossed the music and the Walkman into the refuse bag.

From what he could establish from Ewan's effects, the value of his friend's estate amounted to six pounds and thirty-seven pence. The money was stored in the toe of a venomous shoe.

Seb had returned upstairs with the ancient mobile phone. Everything else in the rucksack he'd buried in the wheelie bin intended for household waste. A collection was due on Thursday.

The bin bags that Ewan had been carrying contained fifty-four manila folders. They were old, a pale green in colour and instigated a memory of school stationery in the seventies. Each folder had been stamped 'Society of Psychophysical Research (SPR) – CONFIDENTIAL'. This was followed by a title: 'Case Studies', a volume number, and then a date. At a glance, most of the folders originated in the sixties.

The actual reports inside the folders were mottled and issued a fragrance of dried damp, but the text was visible. Each sheet of paper functioned as an official form, was identical in design and filled with black type. The headers of each document repeated the information on the front of the file, but the index classification on each report was followed by the name of the subject who'd given testimony. Some of the same names appeared across multiple reports in the first few folders.

Randomly removing reports from the bin liners, Seb read haphazardly but compulsively. His reaction became fascination combined with horror.

[SPR. Vol. 7. Case No. 28. 1963. Mrs K. Harlow]
*I found myself at a great height again. I looked
down upon the world from a distance that I found
terrible. So much so that I came to quite shaken, and
gripped by an impression that a vast expanse of*

*black space had just surrounded me. The tiny white
bed from which I had risen had been visible below.
And yet, I knew, in some other form, that I had been
inside that bed the whole time.*

[SPR. Vol. 10. Case No. 107. 1963.
Mrs Ruby McDougal]
*H and Diane have congratulated me on my first
successes. This comes at a time when I feared I had
disappointed H, and all of the others who have
persisted for so long. I cannot tell you how much
their approval has meant. But they assure me that I
am at the threshold of the truly wondrous, and am
receiving the early intimations.*

*And yet it happened as I was resting after a long
and fruitless day, in which I was sedated twice with
two inducements. The second dose made me terribly
sick, frightened and paranoid. But as I lay down that
evening, I became aware of being entirely raised up
and off the bed. At least two feet of space existed
between my body and my consciousness.*

*The second time, I was again completely
exhausted in mind and body, and suddenly found
myself to be hovering over the bed and looking
down at myself. I looked into my own eyes and
knew at once that I was absent from them.*

*I sat up, but my body remained prone. I lay down
and repeated the action twice, but I stayed detached.*

The same woman had filed over a dozen reports across two
years. Seb could only assume that she'd been a patient in a

facility, or the subject of an experiment. Or perhaps all of the information was submitted by volunteers to be collated by this SPR.

[SPR. Vol. 16. Case No. 79. 1964.
Mrs Ruby McDougal]
I saw the room as it had been, though it was much brighter, clearer, with every object illumined from within and made vivid, almost sparkling. The dust motes were a cascade of gold before the window. My face upon the bed was the most surprising thing. Without doubt that was my head upon the pillow, and yet my face seemed so different to the one that I had looked upon in mirrors, so many times before in my life.

The room I fell asleep in had been dark, but during the experience the room could have been bathed in an unworldly form of moonlight, or illumined by the glow from a soft and magical nightlight. The light was opalescent. But when I saw myself inside the bed, I panicked and woke with a jolt. I opened my eyes and the room was black. Nothing inside the room was visible.

Seb discovered that the same woman had progressed to mastering an astonishing feat.

[SPR. Vol. 12. Case No. 29. 1965.
Mrs Ruby McDougal]
I stood in the room and watched the session. They were all sitting and continuing with the

*formulation of the image-making while repeating the
renunciation. But I had already left my body and
stood behind myself.*

*I instinctively became aware of H and turned to
see him and Katie. They were outside the room,
standing at the window and were smiling at me.*

*I felt superior to the other people around me for
the first time in my life. Suddenly, I knew that I must
get past my husband's decision to leave. This is what
we had come here for. This is what I had stayed for.
All of our sacrifices to this point were worthwhile.
My sense of succeeding and of belonging created an
emotional reaction of such force that I returned to
my body with a jolt. When I looked up, I was sat
upon the floor again, amongst my group. I looked to
the window but could see no one outside.*

*How is it that H and Katie can stay outside
themselves for so long? If it kills me I will master
this!*

Seb abandoned Ruby and picked up with an individual who,
he later discovered, had been the subject of over one hundred reports.

[SPR. Vol. 18. Case No. 31. 1964. 'V']
*As I ventured further than my room, the whole
house was alight with the same misted radiance,
pearl coloured, tinged with grey. My individual
senses became one, what H calls the 'supersense'. I
could see everything in the building, but through
everything too, through the very walls if I wished. I*

felt as though I could see the outside and inside of every simple, ordinary object, while instinctively understanding its form and texture. No barriers stood before me. Whatever was behind me I already knew was there without looking. The feeling was incredible.

The world was the same but fundamentally changed. The world was charged with an energy from somewhere else entirely.

I could have been joy incarnate. My very being was so buoyant, and I was in command of four dimensions.

When I thought of my husband, whom I had left in the bed, I at once came to be standing beside the bed in our room, and looking down upon him as he lay next to my physical body. That had never happened before, but I pitied my poor body and its sense of vacancy, while wishing for my husband to wake and to see me.

My mind has never been so clear as it was that night, so active but unstained by doubt. All was comprehensible instantaneously – myself, the world, my relationships, the past, the point of everything. It was incredible and yet I was entirely passive, a mere observer, and not thinking of my environment analytically at all during the experience.

I saw three other forms drifting in the corridor outside our room. And we were the light! We, the apparitions, lit the place. But my shock at seeing others ended my projection. When I came to, it was as if my mind had suddenly filled with shadows and

*was encircled with those familiar bands of
discomfort, that formed from tension and anxiety.
All of my fears were back in place.*

*Nonetheless, Diane was very pleased with my
account in the morning. She tells me that my vehicle
of vitality is loose and immediately advanced me to
the adepts. I have not been more thrilled by anything
in my entire life. She says she wants me to attempt a
journey further afield, maybe to one of the test sites,
and to report back on what I see there.*

H, Diane, the adepts, the building, test sites . . . Seb's mind
groped for more specifics and context, but the background
remained opaque. The documents were focused entirely upon
the sensations of the case studies, and the very experience of
this curious disassociation within a patient's consciousness.
He assumed that there was no need for the subjects to
explain the purpose, the theory, or the history of a project
that they were already familiar with.

He wondered how these files had come into Ewan's possession. The SPR reports were all written either before Ewan
had been born, or when he was a child. But this was material that Ewan had wanted him to integrate into an
autobiographical book, to augment his own testimony.

Seb removed all of the files from the first bag. Carefully,
he placed the folders into chronological order, spreading them
across the floor of his office. And began reading from the
beginning, replacing the files around his feet as he progressed.

By the time he had finished the contents of the first bag, it
had become dark outside without him noticing nightfall. He

stood up, feeling uncomfortably exposed with all of the curtains and blinds open, and moved into the lounge to fix himself a strong drink.

The cold smell of the sea had filled the top floor of the house. He closed the balcony doors and began drawing the blinds for the night.

As he read the reports, he had realized that, had he read them only a few weeks before, he would have scoffed at the accounts and felt awkward on behalf of the narrators and their tone of sincerity within such a scale of communal delusion. He even imagined himself groaning out loud, as he'd always done when imagined experiences were transformed into beliefs. But he now acknowledged he had been affected in a way few would understand. He imagined his experience of the files was similar to someone reading voraciously about a serious illness that they'd just been diagnosed as having.

Seb sat in the living room and stared into space for a long time afterwards. The lost voices of the SPR continued to speak excitedly within his memory. They seemed to revolve, chattering like a crowd.

. . . Silver light turning fast, raising my body into the air . . .

. . . I could penetrate the walls with ease . . .

. . . The inducements are far too strong, but H insists that my fall was a blessing because it led to me looking down upon my body from somewhere beneath the ceiling . . .

. . . So this is vitality. This is health. I had been ill for so long and in pain that I had forgotten what it was like to be well . . .

*. . . I saw the roof of the facility and the signs
that had been put there for those who can reach
such an elevation. I reported back on exactly what I
had seen. Though H is ill, he held my hands and
tears glistened in his eyes . . .*

. . . The spiritual body has no weight at all . . .

*. . . the sensation on entering the blackness is now
quite wonderful . . .*

*. . . Once I let go of my fear I feel like an animal
freed from captivity. Beyond the darkness, I am
assured there is a light everlasting . . .*

*. . . To think is to move now. My bilocation is
becoming instantaneous. H and Diane are paying me
a great deal of attention. I feel the other girls are
becoming frightfully jealous . . .*

*. . . Exultation . . . Exhilaration . . . Radiant light
. . . my spirit-body freed . . . peace and vigour . . .
the flow of energy . . . in the air but facing down and
seeing my body that still writhed and twitched in its
pain . . . my etheric form . . .*

Some of the testimony had made Seb mutter out loud
because it induced the full force of a recent dream that had
been far too vivid. These sections of the reports he'd also
transcribed into a notepad.

*My spirit-body bled through, and nourished the
silver cord, it grew thinner in the middle and then
detached, became vaporous, disappeared . . . from
the ceiling, up near the corner, came unto me a*

rushing and a force that presented an opening,
an aperture. I glimpsed a figure inside . . .

Over and over again the same experiences were described,
though in ecstatic terms and with a sense of triumph that
Seb could not share with these distant witnesses. How had
all of this contributed to Ewan becoming an unwashed,
homeless alcoholic, who was found dead in a guest house
with six quid to his name?

The silver cord has begun to appear for me too. It
flickered into life last night for the first time. And I
sensed more than saw the slow dark river. I was
delighted when I came to. I wept and embraced my
friends. If I can return there, to that place, then the
detachment, the sinking, the heavy, heavy sinking
that they all speak of, will occur. My renunciation to
the deep is possible.

At the repeated references to 'the silver cord', the 'dark
tunnel', the 'slowly flowing black water', Seb was unable to
stop imagining people being lowered into water they could
not see the bottom of, by means of a disintegrating rope.
Water driven by a swift current, its passage a subterranean
sinus. Perhaps this was a sewer pipe beneath the afterlife, or
a burrow into Hades.

Hadn't Ewan mentioned Hades?

He had seen this place too.

Seb sensed no coercion either, only voluntary participation, and an admiration for this 'H' and 'Diane'. At times,
the devotion bordered upon deification.

The files were also incomplete and must have been part of a much bigger archive. 1967 alone had a file titled Volume 50, containing only the testimonies dated in July of that year.

Throughout the day, he'd gradually developed a sense of a group of people within a larger community who had come to believe themselves special, even superhuman. They were encouraged by H and Diane to believe it too. A community addicted to a process, and the concentration of their entire will was focused upon repeating it. Another thing that reminded Seb of Ewan.

The 'inducement' must have forced the process. Possibly drugs, but nothing pharmaceutical was ever mentioned. There was also a great deal of contextualizing these experiences as part of a 'spiritual', 'mystical' and 'cosmic' order, with much reference to the 'spiritual body', and that was indicative of the time. People had become 'assured' of the existence of a hierarchy involving other 'spheres', 'realms' and 'dimensions'. A fair number of people too; he had records from at least fifty different individuals who'd participated in the SPR experiments. The names in the later files were different from those at the beginning. One woman, however, who was only ever referred to as 'J', seemed to have lived with 'the Society' for six years.

Seb also suspected a high dropout rate.

'My psychical evolving' and 'My renunciation of self has been ongoing for a long time' and 'My concentration within passivity' were phrases that suggested the terminology of a cult. Here was a belief system possessing its own idiom, ideology, and terminology that also postured as something scientific.

There was a great deal of 'as H directed' in the files too.

H? Who was this 'H'? Hazzard? Could 'H' be an actual reference to M. L. Hazzard, the obscure mystical writer that Ewan had been so enamoured of? Surely not. Seb was no expert on the obscure writer, but was sure that Hazzard's connection would have been more well known within the horror and weird field. He'd never caught a whiff of it.

The collective voice of the reports irritated him. There was far too little that distinguished one person from another. The subjects of the reports appeared to be speaking in a group voice. Maybe the transcription of the notes accounted for that. But there was an obsessive and narcissistic quality to the testimonies too, until the recorded ecstasies became morbidly boring.

Seb went downstairs to bed and found himself on the verge of a profound sadness. He became tearful, but didn't know why.

He left the house's lights on.

The illumination in his dream was not the same as the electric light in his home.

His house featured in the dream. But his home suffered a recreation by something too alien, unpleasant and insistent to have been within his mind's capabilities.

The nightmare was suffused with a dim, bluish light, the origins of which he had not been able to determine for a while. The glow had partially illumined his chest of drawers, the mirrored wardrobe, the steel light fittings, wooden blinds, the previous day's clothes folded over the end of the bed-stead.

His own presence within the room was unconnected to

an unfolding scene typical of a dream. Dreams did not have such extended pauses either. Nor were they still-life studies.

A profound sense of expectation had made Seb as anxious as a child separated from its mother.

The floor of his room was covered with liquid. Black water that reflected no light. As soon as he became aware of the water he also heard the distant hush of a current.

The first figure to appear in the doorway of his room passed down the corridor outside without noticing him. At the sight of it, his heartbeat had occupied his mouth.

Exhausted, bent forwards, wading through the black water that made no sound about the figure's knees and produced no ripples, a terribly thin woman had passed his room.

Black hair offered the only relief to her pallid form and had concealed most of her face. The lank hair was plastered to her scalp. A thin vapour, similar to what drifted from frozen food introduced to room temperature, wafted from her back and coiled behind her, then vanished. Her bloodless flesh exuded a faint grey light and the outline of her silhouette had perceptibly blurred as she staggered past, moving at an irregular speed, one much slowed, as if gravity worked against her meagre frame. She was there, in the doorway, and then she was gone.

A second figure passed the door moments later, but on all fours. It's emaciation and unhealthy complexion were the same as the first figure, though this one's hair was patchy. What wisps remained drooped like wet bootlaces from the back of a livid scalp. It had once been a man and the definition of the body had shifted in space, just like that of the first figure, before settling again and then blurring once its slow and painful passage continued out of sight. A stubby appendage had hung beneath that figure's solar plexus. The protrusion was like a dead tongue extending from the middle of a body.

Other figures were soon drifting by, but Seb had no sense they followed those who had gone before them. All appeared isolated, their sufferings insular.

Eventually, one of them paused and fumbled about the doorframe before coming inside his bedroom. The visitor was an aged woman, more bone than flesh, her joints pressing out her whitish-blue skin.

Her nostrils and eyes were pitch black. She whimpered piteously and padded her palsied hands against the walls as if the room had been a sudden, strange and unexpected revelation. Seb retained the impression that she only sensed, rather than saw him, sitting in his bed and paralysed with fright. But she had wanted to find him.

At this point the room and even the building altered. The house was still familiar, though rendered almost as a photographic negative. New objects appeared. A cushioned easy chair of indeterminate colour and pattern came to exist in one corner. It was covered by an old blanket and several discarded newspapers. None of which belonged to him.

A second figure came inside the room. Its white arms were spidery on the dim walls that they traversed, scratching and near clawing for something that made the creature whinny with either excitement or desperation. At that point in the dream, Seb was choked with a terror that the apparition might turn and face him. And yet he never awoke.

This form also exuded the faint vapour and displayed the thick nub, or dead remnant of an appendage about the solar plexus. The silhouette blurred out during its quicker movements closer to the bed, before settling again when it came to be still.

An iron-framed hospital bed appeared alongside Seb's bed. The bars were painted white, the bed linen was white, the legs ended in casters.

He experienced an unaccountable sense of his parents, as if they were close by, and he cried out for his mother and father. This was heard by the visitors. The elderly woman, who had come inside the room first, dropped to her knees in the black water, but without making a splash. She then clutched her long hands to her wasted face and emitted a groan, a sound filled with a misery so deep that Seb's own anguish was reduced to that of a child merely suffering a bad dream.

Two other naked forms waded inside the room, hurrying as much as their wasted legs would allow. They had heard him too. And as the space filled, the walls of Seb's room became increasingly vaporous, vaguer, dissolving away entirely where the blue-grey light had failed in the inkier corners. This very light, he finally came to realize, was emitted by his own form.

Soon he was looking at wet bricks around his bed and a curved ceiling above his head. The articles of his own furniture had disappeared, along with the hospital bed and the easy chair. The gushing of the water, as it funnelled through the dark bricks, became louder.

This was no longer a room in a house, but a tunnel.

The four figures about the bed groped closer.

Seb covered his face so as not to see their eyes.

A croaking, female voice made a sudden, desperate

entreaty. 'Which sphere is this? Can anyone tell me which sphere this is?'

'I can't get back,' another voice called out.

Nothing touched him, but a third voice filled one of his ears. 'Is this the second death? This is not my greater self. Where are the everlasting arms?'

The voices barked and echoed in the long, brick tunnel, an old sewer, and one cold and disturbed by a wind.

'I can't get back!'

'Can you help me? I know you are close. Where is the light? Do you know?'

'I can't get back!'

A wind came from an aperture that never became visible in the distance to which they had all been struggling, barely upright or on all fours. The water flowed away, around their thin limbs, and continued into the darkness.

When they reached for Seb's legs, he screamed and the light in his own form went out.

A final voice spoke from the void, and with a weary resignation. The words became fainter as if the speaker were moving away from him. 'A time of darkness.'

14
Greylands

Once Seb had read the SPR files, he organized Ewan's papers. As much as it was possible to systemize such a disparate hoard of fragments.

He'd not suffered another vivid dream either, for six days and counting. Which was just as well, because the last one had felt too unlike a dream. Seb had subsequently tried to convince himself that the nightmare had been an aftershock, and not an attachment. A week without Ewan, and the house had also returned to its natural state.

As Seb had deciphered Ewan's jottings, so disturbing had he found their contents that he'd given serious consideration to their destruction. Twice he'd stopped short of consigning every scrap of paper to the recycling bin, and only hesitated because what he managed to read had cultivated more of the green shoots of his desire to *really* write again. *What a story this would make*, had been a thought on repeat. And maybe he could even claim the story was factual, as Ewan's beloved M. L. Hazzard had done with his own obscure works. No one would believe Seb either.

His desk and the floor of his office were soon covered by SPR files and stacks of Ewan's dog-eared notes, date-ordered where possible. The jumbled dossier that Ewan had left behind, and its considerable marginalia, had taken Seb five long days to struggle through. The unreadable parts comprised two thirds of the documentation and had been consigned to a separate cardboard treasury box. So severe was the text's illegibility it might have been coded, but without the author to decipher the text, some sections would remain a permanent mystery. Even though most of that consignment had been illegible, Seb worked out enough to know that every sentence began with a thickly scored 'I'.

The piecemeal journal was entirely handwritten, in a variety of biro colours. At the bottom of the bag Seb had found some small pens, the type that Argos stores put out for customers to fill in their order tickets. Even a pencil had been employed at one point.

Cheap A4 pads, photocopying paper, flyers for National Trust properties and bus timetables had been used by Ewan to record his thoughts and experiences. All of the paper was smeared with grubby fingerprints and some pages had been obliterated by stains. A few folios were stuck together with what Seb hoped was food. He'd even uncovered a Hello Kitty notepad that Ewan must have found, or stolen, before tearing out the pages used by the previous juvenile owner. That spiral-bound notebook had entries dated within the last year, but stank more heinously than anything else, as if Ewan had kept it close to his unwashed flesh; perhaps hidden from sight like a prisoner of war concealing a journal. But concealed from whom, and why?

Seb guessed the archive amounted to a decade's worth of hastily written notes. Those dated within the last two years appeared on pieces of paper that gradually diminished in size, the handwriting matching the shrinkage of the paper.

The entire mess demonstrated a confusion and convolution that Ewan had expected him to transform painstakingly into an interesting book, before evangelizing the work for the 'author's' sole benefit.

But, God, how he had died ... Thoughts of that nature had to be suppressed. And yet, the irony was not subtle. Here he was, working his way through Ewan's archive and thinking about a new book, though never the one that Ewan had planned.

Seb's impression of the bigger picture surrounding Ewan's life also remained frustratingly vague. A direct connection between the projecting subjects of the SPR in the sixties and what he had seen of Ewan's last two weeks remained elusive.

No records had been dated to indicate the month preceding Ewan's arrival in Torbay. The sections Ewan had dated Seb managed to translate more easily. They may have been written at a time when Ewan was lucky enough to write on a stable surface, like a table.

Ewan's accreditation of his whereabouts during his experiments was also inconsistent, though Willesden Green, Wisbech, Kettering, Yeovil and Gloucester were mentioned. 'A caravan/Barmouth' featured intermittently too, six years before his demise in Devon.

The contents of the *stable* period ranged from a grotesque self-importance, to screeds of dull, hyperbolic descriptions of 'my gift'. But what else did Ewan have to write about, once he'd rendered himself unable to function in the real world? Which must have increased the attraction of his 'gift' as an escape route.

Look where it got you.

It was possible that Ewan also considered himself to be

two people: a higher self that roamed beyond space and time, and the wretched, physical form, or 'prison', that hunted for intoxicants and endured a miserable, transient existence.

Drug use was a constant theme in the jottings, as were his difficulties with finding MDMA, his substance of choice. Legal highs he embraced as something of a divine intervention at one point during his mission. He had been staying somewhere in Yeovil, and then Gloucester, and like an amateur chemist Ewan had combined all kinds of compounds to 'really burrow down and go much further, to stay for longer'. And yet Ewan's diary proved that he had little control over when these *out-of-body* episodes occurred.

As for travelling beyond the remit of his 'physical prison', he rarely appeared to make it beyond his mother's spare bedroom, or from the other demoralizing places that he'd inhabited. For two years the separation 'never happened once'. Ultimately, Ewan's projections had remained random, unpredictable and fleeting for the best part of a decade. He'd remained a man unfilled and underfed by the experience, famished, even starving at times for a salvation that slowly ruined him.

How the random acts of disassociating his consciousness had progressed to Ewan's evident ability to enter the state at will, to control it and to appear as an apparition, was the missing link. Had Ewan found a mentor, or even a substance, that allowed him to take his inconsistent ability to the next level? This SPR and its inducements offered the only clue.

What was legible in what he took to be the later, more inconsistent periods culminated in what Seb hoped were the psychotic fantasies of an addict. And only within these did Seb discover anything relating to what might have entered his home during the last night of Ewan's intrusion – the very *form* that had brought death to Ewan in Paignton.

Written in black ink, inside the Hello Kitty jotting pad, were sections that Ewan had entitled: *The Greylands*.

It was like a blackout. Different. Everything went dark. A loss of consciousness? Complete darkness. Was this the time of darkness that they had told me about? But this was more like a void. More than darkness. It was nothingness.

Consciousness returned. I moved out of the void and was rushing through the cold, in a wind. But I came to be inside the house again.

Partial awakening with only dream-like awareness inside. I was half in the world, but it was very dim and not properly formed, even formless in places. Something always unreal and misty about these rooms. I was only half aware, but the edges of door-ways and furniture were vague. Objects doubled, or one thing went over another, like two images in fog. Some of the images belonged to me and I saw things that I owned as a child. So was I projecting that? Never experienced that before. Not what I expected.

But I was definitely still in the building and able to move about more freely.

Another fragment in the Hello Kitty pad suggested a location with a physical basis. It reminded Seb of the SPR reports about the tests set by the mysterious 'H' and 'Diane'. Other participants were mentioned but only referred to as 'they'.

Found the place. The corridor of black doors. Awake but dreaming in the mist. Couldn't stop the fear. Was like being a child again. Suspected I was close to something dangerous [text illegible].

Must still be inside the soul-body veil, but never seen this sphere so clearly before. Found the correct room, third on right, and passed inside. Stayed clear from the black windows and slowly seemed to descend to the floor like I was growing smaller and dimmer.

Saw the painting in there. Boy sat on chair with light-coloured hair, holding a bear. Under painting was the same chair with the same bear on it. Actual toy was older, worn to cloth in some places.

There was a row of toys lined up on an old sofa. Before I could look at them I was hit in the face by something soft. A nightgown. Child's nightgown. Very old and white. It had seemed to hover or float in the corner of my eye, and then it came across the room fast and covered my face. Terrifying!

Fell back into void and woke in the bedroom.

They were very pleased with me the next day for identifying some of the contents of that room. HE was there, they said. Apparently, HE was with me the whole time. 'HE helps those who come inside his house.' They keep repeating that.

I mentioned the nightgown and they said it was nothing to worry about. A sign of acceptance, a little trick. 'HE likes those', they said.

Reports of Ewan's *assessment* continued on the several pages that had come loose from the Kitty pad. Seb had found them at the bottom of one of the bin bags.

Fifth time in corridor with the black doors, but fear is still the same and I was not fully conscious again. Something is holding me back. I'm half asleep and sluggish and a bit [text illegible] confused. But I found the room with the playing cards on a card table.

Read the cards. Found the bookshelves and the little table with the three ornaments – glazed cockerel, two white ceramic bowls with lids, blue flower print. Saw drinks trolley and counted the bottles.

Have never stayed outside my body for so long.
[Text illegible]

Aware of a presence in the sitting room. Not pleasant experience. Started to think of a hat, or dream of a man in a hat, wearing dark glasses and leather gloves who was staring at me. Suit and tie. Pale face.

Then the man was inside the large mirror over the fireplace, but not visible inside the room with me, but I could feel him inside the space.

Heard words inside my head. 'When the door opens, go through it. Cast thyself down.' But I couldn't see beyond the doorframe in the corner of the sitting room. He must have meant that one. There wasn't another door. Does that door lead to another corridor up there? House is confusing and always so dark. Door was already open, but leading where? I could see it behind the piano with all of the framed photographs arranged on top, but could see nothing through the door that he wanted me to go through. Made me anxious.

[Text illegible]

Had that been HIM inside the sitting room? I asked them in the afternoon when we were eating (food is terrible here). They smiled and said it wasn't for them to say.

On the day that he'd deciphered one particular cluster of notes, a fragment had frightened Seb enough to stop him working. He'd left the house and spent an evening at a restaurant, followed by the noisiest pub that he could find in the harbour, before dragging his feet back to the house close to midnight.

Bedroom. Big bed with quilted covers. Metal bed frame. Could have been inside a museum. Walked through the room and into an adjoining dressing room. It was filled with women's clothes in alcoves and on stands, like artist's busts – fur coats, dresses, lots of shoes, hat boxes. A table with cosmetics and bottles. All very old. From the war, 1940s, and the 1950s, I guessed. Don't understand why it's there. Whole floor of the house seems preserved, but from before HIS time. But this was where HE lived, in this sphere. They said that this is where HE was.

[Text illegible]

ADAM NEVILL

Voice inside my head said, 'Come out of there! Gentlemen don't mooch through ladies' things!'

I couldn't turn around and go back through the bedroom. Knew the bed wasn't empty any more and I became frightened. Could sense that it had become occupied. Don't like the tricks at all.

[Text illegible]

I tried to end the experience but couldn't. Have tried before in those rooms. Not possible to get off that floor of the building at all, unless I am inside the corridor of the black doors. It ends only if HE lets it end. That's what I suspect. But I had to walk through the bedroom, past the bed, to get back to the corridor of black doors to have any chance of getting out. I kept my face turned away from the bed.

Feelings of loathing and revulsion and rage filled the room, but these were not my emotions or my projections.

Bad scene. Angry room. Angry woman inside.

Why wasn't I told about her?

Saw a bit of her in the mirrors on a dark cabinet at the end of the bed as I left. Very pale, very thin form. Dark glasses like HE wears, and her head was covered by a headscarf. She was sitting up in bed with the bedclothes pulled down to her waist, but showing her little breasts. Nipples and fingertips were black.

Was that Diane?

The experience only ended when I'd returned to the corridor of the black doors.

In the morning I refused to go upstairs in the building again. No way.

They said that was okay. They said I could go outside instead.

Very surprised by that. But I do want to try the next sphere. I told them that I came here for that.

The final two segments that Seb translated suggested to him that Ewan had placed himself in grave danger by continuing with the unpleasant trials, and that he was, more or less, being played with or tormented by his guides, or hosts, or whatever they were. This made Seb wonder at Ewan's motivations for arriving in Brixham. Perhaps Ewan had reneged on some agreement, or even an association with something that he'd realized was not in his best interests as a projector, but too late.

[Text illegible]

Don't like the house at all now. Really bad feeling inside and it makes me feel ill. There is no light at all, even in the windows. Just very grey outside, or completely black, or a heavy fog curls and breaks on the window panes. So how can that be the next sphere outside, and this the entrance? There is no light.

They've been saying 'Patience, patience, patience,' so why are they letting me go outside now?

Tired of the trials though, and the tricks.

[Text illegible]

Spent the day reading the files again. So many. Incredible. But this is not the same place it was once.

Those still here don't know exactly, or won't tell me,
where all of the others are now [Text illegible]

Some of them are in the highest sphere, I am told.
They must be because they were already old in the
1960s.

'Some still come here. You'll meet them soon.' But
they won't say when.

[Text illegible]

Just us here, and what comes into the second
floor. Something not right about the whole deal.

[Text illegible]

While taking breaks from Ewan's papers, Seb conducted internet searches for the Society for Psychophysical Research. His slender breakthrough came in the form of comments referencing the society in relation to other similar organizations in the 1960s. But the same secondary articles also led him to the eureka connection with the writer, M. L. Hazzard.

The SPR had no entry on Wikipedia, but was mentioned as a footnote in a long entry on 'Astral Projection'. It seemed the SPR had been one group, amongst scores of similarly titled societies and organizations, that had flourished from the late Victorian interest in travelling clairvoyance until the 1970s. Many were purely occult organizations, like the Golden Dawn. Others had blended psychology with science and the supernatural. The SPR took its place in the latter category.

On most sites that referenced the SPR, the information never progressed beyond the approximate dates of its existence, in the sixties. There was no mention of the society's dissolution or start date.

Three commentaries did mention its founding by 'a writer, M. L. Hazzard'. On an occult site, Hazzard's theories about 'planes and spheres' were referred to once, but without expansion.

Two postings on 'Astral Projection' websites were critical of the SPR. But the dismissal in the first piece never extended beyond a reference to it being 'discredited and disreputable'. The second post commented on Hazzard's 'disgrace' without specifying more than 'embezzlement' and of 'defrauding members of the society'.

No publications seemed to have been produced by the society either, nor were there any available records that tried to formally define its practices or aims. The group appeared to have left almost no trace of itself, at least within the public domain.

It struck Seb that the publications of the British organizations of the time that bore similarities to the SPR may have contained more information on Hazzard's group, but without recourse to the indexes of the books they'd produced, he'd never know. Nor would he ever reach the end of the published journals and annals from the groups that operated in the same period. There were hundreds of these publications for sale on used-book sites.

He'd also developed an impression that academia's interest in the phenomenon had never waned. But it repeatedly and comprehensively dismissed, or attempted to dismiss, all of the ideas posed by astral projectors, occultists and pseudo-scientists, like the SPR. Extensive research into the subject had been conducted by several British and American universities, including Cambridge, and recently too. A broad range of physiological causes for the phenomenon were cited. A damn shame, it seemed in hindsight, that they never put the SPR in a laboratory.

Strangely, as often occurred whenever Seb tried to research anything online, he'd also found himself gradually moved away from what he wanted to know. Anything close to relevant about the SPR was inevitably old and buried in the archives of long-abandoned websites. But he did have more luck online when searching for M. L. Hazzard.

The Wiki entry on Hazzard was brief but far more interesting because it had been edited by someone frequently, and recently. Seb quickly recognized four of Ewan's online reviewer monikers too. So had Ewan considered himself to be the proprietor of the writer's legacy? If so, why was so little information included in the entry?

Hazzard was listed as the 'unique and influential author of two collections of strange episodes based upon the author's actual experiences, while employing his extraordinary ability to travel outside of his physical body'.

Hazzard's books were listed: *Sinking in the Dark Room. Rising in White Light* and *Hinderers in the Passage*. The revelation of the title of the second collection gave Seb such a shock that his vision had blurred. He'd gone and fetched a drink, which he'd consumed while sitting on the toilet, after feeling a hot, urgent need to find one in a hurry.

When he'd calmed down and returned to his office, still dabbing his brow with tissue paper, he'd forced some composure and continued his consideration of the Wikipedia entry. Hazzard wasn't *influential*. He'd hardly been read in his lifetime, let alone afterwards. *Unique* was also an attribute that Seb, at one time, would have considered debatable, though he didn't question it now. The year of the author's death was cited as 1982, 'from cancer'.

Once he'd worked his way past the sales information for the surviving copies of Hazzard's two anthologies, on antiquarian and book collector sites, and on sale for eye-watering sums, Seb discovered the occasional reference to Hazzard's curious stories amongst weird tale aficionados.

Most posts of that nature had been online for years. The fact that so few people had read Hazzard's work, beyond the two anthologized short stories in the early seventies, must have been responsible for the paucity of discussion amongst the writers and collectors who frequented the message boards.

A more recent thread, though still eight years old, on a 'Classic Weird Stories' forum began with a question: 'Anyone read the book: *Theophanic Mutations*? I hear there's a section on M. L. Hazzard and his cult? Didn't even know he had one.'

The thread lasted for two pages:

'Aren't we his cult? Or still trying to be?'

'You gotta write more than two stories to have a cult.'

'He wrote two collections.'

'True, but who's read them?'

'And it wasn't a cult. It was a research group that studied astral travelling.'

'Still no ebook editions.'

'You'll be waiting a while. Last I heard his stuff is still in copyright. No relatives can be traced.'

'Why doesn't someone scan his books?'

On the second page of the thread, someone calling

himself Charles the Dextrous Warden of the Weird claimed to have read *Theophanic Mutations*:

'Yes, read it. It came out in Numinosity Press, when they were still going. Limited to 300 copies of a pretty shoddy trade paperback. I was sent a review copy. Good read for the best part, though. Most of it is about The Golden Dawn and The Temple of the Last Days, rehashing the Levine book, but with more detail about their weird-ass medieval belief system. The section on Hazzard is pretty far out. Apparently, he was a con man and his organization – which was a kind of cult btw – shook a lot of old ladies out of their cash. He seemed to have been something of a scientology, sociopath type. Very dodgy guy who used all kinds of aliases. Author makes some outrageous claims. Definitely worth checking out, though, and it made me want to read Hazzard's stuff, which remains, as we all know, frustratingly unavailable.'

Seb found only six copies of *Theophanic Mutations* on sale, from between seven hundred and nine hundred pounds. It had been published eleven years before. The author's name was Mark Fry and his website was still current: a WordPress site called 'Noise, Notions and Notations'.

Seb found the site comprised of reviews of electronic noise, obscure films, small press occult publications, psychic geography, folklore and art, or anything weird that attracted Mr Fry.

Seb used his credit card to buy the cheapest available copy of *Theophanic Mutations* from Abe Books. What choice did he have? Losing seven hundred quid was less money than he imagined he would have lost had Ewan lived. He'd have to wait two weeks for it to arrive, though, because the seller lived in New Mexico.

He then introduced himself to Mark Fry in a message via his website, mentioning his interest in Hazzard's SPR. In order to improve his chances of provoking a response, he added the footer from his standard author email and mentioned that 'some SPR files have come into my possession'.

Once he'd progressed as far as he was able to with internet searches, the phone recharger for Ewan's old Nokia phone arrived from an eBay seller and Seb charged the handset.

Even though the screen was faded in the lower half, and probably damaged, Seb was able to operate it. There were seven contacts in the address book, but the text messages had been deleted. The phone was too old to have a camera or graphics, and the memory was minuscule.

The first three numbers he'd called – 'J', 'Dizzy', 'Ace' – were disconnected. The fourth number for a 'Baz' rang out twice before the call was answered. A rough male voice exploded inside Seb's ear the moment the call was accepted, the words frantic and near breathless with anger. 'Ewan! That you? Ewan, you cunt! I'll fuckin' do you! Where are—'

Seb had hung up and found himself shaking for a few seconds. The lingering effect of Baz's threat flooded his imagination with the sensations and notions of sleeping rough in damp, filthy rooms, crashing on couches that stank of cigarette smoke, owing money, being cold, hungry, hungover, strung-out, skint, depressed, unwell, tired . . . His appetite to delve any further into Ewan's past faded. Seb deactivated the handset in case Baz called back.

He went out to the balcony afterwards. The grey clouds

had blown over. Sunlight had transformed the water from the earlier colour of ash to a near-luminous blue and produced a glare from the tiered rows of white buildings bordering the harbour. For a few moments Seb felt delirious with gratitude for what he had, for who he was, and for where he lived. And he experienced a tremendous relief that Ewan was no longer alive. He was convinced that the man would have destroyed him.

15
Discarnate Inhabitants of Hades

Seb sat alone on a bench on King Street, in Brixham, embedded inside one of the alcoves that overlooked the old harbour. The tide was high and the water bristled with masts.

Gentle and soothing was the sun's warmth upon his face. Drowsy and coddled with two pints of Cornish bitter, his thoughts became adrift from the last month, and he recognized the first sign of contentment in weeks. Another comforting, familiar glow spread outwards from a belly full of fresh crab sandwiches, the satiation softening tension. Once again, the sea air seemed capable of nourishing his soul.

Rising up across the harbour and behind his bench, the old stone town teetered upon the edge of the narrow roads that bisected it. Successive levels of ice cream and candy-coloured houses, pink, yellow, white, and sky blue were cut into the cliffs and remained exotic to him after two years a resident. A great shelf of cloud, like a movable ceiling on a sports stadium, inched over the bay from Torquay, but still had some way to travel.

Closer to the shore the sun transformed the sea a green that closed on becoming turquoise. Out past the slipway and

219

lighthouse the water sparkled white gold and heralded the coming of summer. Life could be good again.

Eight days without a nightmare. A week and a half since Ewan had died.

One road in and out of the town and open sea ahead. Natural defences. A town not cut off, but annexed, the architecture and topography remaining unique in the bay. Still a working port with its own fishing fleet and ferry services. An old and established community and he'd been able to live on its edge, like a tourist or retiree, with no shared history. He'd never felt isolated, he'd felt safe. The infinite horizon of the bay made anything seem possible. An insidious, encroaching misgiving that the place had become a trap, he suppressed. And until Mark Fry made contact and *Theophanic Mutations* arrived in the post, he intended to divert his thoughts away from Ewan's legacy.

At the edge of his vision a figure joined him on the bench, a rustle of a yellow waterproof coat announcing someone's arrival.

Unusual for someone to join him there, because he rarely saw anyone use the bench, and the enclosed nature of the walled terrace also suggested the existing occupant's desire for seclusion.

Shielded by sunglasses, Seb's eyes remained fixed upon the sky. Pulling heavily on his electronic cigarette, he released a cloud of blueberry vapour to engulf his head like a smokescreen.

A blob of yellow Gore-Tex and a pale head intruded into his view of the glittering horizon. 'You must get inspired here.'

The voice startled him. A female voice, one slightly juvenile from a touch of excitement, as if altered by a trace of helium. *Cartoon voice*, he thought unkindly.

When Seb turned his head, the woman was looking out towards the quay and appeared distracted. He didn't consider himself famous and, despite appearing on television a few times, he'd never been recognized in public. His likeness was only familiar to those in the genre-fiction world. He wondered if the woman was even addressing him as an author.

'It would be a dull mind that this view failed to move,' he said, trying to sound good natured, though what he said was stiffer with a challenge than he'd intended. He kept the stranger in his peripheral vision.

'Still special to you.'

He found her familiarity irksome. The tone wasn't so much rude as subtly challenging, slightly arch, and perhaps judgemental.

'Of course.' Seb frowned, hoping to compel the woman to explain her comment about inspiration, which now suggested both a general statement about the view, and something uncomfortably intimate that might threaten the bounds of small talk with a stranger.

The profile of her round face broke into a smile. 'I suppose that it might be dull to someone who looks at brighter light.'

An unpleasant sentiment, considering recent events. Now she had his full attention.

Her plump face was made unusually smooth by a lack of colour and conjured infantile associations. It also made her age hard to gauge. Maybe she had one of those faces that never relinquished a younger self, permanently trapped in surprise by the ageing process around the core expressions.

He suspected her eyes conveyed an amusement at his expense. They were startling in their size, intensity and unusual colour. So pale was the iris, the faded blue was in danger of vanishing into the white sclera.

She wore no make-up and her white eyebrows were thick and untrimmed. Her top lip was also furred with the white hair of her unkempt eyebrows. The only colour in her face was the shiny skin beneath the eczema covering her eyelids.

And now he'd taken a closer look at her, he came to believe that too much hair sprouted from the top of her head, as if every square inch of her scalp was overburdened with an excess of hair follicles, producing the pale thatch. He'd not seen the hairstyle on an adult before. It made him think of a Saxon helmet cut from a bushel of straw.

The fringe was slightly asymmetrical too, as if cut in a straight line with a ruler that had slipped at the final moment when the scissors closed. At the back and sides, the length had been messily cropped into a crude attempt at a bob. The style might have been evidence of an individual's lack of interest in fashion, or a sign of a personality disorder.

Seb was no expert on hairstyles, but the chance of it being in vogue was undermined by the unflattering statement her clothing made. What looked like a man's padded raincoat had been complemented with corduroy jeans in poor condition. Her outfit covered a bulbous torso carried atop broad hips. Battered grey hiking boots concealed feet small enough to be ridiculous.

Seb cleared his throat. 'I've never heard that said about a beautiful day before.'

This clearly pleased the odd figure. The movement of her body on the bench made Seb restrain himself from recoiling, and he found it necessary to breathe through his mouth. The rustling of her coat had disinterred a miasma imprisoned from a place that was damp. The odour that impregnated her clothing not only carried the scent of neglect but was thickened with a hormonal fragrance; a taint of oils and secretions that should have been washed away. Seb knew where he'd smelled similar before.

The woman's eager face maintained a grin lit with expectation. She seemed pleased with herself.

Seb moistened his mouth. 'Do you know me?'

The woman shook her head emphatically. Another gesture that suggested a strange immaturity. 'No, but I'd like to.' As she spoke, Seb was stricken by a glimpse of an incomplete set of yellow-brown teeth.

'What . . .' He was no longer sure of the question he wanted to ask.

The woman laughed.

'You've read my books then?'

A rapid nodding made the longer strands of her thatch sway. The bleached eyes widened with excitement and added weight to his suspicion that the woman was unstable.

'So, what can I do for you?' Seb suffered the uneasy feeling that interaction would lead to some kind of entrapment. 'And how did you know I'd be here? Did you follow me?'

'I came to extend an invitation. We'd like you to take part in something. An event.'

'We? I'm sorry, but who are you?'

Another two questions she didn't answer. She remained committed to extracting a response to her invitation that he was clearly disinclined to give. She issued more of the irritating giggling. But a small hand was tentatively extended towards him. The fingernails were chewed back to tiny half-moons of pearly cartilage, embedded inside red nail beds. They looked sore and gnawed rather than bitten. Her fingertips were also wet from a recent trip to her mouth. Seb hoped she would drop the little hand. He had no intention of touching it.

'I belong to a group that appreciates ideas. Shall we say, ideas that reach into unusual places. Even if most *books* are always wide of the mark.' Again the giggle and Seb was sure she was referring to his books. 'You'd be amongst friends, Sebastian.' Her hand remained poised in the narrowing gap between their bodies.

Never fond of public speaking, to which he found himself emotionally unsuited, Seb still occasionally took part in literary events, though he'd never been approached like this before.

And that smell.

'Is that so? I'm a little busy right now. New book.'

'New book! How exciting. That's precisely what we want to hear about. Your plans. What's it about? We'd love to know.' The surprise in her voice was forced, the curiosity insincere. He knew she had no real interest in anything he had written. This was someone who wanted something from him.

'I never discuss the details of works-in-progress.'

'A secret! A shame. What a shame.' She'd phrased this as if his refusal to open up was to his disadvantage.

'For who, me?'

'Don't you like to meet your *readers*?'

224

'I always have time for genuine readers. So why don't you send me your details by email. You'll find an address on my website.'

Her eyes became busy with mischief and she wrinkled her nose in disappointment.

'You are enquiring about a reading? A talk?'

'Mmm. That sort of thing, yes,' she said, but only after a pause as if the idea was only being recognized as a possibility because he'd just suggested it.

'You don't seem so sure.'

'Having you with us is the main thing. The rest can take its course. I think the best connections are made that way, don't you?' The unnerving stare was now offset by astigmatism in her left eye, the effect suggesting mania more than a misshapen eyeball.

It was time to close the conversation. Seb slipped his unread book inside his rucksack. 'As I say, best to send an email.'

'There'll be a lot of people there. We're a big group. There was a lot of excitement when we learned that you were a *local* writer. Perfect, we thought. And so close. Why not ask him to come a bit closer?'

'Local?' As strange as the baffling figure was, Seb wondered if he were being paranoid. He'd never seen her before, or knew of any local reader groups, but that didn't mean they didn't exist. 'I'll take a look at my diary. Anyway, must get on.' Seb stood up.

'*He'll* be there,' she said, and suppressed a giggle.

'Who?'

'And him.' The woman gazed beatifically into the distance. Seb followed her eyes to the far side of the docks. And within the distant panorama of holidaymakers spread out before the pubs, gift shops, restaurants and slowly moving traffic on Quay Street, his eyes located an utterly motionless figure, dressed in black.

Across that airy gulf, spiked with masts and busy with wheeling gulls, he was being watched by that distant smudge of face, a bone-white face. The shoulders of the figure were slumped as if the man was in a deep despair.

Within the projected gaze came a flood of sadness, accompanied by fear. And Seb knew that he was looking at a distant apparition of Ewan, though one much worsened by recent tragedy.

'Who?' Seb's voice came out of his panic.

The cooling of the air and the dimming of the sunlight was sudden. The sounds of the harbour vanished as if his ears had suddenly been crammed with the foam plugs that he used on trains and planes. A shadow filled his eyes. The world around him became far less distinct, as if it had been engulfed by a pall of unnatural dusk, or cast into shadow by a strange occultation of the sun. But at the corner of his vision, the light suggested a painful and blinding contrast. Seb clutched at the railings.

'You'll receive a warm welcome. This is a wonderful opportunity.'

Struggling to catch his breath, Seb closed his eyes, then blinked and peered again to Quay Street.

The lone figure was gone from where it had stood so forlorn and abject.

Near gasping for breath, Seb slumped at the railing and let the remainder of the spell pass.

When he looked about himself the woman in the yellow

raincoat was already on King Street and moving away in the direction of Berry Head. He could see the top of her messy head as it passed between the flowers and gaps in the hedgerow. The last he heard from her was a muted giggle, as if she was sharing a joke with someone who walked beside her.

16

A Dark, Slowly Flowing Flood

Hello Mr Logan

Sorry for the late reply. I've been away, but it's not every day a renowned horror writer writes to me about my book! I'm amazed you've even heard of Theophanic Mutations. I was in two minds whether to reply to the email because I assumed it must be fake. I checked your website and saw that this email address matches the one on your contact page.

What's equally surprising is that you have SPR files. You'll know from my book that I was only able to track down three people who had an involvement with the organization, and who actually knew Hazzard, and they all attested to the fastidious record-keeping that went on at Hunter's Tor Hall, and also confirmed the presence of a large archive. But where the 'library' eventually went to is a mystery.

Your revelation has come over a decade too late, though! I did my best with what little information I could find at the time I was researching the book, but it was scant. Unfortunately, all three of my contacts have since passed away (they were elderly when I interviewed them).

If I'm honest, there was never a great deal of interest from publishers for the material, which is why I went with an indie press. Even though the SPR was new ground, I never found enough to justify an entire book dedicated to the organization. That's why the SPR only forms one third of Mutations. My efforts to publicize the book were not helped either by Hazzard's collections being out of print. But I still wish I'd had access to your files!

I assume you've been out to their old HQ? It's in Devon. Your website says that's where you live. Am I right in thinking that you're researching a new book and thinking about basing something on them? I'd like to read that. But for verisimilitude, you'd have to make it very weird indeed.

If our paths ever cross, I'd like to see those files, and also learn how you came into possession of them.

Best

Mark Fry

The message had been sent earlier in the day, but while so shaken after the encounter on King Street, Seb had not checked his messages until the early evening.

And *it* was not over. Ewan's passing had not called time on his unwitting and unwilling association with whatever his old housemate had been involved in. Even worse, he was being pursued again. He must have been followed to that bench on King Street, and that odd creature probably knew where he lived too.

So was she and Ewan part of the degenerate dregs of whatever Hazzard had started in the sixties?

Hazzard was long gone, but if a relic of the SPR still existed, it would also explain Ewan's possession of their official files.

Seb feared there might be more of *them* too, and perhaps watching the house. *Do they even need to be physically present?*

They had also murdered Ewan, in effect, by using an assassin that left no evidence beyond what was etched into a victim's death mask.

What did they want with him?

Ghost-writing Ewan's manifesto was off the table, and it was hard to imagine a reading and Q&A sufficing to keep them away. Much more was involved. The woman on King Street had mentioned an *event*, a meeting.

I think you're fucked, that's what Ewan had said.

Had the woman also implied that Seb would meet 'Him' too, before Ewan's dreadful form had appeared on the quay? *Him?* Who was 'Him'? *Hazzard?* He had been dead for decades, but considering what Seb had seen in the last few weeks, any assurance offered by a death notice was disputable.

How had this happened, so quickly?

He didn't know what to do, or where to go. And the SPR was in Devon. Mark Fry had said so. There was even the mention of a house in the email: Hunter's Tor, their 'old HQ'.

Where the hell is it? Seb used combinations of keywords to squeeze something, anything at all, out of the internet, but came away with nothing.

If the author Mark Fry could tell him where the building was, he'd have a start at confirming the group's persisting existence. Maybe this Fry could tell him other things too. If anyone could explain the peril that he was currently in, then it was this connoisseur of the weird and esoteric. Forewarned was forearmed.

Seb replied to the email.

Mr Fry
    Thank you so much for your message. This might sound unusual, but could we speak today?

Seb added his phone number to the mail.

This is a matter of urgency and I would be enormously grateful for any time you could spare to clear a few things up. Afraid I haven't read your book yet (it's still on order from the States), and I had no idea until I read your mail that the SPR were based in Devon. Whereabouts? Can you tell me? This might explain something of a personal nature that I have recently experienced. I also know almost nothing about the organization, or M. L. Hazzard, and have only discovered information about his society within the last fortnight.
    Kind regards
    Seb Logan

Mark Fry wrote back within the hour.

I'm just about to finish some lesson planning. Full day of classes tomorrow. No rest, aye? But I could

call you in an hour or so. Or is that too late? That
would be eleven-ish.
    Mark

Seb quickly agreed to the time, then headed to the drinks
cabinet.

'Who was he?' Mark Fry repeated Seb's question, and followed it with a chuckle. 'Hazzard used so many personas, I
don't think he was ever one person for long enough to establish himself as a single personality. And I doubt I uncovered
them all. Every time something didn't work out for him, he
just reinvented himself and started over. He may even have
been a composite of shifting identities with unique personalities. But I can tell you that he began in life as one Ernie
Burridge, and that he ended life as his literary pseudonym,
Montague Leopold Hazzard.'

'I had no idea.' Seb near clawed at the phone to extract
the information.

Mark Fry had called Seb at eleven p.m. and spoke in a
soft northern accent. He embellished most of what he said
with an irrepressible chuckle. Seb took to him immediately.
He might even have fooled himself that this was the first
friendly voice he'd heard in years.

'I don't think anyone knew much about Hazzard when
he was alive, Mr Logan, let alone after he died. At the time
the SPR was active, most of those involved probably didn't
know who they were dealing with. By then, Hazzard was a
much better confidence trickster and was covering his tracks
more effectively.

'The SPR were a very different animal to most other cults

of that time too. As far as I could tell, no one ever broke silence from within the SPR. That was odd, considering what they were up to. Temple of the Last Days and the Process Church were similar in that respect, though in few others. And the SPR didn't go out like the Temple and there were no Manson Family trials. They barely left a trace of their existence.'

'Why the silence, the secrecy? This was a criminal organization?'

'Well Hazzard had learned some hard lessons when he'd fallen foul of the law in the past, and had learned to conceal his past, I think. It was a different time in the UK too. Not so much public scrutiny. As for it being illegal, you know that he did time in prison?'

'No, I didn't.'

'Sorry, you haven't read my book. And probably none of his stories beyond the two that Pantheon anthologized. That right?'

'Yes. This is all news to me. There's almost nothing online.'

'You're not wrong. But his writing was never more than a footnote in his life. Not enough money or adulation in it. He found being a cult leader, because that is what he was, far more lucrative when he hit his stride in the sixties.'

'If you don't mind me asking, what's your connection, Mark?'

'Goes back to my teens. I was fascinated by his stories when I was younger. Me dad had both Hazzard books, and later on, when I realized that no one knew anything about the guy, I started looking around to see if he'd written anything else, and that's when I discovered the SPR connection.'

'I see. You mentioned prison.'

Mark laughed. 'Oh, he was a right scoundrel, but it all caught up with him in the fifties. The first time he went down it was because he'd forged a birth certificate and was masquerading as an aristocrat. A minor baron and war hero. He even had a coat of arms on his cards, his cane, cigarette case and watch. He was running a bogus mental illness charity for victims of war, the servicemen, and the refugees coming in from Eastern Europe. Collected subscriptions, that kind of thing, through soirees in West London and newspaper ads. When he was rumbled, he went down for fraud by deception. Conned about three grand out of people.

'I found all of that in records from Bow Street Magistrate's Court. He had been in the war, though, in North Africa. He was a private, in Signals, but other than getting shelled once in Libya, he didn't see much action. He came close to a court martial, though, for desertion while on leave. But he was dumped in a psychiatric hospital in England for a year, then kicked out in 1944. He managed to get himself discharged from the army on a medical. According to his military record, he'd had a breakdown.'

'And he came out as an aristocrat?'

'No, that was later. What I could find about him in the late forties and early fifties was sketchy. He did some course at a technical college but never finished the year, though that never stopped him putting BSc after his name. Worked bars in holiday camps for a bit, too. Was a waiter at one point in Margate. An entertainer at a camp in Yorkshire. Most of his stories in the first collection were set in these places, so they are partly autobiographical. That's what made me look at those places first, where employment records existed. I found some other stuff in the courts where he'd been charged for various things, mostly non-payment of bills, and once for impersonating a woman.'

'You're kidding me.'

'He was rumbled while in drag, in a restaurant at a rural hotel. I'd say he had problems with his gender identity. I cop a lot of that from his stories too. Lifelong transvestite. And he seems to have drifted back to London after that bust, where he went bankrupt following a spell working in a care home for the elderly. That job didn't last long, but he did get married to a patient's relative, a widow, a fairly unsuccessful stage actress. With her, he drifted through various flats in London, pretending to be 'money', but never paid the rent or electric anywhere they stayed. I found three eviction notices for non-payment of rent in Kensington, with their names listed. He was going by the name of Robert Beaumont at that time and trying his hand at acting. He couldn't pay the fines for his unpaid bills either, and that's why he went bankrupt.

'His wife was a lot older than him and when she died, the baron was born. Picked up some stage-craft from his wife, I'm guessing. Maybe a decent wardrobe too for his female persona, whom he called Diane.'

'Diane!'

'Yes . . .'

'Sorry, please go on.'

'Sure. Well, after the baron scam had run aground and he'd served his six months, he'd become interested in psychotherapy and hypnotism. Changed his name to Magnus Ackermann, enrolled on a course in some kind of cognitive therapy, and another in hypnotherapy, and either failed the courses or didn't finish them, because his name wasn't on the list of graduates at the colleges he'd enrolled at. Though that didn't stop him calling himself a doctor either, or putting MBSH after his new name. He added DPsy later too, for the SPR, to make the group look more prestigious. But he had no degrees. His whole CV was fiction.'

'So the SPR came out of the hypnotherapy?'

'In part. But his treatments and theories needed fine-tuning before he pulled off something as ambitious as the SPR. So he was still serving his apprenticeship in manipulation when he set up the hypnotherapy practice in Mayfair. That was in a swanky apartment to attract a wealthy clientele. And he aimed these treatments at vulnerable women. The bereaved, ill, depressed, divorced, anxiety sufferers, you name it. Rich, elderly women remained his core market until he died. Charged a tenner a session too and got away with it for a couple of years. Used to advertise in the *Observer*, *New Statesman*, even *The Times*, who eventually exposed him as a fraud.

'The second time he was sent down, he wasn't done for faking his qualifications but for obtaining credit under false pretences. Over twenty people pressed charges. Other domestic stuff was added to the charges too, non-payment of rent, bills, the usual Hazzard routine. And he'd concealed that he was bankrupt when going into business too.

'He went down for three months the second time and finished the stories in his first book in prison. So M. L. Hazzard was actually born in Her Majesty's Prison Belmarsh. He was published modestly over the next couple of years, and he used to harass people like Colin Wilson and Arthur Koestler for help. They even mentioned him in some interviews.'

Seb's thoughts spun, but the revelations brought some

relief. 'I've only read two stories. I remember them being creepy, but the writing wasn't quite there.'

'No, he was no Algernon Blackwood, but there's an authentic strangeness in them that I lapped up.'

'But from prison to the SPR in Devon? That's a big leap.'

'It was. But he must have been encouraged enough to take the therapy angle to the next level, which was the SPR. From what I can work out, he picked up some tips from the woman who became Sister Katherine of The Temple of the Last Days. This was from his time in Mayfair. They once knew each other, years before she went to France. Hazzard adored women too, the glamorous, older, aunty types. That's crucial to his whole make-up. You can tell from his stories. But what I think he really wanted was to become a woman. I don't think I've ever come across a person so desperate to escape who they were. I don't think Hazzard was ever comfortable inside his own skin. You could even say that he dedicated his life to escaping it, and literally. I think that might be why he embraced psychedelics as genuine gateways, doors to perception and all that.

'But the SPR was set up mainly for his own enrichment. When he was in prison he'd re-established contact with some of his old clients. A couple of his patients in Mayfair were still smitten with him, and he corresponded with them while doing his time. Maybe they thought his treatments were effective. One very gullible woman was called Prudence Carey. She'd lost her husband in the war on a submarine. But Prudence was loaded. Old money. She owned Hunter's Tor Hall, in Devon, and that's where Hazzard went after he came out of Belmarsh. And, as far as I know, he lived there until he died.'

'Dear God.'

'Oh, it gets much better. Prudence became a kind of patron, so that Hazzard could write his masterpieces and develop his *treatments* and ideas. She'd had out-of-body experiences all her life, which he must have helped her develop in Mayfair. The disassociation of the consciousness and projection of the astral body towards Summerland, as they called it in the SPR, was central to the Mayfair operation. This is all in the court records. And that's how he must have reeled Prudence in. She wasn't alone, either. Hazzard became a kind of a guru.'

'A cross-dressing guru of the afterlife. And people fell for this shit.'

'I think he was basically promising people an assurance of life after death, yes. Or his version of the afterlife for a tenner a session in Mayfair, but at a much higher price when ensconced in Devon, and in very prestigious surroundings. Apparently, there were peacocks wandering the grounds. They also had a chef at one point.'

'Good God.'

'Of course, his residencies were sold as a cure-all for the earthly troubles and illnesses and to some very malleable and naive people. All operated on word of mouth amongst the wealthy. And with Hazzard as the gatekeeper of paradise, everything else in life often became irrelevant to his followers.'

'To the desperate. And he actually got away with it?'

'For a good long while. Nice earner too. But when my contact, Liza, was there in the early seventies, it was all going to hell. That's when the second Hazzard book came out. It's bloody dark too. I reckon he was writing the second book as things turned against him at the Tor, and he must have tried to cash in on the horror boom. His stuff was always too plotless, though, for any but a tiny number of readers.'

'But this projection, and the astral body stuff, he started *that* in Mayfair?'

'No, he'd been at it for years. He had his first out-of-body experience in the army, in the war. He was suffering from dysentery and claimed to have detached from his body in an infirmary. This is described in his story, "Looking at Myself from Nothing". He claimed that while he stood beside his bed, he'd watched a medical officer inject his body with saline. And he had another episode in a dentist's chair after the war. An even more powerful one too, after a motorcycle accident in London in the fifties. That's all in his first collection. You know he always claimed the stories were true and not fictitious.'

'I'm getting a gist of that. What did you make of his claim?'

'I think Hazzard was convinced that a soul could leave its body after a shock, or if the soul thought that the body was dying, or had died. Most of his early experiences are in the story, "Sinking in the Dark Room. Rising in White Light". Of course he claimed he could go much further over time, and that he'd learned to harness and control his "gift", as he referred to it. But he kept all of that for the SPR. Its unique selling point. This was something he claimed he could teach, this gift.

'Prudence even helped him get funding for SPR research, with her connections. But, of course, no one but Prudence knew about his past, because he was M. L. Hazzard at that point. The bogus aristocrat and fake doctor had been buried, but I don't think she was troubled by his past.

'He and Prudence Carey started retreats at the Hall, correspondence courses too, in the early sixties. He'd developed some technique that involved fasting and hypnosis, while using some psychedelics that he'd tried in London and then medicalized into his "formula". There was meditation too, with the cultivation of an image and mantra that could, apparently, induce the experience and get his customers closer to the paradise belt. All of this I learned from Liza.'

'How much of this syllabus do you have?'

'Bits and pieces from hearsay and the short stories. Most of my book is based on assumptions, to be honest, but they're as informed as I could manage.'

'Hazzard never wrote a manifesto, anything like that?'

'I don't know. What I've pieced together of his ideas mostly came from his stories. I think they are a formalization of his theory, or as close to it as you can get to one. Liza's interview pretty much attests to what Hazzard wrote about his *cultivation*. In fact, Liza's interview reminded me of Hazzard's stories. They're cut from the same cloth. And remember, Hazzard refused to even call them stories. To him they were *strange experiences*.

'But Hazzard also built all kinds of stuff into his spiel. Ideas ranging from the Hindu soft body to the vital body of the Rosicrucians. He used Greek and Roman mythology, Elysium, Hades, and stuff that was popular in the sixties, from the East, to give himself a zeitgeist and some gravitas. His adepts did most of the teaching on the retreats. There were two women in the early seventies who called themselves

Alice and Fay, and they were the equivalent of enforcers at the Tor.

'You have to realize too that his patients had to dedicate to a long haul, and cough up the cash for months at a time, before getting a private session with Dr Hazzard, or even Diane if they were lucky. And those private tuitions didn't come cheap.'

'Do you know what he was he like, I mean, as a person?'

'My contacts hardly ever saw him. But they said he was some kind of David Niven type. Sharp dresser. Shades, pork-pie hat. Very posh. Came across as fussy, brittle and prickly. Bit superior. *Assured*, one of them said, but always with a promise of confrontation in his tone. He was said to have a penetrative, intense stare, too, that could be absolutely withering if anyone challenged him. Or if he took a dislike to someone, and that was, apparently, a common occurrence.

'The narrators in his short stories, and they're all written in the first person, are always self-important and easily offended. I get the impression that no slight would ever be forgotten by old Hazzard. Achieving his will over others was paramount.

'He also had two sports cars, one for him and one for his female persona. He'd greet people either as a man or as Diane, do his emotive pitch and then piss off upstairs. He had one entire floor to himself. But Diane was very posh, apparently, always immaculately done up. Quite convincing, Liza said, because Hazzard was small for a man. And this was when Hazzard's life seemed to get even more interesting, at the Tor, but the trail of breadcrumbs thinned once he was off official radars.'

'But you found some people, some members?'

'Survivors, more like. But no one from the classic period in the sixties. They must have died by the time I was researching. And I only found three people who were involved with the SPR at the Tor. Liza, and two women who weren't there for very long. They freaked out and got very frightened of the whole deal, but this was after it had been going for years. I'm pretty sure they had psychotic reactions to the "formula". But Liza put me in touch with them. They all kept in touch after they left the SPR.'

'How did you find her, this Liza?'

'I posted an ad in a mind, body and spirit magazine. But that's not her real name. She didn't want me to use it.

'She was only at the Tor for a few months, towards the end, a couple of years before Hazzard died. But what she told me was still pretty incredible. I don't think Liza ever recovered from her experience either. She came away traumatized. And even as an old woman she was still terrified of *them* finding her. Which they did, in her head, if you know what I mean.'

Seb swallowed. 'How so?'

'She said they would visit her occasionally as she was falling asleep, to let her know that they were still watching her. Crazy. But in reality they left her with nothing but a failed second marriage, estranged children, bankruptcy, terrible night terrors and bad health. She was my main motivation for writing the book, and I dedicated it to her.'

'Do you think that something might have happened there?'

'What do you mean?'

'That it wasn't just a scam. You know, maybe there was some validity to what Hazzard claimed?'

Fry laughed. 'You're pulling my leg! It was a scam. The whole thing was a Hazzard cash cow, make no mistake. He was totally unethical and unscrupulous if it served the interests of the society, which of course were his interests. He was the sole beneficiary financially. There was some kind of complicated pyramid scheme going on through subscriptions and exorbitant fees.

'According to Liza, people suffering from prolonged illnesses always produced the best results, in combination with fasting. How convenient. Hazzard's subjects were often ill, or even terminally ill, and desperate. But they were always well-off. I don't think it's unlikely that he hastened a few ends either with his unconventional treatments, but that's speculation on my part.'

Seb was almost lost for words, but not quite. 'It's incredible that he got away with it for as long as he did.'

'Liza reckoned he'd basically imprisoned and terrorized some of the more infirm and elderly members too, who were paying him huge fees to live there. And if anyone caused trouble or challenged him there, they were kicked out. No refunds. But Hazzard was clever enough to choose his patrons and patients carefully. He vetted them for their suitability for manipulation, coercion, and intimidation if it became necessary, before he signed them up. But nothing ever got physical. He left no bruises that you could see. The damage was deeper, from psychological bullying. He got them hooked, Patty Hearst syndrome, gaslighting, the works. He even got Prudence to change her will and leave Hunter's Tor to him when she died. She passed in the seventies and

243

that pile on Dartmoor was still legally Hazzard's when he followed her.'

'Dartmoor? It's on Dartmoor?'

'Sure is.'

'But . . . do you . . . ? I mean, did Liza think that she could actually leave her body? That there was some basis of truth to what Hazzard claimed?'

Fry laughed again. 'Let's just say that there was no doubt in Liza's mind that the experience was real. And the other two I interviewed thought the same thing. They were all convinced because they'd all done it, repeatedly. *Projected*.'

'But you aren't buying it?'

'That? All fantasy. Isolation, the creation of an environment and atmosphere, sublimation to his ideas, the selection of susceptible people. Just add hallucinogens, fasting and mantras and you can make people believe anything. He must have been pretty convincing at his peak too. But it was all in their heads.

'My book never set out to prove that there was anything valid in Hazzard's claims. What I was interested in was the theory and why people believed in it. What they think they experienced, that sort of thing. The culture in isolation, the esoteric parts of it, were pretty interesting. I just wish I'd written the book earlier when more of the SPR were alive and might have spoken up. By the time I pitched in, the anecdotal evidence was really thin. Which is why your files have me intrigued. They're real, not fake?'

'Letterheaded. I think you of all people will find them convincing.'

'How many do you have?'

'About three hundred.'

'You are shitting me.'

'No. They're called case studies. They go up to the early seventies. Hazzard is mentioned in a few of them too, but only ever in capitals, as if he was a god.'

'I would love, just love, to get my hands on these.'

'Mark, where exactly is Hunter's Tor Hall on Dartmoor?'

'Off the A38 somewhere, about halfway to Plymouth. It's quite isolated. I stayed in Totnes and drove to it from there.'

When Seb had recovered sufficiently from the impact of the revelation of just how close Hunter's Tor was to his home, he couldn't resist manoeuvring himself nearer to making his own confession. 'Mark, I think they are still going.'

'The SPR? No chance.'

'I don't think they ever stopped.'

'Not possible. They've been gone over thirty years. Unless someone is using their name, revived it or something. Though I don't know why anyone would.'

'This is what I intend to find out.'

'I went there, to the Hall.'

'You did?'

'Yes, and it's derelict. Boarded up. Fenced off. When I was there it had been closed since the early eighties. Some locals told me. They called it "the college". So there's been no one there for decades. I think the organization must have gone down when Hazzard passed. It was all going tits-up by the middle seventies anyway. And I'm going back to 2004 when I was there.

'The building was owned by some holding company that listed the building as a college. Might still be, for all I know. I couldn't get any kind of response out of the holding company when I tried, either. I took some pictures, though, but didn't get a plate section for the book, so the photos were never used. Pictures were too expensive for the publisher.'

'But you went inside?'

'No. Couldn't even get through the fence. It's got massive grounds, but you can see it in the distance in a couple of places. The best thing were the gates. Over the top of the railings there's this iron plate with an inscription on it: *Let us go out of ourselves. Let us enlarge.* I loved that. Really nice touch.'

Seb finished another drink and gripped his own hair painfully. 'You have recordings?'

'A few hours of them. I spent a full day with Liza.'

'Could I . . . ? This may sound strange, but I'd really like to listen to them.'

'Afraid I wouldn't release the original tapes. They're on cassette. I've been meaning to transfer them to disc, but haven't done it yet.'

'You have a transcription?'

'Only for the bits I wanted for the book. Most of it didn't make the final draft. But, I'll do you a deal: if you let me read the SPR files, you can listen to poor old Liza, Virginia and Flo. It is quite upsetting, though.'

'Done. When are you free?'

'Well, when did you have in mind?'

'Tomorrow.'

Mark Fry laughed. He thought Seb was joking. 'Half-term in a week. We could sort something out for then. I may have a couple of days free.'

A week? Seb didn't want to imagine what could happen in that time. 'Maybe I could get the train up to you and I'll get a room somewhere, and while you're at work I can go through the recordings. *Tomorrow*?'

There was an awkward moment in which Seb sensed the man's discomfort. 'I hope you don't mind me saying, Mr Logan, but it's quite an odd request. What's the hurry?'

'Seb, please call me Seb. I know it's strange and an awful imposition but . . . I need to learn as much as I can about the SPR, and Hazzard, and quickly. I've no time.'

'This isn't a book. Research?'

'No. Well, not right now. That's not the main reason.'

'Then I don't understand the urgency. I mean, you've only just found out about all of this.'

'This is going to sound odd. Christ, how do I explain this? I'm being threatened, blackmailed, I think.'

'Bloody hell.'

'By an old friend, who died.'

'I'm sorry, I think.'

'He was trying something on. I mean, he was trying to use me for his own reasons. But he'd spent years, literally years, trying to master projection. He was obsessed with Hazzard too. And he . . . well, before he died, he came here with these files. That's how I have them. And his diary. I guess you could call it that. Hundreds of fragments, and what I can read of them suggests that he'd been engaged in something very strange.

'Mark, I believe he was there, at the SPR property. He must have been. And he wasn't working alone, because now I have someone else bothering me. A very odd woman. I just want to know what I am up against.'

'Your friend, and this woman, they said they were from the SPR?'

'No, neither said much of any use. They were very careful about what they told me. But I'm piecing things together from these papers. And if I can get access to your notes, and these recordings, I might be in a better position to know what to do.'

'Have you called the police?'

'No. Yes. Earlier. It's hard to explain. I don't think they'd understand what this is all about.'

'I see.' Though Mark clearly didn't, he was still intrigued.

'So, would that be possible, my coming your way? I won't bother you at all. You can have the SPR stuff while I check out what you have, and then I'll leave you alone.'

'Well, I've a full week on. Lot of lessons.'

'I won't get in your way, I promise. I'll go through the recordings while you're at work. And I'm happy to spring for a good dinner. Anywhere you want to go. And when you've more time, you'd be very welcome to come down here, for a holiday. It'd be my treat.'

Again the uncomfortable pause.

Seb tried again to reassure Mark. 'God, I must come across as a really strange bloke. But I'll explain more to you when I see you.'

This made Mark laugh. 'I'm not going to disagree with you, but if you really think my stuff will help you out, then I'm not going to leave a fellow explorer of the weird hanging in emptiness! Let me give you my address. Can I also say, it'll be a thrill to meet you.'

17

There Were Two of Me in that Room

Their reactions to the material could not have been more different; it was akin to one man shrivelling with fear at the sight of a large snake, while another declared it a beautiful creature.

Mark Fry closed a file and replaced it on the table in Seb's hotel room. He picked up another and began to read, his lips and head moving as he consumed the text.

No sooner had Seb led Mark to the treasury boxes that held the files than the man had become elbow deep, before gazing at the documents with a mixture of wonder and nervous excitement. 'This is amazing stuff. The mastery of the super-consciousness. It's coming through at a glance. That's what Hazzard was after.'

Seb had met Mark Fry at five in the hotel bar, and though incapable of putting people at ease because he came over like a box of scissors electrified by static, he'd invited Mark up to his room. And now stood to one side, content with watching the man's rapture. 'Super-consciousness?' he prompted.

Mole-like, his head shaved but silvery at the sides, his skin naturally dark, Mark nodded his head rapidly, blinking his small watery eyes behind silver-framed spectacles just as fast. As his black denim jacket swung open, Seb got a better look at Mark's T shirt: Neurosis, *Through Silver in Blood*, now faded black and stretched by a loose stomach that exceeded his belt. 'He was looking to control his super-consciousness in order to find the paradise belt. The celestial spheres.'

Mark struck Seb as a naturally amiable character so the sudden intensity was a surprise. The presence of the SPR files were also making the man jitter.

'There's not much in there about him,' Seb offered. 'But I sense the people have been guided or tutored, and been given a terminology to frame their experiences.'

Mark agreed with a nod. 'At least he didn't try and turn the SPR into a religion. I think he had that in his favour. He kept it pseudo-scientific too, even if it was for the sake of appearances to get funding. He never believed science or cosmology were ready for his discoveries, which couldn't be observed or measured by conventional means. I'm guessing most of these case studies were written by women too.'

'Most don't offer a name. But maybe they are, from what you've said about his methods.'

'He was a con man. A total narcissist.'

'I find it difficult to take seriously. I can't help wondering why so many did. It's the terminology. Soul-bodies. Vehicles of vitality. The double. Astral body. And my friend, Ewan, used the same terms, so I'm certain he had contact with the SPR, or whatever has assumed its ideas. He was a fervent believer in the soul too. That death wasn't an end.'

'They all were. You said I can take these away?'

'Of course. I need to take them back with me, so copy or scan them tomorrow, if you can. I don't know for how long I'll have them.'

'Thanks! I want to go through them all, carefully.'

The only way Seb could think of disentangling himself from whatever Ewan had embroiled him in, was to arrange some kind of handover of the files with the odd woman who had appeared beside him in King Street. The thought of it made him feel ill, but he'd been unable to come up with another plan. Assuming she had a connection to Hunter's Tor Hall, he felt far better paying her a visit than waiting for her to appear near his home again. He'd take his cheque book too, in case a donation might both improve his standing and hasten his exit strategy.

He finally popped the question that was burning through his mind. 'Mark, I know you think the SPR members were delusional, but can I ask you what you made of Hazzard's hinderers?'

Seb imagined that Mark had never enjoyed more than a limited audience, because he immediately relished the opportunity to expound. 'Oh, now you're getting somewhere. The hinderers. Marvellous! It's quite complicated, but in his stories, Hades and paradise kind of interpenetrate the earth. In the same way that we are supposed to have these corresponding forms, the body, the vehicle, and soul-body, that interpenetrate each other, these other realms are also here at the same time as us.

'So the inhabitants of Hades and paradise are never far away from us in the real world, but you can't measure the distance physically. And Hazzard believed that discarnate soul-bodies are all around us, all of the time, but most of us can't see them. The incarnate and discarnate are all overlapping, all of the time, in different spheres that exist simultaneously in the same place, but don't interact.

'Mediumistic people, clairvoyants, like Hazzard claimed to be, were able to see or even feel the crossovers, at certain times or when they were prepared. I loved all of that. Great stuff. It's like this whole mystical mythos he used for his fiction, and he was very consistent. He never wrote about anything else.

'Oh, I have these for you.' Mark opened his rucksack and removed two books in protective plastic envelopes. He placed them on the table. 'You can borrow them. But please, please, guard them with your life. They're irreplaceable. You've seen the prices online, and these were my dad's too.'

'Of course. I'll return them before I go home.'

Seb looked at the covers. Pulpy oil paintings. The first collection, *Sinking in the Dark Room. Rising in White Light*, featured a wraith-like form levitating from a bed in which a woman lay screaming. The second, *Hinderers in the Passage*, was pitched as '17 Blood-Chilling Tales of Supernatural Horror', which Seb recited without a trace of irony. On the book jacket, a clawed hand appeared around the side of an opening door. The silhouette of the door was lit by a luminous, ghostly light.

Mark grinned. 'Yeah, cheesy, I know. Sign of the times. And you know Hazzard hated horror. He felt it misrepresented his ideas. But what else did he think he was writing for that second book?'

Mark stacked five old cassettes on the table as well as a box file, then removed a tape recorder from his bag. 'These are Liza's recordings, the better stuff. I'll transfer the other two to disc tomorrow so you can take them with you. How long do you plan on staying?'

'I'll start on these tonight, after dinner. I have all day

tomorrow, so I hope to be finished by late afternoon. I've booked a train for seven and I'll return these before I go.'

Mark nodded and said, 'I can swing by and pick them up. Nice room, by the way,' perhaps seeing the place properly for the first time.

His rucksack remained half-full. Through the elasticated rim of the bag, Seb saw the cover of his novel *Occupied*.

Mark caught his eye. 'Hope I'm not taking the piss, but would you mind signing my books?'

Seb smiled. 'That would be a pleasure. Then we should eat.'

At the table in the restaurant, feeling giddy from the first bottle of wine, Seb carefully leafed through the first Hazzard book, *Sinking in the Dark Room. Rising in White Light*.

He read the epigraph 'No sudden heaven nor sudden hell for man – Tennyson', and then he checked the contents page:

Sinking in the Dark Room. Rising in White Light
Through the Mist
This Prison of the Flesh
Thousands of Invisible Cords
In the Body of my Resurrection
Born Through a Cloudy Medium
My Soul Rose Trembling
A Tight Glove Pulled from my Finger
She Beckoned and I Followed
Shed the Body's Veil
Carry Me Softly on Shoeless Feet
The Discarded Coat

He'd not read any of them.

'That book is more mystical,' Mark offered around a mouthful of steak and jacket potato. 'In the preface he explains that the stories came from "a greater power than exists in my pen". A typical Hazzard flourish. A Hazzardism, I call it. But for a horror man, you'll be more interested in the second collection. *Hinderers* is very dark. His output evolves from the mystical to a psychic and spiritual horror across the two periods in which he was published, which spans about twenty-five years.'

As the waitress arrived to offer the dessert menu, Seb removed the second collection from its protective sheath. Seb ordered coffee. Mark had tiramisu and coffee.

As Mark had attested, the titles on the contents page of *Hinderers in the Passage* suggested a change in tone, and one that effortlessly formed unpleasant images within Seb's memory.

A Dark, Slowly Flowing Flood
Down the Last Valley
The Same Event in a Converse Direction
Many Communications Must Remain in Doubt
This Coat is Too Tight
A Sack with a Narrow Opening
Discarnate Inhabitants of Hades
Indeed, I Have Seen my Sister
I Can See in an Absence of Light
Greylands
Cast Thyself Down
Hinderers in the Passage
A River of Darkness

Broken Night
Flight from Malignant Forms
Second Death
Incertitude

Mark noticed the change in Seb. 'You all right, Seb?'

Seb nodded, but kept his response vague. 'Reminders.'

'Of?'

'Ewan.'

'The guy that died. I didn't want to pry. But you said he was into Hazzard in a big way.'

'You could say that.'

'Was he a writer?'

'Not really. But he had ambitions in that direction.' Seb cleared his throat. 'I'd like you to read his diary. The more legible bits. See what you make of it.'

'It would be a pleasure, I think. If it's Hazzard-influenced.'

'And I'm sure the last parts were written at this Hunter's Tor.'

'I'll look at his stuff, but I seriously doubt he was there.'

'You haven't been there in ten years. But you've read Hazzard's stories, and Ewan did. If someone was determined enough to find out more . . .'

'But they'd have to be crazy to follow in Hazzard's astral footsteps. Wait until you read the second collection. That's enough to put anyone off.' Mark chuckled. 'Here. Let me find it.'

He picked up the copy of *Hinderers*. 'Very last story. This is how Hazzard closed his account as a published writer.'

Mark sat back and began reading from the end of the book. 'I never cooperated with the divine plan. I have died

255

too many times and walked the in-between land. I forced death. I went beyond space and time, beyond the earth. My own nature inhibited my greater self. My spirit never fully left matter and yet I believed I had found eternity. We are ever conscious of the third sphere, Elysium, Paradise, Summerland, but we can never ascend. Its rays merely warm our cold flesh in Hades. We are the super-physical who are trapped beside the temporal.'

18
Born through a Cloudy Medium

[Tape 1. Recorded 2 September 2004. Liza]

[Liza]: I'd been fasting for two days. Nothing but water. That was how you began the cultivation. You were already lightheaded, weak, and dizzy, before you started. But I think I was always too anxious about the medication. Some never needed it, the formula, and Alice and Fay were always on hand to reassure you. But they were always quietly insistent that some of us took it.

At that time, I also remember how I'd started to look about myself in the room that was called Elysium. This was at the Tor. You see, all of the rooms had names that carried promises. And in there I could really see how frail Margaret and Lizzy were. They were very old at that time, and they'd both been there for years. That is when the Tor began to appear to me like a retirement home, in which the residents were sedated. Drugged and controlled and then led back to their rooms, where they would wait, alone, to *cultivate*.

It was in your room that you would focus on the image and begin the words. That's where we did the cultivation, alone. Never in a group like they used to do, only in our rooms, to cut out distractions. We'd practised rhythmical breathing every morning for months, right from the start of a residency. The breathing was vital to clearing the mind. You had to start there.

[Mark Fry]: What were the images that he gave you to focus on?

[Liza]: The river, always. The river and the tunnel, the silver cord. You have to understand that what is left, what is buried behind consciousness, still has properties, thoughts, feelings, though they are different. It's all a part of you, but not as you have ever known yourself to be. But this part of us can be induced by desire, by the will, if you are prepared. The vital body can rise or fall.

[Mark Fry]: How did it start, the projection? Can you describe it?

[Liza]: When it eventually began to happen for me it was always a drop, like a sudden fall, as if I'd tripped. And then I would sink.

I remember my first few projections quite clearly. Some people went up, but I sank through the bed. Went down. And then I would find myself close to my bed in the darkness. The building was always very dark, like a photograph or film that had never been lit properly. And it's very strange because the only light came from me, from what I was in that form, what I had become.

Inside this light I felt as if I was intoxicated. What I could see swum around me. The room was blurred and poorly defined. I had a very poor sense of balance too.

[Mark Fry]: What could you see when you projected?

[Liza]: I could see what was closest to me more clearly. But I couldn't see for any distance. I could always hear water too, the river, the psychic stream, but when I found it the water was black.

I also suffered a terrible feeling of anxiety, of foreboding the whole time that I projected. It wasn't what I expected, but I was told that this was inevitable at the start.

If I ever saw myself, my body, back inside the bed, I would always return. Just black out. That's what it was like. And then I would come to, inside my body, feeling ill from the formula. The side effects, the nausea, could last for days. It was very strong. You had to pace yourself and recover between each projection. No doubt at all in my mind now that what we were taking was illegal. And I started to suspect that all those reports and stories in the archive were lies. The ones from the sixties. Why had so many people had such incredible experiences while we only struggled in the darkness? I always asked too many questions. They weren't welcome.

[Mark Fry]: Did you see anyone else when you were projecting?

[Liza]: Oh, yes, once I began to make it outside my room. That was in my fifth month at the Tor. But I never saw these others clearly. They were in the hall outside. Two very dim figures. There were only seven of us in residence at that time, but I was quite sure that the two I saw were not the projections of those in residence. They were not aware of each other, or of me. I tried to call out to them. But it was like calling out in a dream to deaf people. I had no voice. No strength. Everything was slow and laboured.

HE claimed that I was in Hades when I projected. This is the sphere closest to where we are now, but we were also told that it was possible, in time, to go further. Much further if you persisted, and if you worked at loosening your vehicle of vitality. Otherwise you remained earthbound. But the cost on your health, let alone the financial cost, became more and more obvious the longer I was there. I'm afraid I lost my faith in HIM.

[Mark Fry]: Did you ever go any further than the Tor?

[Liza]: Only once, and I never wanted to try again.

[pause]

[Mark Fry]: Can you tell me about it?

[Sound of Liza clearing her throat]

[Liza]: I was ill at the time. I'd had a chest infection that became quite serious. It was very cold at the Tor, and damp. You had to wrap up, you know. The cold seemed to get inside your bones. Even with the fires going you never warmed up. I used to think it was the moors, the air, the atmosphere. I'd say it rained there at least four days each week. But I wasn't so sure by the end. I wasn't certain of a great many things, even of who I was, or who I had become. I lost sight of that, and what was important, or should have been important to me. But I missed my husband, Eric. He was my first husband. I think I went mad when I lost him. I never stopped grieving. I never have.

[Mark Fry]: But you managed to travel further, just this once?

[Liza]: Oh yes. I was feverish with an awful cough. And I had been resting and it happened, just like that. I projected.

I'd been thinking of my daughter because I missed her terribly and I was regretting everything that I had done. I wanted to see her quite desperately. And I remember the sinking feeling, though that time I sank deeper, and more suddenly.

Then I was moving. I was travelling through the darkness. At speed across fields. I think they were fields and that

I was in the countryside but I could barely see a thing. One could have passed it off as a dream. But I became very aware of her presence. I could actually sense her all around me. My daughter. My feelings for her, and how much, how intensely I loved her as if she were a small child again . . . It was like I was *flooded* with her. It was the most intense connection.

I then became briefly aware of her, as if she were no more than a few feet below me. That's when I actually saw her. She was asleep and it was as if we were in the same room, but I was unable to speak to her.

I became too upset, too eager to communicate with her and I was returned to my sickbed at the Tor. But this sense of her, of how close we had once been, persisted. It lingered for days, and when I was well enough I called her. They listened to your calls, Alice and Fay. From another line they listened to the calls. But it was the strangest thing, on the night that I'd seen my daughter, she said that I had been in her thoughts too, and that she had been very worried about me. She said she had called and she had written to the SPR, though I had received nothing. So why do you think that was?

Anyway, I told her that I had been ill and that I had a sense that we had come together across a great distance. She never believed in what I was doing and had always disapproved of the SPR. It was what finally estranged us. But she admitted that she had felt a presence in her room, on the very night that I had projected. She was living in London and she had awoken feeling terribly hot and frightened. And she had been unable to dispel the idea that there was a presence, some *thing*, inside her room with her.

She turned on the lights, but still believed that the

presence remained there, in her room. She said she was paralysed with a sense of dread, as if that emotion, the dread,
had occupied the room. And she knew that what had entered
her room was in pain. She said she'd thought it was drowning, or that it couldn't breathe, and she believed that it was
me, or was somehow connected to me.

This upset her for days because she had sensed me, her
own mother, in terrible distress. And she had feared for me,
at some deep instinctive level, after the presence had passed
away. I even remember the word she used to describe the
episode. She had said it had been 'horrifying' for her. *Horrifying*. It had not been a pleasant experience for me either.
Quite the opposite. It left us both shaken and very upset.
And it worsened my doubts about Summerland. Elysium,
ha! This was HIS fabled paradise belt that we were supposed
to find? It was horrid.

I left the SPR not long after. It was the furthest I'd ever
travelled and the very last time that I consciously attempted
the procedure. But I'd gone too far, you see. It was too late
to stop by then. I'd loosened something inside myself. It's
hard to describe, but for many years, I could not prevent
myself from sinking into the darkness again, over and over
again.

When I think of how many times we practised the cultivation, it was as if we were programming ourselves. I think
that was the whole point.

The image was always of the silver cord in the slow, dark
river. Silver light turning fast, faster and faster and making
me sink. With the water all around, the psychic stream. And
then we were the light, the turning light, and we released
ourselves from our bond and we focused on the sinking, the

heavy, heavy sinking into the black and peaceful water. This represented the renunciation of the will to the deep.

I've never been able to stop the sound of that water running through my sleep. It's always in my dreams.

[Mark Fry]: So what happened when you left?

[Liza]: Oh, they weren't happy. Alice and Fay were very manipulative. I only managed to extricate myself by pleading poverty. I told them that I had run out of money, and they demanded proof. Can you believe that? I had to produce bank statements. I had to sign an official document of confidentiality on entrance too, and another on exit. I was threatened.

[Mark Fry]: How so?

[Liza]: Oh, it was all very subtle. They said they had attracted *others*, who would never ascend. *Hinderers*. The defective. Hinderers, who had been drawn there, to HIM. And they said that if I betrayed the contract of silence, there would be consequences that they had little control over. These others, the *hinderers*, were very protective of HIM.

[Mark Fry]: Did you believe them?

[Liza]: Of course. I had no doubt at all. I'd seen things, those figures outside my room, and I could sense them at the Tor, and more of them the longer that I was there. There was something wrong with the place. With that entire area. Not only inside the house.

And right at the end, Alice told me to never forget that 'some of the dead are still in place'.

19
Stand Beside the Door
and Let It Take You

Seb stopped the tape recording of Liza. He reached for his drink. 'Ewan. You bloody idiot. You bastard.'

Seb was drunk. Three large glasses of whiskey on top of three glasses of red wine. There had been beer earlier too, in the bar before dinner. How many pints? *Two, no three. Only two. Four?*

There was a judder about the edges of the furniture, the edge of the wall that led to the bathroom.

Slow down.

He looked at Hazzard's books on the table.

Something insidious had placed itself between his life and the sun. A minor writer and cult leader who had been dead for over thirty years.

Impossible.

The situation was preposterous. Fiction was becoming fact.

But what could *they* want from him now? What did they *expect* from him? And why him, anyway? Because he knew Ewan? Had Ewan infected him? That horrible misfit by the harbour with her doublespeak: had she guided Ewan? But *what* guided her?

He had no answers.

Seb gulped at the bourbon until his glass was empty, sat back and winced through the after-burn.

He put the news on the television, the sound muted. He needed to keep close some evidence of a real world governed by natural laws, one filled with a predictably chaotic humanity.

He refilled his glass and took to pacing the room. From out of despair his rage unfurled. He felt unstable and capable of violence. Restraint unwound over a core of vengeful paranoia, suspicion, and a bile that he flung, in his imagination, at a dozen faces with whom he'd clashed as a professional writer. He wanted to destroy something, to smash it. But what? His battle was with the intangible, the unpredictable; the unpredictably intangible. Something that could appear at any time. Motives unknown. Intentions malicious. There were entities capable of killing a man by manifestation alone. *Through sheer terror.*

Had he brought this upon himself, by wanting to be left alone, to live differently? Was that no longer allowed?

This was going nowhere. He capped the whiskey bottle and decided to get ready for bed. The spirit was making him feel unlike himself, impulsive, hot, and full of destructive compulsions.

He felt absurd too, foolish, and self-pitying. Perhaps he was so worn out that he'd gone past the ability to think meaningfully. His thoughts were dispersing. They now seemed feeble and nonsensical.

Seb clumsily switched the TV off, stripped to his underwear and lay down. Made himself comfortable before using the switches beside the headboard to douse the lights. After that, he must have fallen asleep.

Until a recurring swoop beneath his closed eyelids made vomiting a concern. He opened his eyes several times and directed his unstable focus upon the red light of the television standby button, until the rotations in his vision calmed.

The dream he then stepped into was no less unsavoury than the state of mind that produced it.

When he next awoke he had a vague recall of having dreamed.

The only details retained by his intoxicated mind came as a sense of having been within a chattering crowd in complete darkness. A lightless space in which a great many bewildering requests had been made of him. And there had been a noise like a wind, or maybe it had been water rushing through an enclosed space.

He sat up in bed and switched a light on. Realizing just how disoriented and dehydrated he was, he clambered out of bed and went into the bathroom to gulp down three glasses of water, something he wished he'd done before going to bed. By suppressing his body's urge to expel the contents of its stomach, he knew he'd assured a more severe hangover, and a lengthy period of feeling toxic the following day. He'd been careless with drink, and at a time like this. He returned to bed angry with himself and passed out.

Can you ask my daughter to come and fetch me?

He thought this had been spoken from inside another dream, and then was certain the voice had come from inside his actual room. Perhaps it had been spoken in the bathroom from where someone was now running a bath?

They buried me over there.

'Where?' he replied aloud to the woman sitting beside his

bed. He didn't see her face, or any of her body because the light that issued from her was too dim. From her voice alone he knew that she was elderly and upset. He could smell her perfume too, something similar to dead flowers.

The work must be completed. And then we will discuss terms.

'Definitely not. No. No. No,' he shouted down the dim, white corridor that formed at the end of his bed.

Paint flaked from the walls of his room. The ceiling was stained yellow with water rings.

I am making progress on the fear and dread.

'You shouldn't even be in here,' he said to the woman who now stood beside the bed. She'd come from out of a door further down the white corridor, three times. The third time she'd made it inside his hotel room. She wore a long satin dress, a headscarf and dark glasses. A fur stole culminated in the face of a grinning animal, a horrible fox. Something black stained the front of her gown too, like the residue of a wound. There was a faint light behind her, or around her. But surely this was also part of the dream. He knew he was dreaming, but his level of awareness was unpleasant.

Sink. Heavy, heavy. Sink deep.

Legs going heavy. Sink downwards and stand free. Reduce breathing. Blank mind. Blank mind. Blank mind.

Enlarge yourself. Float out.

From here to there, and back again.

. . . sinking, heavy, heavy . . .

. . . everything's gone black . . .

Let us go out of ourselves!

267

In delirium Seb felt his feet moving upwards and towards the ceiling.

No, his legs were still upon the bed. But he was clutching the mattress with his fingers to prevent himself from rising.

. . . we are the soul-bodied . . .

Thin Len was so tall and he went through that nursery on all fours like a big spider.

Let us enlarge!

. . . this awakening was not like the others . . .

You're never as alive as you are when you leave your body.

Leave your body and walk a few feet over months.

. . . the gliding, the gliding of the double, the gliding, the gliding, the gliding of the double . . .

This coat is too tight . . .

Cast thyself down!

I can't get back!

Is this the second death? This is not my greater self. Where are the everlasting arms?

I can't get back!

Can you help me? I know you are close. Where is the light? Do you know?

I can't get back!

The voices filled the room, overlapped each other, rotated, repeated. Seb had been listening to them for hours, or only heard them once. He didn't know.

The room was bigger than it should have been. It was a building cluttered with dark and heavy furniture. High ceilings soared above his head, then went further and further upwards.

He was inside a tunnel that smelled of wet bricks and stagnant water.

No, he was inside his hotel room.

The old house again.

No, he was outside in darkness, beside a river.

The room, this was his hotel room!

There was nothing there at all, nothing there at all . . .

He was in a field of black grass. The air was misty.

The room, in the hotel.

The old building with high ceilings, furniture everywhere.

The hotel room.

A corridor of black doors.

Seb sat up in the very bed that seemed intent on releasing him into the air. He whimpered at the darkness that pressed upon him from all sides.

They let go of his hands, but his fingers remained as cold as their own had been, those people who had been sitting beside him.

He threw his body back against the wall and shouted, 'Get out!'

Fumbling at the stiff, plastic light switches, he became aware of a glimmer above his head. Before the first light came on in the room, he looked up for a fraction of a second and saw a pale smudge submerge into darkness, as if it had been enveloped by water flowing across the ceiling.

You're dreaming. That's all.

There was no one in his room. The walls, floor, bed, desk, and chair were now present again. The silencing of the voices was absolute. Everything visible was now contained within four walls and held in place by gravity. That realization made Seb gasp and he was close to sobbing with relief.

He got out of bed and turned every light on. Blinked, and then blinked some more.

3:00 a.m. on the screen of his phone.

Seb held his face for a while, pulling his eyelids down as far as they would go before pain became an issue. He touched a wall with a shaking hand. Belched, sat back down on the bed, his head sunk between his knees, and he told himself that he'd only been dreaming of those places and voices. He could not accept that a dream in the dark had the ability to replace the world with another place – a teeming space, and one peopled so quickly.

With what? Memories, bits of things he'd read, or had they been suggested to him? *They hinder.*

He didn't want to be inside the room. He tugged jeans on. Staggered through the vestibule beside the bathroom to the door of the room, using his hands against the walls.

Unsteady on his feet, his balance shot, he didn't know where he was going, but he wanted some other place that hadn't been filled with voices. He really had to get out, *just out and into* . . .

The corridor outside his room, on the third floor of the hotel. Pale blue carpet, cream walls, ceiling lights.

Aiming for the landing before the lifts, he was surprised to see that the two fire doors down there were closed. The glass fitted into the top half of each door was reinforced internally by wire mesh. *Fire doors, they were usually held back, but at night they must close.* But someone was visible through the single pane of glass. Seb stopped moving. *A night owl, night porter, someone with an early start. Sun will be up soon.*

Whoever was wearing the dark coat moved away, and

swiftly, across the floor of the landing on the other side of the glass. They turned and vanished into a lift or onto the staircase. *There is no staircase on that side, just the two lift doors.*

A faint bump behind his back brought him about quickly. He lost his balance and lurched sideways, but caught sight of the origin of the sound. He'd seen whoever had just withdrawn their face from the panel of glass in one of the doors that sealed the opposite end of the corridor. *That* passage, beyond those fire doors, contained the staircase. Yes, he remembered now. But didn't want to go down there because someone had been watching him. As they had moved backwards quickly, the smudge of a pale face had closed its mouth. An aperture disconcertingly dark and wide as if it had been in the act of calling out but soundlessly.

Seb moved his head from side to side on his shoulders. He tried to see through the reinforced glass panels and into the spaces beyond to identify who was on the other side of the fire doors.

And it was then he saw something move again through one glass panel. What appeared to be the back of a dark coat retreating, while seeming to shrink in size. It was as if he was watching a figure moving at speed, and across a distance much longer than the one that existed beyond the closed doors.

Maybe what he'd thought was movement behind the glass panel of the fire door was his own reflection as he'd turned around.

Please let it be.

Perhaps the face had been a part of his mirrored flesh too, and the open mouth some dark feature of the corridor beyond, superimposed through the refraction of light. Maybe he'd even mistaken a fire extinguisher for something else?

Under closer inspection, the panels in the fire doors now revealed no movement, or any other sign of a presence beyond the glass.

Above his head the lights buzzed at the end of his hearing. He could smell the fragrance of carpet cleaner. It reminded him of an airport lounge, or a boardroom. A sense of stillness and emptiness within these communal corridors made a mundane entry into his awareness.

At the same time, he became aware of how cold he was while standing shirtless in a hotel corridor.

20

A Tight Glove Pulled from my Finger

'Bad night?' Mark Fry came into Seb's room, smiling. He probably believed a hangover responsible for Seb's downcast face and crumpled appearance.

Mark taught sociology and film studies classes at a local college of further education and his classes had finished in mid-afternoon. For this Seb was grateful because he didn't want to be on his own.

He looked at Mark with a dour and humourless expression that encouraged Mark to straighten his face. Being unable to explain to Mark why he was a wreck was frustrating but the least of his troubles.

Seb nodded at the recordings. They were stacked on the table beside the tape player and Hazzard's books. 'All yours, Mark. And thank you again.'

'My pleasure. I pulled some favours with the admin staff and they copied the SPR stuff for me this morning.' He parked the wheeled case that he'd brought with him beside the table.

With his foot, Seb tapped the large treasury box he'd left under the table. 'I'll leave Ewan's notes with you for the time being. See if you can make out more than I managed.'

'I'm an expert at reading poor handwriting. Years of

practice. Everything is typed now, though the quality of the content hasn't been improved by Microsoft Word.'

Seb was too preoccupied to smile.

'Were they of any use?' Mark asked, as he raised *Hinderers in the Passage* from the table.

Not a question that was easy for Seb to answer. He'd read parts of each collection after starting on them at around four a.m. He'd not attempted to return to sleep following the disturbance and had sat alone in his room with the television murmuring, drinking endless cups of coffee until Mark arrived.

The best two Hazzard stories, which resembled plotted short fiction, were the two stories that Seb had read years ago. Structured narratives, found in traditionally told stories, were absent in most of Hazzard's work. The majority of the tales were better defined as surreal, weird imaginings, filled with ghastly images. Plots were added to some of the stories in the first anthology, though awkwardly, as if the recorded experiences were unsuited to logic.

The earlier stories were akin to cosmic fever dreams in which distant, astral shapes communicated with the narrators through sensations, and often before a background of blinding light.

The narrators were inveterate spies. Voyeurs with unscrupulous motives who often enacted revenge on earthbound rivals through the projection of malign versions of themselves. If the stories were biographical then the manipulations of Hazzard's 'astral body', his *gift* no less, had never been put to positive use. In this respect the author appeared to have been a mentor to Ewan Alexander.

Had he read the books with innocent eyes, Seb might have been impressed by the author's resistance to spells, rites, and rituals to evoke the supernormal. Unworldly phenomena was just *there* without question, and was always *becoming* within the ordinary world for those with special talents, those who had accessed other planes in a dreamy loosening of their consciousness.

Mythology was often referenced to attest to the existence of other places. Realms that folklore had long tried to encompass, or to explain. Hazzard had definitively explained the ghost, poltergeist, premonition, revenant, demon and angel. At least to himself.

The author always recounted stories from the point of view of the *ghost*, the astral double. The leaps of the imagination into fantastical spheres and celestially lighted realms had reminded Seb of Machen's *Hill of Dreams*. But Hazzard's spectral visitants were depicted as visionaries, explorers, sirens and femmes fatales, or playboys turned revenant. Authorial wishful thinking, perhaps, which failed to rid the works fully of the ordinary, mundane and unpleasant settings in which they must have been written, like prison.

The fetishistic adoration of female archetypes and their fashions, and the sinister voyeurism, persisted in each anthology.

By the last four stories in the first collection, the celestial light was dimming from the ethereal landscapes and had become grey and misty before fading to black; places filled with shadowy forms and strange cries from unseen faces.

The rising and flying 'doubles' stopped soaring and ascending to the heavens, their inner power and sense of greatness diminishing to what appeared to be a sickening habit. They began to stagger and crawl, not fly. Eventually, the narrators became captives to something they accessed against their wills. They were no longer tethered to the body or to the earth and its conditions. They were stricken and only saw one ill-defined region superimposed over another.

By necessity, life then became a struggle to keep the darkness from intruding upon the world. And separation from the body could happen randomly, at any time. Leaving the body became a permanent affliction, and the very promise of a dreadful destination. But it had all stirred a sense of awe within Seb too.

As Mark had alluded, the tone of the stories altered radically in the second volume. Those tales didn't suit beginnings, middles and ends either, because all three conditions were often the same thing and there were few resolutions to the situations described.

In Hazzard's final stories, the transcendent quality of the first collection had entirely degraded into the grotesque. An obsession with piercing light had conversely become an obsession with light's absence. A peculiar terror akin to vertigo and of falling into the sky from the earth, and then falling even further beyond the earth's atmosphere and into a cold and endless space, was a dominant theme. As an idea, travelling through space at dizzying speeds was soon replaced by a confinement in dreary rooms. Memories of places and situations were stuck on repeat.

The scale of infinity was transformed into an enclosed maze without end or purpose. The damp tunnel became a much-used metaphor. This was also the very realm that Seb now appeared to be glimpsing against his will.

The final tales degenerated into pure studies of claustrophobia, panic, shock and fear, but all leading to a terror that was mindless in the narrators.

Much of the horror came from the characters accepting their inevitable confinement within the 'greylands'. They were witnesses, near-passive observers, not active entities in control of their destinies. The end.

But there was tension and suspense, though it never arose from a character's resistance to such a ghastly fate, but through their full acknowledgement of the dreadful eventuality before it occurred.

In the stories 'Broken Night', 'Flight from Malignant Forms', 'Second Death' and 'Incertitude' the astral doubles had even watched their earthly remains buried and cremated, then crawled around gravesides and the dark places where their ashes had been sprinkled, unaware of how long they had been keeping vigil beside a door that had closed forever. Eventually, they forgot who they had once been. The spiritual entropy was the most terrifying thing of all for the reader to grasp.

The tales were often master classes of apprehension, but few would have been as affected by Hazzard's literary output as Seb had been. You had to be a participant in the subject matter for the writing to achieve its full effect.

There were a few lines in 'Flight from Malignant Forms' that Seb doubted he would ever forget: 'In the greylands we found others in different form. They wept in our faces or clawed us from out of the mist. If they are angels or the souls of the departed, then none should be hasty for the dark.'

Hazzard must have wondered if he were shouting down a well when he wrote the books.

Even with Mark Fry in the room, Seb was still fighting a need to collapse onto the bed. Tiredness and the nauseous dregs of his hangover had made him too weak to do much beside remaining prostrate all day. His hands were shaking again.

He knew how uncomfortable he was making his visitor. Perhaps Mark thought him an alcoholic or mentally ill, and perhaps he was both of those things.

'I have to go there,' Seb said quietly.

Mark never spoke and was probably suppressing a mad giggle. Seb wouldn't blame him.

'I need to take the files back. Find out what they want.'

'Sorry?' Mark ventured.

Seb faced the floor as if in defeat. 'They were here. Last night. They followed me here. They can follow me anywhere. In the stories . . . There's a connection between the stories and me.' Seb pointed at the two volumes of stories. 'I am the image that *they* focus upon. *He* knows about me. *He* knows.'

'Who, sorry?'

'Mark . . . There's a lot that I haven't told you about why I am here. Why I am not at my best right now.'

'The blackmail?'

Seb nodded. 'Yes. But you wouldn't believe me.'

'I'd like to hear it, all the same.'

Seb laughed humourlessly. 'Oh, you'd get a kick out of it. It'd be weird enough for you, all right. It'd be cool.'

Seb then paused to wonder about his reputation. Mark was a writer. Would Mark find the temptation too great to resist going online to mention their meeting in social media, to write an article about his visit?

Seb Logan has lost the plot. His unhealthy obsession with a minor horror writer, astral projector and leader of the nefarious SPR cult led to the author's unravelling in a hotel room in Manchester.

How could he think of his reputation at a time like this?

Seb felt guilty for thinking so badly of the man who had been nothing but friendly and helpful, particularly given the sudden and odd appearance he'd made in Mark's life. 'I'm sorry, Mark. I'm going through . . . a lot right now. And I'm not sure what to do.'

'I'll keep confidential, if that's what you're worried about.' Mark sat down upon the chair drawn out from the table. 'It hasn't escaped me that you're under a lot of strain, Seb. I thought it might have been about your writing, but I am guessing this is something personal that I have no right to ask about.'

'Neither, really. It's not what you think. I wish it was. I've never experienced anything like this. It's just not normal, or logical. It shouldn't be happening, but it is. And it started when Ewan appeared . . . I'm sorry. I probably shouldn't say any more.'

Mark fidgeted. 'I'm a good listener, Seb. And maybe I can help. You never know. Try me.'

When Seb had finished his account it had gone six and he was close to missing his train. He realized he didn't care. He'd come loose from the world he knew. At one time catching a train would have caused him paroxysms of anxiety. But the train would take him home and from there he must journey to *the Tor*. That was inevitable. Like a character in

279

one of Hazzard's stories, he must seek his fate in the unknown. He must go and find whatever was still in place, what it was that had been left behind.

Mark's mouth was actually open. Seb had deliberately avoided the man's eyes, so as not to have been put off while he recounted the events of the last few weeks to this aficionado of the esoteric. Any flicker of discomfort, disbelief, or even mockery in Mark Fry's expression might have shortened or tempered his confession. But when he'd eventually returned his gaze to Mark, his visitor was clearly unnerved by a story that should have been treated with hilarity, scepticism and a concern for Seb's mental health. Surely there was a limit to the amount of rope that Mark Fry would feed out before calling time on crazy Sebastian Logan. 'That's pretty incredible,' was all he said.

'Please don't tell me that you believe me.'

Mark narrowed his eyes and lowered his voice in the manner of an official about to impart grave news. 'Seb, I'd be the last person to judge you, but what people think they have seen and experienced, and what they have actually seen and experienced, are often the same thing to them. And I'm less inclined to care about the difference than most people are.'

That was probably the best reaction he could have received from anyone. You withdrew from the mad or you humoured them. Mark had opted for the latter course.

'And considering what I am known for, Mark, the books I write, you can imagine how impossible it would be for any rational person to accept what I have just confided in you. They'd see a connection between the two things. Cause and effect.'

'But you think that going to Hunter's Tor will stop this? These dreams, the visions? Maybe it'll be like some kind of catharsis? You'll see that the place is derelict and harmless and that will help you . . .' Mark winced and rephrased the end of the sentence. 'Deal with the visions, I mean.' He'd wanted to say hallucinations. 'I'm not judging you, Seb. Please don't think that I am. But have you seen a doctor? Had a scan and stuff?' That had been hard for Mark to say and Seb didn't hold it against him.

'Nothing wrong with my eyes. No headaches, symptoms, head injury, contributing illnesses or conditions. I'm a bit reclusive, but there's nothing in my lifestyle to explain this if it's *all in my head*. It just started happening, a few weeks ago, when Ewan arrived. And then he was actually killed. But not by anything living. And it's getting worse, Mark. Last night . . .'

'You were going to say something.'

'It's like I am being summoned, you know? My presence is required, somewhere. All signs are pointing to the Tor.'

'An empty building. It might even be in use now for something else. Who knows? I haven't checked, or even thought about it much until now. National Trust might have it.'

'They don't. I looked. It's not even on a Google aerial map as anything but a blurry image of something grey. There is nothing online about that building or its legacy. It's like it doesn't exist. Don't you find that odd? It's as if anyone aware of the place, and I mean aware of what it was used for, is no longer around. And when they were around, they were too terrified of that place to say anything about it. Besides Liza and her two friends, at the end of their lives. But Liza also says, quite clearly, that it never ended for her.'

'What . . . I mean, what would you do, when you got there?'

'I don't know. But I'd leave those behind.' Seb nodded at the case containing the SPR files. 'And if this woman, and whoever else Ewan was dealing with, are present, I'll ask them what it is that they want from me. But I have to go. As soon as I get home, I have to go. To make them leave me alone, somehow. Them, and whoever it is that is *with* them.'

The hinderer. Head in a sack. Moving like a dog against the wall of your home. Thin Len . . . 'Oh, Jesus.'

Mark leaned forwards, his small eyes widening behind the oblong spectacle frames. 'Amazing.'

'What?'

'This! This whole thing. I mean, you actually think that Hazzard is behind this. That he's projecting at you. From the grave. I love it. I'm sorry, but I love it.'

'I'm glad you find it entertaining.'

'No, I really didn't mean it like that. And I'd like to come with you.'

'What?'

'I know the place. Where it is. Would you mind?'

Seb nearly wept with relief at the mere notion that he might not have to go alone to an isolated building on Dartmoor, and to a place that must be the very generator of his nightmares. He wanted to grab and hug Mark Fry, but then recalled the images of what he'd seen inside his own home. These images combined with the residuals of his recent dreams and he knew he'd be putting Mark in danger by allowing the man to accompany him. 'I can't let you come with me.'

'Why?'

'Because I think you'd be putting yourself in grave danger, Mark. Maybe even as much as I am in now. I wouldn't ask a best friend, even a family member to do this for me, and I hardly know you. I don't . . . this will sound funny, Mark, but I don't want you on my conscience.'

'Please. Call it professional curiosity.' Mark then looked around himself, as if casting about the floor for the words that he wished to express. He tapped the two Hazzard books on the table. 'Look, I haven't been this excited about the SPR in years. Not since I saw your files. That whole project was incomplete for me. I barely scratched the surface of what was going on there. I know almost nothing about its peak years, in the sixties. But since you pitched up – you, Sebastian Logan, of all people – I've been so bloody excited by this again, and by Hazzard. It's like Christmas. How many opportunities does a man like me get to hang out with one of his favourite writers, and to go with him to the place where Hazzard ran his cult?

'If someone is there . . . if there are more files. Evidence. Just, wow. Wow. Fucking wow! It would actually be cruel if you prevented me from tagging along. I'd be going of my own free will.'

Seb started to grin because he knew that Mark Fry wasn't exaggerating. It would be an act of cruelty to deny him participation.

Wasn't it Seb that they wanted, not Mark Fry? And Mark knew more about Hazzard and the SPR than he ever would. Mark also knew how to find Hunter's Tor Hall. Seb looked at his watch. 'I want to go tomorrow.'

'If I come down with you, I can still be back for Sunday. That gives me time to do the lesson planning I need to do

before next week. I can do my marking on the train home.
I'll just need somewhere to crash for a night.'

'There's one more train after the one I've missed tonight.
How long would it take you to get a bag together?'

21
Flight from Malignant Forms

'Hazzard had a couple of disciples. Other writers,' Mark offered as they chugged out of Exeter St David's station, where the service had deposited most of the remaining passengers. 'Did you know?'

They sat across from each other at a table in the middle of the Quiet Carriage at the rear of the train. Night had fallen. Beyond the windows the world was a blur of orange lights, half-seen landscapes, unlit industrial and agricultural buildings, a greyland. Between them on the table were strewn a litter of empty sandwich packets, coffee cups and four bottles of Doom Bar from the catering service. Victuals that had sustained them on the evening train.

'Disciples? Which writers? Horror writers?'

'Not really. Have you read Bertrand Webster?'

Seb shook his head. 'But I know the name. He wrote science fiction?'

'That's what he's known for. There's a Masters collection coming out of a Bertrand Webster series. But he wrote three stories in the Hazzard vein at the end of his career. They came out in a small press, in the mid-nineties, but were picked up and reprinted in some 'best of' genre anthologies. When I read them, I was sure they were Hazzard stories, but they couldn't have been because Hazzard was dead when they were written.'

Mark sat back and narrowed his eyes to a squint as if to aid his recall. 'There's one called "A Mere Sense of Identity". And one called "The Long Dim Tunnel". But "Wandering Down Eternal Corridors" is the best of the three. That's very creepy and strange, about a building that never ends, full of the dead who don't know that they're dead. In fact, all three stories have "hinderers" in them. Hazzard's best creation. Webster never wrote any horror, except for those three stories, which is a pity, because he was bloody good. But in the author comments at the end of the small press book, he called Hazzard "the criminally neglected master of the Strange Experience". I never found out if Webster was part of the SPR, but I suspect he might have had a connection.'

'You didn't track him down?'

'He was dead when I looked. Alcoholic, someone said on a message board. Drank himself to death in the late nineties after dropping from sight. The other writer, Moira Buchanan, topped herself in the late eighties. Don't know much about her, but her Hazzard-influenced stories are really strange too. At one time, Buchanan wrote these big sagas about families in Scotland for libraries. All of her books are out of print now and there's nothing supernatural in them at all. I read two of them and they were more like Gothic romances than anything else. But she dedicated her three horror stories to Hazzard as "the Master". Right at the end of her career.'

'Which is what M. R. James called Le Fanu.'

'Yes, but these two fairly minor pulp writers bestowed the same august title on Hazzard. Maybe they were both affiliated to the SPR. I doubt I'll ever find out. Moira Buchanan's horror tales are exactly like the final Hazzard stories in *Hinderers*. I can dig them out for you. "Come to Light" was the first one. "The Earthly Dark of the Burrow" came next and is very good, very claustrophobic and mad. And there's one called "Before I Knew I Was Dead". That was the last thing Buchanan ever wrote, apparently. Very depressing story as she succumbed to suicidal thoughts.

'Strange that one writer drinks himself to death and another commits suicide, after each writing three stories in Hazzard's voice, which were entirely different to anything they had ever written before. And they both called him a master, like he was *their master*. I love that kind of thing, though. People fell under his spell, I guess. Like Ewan, but for him it was only through reading Hazzard's obscure stories, years after *the Master* had died. That's really freaky.'

'Isn't it.' The unnerving connection between Ewan's desire for Seb to write a book for him and the mimicry of Hazzard's voice in another two writers, whose lives ended in miserable, tragic circumstances, confused and unsettled him even more than the contents page in the anthology had done the night before. The very pressure of unease's gravity grew denser and Seb found himself slightly short of breath while Mark enthused about the literary connections.

Mark stood up and moved out from behind the table. 'I need the loo and am going to seek out another bottle of Doom Bar. Might as well make a night of it. You want anything?'

Seb shook his head. 'No thanks. But take this.' He gave Mark a ten-pound note. 'No arguments. I'm covering all of your expenses.'

'You don't have to.'

'Mark, I want to. And I'm feeling as guilty as hell, as well as being really glad that you're here. I'm still conflicted about this, but I owe you one.'

Mark smiled. 'Any time.'

Seb settled into his seat. For once the Quiet Carriage was fulfilling all that it promised. He wasn't even sure how many people were still aboard the train. He couldn't see any passengers, but across the aisle some bags were visible in the overhead racks. Warm air and the gentle shifting of the carriage produced a lulling effect.

Seb opened his eyes. Exhaustion had overrun him and he'd fallen asleep and then stumbled in his dream, as if one of his legs had suddenly become shorter than the other and pitched him over.

The train might now have been rolling through the countryside close to the Teign estuary. From the position of his reclined head he could see no lights outside. Perhaps they were in a tunnel or an unlit seascape existed outside. He yawned.

Mark hadn't returned from the buffet car.

Two rows away, towards the end of the carriage, he became aware of the top of a grey head, the hair completely white. It had risen and then sprouted over the back of the seat and appeared unhealthily thin and unkempt.

Seb had no recollection of anyone occupying that seat before now. A sudden image of an elderly form pushing itself up the backrest, as if to peer over the headrest like a naughty child, made him tense.

Across the aisle, the windows were mostly obscured by the headrests. But the panes of glass were blackened by an absence of light outside the train, so the visible portion of the windows were mirrored and reflecting the carriage across the aisle, at head height.

Seb still needed to squint, and lean across the table, to better make sense of who sat in the chair two rows away. What he saw reflected back at him from the glass suggested a ball of screwed-up newspaper. Without any doubt, the blurred, grey thing was also responsible for the colourless hair drooping over the chair back.

Slowly, Seb got to his feet, the edge of the table keeping him bent at the waist. 'Anyone . . .' he said, but had no idea how to finish the sentence. A tiny prickle ran up his back.

The reflection of the papery lump seemed to be moving in a way that suggested a hinge action within its form, like a jaw opening and closing. The white hair also moved, as if caused by the motions of a mouth working at the air.

Seb slid out from behind the table. Better to leave the carriage than verify the existence of a creased face, or a body in a far worse state below the chin.

The reflected head also rose as he stood upright in the aisle, though it remained facing forward and continued to work its mouth. This seemed worse than the head turning around, as if it could sense him without the use of its eyes. And when the pallid scalp became more visible, and when he saw how the pate was stained by large, black moles, from which the sketchy fronds of dead hair protruded, Seb lurched for the door at the front of the Quiet Carriage.

He got into the vestibule between the carriages. And stopped when a hot waft of effluence spilled from the toilet on his left.

The train rounded a bend at speed and he careened like a drunk to the next door.

The carriage ahead, Carriage B, promised a welcome sense of occupancy. Several people had stood up and were reaching for their luggage from the overhead racks, down at the far end. Perhaps the train was approaching Torquay, which would mean they were nearing the end of the line. This could all stop and he'd be safe with Mark Fry. *Maybe we'd be better off sleeping in the same room tonight.*

Seb was just about to punch the green button that would open the sliding door into Carriage B, when he managed to get a better view of the people at the end of that carriage. What he saw made him unwilling to look at them for long.

They seemed in no better physical condition than the thing inside the Quiet Carriage. Those thin arms no longer appeared to be reaching for their luggage, either. Whoever was down there was raising their arms either to indicate distress and a summons for help, or it was some form of mad elation. Perhaps it was both. And for a split second, Seb believed that he had seen something soft and silvery hanging at the waists of what he'd just mistaken for a group of passengers.

He fell away from the door and turned into the stench of faecal sewage. There was a sound of gushing water as if the toilet was flooding from both pan and sink.

In the other direction, whoever he had seen in the Quiet Carriage was on all fours now, and either crawling, or searching for something, on the floor, towards the end of the aisle. Seb saw evidence of what might have been withered legs and a spiny back before he closed his eyes on the world around him.

The door to Carriage B shuddered open.

Seb cried out, 'Please no,' in a voice that would have filled him with shame in ordinary circumstances. His entire body flinched with such force that his feet left the floor at the height of a few millimetres. The colour of true terror, he realized uselessly, and the cowardice that it induces, was not yellow after all: it was as white as a bloodless face that could only mutter to itself. And that was the kind of face that he presented to Mark Fry as he came through the door, holding a bottle of Doom Bar and a plastic pint glass.

Mark stepped back. 'Shit! You jumped me.'

As he took in the panicked statement of a man, pressed against the door of a moving train, as if he wished to get off before the next station, Mark followed this with, 'You all right, Seb?'

22

Carry Me Softly on Shoeless Feet

'See it?' Mark Fry pointed at the top of the gate.

Seb nodded. He'd seen the signage poking through the treeline as they approached the Tor. Reddish iron flaked through paint bubbling off a decorative feature that arched over the gates. The inscription remained clear. 'Let us go out of ourselves. Let us enlarge.'

Dark ivy re-skinned what was visible of the boundary wall. Nettles, brambles, unkempt shrubs, weeds and long grass encroached over the stone posts and erupted through the bars of the gate. During their passage to the edge of Hunter's Tor Hall, many other signs of a growing remoteness and wildness had combined to ratchet Seb's anxiety to the foothills of panic. A feeling that he struggled to quell, even after frequent stops to drink water and urinate behind trees. Delaying the inevitable only made the inevitable worse.

Early that morning, after leaving the A38 between Buck-fastleigh and Ivybridge, they'd headed into the interior of Dartmoor until they were moving slowly on B roads. Eventually, the satnav screen was entirely green save for a minor road they'd crawled along in the direction of the Hall. Google Maps on Mark's tablet and Seb's smartphone, augmented by Mark's ten-year-old recollections, had got them as close to the estate as was possible by road. The last of the tarmac scratched a thin line through ten miles of hilly farmland, visible in glimpses through the trees enclosing the lane.

After their frail phone signals had flickered their last, Seb had pulled onto a grassy verge at the side of the lane. From there they had walked for over a mile, on the remnants of a stone-chip path, often forcing their way through the prickly, damp verdure, to arrive at the gates.

Mark swallowed a half-litre bottle of water and gasped. 'There's a slope on the other side of this wall that goes up to the house. I'm guessing what's left of a driveway does too. That's all I saw last time from higher ground.' He turned around and pointed. 'I climbed a hill over there. This house was in the distance, a big white place. And I followed this wall as far as I could in both directions, for about half a mile each way. The bracken was so thick and I didn't have a ladder so I couldn't get inside. I ran out of light and time.' He'd kept up a near-relentless banter ever since they'd left Seb's house, and Seb had found it a welcome distraction from the successive waves of nauseating anxiety that he'd endured.

There was no need for a ladder at the Tor now. If the gates had been chained shut when Mark was here ten years before, they weren't any longer. 'No lock,' Mark said as they inspected the gate.

'Because they know I'm coming.'

Mark looked at Seb, his expression quizzical but softened by uncertainty, and even sympathy. His struggle with Seb's claims about what had appeared on the train, at his Manchester hotel, and elsewhere, had continued through the evening and into the morning they'd spent at Seb's house in Brixham.

'That woman?' was all Mark said, quietly.

'She's expecting me.'

'Well, let's find out if anyone is in, eh?' Mark said cheerfully, though it sounded forced.

Pushing and lifting one gate between them, they made enough of an opening to squeeze into the grounds.

The overgrown thickets they then crashed through must once have been part of a landscaped woodland garden. Seb was no gardener but he recognized some of the plants, the rhododendrons, azaleas and camellias. They grew untamed about the feet of the larger trees. Deeper inside, the vivid purple buddleia flowers reached out the undergrowth, and swathes of pink and rose-red verbena erupted upon a mass of stems where the shrubs were better spaced. The air thickened with the hum and frenetic antics of bees. Had the circumstances been different, Seb may have found the untamed gardens beautiful.

It was hard going through the lower levels. They couldn't see for more than a few metres in any direction. Nothing had been topped or felled for decades. Only the crunch and slide of gravel beneath their feet provided any indication that they were still on the original drive. After a few hundred metres further in, an expanse of grass became visible through a border of overhanging tree branches.

'Look here.' Mark touched the white stone rim of a pond, the water entirely covered by vegetation. Part of a stone bench emerged from the undergrowth concealing the water. Further along, the stamen of a cast-iron fountain, resembling an open flower, appeared close to another concealed water feature. Relics of former follies and grottoes built by Prudence Carey's family, and now reclaimed by nature.

All Seb knew of the Carey family Mark had told him the previous evening. In the 1920s a business empire of grand hotels had enabled Prudence's father to buy a near-dilapidated eighteenth-century country house. It now appeared the property was determined to return to a pre-restorative state.

'Impressive,' was all Mark offered when the house finally came into view upon the summit of the hill.

Seb's own first impression of the house was that it proved its Georgian origins, probably Neo-Classical Revival. It wouldn't have been out of place as a temple in Rome or a museum in London. A large building, simply designed and undecorated. Typically Palladian style with strong, vertical lines, squat windows on the lower ground floor with long sash windows above. A pillared portico framed a grand front entrance.

The spectacle also called for an awed consideration of Hazzard's ambition. The cross-dressing con man, the dishon-ourably discharged private from the Signals Regiment, the convict and former barman at a holiday camp had dispos-sessed Prudence Carey of her family seat with his talk of projection and celestial spheres, astral doubles and paradise belts. Many others had flocked here to hear the gifted 'doctor' speak, and to maintain his lifestyle. A lifestyle befit-ting a status that he'd elected for himself. Hazzard had genuinely believed that he could fly and he had reached the social climber's mountain peak.

Between the edge of the wooded parkland and the Hall, a series of tiered lawns were now just visible amidst waist-deep nettles, weeds and brambles. The terraces extended to a stone patio, bristling with weeds, that encircled the front of the building.

Mark and Seb trudged upwards in weary silence, moving wherever a path became visible.

Before the front door a final terrace surrounded an oval garden, or what was called a circus. Short borders of masonry formed an avenue, interspersed with garden plots that were a morass of weeds and wildflowers.

Inside the portico the panelled doors were locked. Above them a semicircular fanlight had been designed like a rose and the glass was intact.

Once closer to the walls, Seb noted how the white stucco and paint had flaked to reveal a pebble-dash of dark bricks. Moss stained the paintwork in long beards beneath the ragged gutters.

The ground and first floors were shuttered, though the top-storey windows were uncovered. The glass up there was black and reflective. Not so much as a ceiling could be seen inside.

Staring up and into the inner darkness transmitted a peculiar, unwelcome feeling of exposure, so Seb moved his attention to the slope they had just ascended, and looked further out. The view from the house reached for miles, a vista of great hills, shaded fields and plains, tufted with patches of woodland.

Exploring the rear of the building, they waded through long grass and discovered a disused tennis court, the net rotted away. Curling about a row of cider apple trees, the old chain-link fence was orange with corrosion and had collapsed into metal tongues.

Another twenty metres beyond the court a walled garden

of red brick was intact. Whatever had been planted inside had rioted and thrust itself untidily at the sky. Faint engravings of narrow footpaths, marked by overgrown earthen banks, disappeared into more parkland which obscured the far boundary of the estate.

Hunter's Tor seemed endless, a wild infinity. A place for a mind to stretch unto its furthest reach.

Seb briefly imagined figures dressed in white, sat at patio tables outside the front and rear doors. How they must have surveyed the landscaped gardens and the distant hills. How they must have discussed journeys to places still further afield, invisible to the naked eye, while their bodies had remained inert inside this great white edifice.

Mark removed his rucksack. 'No one here, Seb.' The back of his shirt was dark with sweat. 'Place is abandoned. Hasn't seen any attention in years. All locked up and forgotten.'

Alone, Seb continued further down the path beside the walled garden, seeking outbuildings. On his left, a wooden door with flaking green paint appeared inside an arch in a wall. The gateway was sealed with a corroded padlock, though the bottom of the door had rotted through.

He ducked under a cascade of white blossom, as the path rounded a slope, and then stopped, startled by the sudden, vibrant intensity of an unruly rose garden. Even from twenty feet the vanilla-peachy fragrance of the flowers was overpowering, the air above transformed into a dogfight of butterflies and bees, circling, fluttering, alighting and diving into the pink, red and white flowers. A backdrop of trees with winter-green foliage made the tangle even more fervent.

But how did Seb account for a fresh onset of unease here, so near these flowers? The longer he stared at the roses, the more the ecstatic activity of the fauna suggested agitation, rather than rapture, before such a fragrant bounty.

Overwrought, Seb crouched and uncapped a bottle of water. The exertion of the trek to the Hall, following weeks of disrupted sleep, had taken a toll. His nerves had peaked and crashed like surf all morning. That's all this was. And now he'd stopped moving, the pungent scents and the warmth of the midday sun against his head made him drowsy. He yawned. His eyes watered.

Yet, at the sight of this neglected but thriving rose garden, his feelings continued to oscillate between suffusions of romantic delight and agitation from being so close to it. He imagined he might have walked into a place already occupied, albeit thinly, though with an intelligence, or approximation of such, and that he was now under its scrutiny. He suspected the flowers were aware of him. This was a place he'd never want to be alone.

Seb moved away from the roses and returned to the house to find Mark.

'Seb! Seb!'

Can't he keep his bloody voice down? 'Ssh.' Seb held a finger to his lips.

Mark was stood to the side of the house, his eyes wide with excitement. 'What you said about being expected . . . Look. The patio doors at the back are locked, but this side door isn't. So maybe they wanted you to go through the tradesman's entrance.' Mark chuckled.

Seb's legs weakened as Mark pushed the side entrance open. 'Let us go inside. Let us enlarge,' Mark said, quietly, as if with reverence, which made Seb feel even worse.

Ewan had been here. *They* had wanted him to come. 'We

drop off the files, then hit the road.' Seb wasn't sure if Mark heard him.

His weight depressing the floorboards inside, Mark clicked his torch on.

'Amazing. There's still stuff here.'

And there truly was in the first room they entered, the kitchen. Above cupboards, a dozen shelves laddered to a peeling ceiling. Oddments of crockery and an incomplete dinner set remained in place. A dark blue Aga in a tiled hearth stood at the opposite end of the kitchen. A clutter of pans covered the rusting hotplates. Mismatching bowls and glasses were dotted about an open cabinet beside the stove. Three dozen ancient cookbooks mouldered upon two wooden tables that sat side-by-side in the middle of the floor.

Seb stroked the kitchen surfaces with his index finger to confirm the room was filmed with dust. 'Hasn't been used in years.'

Apart from some soft matches and a few items of tarnished cutlery, the drawers were empty. The room seemed to have been improperly cleared many years before.

No daylight penetrated the shutters on the windows of the ground floor. The hallway beyond the kitchen and empty scullery were panelled in dark wood, creating dour tones that effected a deeper sense of darkness.

They moved beyond the daylight falling through the side door. Their torches created a sepia fog, comprising a myriad of dust particles falling like an endless rain.

The pictures were gone from the walls. Only an empty umbrella stand and a stool with scuffed, wooden legs remained in the hall. Upon the seat was an alpine hat. It had been placed upon a folded scarf of yellow silk. A pair of hand-stitched leather gloves completed the ensemble.

Mark shone his torch on the articles of clothing. 'Do you think they were Hazzard's?' He took a picture.

Seb struggled to hear much besides the rush of blood through his ears. His eyes felt as if they had extended from their sockets to become as large as eggs, white and filled with suppressed hysteria. If he heard a noise beyond those of their feet and Mark's voice, he wondered if his bowels would give out.

In the two larger downstairs rooms at the front, the brownish outlines of missing picture frames were visible. Bookcases covered two walls in one of the large front rooms, but their empty white shelves now foamed with grey dust. The mantles were clear of bric-a-brac.

Dreary spaces, their lines softened by successive layers of cobwebs, the walls stained by the desiccated spore of insects, the floors gritty with rodent droppings; a sense of meagreness and poverty was now suggested along with an incomplete flight.

There were also hints of a Spartan, clinical character to these rooms. It was possible to imagine them being airy once, bright with sunlight, and facing the tremendous view of the moors beyond the closed shutters.

Some furniture had survived in the largest living room: an ancient settee and two large armchairs, the fabric worn on the seats and armrests. One chair had a tartan blanket draped over the headrest, as if it were a ghostly reminder of an old figure who'd once sat there.

After inspecting the first three rooms together, Mark surrendered to his eagerness and began roaming, hurriedly, as if a time limit had been imposed upon their search of the former SPR headquarters. His feet banged about the floorboards and his torch beam excitedly scythed across the walls and doors.

Reluctant to be left behind, Seb followed as best he could, tracking the excessive noise of Mark's feet into a long dining room in which a table without chairs awaited. The cabinets also offered nothing more than bare shelves behind dirty glass. Beneath the window the indentations of a sideboard's legs still pocked a threadbare rug that covered most of the floor.

Mark rushed out as soon as Seb arrived. From further along the passage that bisected the width of the building, he called out, 'Seb! In here! Quick,' as if he'd found what he was looking for. 'Check it out. His study? Do you think?'

That room had once been an office for someone. A desk remained, an antique hardwood. A Remington portable typewriter sat uncovered beside two pencils, a large stone paperweight and an empty blue glass. The shelves above the small desk were empty.

'And look. Still here.' Mark's torch lit up a table beneath the shuttered window. Upon it a cluster of framed photographs stood upright. Mark began to raise them and blow away dust. There were nine portraits.

'That was Prudence Carey when she was younger,' Mark said. 'I've seen that picture before.' It had been shot in black and white and featured an attractive woman with dark hair, seated in a stylized pose, looking over her shoulder. Seb guessed it had been taken no later than the thirties.

Two of the colour pictures captured an elderly woman beside a flower bed, and perhaps this was part of the Tor's now neglected gardens. It had probably been taken in the early seventies. 'I'm guessing that could be her when she was older,' Mark offered.

'There he is,' Mark said so suddenly he made Seb jump. He held up another picture frame and jabbed his pudgy hand at the portrait of a small, smartly dressed man with a slender face, sharp cheekbones and dark eyes. He was handsome in a way that was pretty. 'The Master.'

In another photograph the same figure wore a carnation on the jacket of his suit and stared dreamily into the distance, his hair immaculately styled with brilliantine. It looked like a portfolio shot taken some time after the Second World War.

In another gilt frame the same man, though much older, was standing beside an E-Type Jaguar and wore a pale macintosh coat and a small alpine hat. The print was blanched by sunlight, but Seb estimated that it had been taken in the sixties. Gloves and oblong sunglasses also issued signs of a subtle though deliberate concealment. One hand rested on the roof of the sports car. The dandy grown up.

'So who's that?' Seb asked. The final three portraits featured another woman. Slender, near willowy, her face heavily but tastefully made-up in each photograph.

She wore a simple black dress in one picture and held a glass of sherry. A stole was draped over one arm, the only embellishment that added a theatrical flourish. One eyebrow was also arched in mock-disapproval at whoever held the camera, the eyes alluring and mischievous. She stood as if in the first position of ballet, her sling-back shoes pointy-toed and high-heeled, her slender shins shimmering in nylon. Elegant, quietly glamorous, even sexy, and posed before a large fireplace. Seb had not long shone his torch on that fireplace in one of the downstairs rooms.

The beauty wore a hat and veil in the sole headshot. Behind a gauzy veil, her painted eyes were made feline with eyeliner, and feminized further with false lashes. Shiny, dark and slightly parted lips smiled beneath the veil. The siren.

'Diane? You think?' Mark said. 'The eyes and nose, same as the male persona. See?' He pointed to one of the younger shots of the man.

He was right. This was Hazzard, and convincingly transformed into a fashionable society beauty. Nothing too dramatic or camp. This was an artful mimicry of the female without a hint of the spectacle of drag. It could have been the portrait of a film star.

In the final picture, the transvestite was older and dressed in a long mink coat, the glossy fur shimmering. Her hair was concealed by a hat, or white turban, the eyes completely hidden by sunglasses. A beauty spot had been delicately impressed beneath one eye. Long satin gloves covered the delicate forearms, and patent leather boots encased her legs, adding a subtle charge of the erotic and revealing the fetish at the heart of the persona. Age seemed to have transformed the alter-ego into something more imperious too. The gaiety and prettiness had vanished from this colder, fuller, but still handsome face.

The actual evidence of Hazzard's eccentricity, the split gender and the feminine half, cultivated with such care and enthusiasm, startled Seb. He found it hard to equate Diane with the terminable morbidity of Hazzard's second collection of 'Strange Experiences'.

The life of the man seemed too large to be accommodated

by any experience at his disposal. Despite his perilous situation, Seb couldn't deny the compelling aura that this master of lies and subterfuge, of disguise and theatre, still managed to issue from old photographs. While enmeshed in a tawdry history of under-employment, imprisonment and fraud, Hazzard had also achieved something extraordinary inside a grand country house. He had accomplished something that no robed guru or bearded, self-proclaimed prophet of the same era, had ever mastered in their more celebrated compounds or temples. Hazzard was an original.

'Just bloody incredible.' Mark took photos of the portraits. Then switched his tablet for a small camera that he cupped in one hand. 'You know who should come here and film this? That Kyle Freeman fella. I love his stuff.'

Seb looked at the ceiling. 'Let's go. Upstairs.'

'Let us go out of here and enlarge upstairs.'

'Mark. Please. Stop saying that.'

The bare floorboards became an amplifier of their footsteps. They might have been wearing shoes with tipped heels as they walked into the shrinking circles where their torch beams ended on the brown walls, the circles of light growing brighter as they narrowed, the darkness welling behind their shoulders. Both of them sneezed, as if one had set off the other.

The first floor existed in total darkness. Twelve rooms arranged around a broad corridor that ran through the building widthways, with the staircase opening in the middle of the floor. And like the hall below, these walls were wood-panelled, the doors large and thick with yellowing emulsion.

Every bedroom door had been left open, and inside each room the wood panelling ended at a picture rail. Wallpaper stained brown with age continued to the cracked and flaking ceilings. And, as if awaiting new guests and donors, the old SPR beds remained. All were neatly made with a white sheet folded over a cream blanket. Any other furniture had been cleared, leaving dark patches and scratches on the wooden floorboards.

'This is where they projected from,' Mark said in the first bedroom they entered, his eyes wild with excitement. 'From these actual rooms. Incredible, isn't it?'

It was something, for sure, and Seb's own gaze flitted across the walls as if he expected to see a prostrate shape, still hovering above its earthbound double. He felt no admiration, only trepidation.

A locked door blocked the stairwell and any access to the top floor where Hazzard must have lived.

'Don't! Please. Don't,' Seb said, as Mark heaved and pushed at the door, rattling it within the frame. 'Let's look downstairs again. There'll be a cellar.' Seb realized he lacked the courage to go any higher. Whatever was up there, he wasn't ready to see. He needed to go back down and regroup his wits before Mark forced his way into what remained upstairs.

Near the kitchen, behind a door they'd previously mistaken for a pantry, a staircase descended to a lower ground level and opened into a large storage room. The walls flaked and were lined with rusting pipes and a later addition of strip-lights.

A second flight of shorter stairs rose to a broad trapdoor,

once used for receiving supplies and the fuel required to maintain a large house. Most significantly, the room was lined with long metal cabinets, each labelled chronologically. It was the SPR archive.

Mark wasted no time and began hauling open drawers, his thick fingers soon flicking through the folders inside. He held the butt of the torch handle between his teeth.

'Look here,' Seb said, shining his torch at the floor around two tables. The surfaces immediately struck Seb as too bright.

'What?' Mark asked, without even looking over his shoulder.

'The floor.' It was tracked with scuffs that hadn't been recoated in dust. The surfaces of the two tables were definitely cleaner than they should have been too. One was cluttered with stationery, biros and copier paper, some of it reasonably modern and still in place. 'Someone has been in here, recently.' More footprints became visible beneath the table. A track had also been worn through the dross, to and from the filing cabinets.

Mark rose from his knees, wincing. 'Ewan?'

Seb nodded. 'I think so. That bastard was in here.'

'But look around,' Mark said, smiling, and indicating the emptiness and signs of dereliction. 'There is no SPR any more. Your mate got inside and took some files. And there's far more than reports in these cabinets, Seb. That first one is full of accounts. Bank statements. Utility bills. Receipts. Masses of them going back decades. Evidence of a fully functioning business and household. It's a treasure trove. It's just bloody amazing! The explanation of how the organization was run must be inside this room.' Mark returned to the cabinets.

The squeal of the drawer runners grated on Seb's nerves. 'All undisturbed, Mark, and for so long? How is that possible for a building of this size? No inheritance, will or probate? No further occupancy? I don't buy it.'

From his rucksack, Seb removed half of the SPR files that Ewan had taken from this very room. He stacked them upon the table. From Mark's rucksack, he removed the second half and placed them alongside. The action of returning the documents provided some relief, but it also felt pitifully insufficient, a mere gesture.

Beyond the archive room Seb inspected the subterranean alcoves.

Each brick cubicle was filled with shadow or made grey where rays of sunlight struggled to enter through the dirt-encrusted windows near the ceiling. From what he could make out, the storage spaces were filled with paint tins, stacked garden furniture, some rusted tools, hundreds of empty wine bottles, and all of it coated in cobwebs and dust.

He also found a fire poker, unused light bulbs, an old pith helmet, rotting deck chairs, broken tennis racquets, mattresses soaked by water as if there had been a flood, an old iron cot and perambulator, the fabric mildewed and decomposing.

At the end of the concourse he came across a column of cardboard boxes that were sealed and not nearly as old and speckled as most of the surrounding materials in the basement. The boxes bore the stamp of a printer in Crewe.

Seb tore open the first box and pulled away the bubble-wrap. The container was filled with books. At least two dozen copies of the same book. Another two dozen copies were waiting inside the second box that he tore into. And this was a book written by an author that Seb knew fairly well, because that man was currently standing inside the SPR archive and noisily pulling open drawers.

Theophanic Mutations by Mark Fry, and what must have accounted for nigh on the entire print run of the sole edition of a rare and long-out-of-print paperback.

Confusion made Seb's movements near frantic. 'Mark?' Seb held onto the stack of boxes to steady himself. 'Mark?'

'Seb. Seb. Seb,' Mark called back, but in a suppressed, urgent, hissy voice.

Seb stepped out of the storage alcove and into Mark's torch beam, directed down the corridor to locate Seb. He could see no more than a silhouette of Mark's head.

'We got company!' Mark whispered forcefully.

'What?'

'Ssh! Outside.'

Seb moved to where Mark stood. 'Just seen someone walk past that little window. Up there. Feet.'

'Turn your bloody torch off, then,' Seb said, as he killed his own light.

In silence and darkness, they listened to each other's breathing.

'A security guard?' Seb eventually whispered, and from a hope that what Mark had seen was real and not *something else*.

'No alarms, though. Nothing. Door wasn't even locked. Didn't look like a guard either. I saw a bit of skirt. Must have been a woman.'

'It's her! Come on.'

Seb made his way back up the stairs and into the passage behind the kitchen. Mark followed, but he took his time, as if he was more reluctant to leave the SPR hoard than afraid of what waited for them outside.

23

She Beckoned and I Followed

'We're so pleased that you came.' The same woman with the crudely cut hair, who had accosted him on King Street in Brixham, spoke first. She appeared just as dishevelled as before, and was dressed in the same clothes, the dirty cords and a bobbled fleece inside a grubby, yellow raincoat.

The eyes of the second woman darted between her companion and Seb, assessing the exchange and the facial expressions, as if searching for the right tone, the correct discourse, with which to participate in the opening exchange. She wore a long, patterned skirt with hiking boots. In places the hem was soiled and ragged. The thick rope of her plaited hair seemed coarse, like grey hemp. Unkempt strands formed a fuzzy halo around her lined face.

She appeared expectant and eager to join in, but was also suffering an attack of nerves. Her white fingers twisted and her hands trembled. And if Seb wasn't mistaken, she also seemed relieved to see him.

The two women stood apart at the end of the oval, weedy terrace, before the portico. They had been in that curious position when Seb emerged from the side of the building.

He cleared his throat to get rid of the tightness. 'The files that Ewan took. They're back downstairs. All of them.'

'Thank you. I hope they gave you an idea of what has been achieved here.'

Mark remained behind Seb, and kept silent.

'This has to end . . . I want it to stop, today. I want you to leave me alone. This has nothing to do with me. What was done here. Whatever you are doing now, I want no part of.'

The long-haired woman looked at the floor as if embarrassed by his outburst. But her companion with the helmet of hair smiled with what Seb took for satisfaction. 'We're all involved. We all struggle through the psychic stream. And the current is more powerful in some places, like here, and in some people. But the slowly flowing flood does not stop reaching out, Sebastian. When a roof leaks, the water always finds its way down. It drips onto our heads. A little at first, then more and more. But we all join the flow eventually. The dark, slowly flowing flood. We merely join it at different times. Who can say when that time comes to any of us?'

'Ewan had no right to involve me in this. Whatever he did has nothing to do with me. I hadn't seen him in years until recently.'

'Lucky you,' the woman said, her eyes becoming sly. 'And what a disappointment he was. We hope you won't be. But let's be grateful that Ewan brought us together.'

'What is it that you want?'

'Want? This isn't about us, this is about you, and your potential. We offer nothing but an opportunity.'

'Yes, it is. It really is, Seb,' the nervous woman with the long hair finally spoke up, only to be admonished with a withering look from her friend, who resumed her spiel. 'Do you close yourself off from the truth, Sebastian? Do you fear a vision far greater than anything that appears in *story books*?' She was referring to his work again, and this time as if it were childish. No attempt was being made to conceal her contempt. 'Have you not received an inkling of a place far greater than this?' She spread her arms and looked about herself, as if to indicate the ground upon which they stood.

'Whatever *this* is, I told you, I want no part of it.'

'That, unfortunately, is not my decision to make. I can't grant wishes, but I can guide you in what must appear strange and frightening. But you needn't be afraid, or confused.' She'd widened her eyes mockingly when she'd said 'frightening'. 'And if you see them tonight, and you may do, don't be frightened. They don't know themselves.'

Seb breathed out hard enough for it to become audible. He worried he might hyperventilate and needed to force a swallow to regain control of his larynx. 'What do you mean? Tonight?'

'Please, Seb. You must try to understand what Veronica is telling you. Otherwise it'll always be difficult. It doesn't have to be this way. We don't have much time.' This from the second woman again, her face pleading with him. And *Veronica*? At least he now had a name for the creature with the helmet-hair.

Seb shook his head. 'Have I not made it explicitly clear that I want no part of whatever it is that you are doing? And that goes for whatever you were doing with Ewan that got him killed.'

Veronica leapt in. 'This is why trust is so important. Ewan couldn't be trusted. He may have been gifted, but he lacked other qualities. So it's very important during your visit that we establish a clear understanding of what we are

312

to expect from each other. What we are to give and what we are to receive, so that we can avoid the wrong outcome.'

'I'm not giving anything and I don't want to receive anything. I've replaced your files. If I am forced to endure one more . . . episode, I'll take action.'

Veronica laughed gaily.

Seb cleared his throat, his anger welcome. 'Oh, I'll let others know exactly what is going on here. And what went on here. Bit of exposure. I bet you'd love that.'

Veronica tutted, mockingly, but the amused grin never relented. 'We have very little patience with the indiscreet. That has never changed in the entire history of the organization.' As she spoke she'd looked past Seb and at Mark Fry.

'Organization?' Seb said. 'Stop faking legitimacy. People were terrified here, drugged, driven out of their wits by a con man, who extorted money from them with threats. Maybe some of them even died here. Who knows? But there are ways of finding out. There is always evidence.'

Veronica's nameless companion winced, but continued to concentrate on her feet, hinting that Seb was making a grave error in goading them.

Veronica returned her attention to Mark Fry. 'Mark, perhaps you would like to contribute to our discussion. You've been awfully quiet so far.'

Seb swivelled about and stared at Mark in bafflement. *They knew him?* He thought of the books in the basement.

Mark was biting his lower lip and snaking his head in evident discomfort, looking everywhere but at Seb. 'Veronica, you said you wouldn't mention that.'

'All things change, Mark,' she said, smiling.

Mark glanced at Seb. 'Mate. You better . . .'

'Better what?'

'You have to.' Mark looked at the two women as distaste transformed his face. 'They . . .'

'You know them! You've been in here before, haven't you? You lied!'

'Seb . . . I'm sorry.'

'You bastard!'

'What could I do? You know, yeah, you know what they can do. You think you were the first?'

Veronica beamed. 'Mark knows all about our potential at the Tor, and our capacity to continue protecting ourselves. He has learned things of great importance that continue to be nurtured here, and that continue to thrive. And we have a long reach as you know, Sebastian. I hope you didn't mind our paying you a little visit at your hotel? You might also want to be advised that there is no earthbound place where we cannot find you. And this organization has you *in mind* for something very special.'

The two hooded figures in the corridor outside his room. *The cold hands that had held his at the bedside?* 'You . . .'

Veronica gave him her best yellowy grin.

'Seb. Please, Seb,' the nervous woman said. 'There's no point in resisting your appointment. When *he* makes them, I'm afraid they must stand. He's very specific about who he works with. And it really is an honour to be chosen. This is a very special role we are offering. A place has been made for you, right here. As soon as he found out about you, well—'

'Joyce! If you please!' Veronica's incongruously girlish voice deepened into a tone that struck Seb as even stranger and formidably masculine. They all flinched.

Veronica and Joyce. He had their names now. Even in

shock and fear, he told himself to remember their names. 'Role? What bloody role?'

Veronica's smile returned. The crimson of her rage faded from her cheeks. 'We all have contributions to make to one who has journeyed so far for our enlightenment, for the truths that have the potential to transform our lives, and this world, with a common goal.'

'What? Why am I even having this conversation? You're mad.' Seb made a move for the end of the terrace.

Mark spoke up again, his eyes flicking nervously between the two women and Seb. 'Seb. You have to. Just get it done. Trust me.'

'Done? Get what done?' he shouted at Mark.

Despite the insincere smile on her face, which Seb found more odious as each moment passed, Veronica's tone became more forceful again. 'This organization has to be maintained. You've seen the disrepair on your tour of our building, and our work is at a vital stage that was envisaged many years ago. We approach a critical phase. Appearances can be deceiving, but I can assure you of a great deal of *activity* that continues within our organization. Despite some setbacks, in a world that struggles to understand our mission, many here are still projecting.'

Even though they were close to the hottest part of the day, Seb experienced a horrible sensation of coldness and queasiness. Briefly, he thought of the two obscure authors that Mark Fry had told him about on the train. One had committed suicide and the other had drunk himself into an early grave. Moira Buchanan and Bertrand Webster must have been sharers of the *great* vision too. They had been the recorders of those that still *hindered in the passage*. Mark had only been prepping him.

'There is work to be done, Seb. And urgently.' Joyce spoke plaintively, her fuzzy head tilted forwards out of sympathy, as if she were explaining difficult news to an infant.

Seb backed further away, and from Mark too, who seemed unable to stop a pained grinning, as if he thought the situation tragically funny. The day had turned into a ghastly and absurd practical joke.

Joyce followed Seb, near pleading. 'So many have given so much to the society. And we must all contribute what we can.'

'Money,' he said, but his voice was a rasp. 'You want money. Extortion.' Nothing had changed at the SPR. Blackmail backed up with threats remained the core tactic of the 'projectors'.

Veronica frowned. 'I don't perceive it in such vulgar terms, but as Joyce has explained to you, all vital organizations require funding. Public health, charitable organizations, scientific research, all require maintenance, do they not?'

Seb had never felt even remotely violent towards a woman, but he wanted to split Veronica's skull apart with a brick and then beat Mark Fry to death with the same dripping masonry. His anger was intense enough to make him dizzy. When he managed to speak, his voice retained half its original strength. 'Taking drugs and forcing out-of-body experiences. To travel through the *spheres*. Selling lies about paradise? Harrowing old women with ghastly visions of the greylands . . . This strikes you as significant? Akin to medical research into life-preserving drugs? Are you bloody insane, or just completely without any morals, scruples or ethics?'

Veronica laughed, and even clapped. 'We don't expect you to understand immediately. It's a lot to grasp so quickly. But you must admit that you have been a witness to miracles. And can I ask you to refrain from swearing? *He* despises the foul-mouthed.'

'Yes,' Joyce said, nodding vigorously, her long, miserable face transformed into a mad glee. 'This is the only way to direct you towards our vital cause. We thought you of all people would understand this mission. Perhaps the most important research being conducted anywhere at all in the earthbound sphere is happening right here. So I implore you, Seb, to embrace this opportunity, so that we can work together and *minimize* any further difficulties.'

'Seb. Seb. Trust me on this,' Mark said, now moving towards him, his arms open. 'Take it from me, you really don't have a choice. Just write the book for them.'

'Book?' Seb spun around, losing his balance. He sat down in the weeds. Pieces of gravel pricked his buttocks.

'It was the most marvellous idea. One that was tried before, though by far inferior talents and with limited success. We were very patient with Ewan too, though it appears dear Ewan's visit was not all in vain. We believe he was struck by the very same idea, though one intended for his own enrichment. We had no idea when he ventured out alone, that he had intended for you to be complicit in the theft of *his* legacy.'

'Legacy?'

'God, Seb,' Mark suddenly spoke up. 'If you hadn't called me. You should never have called me. They only wanted Ewan. But I had to tell them . . . about you.'

'You . . .' Seb couldn't follow what Mark had said. He

seemed stuck within the midst of a complicated plot whose story he'd been improperly following.

'I'm sorry, mate. They made me . . . they asked me to get in touch if anyone ever . . . you know, dug around about the SPR, because of *Mutations*. Only a few review copies ever got out. I had to tell them about you. And once they figured out who you were, they guessed what Ewan was up to by gate-crashing your place with those stolen files. If only you hadn't bloody called me, you'd . . .'

Seb closed his eyes to quell a dizzy spell that tried to rotate the big white house, the blue sky and the grass about in his eyes. He wanted to be sick, but felt too bodily weak to throw up.

He'd been off the hook when Ewan died. That was what Mark was suggesting. *If you'd left the bags at the Beach Haven Hotel . . . and not . . . Oh, Christ.* But the potential for his own book had been too tempting, and it seemed they wanted him to write one on the same subject too, though not for his own benefit.

Veronica beamed. 'And this will be the most exciting collaboration. I think Ewan's ambition got the better of him, and things took an unfortunate turn, but this is an enterprise that we now wish to take ownership of. And it has been such a long time since *he* has published. Too long. *He* has so much to share with the earthbound world. His vision will just astound. We're quite certain of that. There has never been a better time to embark upon the next stage of our work.'

'*He*,' Seb whispered. 'Hazzard . . .'

'And you, yes!' Joyce cried out, as if with elation, her drab ponytail swishing like a dead eel. Seb had seen few people in his life so excited. She turned her head to peer at the dark windows of the highest storey of the Hall, and smiled beatifically. 'He wants to begin immediately.'

'He . . .'

Veronica nodded her head slowly. 'Is still with us, yes. He often comes home. Many of the others still do. You'll meet him soon enough, at a time of his choosing I expect. Perhaps tonight. Maybe at another time. We are not his keepers. But it is his wish that you will be our guest at the Tor tonight.' She then raised her chin in an attitude of self-importance and seemed eager to bring the meeting to a close. 'We'll discuss terms in the morning. Joyce, will you show our guest to his room while Mark and I have a little chat.' Veronica then turned away from Seb, as if she were dismissing a trifle.

'We're delighted to have you with us,' Joyce said to Seb, while vigorously nodding her head, coming close enough for him to smell the damp and the sweat clinging to her old clothes. 'Your presence here is just perfect. Nothing could make us happier. Though I hope you brought something to eat. I'm afraid we can't possibly cater for you. We no longer have that facility at the Tor. But one day we'd like to open our doors again, and wider than ever before.'

24

Thousands of Invisible Cords

'If you have *company* tonight, I'd advise against using your torch. Some of our alumni are better formed than others. Or so we find. Most of the time they remain still, though, and quiet. They wait in the darkness. They wait for the light.'

Seb closed his eyes to let that information settle. It seemed easier to endure with his eyes shut. At Joyce's mention of 'company' Seb's scalp had been ready to rise from his skull. And within the frantic din of his thoughts he knew that these minutes alone with Joyce were crucial. Within this brief window before she left him alone, because that is what she planned to do, he must learn as much as he could about his current plight. 'For years. They've been here for years, haven't they?'

'They have no way of knowing how long they have waited for ascent. There is no time over there. What may feel like a few minutes might amount to decades, or even longer. But we all wait for ascent, do we not, in different ways? And all change inside the passage. The longer one remains, the more one *transforms* in readiness for the higher spheres. And transcendence is all that *he* has ever sought. Do you know your way? You've been up here, with Mark, haven't you?'

He no longer found Joyce as sinister when apart from

Veronica. Unkempt, clearly unwashed if he ever stood too close to her, and a woman stricken with bad nerves, but she was as sad and as desperate a figure as he had ever encountered in his life. Alive maybe, but as trapped as those other things, and somehow bound to serve the mad schemes of a long-dead sociopath. Hazzard had been right: Seb recalled something he'd read in the second collection about there being first deaths and second deaths, but neither being conclusive. These women were guided by whatever lingered here. And what he would not doubt was their capacity to end his life, and then to maroon him here in the darkness, forever. The idea brought into his mind an image of thin limbs struggling through the black waters of a misted culvert.

Wendy had also mentioned a discussion that would take place the following morning, about 'terms', so they would not want him to die tonight. Nor had the return of the files been their primary concern. He could only assume from their disingenuous spiel, that the purpose of his stay at the Tor was to remove the last of his resistance to what they had planned for his future. A fate that had been set in motion after Ewan had unwittingly seconded him as some kind of ghost-writer for M. L. Hazzard.

Seb looked at the ceiling. What choice did he have? 'Are there others like you . . . in the SPR? Others still alive?'

'SPR! I haven't heard us called that in a long time. But only Veronica and I have residential appointments now. We keep things going.' Joyce giggled again, near-coquettishly, though Seb failed to detect anything amorous or humorous in their exchange. 'But we've members all over the world. Not so many these days, alas, but our work continues.'

'You live in this building?'

Joyce continued to lead him deeper into the main corridor of the first-floor passage. 'Oh no, the Tor is solely for the use of the alumni. Their work is far from finished.'

'Finished? It's an empty building, falling apart.'

Joyce smiled at Seb, over her shoulder, the lined face and watery eyes alive with a cherished delusion. 'Yes, I suppose it's seen better days in this sphere, but better days will come again, with your help. The earthbound and celestial will mingle again. Have no doubt.'

When she stopped walking, Joyce spread her arms within Seb's torchlight, as if she were offering him access to palatial accommodation of a five-star hotel. 'Take your pick. Bit dusty, but I'm sure you can make yourself comfortable.'

'I'm not sleeping here. I'm not staying here, Joyce.'

'Oh, but you must.' Shocked, she threw her hands to her cheeks. The woman was half-crazed. Veronica threatened him and this one coerced him with her instability. A double-act of lunacy.

Joyce then peered at the locked white door before the stairwell that led to the top storey, and with an expression of fearful expectation that made the lining of Seb's stomach prickle. She'd deliberately drawn his attention to that door.

'Who are you? You and Veronica?'

'I'm not permitted to go into that.'

'You cannot just terrorize and force a person to do something against their will.'

'Oh, but it's not like that. If you only open your mind and your heart, you'll see—'

'I'll see horror and pain and confusion. I've seen enough of it already. There is nothing healthy or sane about this place. And there never was. It's wrong. It's very wrong. And you bloody know it. Hazzard was a criminal. A fraud. His entire enterprise was based upon deception and extortion. And it's over. Long over. Surely you can see that? No good has ever come of what he started, for anyone, least of all for him. He got lucky with something. Something extraordinary but terrible. Something ghastly that should never have been attempted. You cannot possibly expect that anyone sane would want anything to do with it. There is no light. There is no ascent. Not any more, Joyce. What little I know has made me sure of that. And the two of you are maintaining a madman's final scam. So what is the point of carrying on? You are wasting your lives.'

'You mustn't say that. You mustn't say things like that *here*.' Joyce's eyes widened and she struggled to resist them straying once more to the white door at the end of the corridor. And then she looked at Seb and mouthed the word, *please*.

Seb stepped closer to her. Her entire body was trembling. When he gripped the outside of her arms, she dipped her head and collapsed against him as if she hadn't been held in a long time. When she looked up at him, her face stricken with fear, she sniffed back her tears and whispered, 'Please, help us. We need you. We can't fail. We can't fail *him* or he'll never let us go . . .'

'We can leave. I have a car. I'll take you with me. Today.'

'Would you?' she said, and then sobbed.

'Yes.'

And then the woman seemed to remember something crucial and she regained control of herself. She began to smile like an imbecile. 'We've forgone temptation and earthly comforts for a reason, Seb. Our purpose here is greater.

323

We're wedded to that and that alone. You must try to understand. You and I, we couldn't be together. Not in *that way*.'

'What?' Seb released her shoulders. 'I never suggested anything of the sort.'

'Please. Don't be embarrassed. The earthly conditions are full of temptations and distractions, and so much pain. There is only pain and misery when we are earthbound, and we can never truly know ourselves. You know that. We've read your books. Some of them. Well, bits of them. Bits of one of them, at least. But we've read enough to know that you understand this better than anyone. It's in your vision, the pain. We're all earthbound prisoners and it's not possible to ever find our true potential. But there are other places, and it is to those that we must reach into. Like *he* said, "Into wonder we must walk."'

'Jesus. How did you become . . . this . . . ?'

Joyce frowned at Seb, as if he had asked her a stupid question. 'I was called and I came.' She said this with an air of self-importance and her eyes shone with something approaching awe. 'Oh, I was much younger back then. A child really. Nineteen, or eighteen, I don't much remember. And the society had seen better days when we arrived, but the commitment lasts much longer than what we call *life*, Sebastian.'

Seb stared at her with abject revulsion. 'You murdered Ewan. You killed a man. You and Veronica and . . .' Seb looked at the white door . . . 'that thing, up there, and whatever else is still coming out of here. You all did it.'

Joyce recoiled from him and clasped her hands together, squeezing her eyes shut at the recall of something so unpleasant. 'Ewan . . . He stole from us. He was trusted . . .'

'Did he deserve that?'

'He came here with an agenda. That wasn't right. That has never been permitted. Ego, self-interest . . . No, no, no. And he was warned . . . He was warned about what . . .'

'Joyce. You killed a man. How many others have you murdered?'

'He said he was a poet. A poet? But he wasn't capable . . . It wasn't satisfactory. We were all very disappointed in his . . . *ability*. And the drinking!'

Joyce returned her attention to the white door in the passageway, the door that led to the next floor of the dark house. She dropped her voice to a whisper. 'When *he* enquired about Ewan, he was not pleased. You can't imagine . . . And it was with great regret that he called upon *one* who is forever lost . . . but he only did it to protect us. Don't you see? No one has ventured as far as *him*, or discovered so much in the light, and in the darkness too.' For the last two words she uttered, her whispered voice became so faint as to be almost undetectable, but Seb heard her.

'That thing that came to my home,' he whispered. 'How do I . . . get rid of it. You have to tell me.'

'It is not permitted.'

Seb grabbed her arms again. They felt especially thin and unpleasant as he squeezed the near-rotten wool that hung from her old bones. 'That thing, in the hood. Tell me how to get rid of it!'

'Ewan. It was sent for Ewan.'

'Is it here? Thin Len?'

Joyce's eyes grew wide. 'Sometimes.'

'Now?'

She shook her head as her eyes filled with horror. And yet

her mouth displayed a horrible grin, the visible teeth both yellow and grey in the torch's light. 'Thin Len. They hanged him. A long time ago. A thief who was once dismissed by the lady of this house. He worked here. While her husband was away the lady sent him packing . . . But Len came back. Crept back inside this house and he throttled all of the little children in the nursery. The maid, she helped him. She loved him. They were both hanged in Plymouth. Then Len came back again, and he crept inside here like an old dog. He never left that second time . . .' Joyce's eyes moved to the white door. '*He* showed us the story while we slept.' She winced. 'Oh, and so many times, you can't imagine.'

Thin Len. The face in the trees. The whining dog in your home. The crawling of it outside your window.

Seb felt giddy at what had been recounted: a preposterous folk tale to anyone not suffering his predicament. He barely found the strength to speak. 'And Hazzard . . . He has some control of *it*? Can direct . . .'

Joyce's grin grew wider, as if she were proud of her peripheral association with such a vile pact. 'But with you it can be different, Sebastian. Don't you see? Now that you are here you do not need to be *sought*. Ewan brought us together for a reason. We know that now. We're all confident that you're far better equipped to assist *his* legacy. A great literary legacy. We couldn't be more excited.'

Talking to the desperate living dregs of what Hazzard had founded and then lost was making Seb feel about as unstable as they clearly were.

This woman must have been here as a teenager, and perhaps in the early eighties as Hazzard was dying. She'd never left him either, or been allowed to. Maybe she would return after her own *first death* too.

Seb turned about and walked to the stairs.

'Seb! Seb!' Joyce whispered insistently, and she kept on calling after him until her voice was lost in the lightless depths of the old hall.

Outside the Tor, Seb could see Mark engaged in an animated discussion with Veronica. Or, at least, Mark seemed agitated and that accounted for the wild gesticulations that he was making with the one hand that he kept thrusting into the air, as if pointing at the sky. Veronica regarded him with what amounted to a contemptuous indifference.

Seb walked over.

'No. No. Not again. I can't get any more . . .' Mark stopped talking when he became aware of Seb's approach.

Veronica redirected her thin smile towards Seb. 'I hope you have found a room to your liking.'

'Shut up!' Seb barked into Veronica's face. She did nothing but blink and resume a display of her mottled grin; an expression still filled with an unaccountable loathing for him from the first time they met.

Seb seized Mark by the elbow and forced him away from the woman. 'What the fuck? Mark, what the fuck?' He looked into the eyes of a man with whom he'd spent the last three days, realizing that he hadn't a clue who Mark Fry really was. The man's face was pebbled with droplets of perspiration. He also looked about as guilty as anyone could manage.

Mark shrugged his arm free of Seb's hand and glanced at the top floor of Tor Hall. 'I was on notice. Ever since I wrote that bloody book. They made me buy the whole print run, except for a few review copies that I couldn't get back. Shit, I hadn't *heard* from them in years. I thought I was off the hook.'

'You bastard.'

'I had no choice. You know what they can do, you know their reach . . . And you got me involved again. Don't forget that. So thanks, mate.'

'Fuck yourself. Those women on your tapes, what about them?'

Mark swallowed and shook his head. 'This place reached out one final time when my book was published.'

'Webster and Buchanan?'

'Unfortunate enough to have been friends with Hazzard. I don't know much more about them. I think he had plans for them too, but it didn't work out. Or for me . . . but I managed to persuade them that I was no good. They didn't need much convincing. They hated *Mutations*. Doesn't appear that Ewan was up to the task either.'

'To hell with *Mutations*! And it didn't work out for those others, is that so? Funny way of putting it! You know what *happened* to them.'

'I hope it works out for you, Seb. I really do.'

'You could have warned me.'

'What good would that have done? Once . . . once you are part of the image forming. Like I am. Like Ewan was. That's all it takes. If that thing up there . . . if *he* is made aware of us. If he has a sense of us . . . and has an image of us. I think that's how it works. And it can't be undone. I've tried. And no one will ever believe you. No one sane. They'll think you're mad. They'll think you're seeing things. They commit perfect crimes here, Seb. Don't you get it? And they're so bloody greedy. They made me take out loans. I'm bankrupt.'

'You better get me out of this, and fast. I am not staying here.'

'You have to. Where can you go? Home? Manchester? You can't hide anywhere. Neither of us can. Distance doesn't matter. We're in the flood now, Seb. We're in Hazzard's stream. He goes backwards and forwards. Time doesn't mean a thing over there. But you don't have to be swept away.'

'How? How is this possible? It's just not real. It can't be happening,' Seb said uselessly, and more to the sky than to Mark.

'You ask me that? How can I explain this? But you help them and maybe they'll cut you some slack. There's no other way. You have a publisher and readers. You get paid to write. That's what they're after, money, and exposure for his ideas. You think death has shrunk Hazzard's ambition? I'd say it's made it worse. But I tried to explain to them, on your behalf, that it's not all that simple. You know, with books, and with horror always being a hard sell, and your last book about the ship not being so good . . . But they're expecting a film too. So be prepared. You'll have to manage their expectations from the start. That's the first thing you need to do, because they think that you are a big, fat cash cow.'

Seb was almost in tears when he said, 'I don't want this . . .'

'I'm sorry, Seb.' Mark looked at his watch and winced. 'Gotta get a move on. Train to catch. I've a taxi coming. Local driver. Oh, and the locals, watch out for them. Some of them help Joyce and Veronica. Feed them. Stuff like that. "Them up at the college", that's how they referred to these bitches while I was mooching about. I knew something was up ten years ago before I even saw this bloody place. I found boxes of food by that gate. They were left there by people from round here. Some kind of bloody tithe or tribute, I don't know, to sustain the SPR. But there are surviving connections from when Hazzard was alive. Only it's all going wrong, I think. The network they've used for years is literally dying off. They're skint and barely hanging on now. They think you're the answer to their prayers.'

Seb sank to his knees and placed his strengthless hands upon his seemingly hollow thighs. His legs seemed incapable of supporting his weight.

Mark glanced at Veronica, then whispered to Seb from the side of his mouth. 'You can get through it. I did. They made me bring my books here and they insisted I stayed one night. You know, to make a point.' He closed his eyes and winced at the memory. 'They're crazy, Seb. Both of them. They don't even have running water. They use a stream. There's no electricity here either. They exist in some bloody awful cottage over at the back. Place is cut off, but they keep it all going, for him, Hazzard. I don't think they have much choice either. I'm guessing they're all that's left of the last SPR intake before Hazzard died. They've been here for bloody decades, going mad. And Hazzard will not release his last two followers. Don't trust them. Just write the bloody book and hope for the best.' Mark turned away and began moving down the slope, heading for the overgrown lower parkland.

25

The Discarded Coat

They had left him hours before. Not long after Mark disappeared from sight, the two women had walked away and disappeared behind the house, without a single backward glance.

Still dazed from shock, Seb had followed them at a distance, until they passed the walled garden and vanished into the woods beyond the roses.

He'd returned to the Hall, slumped upon a wall before the portico, and sat with the disarray of his thoughts for company. Occasionally, a shiver touched his neck as if a breeze or a cloud's shadow had passed over him.

Even outside in strong sunlight, with a blue and cloudless sky above his head, the prospect of the night ahead had made him experience a physical frailty decades beyond his age. But the consequences of defying these unstable remnants of the SPR didn't bear consideration. If he drove home, then what of later, what of tonight? Something would be sent after him. Was it better to be at home, in his own room, and to have his final cries unheard by any save *those* that gathered about the bed? Would he choose heart failure at home over a night at the Tor? That's what his life had come down to: stay or die.

He was useful to Veronica and Joyce and what they served. That was all he had in his favour: their desperation for money. They had been forgotten and were captives. Mark had said as much, though how much he could believe of what any of them said was open to question. But who else could Veronica and Joyce turn to?

They must have seen Ewan as an opportunity and snatched at him to placate that restless presence on the top floor. He imagined Ewan's bragging about his literary prowess after being caught trespassing. The fool had got in way over his head, had scarpered and lasted two weeks on the run. His last bad scene. Too much defiance from Seb too would fatally stretch the patience of Veronica and Joyce. Seb imagined they made reports to whatever existed higher up the food chain.

When a suspicion that he was being watched from the top windows of the Tor became uncomfortable, Seb went back inside. Indoors, he clung to a wall until an episode of panic passed. He then looked about himself in the musty darkness.

So how was it done? How was a night endured here? Mark Fry had managed it. Ewan too. But when Seb thought of those figures on the train, and of what he'd dreamed into life inside his hotel room in Manchester, he bent double and closed his eyes.

'Oh, dear God.'

They were coming tonight.

Seb collected three blankets from the SPR bedrooms and took them downstairs to beat as much dust from them as he could using his bare hands. He unshuttered the windows in one of the large rooms and spread the blankets on the dirty sofa. One would go beneath him and two on top. Though he didn't expect to sleep.

The light that passed through the grimy glass was welcome and would last until around nine p.m. He even wondered if spending the night outside would be safer, until he recalled a dream of being chased across the golf links in Churston by something with its head covered by a dirty sack.

Thin Len. The strangler. Child-killer.

Indoors it is.

He had most of one bottle of water left, and that would have to last until morning. The apple and banana he'd put inside his rucksack, and the flapjack that he'd bought while stopping for petrol early that morning would have to sustain him, though the mere idea of anything inside his stomach made him nauseous.

Seb also wondered if he should take the opportunity to look at the files in the basement. Maybe he could learn something useful. But his desire to get out of the building became greater. Until the dying of the light he would stay in the open.

Half a mile from the Tor, he came across an ivy-choked cottage, the home of Joyce and Veronica. They'd made no effort to maintain the small gardens. Two greening sheets of polythene had been untidily weighted down with bricks upon one part of the roof.

He suffered a quick and hideous vision of the two creatures being a part of his life from now on, his existence much reduced and compromised while he remained within their orbit. It would be like having two of Ewan around, only it would be much worse. *Even worse than that. When does this end?*

And what came next? A co-written book with all pro-ceeds going to the SPR? Or did they have something more evangelical in mind, so that he would be required to put his name and reputation behind their cause?

Maybe they would accept a cheque now and leave him alone.

No, because *he* wanted to be in print again. That's what they claimed. Hazzard wasn't giving up on the earthbound prison.

How was this material to be narrated, even dictated to him? *Inside there?* Seb looked in the direction of Hunter's Tor Hall and needed to sit down to stop the shaking that came to his legs.

He couldn't have made up a situation as outlandish for one of his own books, but here he was, trying to peer through the windows of a hovel and the home of M. L. Haz-zard's two surviving curators.

Through an open window at the side of the building, Seb spied the interior of a scruffy and overcrowded living room. Two large blue Calor Gas tanks and a twin-plate camping stove were visible. He briefly pondered why they had not made part of the Tor habitable and then he remembered Joyce's reference to 'the alumni'. That alone satisfied his curi-osity about the living arrangements.

He moved off and walked the grounds for a few hours more, using what paths he could find in the woods and over-grown meadows. In places, he caught glimpses of the distant boundary walls.

Eventually, at dusk, the effects of exhaustion upon his nerves encouraged him to return to the Tor, *to wait it out.*

He heard the first one just after nine p.m.

26

A Vast Blackness, Infinity

The sun had all but disappeared. The evening chill was moist upon the grass. And from the grounds at the rear of the building there came a voice. No words that he could make out, but a woman's voice that carried through the otherwise silent and still dusk.

Seb stirred from where he was sitting with his back against the front doors, his thoughts momentarily adrift.

He found no one at the rear of the building where he'd hoped to come across Joyce, perhaps on a scouting mission to make sure that he'd stayed put. Maybe they knew where he was anyway, at any time.

How they communicated with what existed within the Hall, and if *that* was aware of him too, he had to establish before any attempt could be made to severe the connection. The process of projection had taken a great deal out of Ewan. It wasn't easy, and maybe that could be used in his favour too.

When he was nearer to the rose garden, Seb heard the woman's voice again, though it came from much closer to where he stood.

They buried me over there.

There was no menace or threat in the tone, but that had

335

been the voice of an elderly woman, and a tone weighted by resignation. What had been said was horribly familiar.

Seb saw no one, and nothing behind or around him.

The foliage was dark now, the smell of the flowers fainter. He was reminded of the strangeness of his feelings when near the garden earlier.

Voice shaking, he called out 'Hello' several times and circled the oval garden. Went round twice, and wondered why he'd felt compelled to make a second pass of the darkening roses.

No one replied. He never heard the voice again.

The momentum of nightfall encouraged him to return to the building, but as he walked back to the house, a second voice spoke from inside the walled garden. And again, he was sure he had heard the voice of an elderly woman.

Can you ask my daughter to come and get me?

Not a footfall did he hear from within that enclosed area. Not so much as a twig snapping. And yet the more he thought of the voice, which still rang out inside his skull, he also wondered if those words had been generated from within his own mind.

By the time he reached the hall, he was shivering from the cold and had zipped his waterproof jacket up to his throat. Catching sight of the reflection of his pale face and wild eyes in one of the windows that he'd unshuttered filled him with a disgust at his own helplessness.

A dirty, ancient blanket about his shoulders, he sat alone in the part-furnished front room until ten, resting his lower back upon the tall skirting boards beneath the window. His loathing for Ewan, Veronica and Joyce was the only relief from a fear as crippling as a cramp in cold water.

As the light failed outside its dirty windows, his unpleasant sense of expectation gradually evolved into an apprehension about a growing occupancy beneath the roof of Hunter's Tor Hall. He tried to assure himself that only his imagination was being affected by the atmosphere of a strange, abandoned building. But, as much as he tried to use his reason to defeat these impressions of an impending cohabitation, he remained sensitive to a feeling that the stale air was beginning to move itself in vague currents, as if it were being displaced by the entrance of new forms.

From outside the window came the distant sound of a man weeping. This was just after half ten, when visibility was shrinking by a few metres each minute.

What may have been another two voices outside came soon after the weeping passed away, but from separate directions.

Those who had called out gave an impression of being scattered in the gathering darkness and lost to each other. The noises may even have arisen from the beaks of birds, or even the muzzles of animals. One of the cries had reminded Seb of an anxious sheep.

He stood up and turned his torch on. He shone it at the broad window he'd sat beneath, to make certain that there was no one outside. And unveiled a smudge at the window.

His first thought was that it was a face, looking in. A near negative of a woman's face. Or maybe an after-image, transparent and almost part of the light's reflection upon the dirty glass.

Or had it been an illusion partly formed from the grime and the greying air outside?

Within his memory lingered the texture of the hair on what may have been a head, hanging dry and white about empty eye sockets. Seb turned about, in case what he had seen had been a reflection of *someone* standing behind him. His torch flashed across bare white walls.

Fearing he'd given his position away with the torch, he moved across the reception hall to the adjacent room at the front of the building. His breathing was so loud he imagined he was being followed by someone panting with excitement behind his shoulders.

Another face awaited him in the second room, as if summoned to the walls by his light. At a pane at the foot of a patio door, from within the inky surround of night, Seb detected an impression of human features stricken by despair. So deeply lined was the flesh, the head appeared ready to crumble. The piteous thing was also entirely bereft of hair.

The image blended within the grime on the glass and vanished almost as soon as he became aware of it, and he was left wondering again if he had seen anything at all.

He desperately regretted opening the shutters. Perhaps there was a good reason for the windows being blocked. Joyce had advised against using the torch because light was no asset here. Not using it might be the only way to get through the night. *Better only to hear them and not see their faces.*

Get through this he must.

Outside, the distant cries gradually increased in frequency and Seb wondered whether people or animals were passing the front of the Hall. Whatever roamed out there seemed to be lost amongst the long grass of the far terraces, and often wept amidst the beseeching sounds of what resembled words. Words that blended with the nocturnal cries of unsettled birds. Only the sudden howl of an animal in great distress finally forced him away from the front of the building altogether. That was around eleven.

Deeper inside the lightless Hall he ventured.

Sometime before midnight he crept inside an upstairs room, a former bedroom of the SPR. In the darkness he sat beside the door and huddled down.

A long period of time passed that he didn't keep track of. Looking at his watch seemed to make time trickle more slowly or even stop completely.

Inside that empty room he even dared to hope that he'd found shelter. Only within absolute darkness, when he developed a better sense of what he had come to share the room with, did his face and thoughts twist to a rictus.

Eyes swivelling within his skull, he detected a motion up near the ceiling, above the bed.

A terrible palsy came into his hands. His legs felt weaker than they had ever been. He fingered the torch and became better aware of a swishing motion, one gentle and interspersed with short exhalations. This was followed by an involuntary gasp, as if someone had been plunged into freezing water, near the ceiling. He feared a struggle was in progress, *up there*. There followed a raking of the air as if someone was being throttled or was drowning in the darkness.

Soon after, a faint illumination appeared in the air, on the other side of the room and at least six feet from the ground.

Or was that his eyes? It was so dark he no longer knew if he could see a light, or whether a colour was being projected from his own brain to alleviate the void about him. The frail glow didn't increase in intensity, but it was moving. Yes, it trembled or quivered and there grew a hint of moistness within the vague aura.

Witless with fright, Seb turned on the torch.

Whatever half-formed antics he partially lit on the ceiling, and only for a moment before he abruptly switched the torch off, gave him an impression that a form was suspended above the empty bed. And those had been limbs writhing and snatching at the empty air as if eager to reach the mattress below. He might have seen a thin hand too and a smudge of a sharp foot, kicking, or pushing at the empty air.

Might that have been an open mouth sinking upwards?

Seb went out of that room on his hands and knees, groping with his arms spread wide, his passage far too noisy for the stealth that he wanted so desperately. And yet, in the next room that he crawled into, whatever was already inside that space must have turned to him as he entered on all fours.

He heard its feet scrape across a floorboard and the shuffle of a body that wasn't his own.

Without thinking, he switched the torch on, and the beam seemed more intense than ever, a white transparent blade, cylindrical and bustling with dust.

The penumbra of the torch beam's circumference fell across one dirty corner. And in that corner he developed a notion, because he refused to look closely, that the space was occupied by a crouched form. One that may have been facing or looking into the wall. But even in his peripheral vision, he believed the form was both hairless and shivering. Something in that room was as white as a fish's belly and spiny with emaciation. When it appeared to rise upwards as if intending to stand, Seb killed the torch and scampered backwards. But into the wall he crashed, and then the door, painfully cracking his skull during his rout.

A condition of absolute darkness existed in the passage outside, and in that blankness he was beset by the dull rasps of several bodies rubbing against the walls, and close to the ground like dogs.

Seb stumbled to what he hoped was the top of the staircase, then feared a fall and risked a brief usage of the torch that was now jumping in his right hand.

He lit the stairwell and a portion of the passage below. A space empty mere hours before, but suggesting motion now. He had looked down there for little more than a fraction of a second before he killed the light. And in the chaos of his own mind, he then attempted to process what he'd glimpsed.

A blotchy scalp, straggling with wisps of colourless hair. An arm more bone than flesh that had reached up to delicately finger a bare wall. Little jerks of grey shapes near the front entrance, like unpleasant pets impatiently awaiting release. And all underlaid by the incoherent rustle of papery voices that seemed too quiet, or even too far away, from where the sounds emerged.

With his arms wrapped around his torso and his hands tucked beneath his armpits, Seb rocked himself back and forth on the stairs. Lips aquiver, his jaw worked hopelessly at the darkness as he mouthed words of nonsensical encouragement to himself.

Below, in the main hall, from where the sounds of water

now trickled, the dim sheen of the other occupants became visible without the aid of his torch. The only mercy being that they remained vague. But he closed his eyes tight on this sense of a small procession of figures that produced the pale phosphorescence as they fumbled their way blindly through the darkness of the lower building. Very little was revealed by the moist iridescence that issued from whatever hung from their navels, and for that he was also grateful. But from those wet abdominal stubs came the thin light.

Closed doors were no obstacle to these hinderers either. They simply seemed to come through them, or their motions and muffled whispers appeared where walls should have stood. Without light he was no longer sure that he was even inside the building.

My sister. She was . . .

That came from behind his back, from a room at the far end of the corridor. The broken utterance was followed by a faint sob. Seb found the strength and the will to move his legs again. Upstairs was becoming too noisy.

Back on the ground floor he never found any evidence of the water that he now heard bubbling like a brook.

The Passage.

Downstairs, closer to the earth, the Tor's internal darkness was more active than ever. Ahead of him and behind him, glimmers of mercury continued to appear and vanish. Partial evidence of articulated forms passed across his meagre sight, repeating like bits of film stuck in a projector. He wanted to believe his own disordered mind was screening these fragments on the inside of his eyelids, but his eyes were so wide they smarted as if they were open beneath the sea.

There was a great crawling in progress here, and perhaps

towards the vague recall of a lighter place that had once been known. Maybe this was a search for what had been left behind.

When the collective suggestions of the wasted became too much for Seb to endure, he shuffled towards the kitchens with one hand held outwards, while the other clutched at his car keys. But even squinting in the lightless spaces failed to rid *their* movements from within his mind.

Beyond the front entrance of the Hall, and as far down the lower terraces as his torchlight reached, the progress of the external hinderers appeared inexorable, slow, and then somehow too quick for his eyes to follow through the grass, as if they were flickering out of his vision to re-emerge from behind waves of darkness. But in the warm and salty rain that began to fall in the early hours of the morning, most of the hunched forms seemed intent on getting somewhere. Some did no more than stare upwards, but the thought of passing through them to reach his car was unbearable.

Too afraid to risk the night-blackened woods, Seb returned to the Hall. *This* had to stop, and soon, or he would lose more than his wits. He'd begun talking to himself inside his own head, but it took him some time to realize that his thoughts had become audible.

Downstairs was now too busy with the alumni, so this time he went up with his eyes mostly closed and his shaking hands sliding across the dirty walls to find doorways that he wished to avoid.

His eventual discovery of the now-unlocked door that opened onto the staircase that rose to the top floor was incapable of causing him any further alarm. He'd reached capacity. By the time he made it onto those stairs, he also seemed ready to escape from himself. He believed he would soon be forced from his own mind in search of a relief from the unrelenting terror being sustained within his skull. And he couldn't delay this any longer. His presence was clearly required.

Up there.

For a while he even believed himself to be alone in the very place where *he* had once lived: M. L. Hazzard, *the Master*.

Seb flicked the torch on to see where he was standing, and like his old friend, Ewan, he saw that he had entered a corridor made up of plain white walls and black doors. The floor was thick with dust, the air swollen with the silence of its vacancy.

Was the space holding its breath?

He helps those who come inside his house.

Seb rediscovered his voice. From a whimper to a croak to something much stronger, he began to speak aloud. And the sound of his voice was the only thing that kept a sense of himself in place between his ears. Talking also seemed to remind him of the contact between his feet and the floor-boards. 'I came! Are you here?'

Seb fell silent for fear that one of the six black doors might be pulled open from the other side.

He remembered a detail from Ewan's notes, and walked to the third door on the right. Opened it.

In the reflection on the window opposite the door, he watched himself walk into the room.

Inside the room, he saw the painting that Ewan had described. An oil painting of a boy. A boy sat on a chair. His hair was thick, curly and blonde. The child held a bear.

Directly under the painting sat the same red velvet armchair, with the same bear still sat upon the chair, propped up by a cushion. But it was a much older bear than the one depicted in the painting because this one's fur had been worn smooth in places.

Curiously, the room was bare save for what resembled props. A couch with the row of antique toys lined along the length of the seat, dominated by a large doll. This was an unappealing effigy of a baby girl wearing a hand-knitted cardigan over a white dress. Its hair may have been butchered by a child left alone with scissors. The shiny face was wide with surprise.

Another bear sat beside the doll, and then another doll made in the image of an imperial depiction of a Chinese man. The fourth doll was tiny and engulfed by a white smock. Its head was the size of a conker and jet-black in colour.

Upon the rear of an interconnecting door an old lace nightgown, made for a child, hung upon a hook.

To this place, the projectors of the SPR had once been trained to direct their astral bodies. Was that not what Ewan had undergone right here, an assessment? Had this room been some stage in a test? A place of significance to measure progress, before those hapless souls went further out, and beyond those black windows and into a misty void. Was it from here that a waterless stream was used by Hazzard, and from which it became impossible for so many to return?

Seb backed out of the room and closed the door.

In a second room he found the card table. It had been set out for four players. One card was uppermost before each chair.

There were empty bookshelves and a side table with three

ornaments arranged upon its surface: a glazed cockerel and two white ceramic bowls patterned with blue flowers. A silver drinks trolley lay disused and furred with dust.

Seb found the master bedroom to be as it was described in Ewan's notes. It was a woman's room. A large brass-framed bed remained in place, the lace-edged bedclothes neatly made. There was a little dressing table too, draped in white cloth, the top cluttered with antique perfume bottles.

A smaller dressing room was connected to the bedroom.

Seb shone his torch inside and the darkness receded, a shadow of black molasses withdrawing from the light. A wide alcove revealed a line of women's coats and dresses. Hat boxes filled the shelf above the dusty garments. At least fifty pairs of shoes, some heavily worn, covered the floor beneath the clothing.

Diane's room.

And it was always here. Always. Unlit. Behind these walls and in this echoing vastness of an empty building, this was here. Stale, unworn clothes. Furniture recoated with dross.

But was this room also a beacon?

A sudden sense of what reached away, stretching forever, beyond those black windows and above the roof of the Hall, made Seb want to curl into a ball and scream. The beam of his torch wavered as his hand shook.

He'd come up here for a sign, but was now succumbing to an influence. He could feel it. As each moment passed, an impression of the room's past, and of its occasional occupant, amplified within his imagination to a near unsustainable degree.

He felt more deeply uncomfortable inside his own skin than ever before in his life. The tiniest hairs covering his body extended. Their roots prickled electrically. A terrible anticipation of engaging with the unseen presence forced a whimper from his lips.

His expectation was soon similar to a physical pain and he turned clumsily to flee the room. The white beam of the torch cut across the standing mirror in the far corner of the bedroom.

Whatever sat upright in the mirror's reflection of the bed had flesh as pale as a bloodless body found frozen in arctic ice. But the figure was not sat up inside the actual bed, but only in the bed's reflection. His torch quickly confirmed that there was no bewigged head propped up by pillows, with a face painted clumsily, or even ruined to smears by tears, and so large upon a skeletal neck. No teeth the colour of ancient bones were grinning at him now.

Seb panted with relief.

But the room was not done with him and the air filled with a sweet musk. A scent cloud that bloomed to the glutinous pungency of the rose garden outside. About his head came a susurration of something silky.

He then became certain that his feet had risen from the floorboards. Seb even spread his arms for balance. All the blood in his head must have evacuated and left his mind reeling. He blacked out.

And awoke.

From the other side of the bedroom he found himself to be looking back upon himself. There he was, bent with fear, his mouth open in the idiocy of shock, his coat zipped up to the chin.

Seb adjusted his footing to dispel a sense that he was falling forwards. A wave in the sea might have been tipping him over. A queasy sliding of his vision followed, his panic caught in its uneasy wake.

Now he was no longer staring at himself, or outside of himself, but standing in the place on the opposite side of the room that he had just been staring at.

From the corner of his eye, a gliding motion inside the dressing room brought him about.

A sharp inhalation of air was drawn behind his ear.

The flat of a cold hand laid itself between his shoulders.

Seb whimpered, turned and illumined an empty bedroom.

He then directed the torch beam in the direction of the rustle inside the dressing room, to make certain that one of the long fur coats had not just stepped out from the clothing rack.

A black coat draped about a thin form. A pale head wearing a hat and dark glasses.

The torchlight failed to reveal anything.

The cold hand in the darkness touched him again.

Seb lurched for the door and fell into the corridor outside.

The door at his back slammed with enough force to pass a tremor through the entire building.

He sat up on the dirty floor and said, 'Please . . .'

He could hear nothing but the echo of the door slamming. He put his hands to his ears to dull the noise inside. His ears popped and he thought he might be sick.

When the nausea passed, Seb got back onto his feet and stumbled from the top floor. Torchlight raking the floor and walls, he ran through the long shadows that stepped backwards and inside the doors that he passed. And he kept his eyes averted from the fresh movements on the ceilings of the bedrooms. He looked away from the jostling grey patches that made him think of dead, wet skin. Only in the middle room, opposite the stairs that descended to the ground floor, did the urgent sounds of exertion, those exhausted grunts, draw his attention. And in that room he saw another partial form adrift in the air, mostly indistinct save for the stub that protruded like a dead umbilicus from a hollow stomach.

Out through the hallway and the kitchens he fled, shouting to himself to drown out the din of his own mind, and of what groped about his feet in the darkness, muttering.

He found the grass outside and there he fell twice. Back upon his feet, he ran round the house's walls and made it as far as the rose garden. Blind and wretched with fear, he found himself gripped with a need to find Joyce, to seek her protection and to settle Veronica's terms to end the night. But soon, nothing could have persuaded him to venture any further down that gravel track, between the walled garden and the night-drenched roses.

Seb turned off the torch and thought of throwing it away into the darkness in case he was tempted to turn it on again before the sun rose. He would not look upon what now circled the rose beds. And he would not see what moved in such numbers, through the trees bordering the path.

A crowd was feeling its way towards the Tor. All of those who had gathered were close to the ground and talking in incomprehensible voices. He could go no further and they were coming closer. Soon, he would be amongst them.

We'll have to go back, a woman's voice announced from nearby. *There is no light here.*

27
Shed the Body's Veil

The sun had been up for three hours when the two women found the writer in one of the large rooms at the front of the house. He was slumped in the threadbare easy chair that no one had used for more years than they cared to count.

His body was wrapped in an old, but beautifully pre-served, fur coat. His wide eyes did not move as the women entered the room. All of the shutters were closed. A heavy pall of stale perfume hung in invisible drapes about the chair.

The two women exchanged glances, until the one with the long hair began to sniff and dab at her eyes. She then raised her face to the ceiling and muttered as if to something that existed beyond the room. Eventually, she picked up the little rucksack that had been dropped beside the chair and peered inside it. 'Shall I fetch the spades?' she asked her companion.

The one with the short helmet of hair returned her disdainful gaze to the seated figure. She opened the fur coat that the writer had been wrapped inside and placed her hand against the man's chest. 'No. He's still breathing.'

She snapped her fingers angrily before his face but failed to illicit a response. 'He'll come back.'

'Oh, thank goodness for that! Shall I put the kettle on?' her companion asked.

'Please do. We'll pick up with him later to discuss terms.'

THE END

Part 3

THROUGH THE MIST

28
My Soul Rose Trembling

[SIX MONTHS AFTER I TYPED 'THE END']
'We don't like it,' Wendy said. 'I mean, is that supposed to be us? These . . . creatures? This Joyce? And this horrid Veronica? I don't think I've ever read anything as disrespectful in all my life!'

But you do have yellow teeth, and you do smell, and you are mad, and you are blackmailing me and extorting money from me. So what's your problem, Veronica? Oh, I'm sorry, I meant to say, Wendy. *And one more thing, your haircut is crap. I still don't know for sure, but I assume that you do it yourself with kitchen scissors, or maybe with a knife and fork. Or does Joyce – sorry, I mean,* Nat *– step up to the plate with a pair of garden shears and give you a trim? I used no artistic licence in my descriptions of your bloody head, besides changing the colour from a kind of ashy-dusty grey to blonde.*

'Yes, quite!' Nat said, encouraged by her partner. 'And our ideas, the very ideas of our organization, you have misrepresented them. I'm afraid this will do nothing for our reputation as an international society.'

Is that so, Joyce? Sorry, I mean, Natalie. But one never sees oneself as one is. Do any of us? You of all people should appreciate that. Though, as you lack even a shred of self-examination, or anything that could be regarded as reason, apart from the low animal cunning that drives your every move, then you would realize how loathsome, absurd and sinister both of you, and your 'organization', truly are.

And in my defence, I think I have rendered my association with your 'organization' with an unnerving similitude. And isn't this what you wanted: my imaginative interpretation of the wonders within your dear Master's vision, and of his illustrious society of projectors?

Well, that's what you got: the truth. And the funny thing is, as the Master has always claimed about his own less well-known 'work', besides changing a few names and hair colours, everything in my book is also true. It's all true. I wouldn't even call it fiction, I'd call it an account of a truly strange experience.

'I mean,' Wendy said, her face quivering with the anger that hadn't abated since she'd arrived at my door that morning, clutching the manuscript to her body, 'you've spent six months . . . Six months while we have waited and waited for this *book*, and yet you produce this . . . This *Yellow Teeth* thing? And whose teeth are these that you are referring to?'

I cleared my throat. 'Well, Wendy, it usually takes me over a year to complete a novel. But due to the extraordinary pressure of a deadline that you imposed upon me, and the abandonment of the book that I was writing . . . Not to mention the very vivid "material" that I have been privy to since making your acquaintance, I have been unusually inspired and motivated to complete this draft. I was also granted an extension by my publisher to fine-tune those details about the teeth, and other things.'

Wendy entwined her fingers into what looked like a bony mace and shook that knot of hand angrily. 'But you haven't changed all of the names! I mean, you are in it. *You*. You put yourself in the story! This book wasn't supposed to be about you, it was supposed to be about *him* and his life's work. This is unacceptable. It's not what we asked for. It's not what was required.'

'No, it's really not, Seb,' Natalie said. 'You've really been a grave disappointment to us. In fact, I am uncomfortably reminded of a similar experience that we had with your friend, Ewan.'

'Quite, Nat. Quite so,' concurred Wendy, nodding her head to add weight to their position.

Nat's own gorge rose. It seemed she'd waited a long time to *have a go* at someone. I don't imagine it has been easy living with Wendy for decades, and in that wretched hovel in the grounds of the Tor, in the service of him and the alumni of the API, or the Association of Psychophysical Investigation. At least, in the story, I did change the acronym of the API to SPR – not that anyone beyond a handful of people even knew anything about the API. 'You promise so much, you writers. And we've taken such a close interest in you, and we presented you with a marvellous opportunity, and provided access to miracles, and then . . . you produce *this*? You have assassinated us. You let us down, you let the API down, you let *him* down, you let yourself down.'

Wendy now looked at Nat with something approaching surprised admiration, though this quickly turned to what looked like resentment, as if Wendy had wanted to say these very things to Seb, but had been upstaged by her subordinate.

'Thank you, Nat,' she said in such a way as to prompt the end of her colleague's participation in the discussion.

I fought to suppress a smile of satisfaction. My revenge had been sweet and all that I'd done was write an accurate account of my recent experiences. But it would have been foolish to goad them any more. Despite the tone of the novel, I was sure that the publishing advance would deter them from taking revenge. There are times when being a disappointment as a writer is advantageous because freedom is the by-product. 'You asked for an interpretation of my experience of your organization, Wendy, and from the very moment that Ewan reappeared in my life. You wanted me to depict what you have devoted your lives to: *him*, Hazzard. Well, this is the honest result. I'm afraid I see you in a way that is remarkably at odds with how you perceive your-selves. And I can only write what I feel compelled to write. I'm afraid, as I told you, I cannot write to order. I have more integrity than that. And it's not as if *he* can even read it. So be grateful for what you have.'

The two women stared at me in silence. Their shock and suppressed rage seemed to suck the static electricity out of the room and into their quivering bodies. One of Wendy's eyelids even trembled above that discoloured, egg-yolky eye, and the eyeball appeared to distend from the eye socket. Her forehead purpled and I mused over her blood pressure.

'I know what this is,' Wendy all but spat at me. 'It's a smear. Revenge. A petulant attempt to protest your griev-ances. But that was not what we asked for!'

'Asked for? Is that how you would describe what you have demanded from me, ever since Ewan allowed your shadows to fall across my threshold, and to darken an existence that I was perfectly content with?'

'Oh no. No, no!' Wendy cried. 'We're not going through all that again. If you cannot see this as an opportunity, then that is not our problem. This book –' Wendy tapped the manuscript that she had thrown onto the coffee table – 'is nothing short of a smear campaign.'

'Then sue me for defamation and libel. After the book is published.'

Wendy's thin-lipped mouth worked about her dirty teeth but produced no sound. There was a flicker now in her second eyelid.

'Did you say, published?' Natalie whispered.

'Oh, yes. My publisher has accepted the manuscript. I sent an outline and the first few chapters to my agent some time ago. That's how it works, you see. Not that either of you would know anything about how this business operates. And that *thing* that occupies the top floor of the Tor wouldn't have a clue either, because he's been out of the loop for some time. But my publisher has offered me a new agreement for *Yellow Teeth*. They're very enthusiastic about this book too, and more so than the book I abandoned. In fact, they hope to publish *Yellow Teeth* at Halloween, this year.'

Wendy managed to swallow enough of her bile to speak, albeit in a strained whisper. 'How much are they offering?'

I told them.

'Dear God,' Wendy said. 'As much as that?' She glanced at the manuscript on the table. 'For . . . *this*?'

'Oh, yes,' I said. 'For that very novel, right there. *Yellow Teeth*. The manuscript has been accepted for publication.'

'I see,' said Wendy, the blossom of blood draining from

her face. 'And you took it upon yourself to proceed without discussing this with us.'

'I did. It's my book and my career.'

'Not exactly,' Nat offered. 'We have told you that you mustn't think about your writing in those terms any more. You are to facilitate the reintroduction of a significant set of ideas into the world.'

'Nat!' Wendy barked. 'If you don't mind!'

'I'm sorry, Wendy.'

Wendy turned again to me. 'This money . . . The advance, when will it be payable?'

'The signature and delivery portion within four weeks.'

That made Wendy grin, though spitefully.

Natalie closed her eyes and clenched her hands together as if she were thanking whoever had answered her prayers. 'Wendy,' she muttered in a pathetic voice, 'we can get the roof done . . . Some clothes—'

'It belongs to the API, Natalie, you know that.' Wendy then raised her chin so that she could peer down her nose at me. 'You will make the transfer without any delays.'

I nodded. It had taken a good long while for me to accept that the advance for the new book was gone, and all future proceeds too, if there were any. All would be paid to these creatures that stood before me. They were stealing from me. But by giving them the money, I knew that I was prolonging my life, and any quality of life that I could ever hope to enjoy.

I wanted to sleep again. And by this time in our association I would have done anything, paid anything at all, to have rid myself of Wendy, Natalie, and whatever it was that came and went on the top floor of Hunter's Tor Hall, this

Master that had imprisoned us and directed the killing of Ewan.

I had just enough money saved to support myself for another eighteen months, by which time I would need to secure another book deal, for the book that would follow *Yellow Teeth*.

I stood up. 'And that concludes our collaboration. I have your bank details and you will receive the monies agreed in due course. I'll even send you the royalty statements every six months so that you can see if the book has sold, and if the work has accrued any future income. You can even file the statements in the basement of the Hall, along with all of your other records.'

I showed them the palms of my hands. 'I have done what you asked, so I'll have to ask you two ladies to leave now. As we also agreed, you will never contact me again. Now, I have work to do. A lot of publicity to prepare for, in order to promote *our* new book. You see, it's a requirement for authors these days.'

Natalie sat forward on her chair. 'Leave? But we can't. Wendy, the *other thing*, are you going to mention it?'

Wendy nodded. 'Indeed. I was waiting for a suitable pause in our associate's version of events before I made a start.'

'Start?'

'If you please,' Wendy added, and even raised one calloused hand to silence me. 'And would you sit down. I think it is better if you hear this sitting down.'

'I'll stand.'

'As you wish. But we have been in receipt of a new directive, Sebastian.' She and Natalie both chortled at that. 'And this has come right from the top. The very top of our organization. And you know all about the top, don't you, Seb? The top floor and the highest executive level of our organization, which you were fortunate enough to have *visited* some six months ago. But it has come to our attention, and this is of the utmost urgency and importance, and one that will be treated with the strictest discretion by you, that a new opportunity has been put upon the table.'

'Forget it. We're done. We had an agreement. I wrote the book and that's all—'

'Alas, it is not for you, nor for me and my colleague, to make nor change the rules.'

'You agreed—'

'Circumstances can change. Agreements alter accordingly.'

'No!'

'Our leader's keen interest in returning to public life continues.'

It was time for me to shake my hands in the air. 'He's dead. Gone. You know that. No matter what you believe, Hazzard is no more. No one is interested in him, or his ideas.' I dropped my voice. 'I mean . . . look where it leads. Any attempt to revive the API is futile, and you know it.'

'Oh, really!' said Natalie.

Wendy grinned with the satisfaction of being back in the ascendant. 'He will never retire. He can't, for one thing. But he is very keenly aware of your connections and your ability to act as a broker on our behalf. He is also keen to begin a more direct collaboration with a writer, who will—'

'Forget it!'

'Who will take on certain editorial duties organizing *narrated* material. But the final words will be his and his alone.'

'No!'

'Be seated!' Wendy roared. Natalie jumped. 'Do you not know to whom it is that you speak? Do you still doubt the reach of the organization that we represent?'

When Wendy had finished shouting at me, her body continued to tremble and she made several gasping noises from the back of her throat. Natalie even placed her hand upon her colleague's shoulder, but Wendy shrugged it away with irritation. 'I think it's time for a story. I think a story is the best medium with which to express our new *intent*, and with which to seal an agreement for a new work.'

At that point, I remember holding onto the cabinet below the window, as I had begun to unconsciously back away, towards the balcony door.

This moving of the goalposts was not completely unexpected, despite every assurance that I had extracted from them during the previous six months. I had done all that I could to make them swear that their interest in me would never continue beyond one book, providing the book produced a sum commensurate with their expectations. They were broke and I had already exceeded their expectations.

If the book had not been commissioned, I would have given them my savings, because I had no choice. During the early hours of dawn, one morning half a year gone, in a ground-floor room at the Tor where they found me unconscious, they had also appeared to understand that a person could only endure so much of *their master* and his legacy. One night at the Tor had been sufficient for me. They must have seen that it would be unwise to push me any further in that direction. But the desperate care nothing but for their own desperation.

Characteristically, Wendy smiled with her mouth but not her eyes. 'There is a passage, a stream, that you are aware of, Sebastian. A place through which *he* passes. And the very place in which our former members still gather, and where we too will make our own search, one day.'

'Oh, yes, yes!' Natalie suddenly exclaimed and clutched at Wendy's hand as if this was something to look forward to.

Wendy relaxed into her seat. 'A place where the search for the higher spheres, for the celestial light of the paradise belt, continues. And there, our mentor and guide, our leader, has drawn unto himself a collection of . . . how shall I put this? A host of malignant forms. And even in their unfortunate and most frightful condition . . .'

'And how they suffer, how they still suffer, you cannot believe,' Natalie said.

'Our leader has considerable influence over how *their* activities are guided. Despite your disingenuous nature, I know that you have some awareness of what *it* is that I speak of. And so I would ask you to keep in mind the earthly name of one of the most unfortunate souls who has an associate membership in our current organization. His common name carried some notoriety for over a century, and the accounts of Thin Len's crimes are lurid. He was an idiot, a sadistic imbecile, and a ruthless killer of children in his earthbound days.'

'There is that woman too,' Natalie said, shaking with excitement. 'We mustn't forget her, Wendy. The woman once known as the Grey Lady in some local parts, but Choker Lotty by the press before she was hanged. She was a poisoner whose rage still burns as white as the vapours that she was said to have evoked from her own sister's belly . . .'

'Quite, Natalie. Her sister was carrying the child of Lotty's lover.'

Wendy had relaxed and momentarily closed her eyes after an unbecoming flutter that made her appear even more unstable than she was. 'Your old friend Ewan has met them both since he took his place amongst the alumni at the Tor. And we know that you have encountered at least one of them, in some distant, half-remembered form, and right here too.'

'Yes, yes,' Natalie said. 'I can confirm that Thin Len has passed by *here*. He knows how to find this place.'

'Exactly. The image was shared, was it not, Natalie? The two images were put together, here and *over there*.'

'The image was shared. We deplore such tactics, but in some special cases we're left with little choice. And alas, this connection has already been made.'

'It is said their passage is marked by a gliding, is it not, Natalie?'

'The gliding of the double it is called. And that which manifests, becomes corporeal, yes, yes, yes.'

'But for us to remove this bargaining asset from our ongoing relationship, we would require from you another work. One far more ambitious than the last.'

Wendy looked at the manuscript on the table and curled her lip with disapproval. 'A work that will see you find your utmost potential as a vehicle, a conduit, who will faithfully transcribe the experiences of our patron, and the wonders that he continues to behold. But, our dear Seb, you will not be the author, but more of a secretary, an assistant this time. It is time for a far more substantial and meaningful vision to see print than one that you could ever produce on your own.'

Natalie nodded rapidly. 'Quite. Quite. Yes. And there is a residential component, is there not, Wendy?'

'There certainly is. We would not be remiss in calling this a writer's residency at our beloved Tor.'

At this point I came to be sitting on the floor with my back against the sliding doors before the balcony. But I did manage to say, 'Never.'

'I'm afraid the wheels are in motion, Seb. You are to begin immediately.'

'I can't. Not *there*. Not again. Who . . . who could stand it?'

They meant for me to record Hazzard's strange experiences, but in that place. To actually live at Hunter's Tor and to endure *him* until my mind went out like the minds of those others who, even now, must still be circling the rose garden each night, while seeking the light that will never again shine upon their wretched faces.

'Your accommodation during this residency will be the gardener's cottage. That's far more suitable. It's been our home for many years,' said Natalie. 'We've been very happy there, haven't we, Wendy?'

'We've managed, Natalie. We've coped. Though I believe that our time in our leader's inner circle, on site, is also under review within this little reorganization that we are undergoing. Sometimes the old wood has to make way for new blood. Fresh ideas. New faces. And there's practicality to consider. If you are going to be working together, it makes perfect sense for you to live near *him*. An exchange, in effect. An exchange of living space. Though we'll all be working for the same side, our close presence will not be required quite so much, while you are hard at work on the new book. Our fundraising activities will be far better positioned . . . well, *right here*.'

'It is a lovely house,' Natalie said, and clapped her withered hands like a little girl. 'We've always enjoyed coming here and admired what you've done with the place, Seb.'

'Indeed, Natalie. You could say this house has become a prominent asset to the organization.'

'Indeed. Yes, yes.'

I finally broke my stupefied silence. I'd commented upon their mental state before, but couldn't resist repeating myself. 'You're mad. You think you can take my home . . . and deposit me out *there*, in that place?'

'And we can only hope,' Wendy said, elatedly, 'that you will feel *compelled* to record what will be shared with you, faithfully this time. We can only hope that it does not compromise your *artistic integrity*.'

'Agreed,' said Natalie, beaming. 'Because you don't have any *fucking* choice.'

29
Looking at Myself from Nothing

The psychic stream flows thickly through this place.

Those who have detached and who continue their search rarely bother me while I work. I'm not sure they are even aware of me. But I do see them, and often. Sometimes by day, but mostly at night.

When the sun goes down, I keep to the cottage because when I see *them* now, I see them more clearly, or they are better formed as my time in their presence lengthens.

I'll give you an example. Yesterday at dusk as the light dwindled, I came across a woman on the other side of the rose garden. Or, at least, I saw what was left of her between the vines and thorns. She had been wearing a hat with a wide, floppy brim, but her head was bowed as if she were searching for something about her feet, or even trying to locate her feet. I saw part of a lower jaw, the flesh stretched over the bone, the dirty teeth pronounced. I saw something of an arm, too, and one that was as thin as the branches of the plants that she crouched beside.

But I heard her voice clearly, as if she were still alive, and she said to me, 'It's not far now.'

She then asked if I had 'seen Sylvia', before informing me, 'She's not been well, you know.'

After that, the figure was no longer there at all.

Those I come across are trapped in repetitive trivialities. I often hear the same voices repeating the same phrases inside the rose garden where Hazzard's ashes were scattered by the last handful of his followers, one grey morning in 1984. Or so I have learned from the records in the archive. But there are many here that are best avoided, because they rage blind against the invisible cords that bind them. I cannot endure their antics. I move on from where they thrash in nothingness.

In my sleep, each evening, I follow the sound of the stream and the wet, grey procession until it vanishes. I often find myself trapped before a wall inside the building, the place to which they all scurry in panic or ecstasy.

Sometimes I find myself dreaming that I am far away from the house, but still inside the grounds. I am on all fours, begrimed, and talking to myself as if I have a fever.

Awake, I can never locate the stream. I often hear it, rushing nearby, in various parts of the grounds when I go out to walk. Finding the confines of the study stifling, as I wait each morning for that voice to rise from the unlit, shuttered places that abound inside the building, I go out.

He comes to those who have entered his house in many ways. Sometimes, as I sit still with my eyes closed against the bustling darkness, I await the first image to bloom inside my mind.

There can be nothing for me to write for days, and I kid myself that this intermittent hinderer activity has finally lifted from the dead building and perhaps moved further downstream. Or maybe it has stumbled out of its captivity to enter the light. But it doesn't work like that, not for *them*.

They seem to have forfeited any right to what they sought so many years ago. Their frantic scrabbling at the air to get back inside what no longer lies below, dead-eyed upon a bed, is also made in vain.

The Master's voice, on the rare occasion that I hear it, suggests a fussy and brittle temperament. And sometimes I hear this self-important intonation and, despite the great gulf that divides us, I sense that this presence remains acutely sensitive about its appearance and status, and might be easily offended. I fear that no slight would ever be forgotten. Achieving its will over others is still very important. So I refrain from causing injury.

Hazzard speaks but never manages to complete much of a thought, let alone an actual tale.

He most often adopts the female persona, Diane, and there is just as much mimicry involved in the tone of Diane's voice as there was in Hazzard's original masquerade here, on this earthbound side.

But I have seen Hazzard and Diane. I am sure I have, though it can be hard to tell them apart from the others, who hinder and crawl about the floor here, or who suddenly seize themselves upon a ceiling and bay like hunting animals. Many do nothing but stand and stare, as if forgetting why they are here, or even who they once were. And as they forget *what* they were, I fear they wither. I fear they transform into something baser that is wounded and cornered.

Sightings of Hazzard are as rare as his intermittent communications. Hearing these bursts of his speech is like trying to tune an old radio, with an aerial insufficient to the task of locating transmissions. His narration forms fragments of sentences that seem to be directed at someone else in another time, or even another place, that I partly overhear. But I start typing what I catch, in case it is an experience that is required for *our* collection.

He has found other ways of communicating with me too. After I have awoken in my chair in the front room – and how I dream so vividly now – I wrap my coat about myself and I stumble to the typewriter. Upon the letterheaded paper that has been supplied, I then type frantically, to catch the impressions of *his* visions before they vanish from my mind.

Only last week, after I had just finished narrating an experience that left me weak and shaking, I received a sense that something was *standing* outside the study. *It* was in the corridor between here and the dining room, where I take my small meals.

I know he had been aware of me that time. Perhaps the faint tapping of the typewriter keys had carried to . . . but to *where?* I don't really know.

I moved myself out of the chair and swiftly to the door of the study and I called out what I had wished to say for some time. I asked *him* for mercy. I cried out and said I could not continue for much longer, that the visions were becoming too much, that when they dispersed from my head they drew my mind out from my body.

You see, there are places on this earth that help us to get out of ourselves, that make us enlarge in spirit, and this is one of them.

But in that corridor outside the study, I caught sight of an iridescence that hindered. Rags of a soul-body, and those shreds fled as if Hazzard had been disturbed in his bathroom, and was gripped by a mortification at the sight of his own unclothed form.

Withered were the smears of the Master's legs too. Out-stretched were the bones upon which Hazzard's sharp fingers trembled to a blur. But the fingernails were painted a dark colour, so I assumed that it was Diane that time. I could smell her too, and that day she smelled like the rank water left in a vase, once the roses have all died.

Quickly, she grew smaller in my sight, as if she were skit-tering down a slope that could not have existed inside that passage. And yet I perceived evidence of a black wig, one too static and clumsily propped upon a small skull, as if to re-enact some former period of glamour that was once enjoyed amidst a coterie of admirers.

At other times, Diane is better put together, and when I hear her tipped heels approaching, I make sure to get down upon the dusty floor and to avert my eyes.

At those times, Diane will wear a black wig, a hat and dark glasses and cover herself as much as she is able. To catch sight of her face in a reflection can produce a terrible shock that makes me fear for my heart. The sudden crushing pressure of the air through which she stares, the miasma of the scent, the horrible, queasy flopping inside my belly as if I am being turned upside down, but finding nothing below my feet, is too much to bear for more than moments. One can never get used to it.

Only during those rare appearances do I get a sense that she knows I am here, or at least has a sense that someone inhabits these rooms below her, like a rat. A rat that scratches its fingers upon the typewriter's keys.

When Hazzard comes in his male form, he rises in rooms adjacent to those that I rest within. At these times, I imagine that the double is in a grim mood. I judge this by the sounds that come through the walls. I imagine him squinting too, as if near-sighted, as he pants with rage and utters those bitter, indecipherable exclamations and gropes about the empty rooms, feeling his way about the grimy walls, looking for his past, I think. Or maybe he even searches for another who is no longer around. Who can say what it is that the restless dead still seek?

Alas, the entire collaborative venture is futile, and I have done all that can be done. I have fashioned enough material for three experiences within my first month at the Tor. I have often said aloud, 'These *strange experiences* have no commercial value. Not any more.' I have tried repeatedly to tell him that his ghastly snatches of the numinous are destined for an even greater obscurity than he knew before.

I have called out, 'There is no future for you! Not out there! Not now!' But I don't think he hears because the visions keep returning and forming, and I see again and again the sights that have made my hair whiten, and that have shrivelled me inside and left me trembling and sobbing against the hard floors of the Tor, or slumped upon the typewriter and unable to rouse unless others come and slap my cheeks hard.

Others.

There are others in his service beyond the two women who call themselves Wendy and Natalie, and who arrive at the end of each week to take my papers away.

As 'Mark Fry' said, local people do put boxes of food outside the gates, the food that sustains me. I've never seen anyone make the drop-offs, but I have heard distant car engines and the strident sound of a car horn. It blares three times in the distance to let me know that such basic food-stuffs, and often expired dry goods, have arrived. When I arrive at the gates the car has gone and the box of food is in the grass outside the wall. I think they spit onto the food.

This locally sourced food supply sustained the last of the API too. Their story is in the files. I have read over half of them now.

Such wonders and terrors abound in the archive. The two emotions were inextricable for those who once *detached*.

I suspect that Natalie is a local girl who was once asked to come inside to function as a nurse for the dying Master and who was never permitted to leave. Few names are entered in the later files, but I suspect her real name is Eunice and that she arrived in 1982. You see, there was once a 'Eunice' who changed the beds and bathed the bed sores until the entries in the archive ceased in 1986. She seemed to be the only member of staff who was still carrying out these duties two years after 'the Master' died in 1984.

And I am fairly certain that Wendy is actually the 'Ida' of the files, who travelled here during a rootless period of transience in 1981, and who seems to have since imposed herself as a spokesperson for the API, and heir-apparent to Hazzard's domain.

These two characters, Eunice and Ida, who have remained loyal after his passing, were the very same individuals who must have lit the fires beneath the two remaining and very elderly 'projectors' and acolytes – Faye and Alice – who expired within long comas in the rooms upstairs that were once named Elysium and Summerland. These amateur cremations both occurred in 1984. The coincidence of both deaths occurring in the same year did not escape me, and left me wondering if both 'first deaths' were hastened, and if Faye and Alice were burned alive.

I can only imagine that Eunice and Ida arranged for the disposal of the remains of Fay and Alice so that there were no impediments from the authorities, or distant relatives, to hamper the continuing work of the Association of Psycho-physical Investigation, with its rigorous schedule of projecting, and its sundry fundraising activities. Perhaps they even grew tired of attending to the invalids. But this is supposition on my part.

The ashes of the final projectors were either scattered amongst the roses, or if their bodies didn't burn properly, as had been indicated within records made in 1979 and 1981, when others also suffered the same tawdry fate of expiry and burial at the Tor, the carcasses of the poor old wretches would have been rolled into shallow trenches. Some of those were dug by Ida in 1981. I have to imagine that Hazzard ordered it.

To the API there are first deaths and second deaths, and then eternity. I fear all three, but the latter condition the most.

I suspect too, that one day, Eunice and Ida, under their guises of Natalie and Wendy, anticipate performing the same crude disposal of my own physical remains, once this work has finally destroyed me.

Nonetheless, the sound of my frantic typing can be heard all over the building. One writes to live, and it has always been thus.

I am working on a third strange experience now, drawn from the usual fragments of nightmare gibberish. This latest was given to me three nights ago. I woke, trying to scream, certain that a cold hand had been placed over my mouth and nose within total darkness. On my awakening, the very room was full of the smell of dead roses.

I will give you the first lines that came to me with such urgency, in something of a verse narrated by Diane, in a sing-song voice:

> '*I hang in space above water.*
> *I am pupae.*
> *My face is no more.*
> *I am sure that I came from down there,*
> *So with these arms that I cannot see,*
> *I reach to where the bed must be . . .*'

I put one copy of the completed pieces – as *finished* as they can be – inside the files in the basement for safekeeping, and then I type another copy for my agent, to whom they will assuredly go.

Poor Giles.

30

In the Body of my Resurrection

After my literary agent, Giles White, depressed the buzzer a third time, I imagine that he stepped back from the door and took a better look around himself.

This was just not like *me* at all, and even the closed blinds would be less alarming than the sight of the rear garden. The lawn at the back and the four flower beds that I had once tended so carefully were not so much overgrown as engulfed. The garden had returned to the wild. The sun umbrella on the lawn had not been taken down for some time and the canvas was mildew-green. Beside the front door, bin bags were stacked beside an already full wheelie bin.

Giles had visited the house many times since I'd moved to the coast, but on this visit it must have appeared that the mind of the occupier had withdrawn from the external world. And perhaps to huddle within incessant preoccupations, deep inside the building. Nothing unusual there for a writer, as Giles would know, though not *this one*. Not Sebastian Logan.

He knew that I despised uncleanliness and disorganization. In fact, he may even have interpreted *Yellow Teeth* as evidence of an author working through issues on this very subject. Particularly when considering the years that I had spent struggling on low incomes, while living in bedsits and shared accommodation, and into my forties. Giles knew that story.

The plot of *Yellow Teeth* had concentrated on the theme of intrusion too, but of a particular kind: the imposition of the chaotic and disorderly into the life of the orderly, the unclean forced upon the clean. I'd even depicted myself as the lead character, and a horror novelist at that, living in this very house.

The biographical detail, this casting of myself as the protagonist, had been met with enthusiasm by my publisher. They'd liked the angle of *Yellow Teeth*. Giles had also been thrilled by his own inclusion in the story, as my actual literary agent.

I had told Giles to 'come at midday' in my last message. That had been sent two weeks before, and the last time that I had been permitted to enter my own home. I'd also mentioned that I had been unwell and unable to travel to London, and that 'leaving the area' made me 'uncomfortable these days'. I'd been impossible to contact by phone too, because there is no phone signal at the Tor.

Ten foreign-language editions had already been negotiated for *Yellow Teeth*. Queries about film and TV rights were also stacking up. A decision would have to be made soon about which film production company we chose to go with. Even without the full proposals that I had promised to write, there was talk of a new two-book deal. Deadlines needed to be set down. My editor even claimed that *Yellow Teeth* possessed the strange edge that had been missing since my first two novels. *How dare she?* But, nonetheless, there was urgent business to discuss. Which is why Giles had travelled to Brixham to investigate me.

I imagine out there on my front doorstep, his annoyance became anger – *Does he no longer care about his future?*

He'd have heard a bolt slide through a lock, a chain removed from a latch. Then the door widened to reveal my face. A visage that was hard to identify.

'Seb . . .' Giles didn't know what else to say to me.

How long had it been since I'd washed my hair? And in all the years he'd known me, I'd never worn a beard. Beards were certainly fashionable, though mine suggested anything but the hipster. My get-up that day was hobo.

Though my hair had always been flecked with salt and pepper, it was now the colour of dirty snow, oily and matched by the ragged beard. My appearance was worsened by the jogging bottoms and the stained shirt that I wore beneath the bathrobe. Giles almost suppressed his distaste at the spectacle of my face, and how my features had been narrowed by weight loss, lined with anxiety and harrowed by misery. All compounded by sleeplessness. *And Jesus Christ, the teeth!* He must have noticed my mouth. A mist of halitosis would have clung to the threshold. When was the last time that I had seen a dentist? Within the tangled moustache and beard, my lips had begun to appear too dark. I'd seen them in the windows of the Tor, as the sun faded outside. Giles would have glimpsed the wet, yellow ivory in my poorly maintained mouth.

Yellow Teeth.

He just stared, aghast at the transformation of his once neat, unflashy, shy client, whom he considered a friend.

'Giles. It's been a while. You look well.'

'It has been.' Giles couldn't bring himself to return the compliment.

'Won't you please come in?' I turned away from the door. *I've seen enough*, must have come to the tip of his tongue, though Giles would never be so rude, unless he was talking to an editor.

He followed me up the stairs and into the living room on the second floor.

'A drink?' I mumbled, without even looking at Giles, but I wafted one hand towards the uncapped bottle of bourbon on the coffee table.

'No, thanks.' It was only noon.

Giles also restrained himself from asking for the balcony doors to be opened, but I saw him look at them. The room reeked of fried food, my sweat, expensive perfumes, and what suggested an unemptied kitchen bin.

He took a seat on the side of the couch not filled with laundry that was either waiting to go into the washing machine or had come out and been forgotten about. How did I know? It wasn't my laundry.

Giles peered around the room and at the soiled plates amongst dirty coffee cups and magazines. My bookshelves were all but empty. My framed pictures of the original cover artwork and the movie posters had been removed. 'Your pictures?'

'Gone,' I said, as I eased myself into a seat opposite the couch. The only light in the room was thin and murky, and was cast from the table lamp beside the bookcases. 'Sold,' I said, and I looked at the walls as if trying to recall the pictures.

'Sold? Why?' Giles knew that I couldn't be short of money. I'd always been careful with money – a little tight, if Giles were honest – and even after his fifteen per cent and the tax deductions by HMRC, I could not have been left wanting after the advance of *Yellow Teeth*. The advance had already been earned out by foreign rights sales.

I could only shrug. 'This place too. It'll go next . . .' And then I stopped myself and glanced at the door. As if on cue, a toilet flushed downstairs, followed by a door opening and closing.

I had company.

Right then, Giles noticed that several items of discarded clothing didn't belong to me, a large brassiere and a pair of opaque, patterned tights.

He looked to me for some direction, some explanation, but none was forthcoming. I continued to stare at the dining-room door in anticipation of one who would soon step through it. 'They'll be here soon,' I said, and my bearded mouth settled into a sneer. 'They want to be present.'

'Who?' Giles asked.

I never answered him.

'Seb. Are you . . . I mean, are you all right?'

'Do I look it?' My bloodshot eyes had filmed and glistened with tears. 'Seeing you, my old friend, just brings it back.'

'What?'

'How it was. Before.'

'I don't follow. Before what, Seb?'

And then Giles's attention was drawn towards the door, and to the arched entrance of the kitchen beyond the dining room. Giles even started at the sight of the two women who had appeared, as if from thin air, and who now stood within the two entrances.

The woman with the long hair, dyed a vivid magenta, seemed barely able to contain her excitement, though what she was so ecstatic about escaped Giles. The second woman, with the short blonde hair, smiled at him, but not in any way that could be described as warm. Her expression was close to provocation, as if she had just caught us talking behind her back.

Giles stood up. 'Hello.'

He looked to me to prompt a round of introductions. But I continued to gaze, morosely, at the ceiling.

The woman with the short hair came into the room and sat on the arm of my chair and Giles must have noticed how I withdrew from her presence as she sat down. She wore a black dress complemented by bright costume jewellery. Expensive glasses framed her carefully painted eyes.

The second woman came out of the kitchen, but sat at a distance and at the dining table. She drew out a chair carefully as if she had entered a crowded room while a speech was in progress. She was wearing one of those gossamer, hippy-chic dresses and high-heeled shoes.

'Well. Introductions are in order,' said the woman who'd sat beside me.

'This is Wendy,' I said, without looking at the woman on my left. 'And that's Natalie,'

'Pleased to meet you. Giles White,' Giles said, looking from side to side in bemusement as the room bloomed with the scent of Chanel perfume.

'It's been so exciting to see the last book received with such enthusiasm,' Wendy said. 'And we're delighted to tell you that Seb has been working on something else, something very special. Though we think the publisher can do a bit better with what they pay him for his work. Particularly as there'll be nothing else like it, *out there*.'

I watched Giles shift in his seat. 'Sorry, who are . . . ?' He turned away from Wendy's amused and mocking face. 'Seb, I'm sorry, but we really should be discussing this more formally. Why don't we take a walk? We could pop into that pub we went to last time—'

'What's wrong with here?' Wendy asked. 'And you don't need a pub to get drunk in. Seb's happy to do that anywhere these days.'

I lowered my eyes to the floor when she spoke about me. I felt my thin body shudder within that wretched bathrobe.

'But he's been very busy,' Wendy added. 'Hit a rich vein. You could say he's been channelling something unique.'

Maintaining a stiff smile, Giles struggled to restrain his temper. 'There's material for the new book? Is that so, Seb? I must say, it's all news to me.'

'Well it would be, wouldn't it, with you so far away, with your lunches and things, your authors and parties in London?' Wendy emphasized 'London' as if she had singled the city out for particular scorn.

'Wendy,' Giles said, in a voice that was barely keeping a lid on his crimson thoughts, 'would you mind if I spoke to my client alone? We've some business to discuss. That's why I am here. That's why I have travelled all the way down from *London*. Isn't that so, Seb? To discuss business with *my* client.'

'We have a full involvement in our *partner's* work,' Wendy said. 'There's nothing about Seb or his books, or his agreements with you, that we are not conversant with, Giles.'

'Seb?' Giles said. His bewilderment waged a war with his anger at this woman's manner. And yes, the more he considered the situation, the more aware he became of the tension that the women had introduced into the room. I could read it in his eyes.

Was one of these women my girlfriend, then? He must have wondered. He glanced again at the washing piled beside him. The underwear looked expensive, as did the dresses, though they didn't appear particularly well cared for, strewn about like that, like territorial markers.

He would struggle to accept my romantic involvement with either of them. He would have been equally mystified by what either of them saw in me, in that state.

'Nat!' Wendy said, and so suddenly that Giles flinched. 'The outline, if you please.'

'Oh, oh. Of course. Let me fetch it.' Natalie rose from her chair and teetered into my office.

'Seb?' Giles tried again to reach me. 'Seb, can you tell me what this is about? We've several important matters to discuss.'

I merely shrugged, my posture suggesting the haplessness that I felt.

That was the first time that Giles had looked upon me with pity too.

Nat bustled into the living room and handed the old paper file to Giles. 'The proposal!' Breathless with glee, she added, 'People will be astonished!'

'Will they, now?' Giles replied. He took the file from Nat's outstretched hand. I watched her fingers tremble, and the sight of her yellowing nails made Giles recoil. She'd transformed herself into something feminine, but forgotten to pay attention to her hands.

'Nat,' Wendy said sharply, and glared with disapproval at her friend, if that's what Natalie even was.

'I'm sorry. But it's just so exciting!' Natalie said. She came and sat beside me, on the other arm of the chair. Tentatively, she reached out a veiny, quivering hand and placed it upon my shoulder.

Giles glanced at the folder in his hand. 'API' was stencilled at the top of the file. *API, what does that mean?* I watched my agent's confusion increase. There couldn't have been more than three sheets of paper inside the file. 'Seb, what is this?'

'We've told you what it is. The proposal. Isn't that what you need?' Wendy said.

Giles opened the file and the scent of old card became noticeable in the room. He looked at the letterheaded API folio, all browned with age around the edges. He began reading the first paragraph.

Wendy and Nat extended their heads towards him, like hungry birds inside a dirty nest.

After several minutes, Giles looked up at me. 'What is this, Seb? An outline for a short-story collection?'

'Something far more ambitious than *Yellow Teeth*,' Wendy said, her own grin back in place, while she wrinkled her nose at the mention of my last novel. 'We think he may have missed the point in *Yellow Teeth*. You could say, he may have missed the boat entirely. But that book served a purpose, didn't it, Seb? Kept it all going. Though this is a far more accurate and comprehensive vision of *his* ideas.'

Giles ignored Wendy. 'Is there any more of this, Seb?'

'Of course,' Wendy said. 'Nat. Bring it in. He might as well begin as he's finally deigned to visit us. No time like the present.'

'Bring what in?' Giles asked.

'Oh, you'll see!' Nat said, her voice breaking into a squeal, before she returned from my office carrying a thin pile of printer paper, pinched at the top by a red paperclip. Nat dropped the manuscript in Giles's lap before returning, somewhat clumsily in her shoes, to sit beside me.

Giles glanced at the cover page: *The Hades Intake. 12 Strange Experiences.* It was dedicated to 'Our Master, M. L. Hazzard'.

I caught a combination of recognition, and an even deeper confusion, filling Giles's eyes. He'd recognized the name Hazzard immediately, as he was a character in *Yellow Teeth* – the cross-dressing leader of the SPR. Giles frowned. *Strange experiences*: that's also what the author, Hazzard, had called his own stories in *Yellow Teeth*. 'This is some kind of sequel then, to *Yellow Teeth*?' he said this distractedly.

Wendy raised her thick black eyebrows and answered for me, as she had done all afternoon. 'In a manner of speaking. But this is the best thing he's ever written down.'

'Yes. We're quite a team,' Nat added. 'We share everything.'

Written down? An odd expression, and Giles stiffened when he heard it. 'A team? Seb, is this a bloody joke?' Giles shook his head. 'Seb. This is a short-story collection.'

'Oh, no,' Nat said, correcting Giles. 'They're not stories. They're *experiences*. Strange experiences. And this material has been in the works for some time.'

'Please, begin. We're not going anywhere,' Wendy said, and nodded at the thin manuscript that lay in Giles's lap, which seemed to be growing heavier as each second of the madness continued.

'Begin?' Giles said. 'Seb, you know that Pan won't accept a collection of horror stories. No serious publisher will. We're all expecting a novel. Is this a digression while you work on a new book? A companion piece to *'Teeth?'*

'It's what *he* wants, isn't it, Seb?' Wendy added.

He, an unusual and reverential emphasis on a pronoun for an author too. Wendy hadn't been referring to me either and that really baffled Giles.

Giles raised his hands, palm upwards. 'What the hell is going on here?'

Characters: yes, that's what Wendy and Natalie were becoming in Giles's mind too. And as he reinterpreted the two women in that room, I knew that his scalp had receded beneath his hair. Right then, he must have thought of *Yellow Teeth* – the story of a writer whose life had been taken over by a sinister organization of astral projectors.

Joyce and Veronica. The two women in the story . . . The women of the SPR. And *SPR was very similar to the API?*

Giles began to smile. *A joke.* Yes, he thought it was all a joke. I must have set him up! This was an elaborate practical joke because what he had in his lap was a sequel. And for half a second he was convinced by his own theory.

But the garden . . . the bins . . . and Seb's appearance . . .

Giles and I held each other's eyes and Giles knew in a heartbeat that there wasn't a trace of humour or mischievousness in his client's thoughts.

Natalie and Wendy each acknowledged the moment too, in which the penny had dropped for my literary agent.

Briefly, and judging by his pallor, I think Giles may then have entertained an image lingering from his reading of *Yellow Teeth*. I believe he might have imagined a long form, with its head covered by a dirty sack, crawling along the wall of the very building in which he sat.

He dropped his eyes and read the opening line of the first story, entitled, 'We Are Unshrouded. We Have Enlarged'.

I know the opening line off by heart, because it was the first thing that M. L. Hazzard ever communicated to me, during my third morning as the writer-in-residence at the Tor.

'And out of the trees they come, the thin people. They cry with joy because one of them says she has seen the light. They all vanish into the tunnel and fall silent.'

31
River of Darkness

'They betrayed you . . . See how they live now. See! They have deserted you. Enriched themselves. They embezzle the organization. They have grown rich while you waste away here. Where are they now? Tell me? Where are Eunice and Ida? Where are Wendy and Natalie? Where? Where are they? Where are those who have changed their names to throw you off their scent, and who try to live without your guidance in another place entirely? Do you sense them here, ever? No, because they have gone. Flown. They have left you all alone. They have chosen comfort over the mission! They have no interest in your plight. They have forsaken your greatness.'

I have lain upon Diane's bed, night after night. With my eyes shut tight I have spoken aloud to the darkness when the house is at its most populous. I have said these things and many other things too.

Did you think that when you speak alone that no one hears you? Have you no idea of what glides beside you, briefly, but intent, unsure of itself or its whereabouts, but snatching, with much transformed hands, at the fading echoes of your words that appear in another place, like over *there*?

Trust me, eventually, *something* will hear you, if you choose the right place and the right time.

By day, after so many exhausting nights, I have crept inside the rooms that were once occupied by the living M. L. Hazzard and his female persona, Diane. And upon this insecure ground I have planted my seeds, and I have nurtured them with narratives.

I have laid out the pictures of Wendy and Natalie, all about the rooms. Upon the dresser and the side table, upon the floor and the pillow cases, I have placed their images.

I have fitted their likenesses within the mirror frames from which *he* looks out, and I have placed their faces in the pockets of the empty garments. I have redecorated the walls of Hazzard's rooms with the pictures that I took of these women in my old home. There are no cards left on the card table, only their faces, upturned: Natalie and Wendy.

At the end of each week, when the women collected me from the Tor and took me home from my residency, for a few hours so that I could administer and maintain their deception, I took the pictures and I printed them.

If Wendy went out to shop, or to sun herself on my balcony, and while Natalie was charged with the task of watching me closely, I took pictures of Natalie instead of taking care of the tasks that they had set for me: paying the household bills, corresponding with my agent and publishers, or making purchases with my credit cards to supply each of them with the luxuries with which they have become so fond, since taking up residence in my life and home.

Yes, I took pictures of Natalie with her newly set hair, napping in my room. I took pictures of Wendy asleep on the sun lounger on the balcony, during the high summer months.

I have discreetly taken pictures of those stalwarts of the API dining and drunk on wine, from my wine rack. I have surreptitiously photographed them sleeping and awake. And amongst the pictures of them, I have intermingled the pictures of my home, inside and outside, when it was a place to be proud of, even beautiful. I have taken these images and I have placed the images in another place, so that they can be *seen*. So that two things can come together.

I have recorded my voice too, and one that repetitively intones my case and reinforces their deception. Until its battery fades, I have played the phone to announce details of this betrayal in Diane's dressing room and bedroom, in case *she* ever wearily manages to return and affect her ghastly, but hopeless, occupation of those dim, forgotten and decrepit places that lie in darkness, deep in Dartmoor.

And when she had lingered and touched her once-fine garments with those vaporous bones, there was a chance that she would hear me calling out to the darkness, a place where a certain stream crosses over the land of the living. A place where so many wills were renounced unto the deep.

I plotted with the dust and the shadows, and with those things that still staggered and stooped and crawled through there. Down on my knees did I go, into the nightly stream of the grey and the withered, and I spoke aloud to the lost.

I chattered like an ape about the grave betrayals that had taken place, and of how the living servants of the projectors had abandoned their posts, and left all to crawl eternally in darkness with no hope of light.

I said their names in every corner and empty room: *Eunice, Ida, Wendy, Natalie. Traitors!*

'Help those who have come into your house!' I screamed

in the lowest and darkest places of that building, while clawing my face.

Dressed in Diane's finery, in those stale rags, with my beard flowing and my yellow teeth bared at the sky, I have circled the rose garden for many nights, with *the others*. And I have bellowed out my case. 'Betrayed! Betrayed! Master, you are betrayed!'

And in the black woods where so many crawl and whimper, I have also pleaded my case. 'Doctor, your staff have gone! They ran away! Abandoned you! You are abandoned on the earthbound sphere!'

After eight weeks, I had nothing left to lose save that part of *me* that still glowed and sometimes flickered, a dimming ember that would soon have been doused forever.

I know that I was eventually heard. And I know that the good doctor was most displeased. I filled my ears with rags at those times when he roared, and when he raged.

'Tonight, they will come. Look upon their clothes, the finery. Smell the scents that they have drenched their treacherous bodies with. See those, see *them* who have betrayed you, abandoned you, left you . . . Bring them across and let them answer to these charges. Len! Len! Len! Thin Len will deliver them unto you!'

It had to happen that night, on a Friday when I expected the weekly inspection and the collection of my pages. Once I lit the fuse there was no going back for me.

In the cellars I had found the cans and bottles and containers of white spirit and paraffin and gasoline for the old lawnmowers that must have once roared upon the terraces when Hazzard had been living; when he had stared out from the top floor of the Tor, to survey all that he was master of. And with those flammable fluids I soaked the basement.

The very files of the projectors I used as tapers and wicks, fuses and kindling. Every copy of *Theophanic Mutations* by Mark Fry was reduced to nothing more than a reeking fuel itself, torn apart and laid out in the rooms of the alumni. I soaked everything that was hazardous and combustible.

Perhaps that night when the alumni returned to writhe upon the ceilings, and to crawl through the dim corridors, even they would have seen the lights of the fires like a beacon. I like to think so.

Whether I was to circle the rose garden for all eternity, or to walk from that place a freed but much-changed man, I had decided that Friday would be the day to herald my awakening.

Whatever befell me that night, I knew that I would not spend another night as the only living soul at the Tor. It's the one lesson that the API refused to learn since its inception, that everyone has a limit. And by then, I had truly gone some way beyond my own.

I hid from Ida-also-known-as-Wendy, and Eunice-also-known-as-Natalie.

I did not meet them at the gate at the prescribed time, the usual time. I made them come up, *come back*, to the house.

They didn't like that either. By this time in our one-sided arrangement, I am sure that they never wanted to see Hunter's Tor Hall again, let alone set foot inside the grounds. But they arrived in my car and they came up through the trees to find me. From the top floor, I watched them moving slowly up and through the grassy terraces, one level at a time. And I hid from them.

They looked in the cellar, they looked in the cottage, they looked in the woods and in Elysium and Summerland, and inside every other room from which the projections were once made.

I heard their cries when they saw the signs of my desecration, of the emptying of those filing cabinets, the strewing about of the organization's history.

I heard their frantic footsteps pause at the bottom of the stairs that led up to *his* rooms, and to the white corridor with the black doors.

Like the scratching of mice beneath the floors of old houses, I heard their tense, sibilant whispers. They argued, I think, about who was to venture up those stairs, to see if the writer was hiding up there, where he had been forbidden to go – in the very place they had said was no longer safe for anyone to set foot, not even themselves.

They moved away, and I heard the heels of their new shoes, upon their weary feet, clatter back down the stairs. I suspected they might go for the car, and drive back to my home. Alternatively, they might race down to the cottage to induce the process of separation. A process, I believed, that they had no longer practised with such vigour while ensconced in my home. Perhaps they had got out of the habit, and perhaps it could not be induced so freely now. But they would try to reopen a connection with what was restless here, for sure, and through it they would cajole the malignant and the maleficent to find me.

They went for the car.

From the second floor, I briefly watched them trying to run through the long grass of the terraces.

And I chose my moment.

What I had been whispering for hours I suddenly screamed.

'They are here. Here! Eunice, Ida, Wendy, Natalie, Eunice, Ida, Wendy, Natalie . . . Betrayers. See how they run. They have spent your money! On themselves! Snakes!'

I chanted my poison through each and every room as I fled down to the basement.

I lit up that dusty tomb as I descended, room by room.

The timbers were old and damp, but something in the paint on the walls caught far faster than I had anticipated. The hot embers of the papers slipped through the floorboards. In those cavities, the dross of the ages proved as eager for the heat and light as those who still staggered about those passages by night.

I had no real idea if Thin Len would make an appearance. I had never seen him at the Tor. He'd loped through my dreams and through my home, and reared up in the local woods once, but never appeared at the Tor. Amongst all of the horrors that house had presented to me, that may have been the only mercy that it ever granted.

Until that afternoon.

A day of glorious, golden and shimmering summer sunshine. I could see for miles, right across the plains and hills of Dartmoor, and I could see the tiered gardens at the front of the Hall even more clearly.

As I peered from an unshuttered window on the ground floor, while the house above and around me smoked and crackled and crisped, and even though my eyes smarted and my vision was blurred from the smoke, I saw *him*.

Thin Len.

From a distance, I watched the visible parts of him circle and then fall upon the accused.

How the grass seemed to flatten in the wind, the same wind that fanned the fires of this house into the inferno, the catastrophe that left it charred and black, with half the roof open to the sky the following morning.

I saw Thin Len briefly, a thing dark and long that glided as if swept forwards by the motion of the wind-ruffled grass. A thing that articulated itself like a frantic, damaged insect, when it closed upon those it had come for.

When it cast about them in the tall grass, I heard their cries. That is when I looked away.

Crouched down on the dirty floorboards, I scratched at my scalp like a lunatic, and then stuffed my fingers inside my ears.

I had refused to watch Thin Len take the second one. But I did see him snatch away the first one. Natalie, I think. The sack was suddenly taut on a face at three hundred feet, and up went those arms so tight in the black sleeves. A raggedy scarecrow, striding, flinging itself . . . And then down it seemed to collapse, and up shot the scream of the woman beneath it, and she must have been heard a mile away.

The other woman fell into the long grass, exhausted or too frightened to move, I don't know. I never got the chance to ask.

I hunkered down in the smoke and heat in that room, and I clutched my head and shuddered with a terrible anticipation that *he* would come for me next, and that Len, that very day, would add three more soul-bodies to the nocturnal procession at the Tor.

Coughing, my eyes streaming, and no longer able to abide the smoke, I left the building through the kitchen. I'd left every external door on the ground floor open, so that the breeze could assist the progress of the fires inside. Some of the fires seemed to have petered out once the paper had finished burning, but others must have continued. Eventually, like the master of the house, they must have raged.

Outside, I stood for a long time and waited, with my eyes shut against . . . what never came for me.

Thin Len.

I don't know why, but through the holes in the hangman's hood, on that fiery day, he only had eyes for the ladies.

I hadn't much time to complete the next part of my plan. Perhaps the great house burning upon the hill would have become a beacon, and someone, somewhere within sight, or passing on a distant road, might have called the emergency services. In time, the smoke would have been seen for sure; maybe later that evening when it was still light, and once the fire had really taken hold of the building's timber frame.

With an old shovel, the tool that I'd come across in the cottage, I'd already dug two graves in the nearby woods. To which, in an old wheelbarrow, I transported the bodies of the last members of the API. This was the vehicle that Natalie and Wendy had once used to transport their provisions from the front gate to the cottage, and *for decades*. I took the remains of those disgraced servitors to the makeshift cemetery, but I covered their faces with some old sheets.

With the very last of my strength, I wheeled them into the woods and then tipped each of them into the trenches. Without a word, I shovelled the soil over the lumps that they formed in the dark ground. A place where the sun could not penetrate the canopy of trees, and where the ground was always soft and moist.

After that, I ran.

ADAM NEVILL

Crying like a child, and delirious with what might have been joy, or anguish, or relief, or all of these things, I ran through the grass without looking over my shoulder, lest I was being stalked across the overgrown lawns.

Into the wooded parkland I plunged, crashing past the ivy-smothered follies, and setting aloft the resting butterflies and bees and birds.

I even closed the gates behind me, and then doubled over, sick from exhaustion and terror and elation.

It felt very strange to be driving my own car again. And even stranger to spend that night within my own bed, alone, with no *others* passing about my feet and asking their infernal, meaningless questions. None stood up either, and shivered their sharp backs at the foot of my bed. And none kicked out upon the ceiling, as if tangled in the weeds of black, bottomless waters.

But I did dream.

I dreamed of a slender woman, who wore a hat and had dark eyes part hidden behind a veil. This lone figure of a silent woman stood upon the end of a pier and she watched me as I ran across a shoreline made of sawdust.

My feet sank, and I slipped backwards, and exhausted myself without making much progress, while she remained motionless and watched me.

Perhaps she waited for another to come and join me, in that place where the black sea hushes over the dust of dead wood.

THE END [AGAIN, FOR NOW].

Acknowledgements

The research and case studies collated by Cecilia Green (*Out of Body Experiences*) and Robert Crookall (*The Supreme Adventure, Intimations of Immortality, Case-book of Astral Projection* and *The Study and Practice of Astral Projection*) were valuable sources for informing the ideas within this story. Francis Wheen's *Who Was Dr. Charlotte Bach?* was a fragrant inspiration behind M. L. Hazzard's own colourful past.

Much appreciation goes out to my editor Wayne Brookes, for his encouragement, enthusiasm and his insights, and to all at Pan. Special thanks to John Jarrold, Julie and all at Gotham, Anne and Iona Nevill, my parents, Simon Nevill, Melissa and Darren Thomas, and Hugh Simmons for their advice or support. I want to acknowledge various beauty spots and places around my home in Torbay, which often served as inspiration and as a variety of outdoor offices during the writing of this book. The bay provides.

I'd like to thank the reviewers who consistently support my books and who came out swinging for *Lost Girl* – a novel about different kinds of horror: Jim McLeod and Kit Power of 'Ginger Nuts of Horror', Sean Kitching at 'The Quietus', *SFX*, Charlie Oughton and *SciFiNow*, Slash, Eric Brown at the *Guardian*, David Mitchell at the *Independent*, James Lovegrove at the *Financial Times*, Fred McNamara at *Starburst*, Sapient at 'Pop Mythology', Pablo Cheesecake at 'The Eloquent Page', *Dirge Magazine*, Anthony Watson of 'Dark Musings', Des Lewis at 'Dreamcatcher: Gestalt Real-Time Reviews', Pam Norfolk at the *Lancashire Evening Post*, Marie O'Regan at 'SciFi Bulletin', Alex Cluness and all at Literature Works, Tor.com, Theresa Derwin and 'Terror Tree', Maxine Groves, Sheila M. Merritt at *Diabolique Magazine*, *Upcoming4.me*, Carrie Buchanan at 'Horror Blog', 'Steph's Book Blog', Nathan Ballingrud, Ted E. Grau, F. R. Tallis, Jason Arnopp, Gary Fry, Gary McMahon, Mark Morris, Rich Hawkins, Patty Dohle, Matthew Fryer, Jonathan Wood, Diala Atat and Ruba Naseraldeen at the Dubai Reading Group, the British Fantasy Society, Sci Fi Weekender 7, *Nightmare*, John Connolly, Brian J. Showers, Paul Melloy, Mathew Riley, Toby Clarke, and all of my mates and the sharers on social media.

Finally, I want to project my gratitude to the readers who have hindered in my sphere, and who have followed my terrors this far, and also to those who are only beginning their association . . .

LOST GIRL

How far will he go to save his daughter?
How far will he go to get revenge?

It's 2053 and runaway climate change has brought civilization to the brink of collapse. Billions are threatened with starvation, and mankind is slowly moving north in a world stricken by war, drought and superstorms – easy prey for the pandemics that sweep across the globe. Easy prey, too, for the violent gangs and people-smugglers who thrive in the crumbling world where King Death reigns supreme.

The father's own world went to hell two years ago. His four-year-old daughter was snatched from his garden when he should have been watching her. The moments before her disappearance play in a perpetual loop in his mind, as do nightmarish fantasies of who took her, and why. But the police are preoccupied. Amidst the worst European heatwave on record, a refugee crisis and the coming hurricane season, who cares about one more missing child? Now it's down to him to find her, even if it means going to the worst places imaginable, to do the unthinkable . . .

'Nevill ornaments his tale of brutality and bloodshed with florid Gothic prose . . . There's acute psychological insight amid Lost Girl's squalid inferno, and the author's vision of our near future is horribly plausible'   *Financial Times*

NO ONE GETS OUT ALIVE

Darkness lives within . . .

Cash-strapped, working for temping agencies and living in shared accommodation, Stephanie Booth feels she can fall no further. So when she takes a new room at the right price, she believes her luck has finally turned. But 82 Edgehill Road is not what it appears to be.

It's not only the eerie atmosphere of the vast, neglected house, or the disturbing attitude of her new landlord, Knacker McGuire, that makes her uneasy – it's the whispers behind the fireplace, the scratching beneath floors, the footsteps in the dark, and the young women weeping in neighbouring rooms. When Knacker's menacing cousin Fergal arrives, the danger exceeds her darkest imaginings.

But this is merely a beginning, a gateway to horrors beyond Stephanie's worst nightmares. And in a house where no one listens to the screams, will she ever get out alive?

'Adam Nevill has forged his reputation as one of the UK's best horror writers by writing elegantly stripped down, deceptively simple novels. *No One Gets Out Alive* starts off as a similarly pared back take on the ghost story, but blossoms into something much grander in scale'   *SFX*

THE RITUAL

*In the forests of Scandinavia, an ancient presence
starts its nightmare hunt once again . . .*

Four old university friends reunite for a hiking trip in the
Scandinavian wilderness of the Arctic Circle. No longer
young men, they have little left in common and tensions rise
as they struggle to connect. Frustrated and tired, they take a
shortcut that turns their hike into a nightmare that could
cost them their lives.

Lost, hungry and surrounded by forest untouched for
millennia, they stumble across an isolated old house. Inside,
they find the macabre remains of old rites and pagan sacrifices; ancient artefacts and unidentifiable bones. This place
of dark ritual is home to a bestial predator that is still alive
in the ancient forest. And now they're the prey.

The four friends struggle toward salvation, but death
doesn't come easily among these ancient trees . . .

'This novel grabs from the very first page, refuses to be laid
aside, and carries the hapless reader, exhausted and wrung
out, to the very last sentence'   *Guardian*

'Horrifyingly scary . . . Nevill sinuously ramps up the
tension'   *Sunday Times*

LAST DAYS

Winner of the August Derleth award
for Best Horror Novel

They never let you go . . .

In 1975, a massacre took place in the Arizona desert which shocked the world. The Temple of the Last Days, a cult whose rumoured mystical secrets and paranormal experiences lay concealed behind a history of murder, sexual deviancy and imprisonment, came to a bloody end after a night of ritualistic violence. Now their story wants to be told.

Kyle Freeman is an indie film-maker with no money and few options, so when he lands a commission to make a documentary about the sinister cult and its mysterious leader, he jumps at the chance.

As he travels from London to France and then Arizona, tracing the path of the Temple of the Last Days, uncanny events, out-of-body experiences, ghastly artefacts and nocturnal visitors plague him. Finally he discovers the terrible secrets the cult died to protect – but is it too late to escape their hideous legacy?

'The British horror master's fourth novel sees him in top form with intelligent storytelling, an authentic, authoritative voice, and myth-building akin to Clive Barker at his most ambitious'
Rue Morgue

extracts reading groups
competitions books new
discounts extracts extracts
competitions
books new books reading groups
events books extracts events
new extracts reading groups
interviews
discounts
new books events
events new
www.panmacmillan.com
extracts events reading groups
competitions books extracts new

Georgina Public Library
90 Wexford Drive
Keswick, Ontario   L4P 3P7